The Wyrmstone

The Wyrmstone

2nd Edition

Lisa C. Murphy

Denny Creek Press

The Wyrmstone
2nd Edition
Copyright 2018 by Lisa C. Murphy

ISBN Paperback: 978-1-946832-04-7
ISBN Kindle: 978-1-946832-06-1
LCCN 2nd edition: 2018900482

Denny
Creek
Press

Kirkland, Washington

Originally published by
Crispin Hammer Publishing Company
Copyright 2013 by Lisa C. Murphy

Dedication

To Devin, Kris, Connor, Blake, and Michael;

As boys they went into their imaginations, only

to emerge years later as fine young men.

Notes on the Second Edition

This book was originally published in 2013, and rewritten in 2018 as it was transferred to Denny Creek Press. It is not often that an author gets a second chance at their novel, and I and my characters are grateful to have been allowed complete liberty to make changes. I hope my readers agree that my efforts have added to the adventure.

Acknowledgements

Dreams are woven of threads, offered by generous friends. I'd like to thank my son Devin, who let me pester him endlessly about the universe of fantasy gaming. A grateful kiss to my husband, Mark, who never wavers in his enthusiasm for our life together. I owe a deep debt to my readers: thanks to Kay Morison, Carolyn Rose, Dr. Jim Macon, Craig Danner, Michael Peñuelas, Dr. Michael Martin, Dr. Anita Peñuelas, Dr. O.T. Murphy, Barbara Appleby, Betty Krier, and to M. Carolyn Murphy and Beth Epstein, both whom we miss and love. I deeply appreciate Giancarlo Rossi's translations to Italian, and Evan Dunn's excellent help with Latin. Without Brock J. Binder's advice I could never have gone to jail convincingly; thanks for the vicarious peek inside. I send a hug of love to my first writing teacher, Mr. Tommy Trosey, who showed me the world beyond neat, sweet, and petite. And to the attentive, keen-eyed readers of my writing group, Kay Morison, Karen MacLeod, Cindy Wyckoff, Dr. Jim Macon, and Pam Binder: you steer me off the rocks and into the open sea. Thank you all for encouraging me to dream.

Prologue

My brother was a goodhearted fool who lived and died by the stupid things fools do. As the eldest, I was entitled to the succulent lands of Tuscany that my father had civilized, one bloody war at a time. But my father's will allotted his vast estates to my bland-tempered brother, and I inherited nothing but a sorcerer's staff.

Having no resources with which to correct this slight, I stayed my tongue, biding my time. Then in 1201 my lord brother decided to marry. He was showered with gifts, and came into possession of an amethyst.

The gem was the size of a snake egg and as purple as a bruise. Skilled fingers had cut it flat on the back, and carved its face into the six facets favored by Yvess, the Highland dragon empress. My brother brought it to me that I might charm it, to bring his flushed and delicious wife many offspring. He did not know the legend of the gem. But I did.

So I indulged him. I bound the gem in a tangle of golden roots as grasping as the sweet fig of a girl who had captured his heart. Into that gold I carved a spell to grant pregnancy and powerful sons. Then, I indulged myself.

Since my father's death I had secretly watched the dragon, but had not dared to approach him. Even a young dragon of a thousand years can dominate an unwary sorcerer, and this was the ancient Lowland King, a Great Wyrm of the swamps. I was cautious not to alert him to my interest, admiring only from afar the impressive swath of crushed villages that trailed behind him, undeterred by my brother's army. Adrikhedon, they called him: Dark Destroyer. A fit implement to relieve me of the brother who chafed against my skin. This dragon would be mine.

While my brother wasted his last days planning a wedding feast, and his final nights dreaming of his bride's maidenhead, I read my father's sorcery texts. On the wedding night I retreated to the dungeon. In a cauldron of pounded lead I sacrificed our family's most potent relics: the legendary sword Deathwish, proven against the Highland Emperor Wyrm; a cinnabar vial of the lethal Night Veil, stolen from Arabic alchemists; and a black drop of dragon's blood, dripped from the vial concealed in my father's staff. Drawing on all I had learned from moldy books, I melded these into a Mist of Forging.

Bring me Adrikhedon to do my will. Deep in the dungeon I sucked in the searing hot vapor, and blew the acid breath of my soul's desire into the tangle of gold that gripped the stone.

Out from the stone flew Yvess' dragon guards, roaring with protest, frenzied for slaughter. Huge ghostly horrors, they swirled above in the dusty rafters, shrieking with lust to get tooth and claw into me. I trembled, shielded by my thin cloak, cursing my father for having taught me so little. I had known the stone was strong; legend said it was enchanted by Yvess herself, and she is the sovereign of magical illusion. But I had not foreseen such powerful resistance. I had but seconds to dominate, or die.

There is an abyss where lives the soul of man; half beast, half human, the soul crouches, forever twisting, now toward heaven, now toward hell. A sorcerer can reach but once into this darkness, and whatever he grabs to sacrifice will never be his again. With clawed hands I ripped from this abyss the human I had so little use for, and thrust this scrap of myself into the gold.

"Go," I panted, holding aloft my father's staff. "Crumble to dust wyrms of Yvess, for I, Pancrizio Sovrani, claim the power of this stone."

With screams of ire the creatures lunged. Mist of dragon breath on my neck. The prick of talons over my heart. But my staff prevailed; inches from my throat they folded, drifting like so many cobwebs in the dungeon dampness. And then they dissolved into ash.

Dawn of my brother's first wedded day, and a lone rooster croaked at the timid sunrise. Soaked in sweat and vigorous with my mastery, I held up my prize: the Wyrmstone was complete.

"Adrikhedon," I whispered. I climbed the twisted staircase from dungeon to tower, arriving at the bridal chamber. "Adrikhedon."

The dragon came immediately, green and terrible. Lords, guards, and riffraff alike slept off the wedding wine as it hovered. It exhaled once on the thick walls of the tower, searing a gap through which it poked barbed jaws. In one slobbering bite it seized my brother by the neck and lifted him skyward as he thrashed.

I tossed aside his screaming wife and stood in the mangled hole. My father's staff poured forth foul darkness from my right hand, and the Wyrmstone streamed a milky light from my left.

"*Adrikhedon, proch mandatum niss calx sna rů gethrix, draŭtox.*"

My Draconic was mispronounced and far too softly spoken. The dragon hovered, turning his golden gaze on me. He shuddered with such a violent retch of hatred I thought he might drop my brother's corpse. For what seemed an eternity he hung aloft, wings flapping foul air over my head, short swords of teeth bared. His glare ate at my will, probing the power of the stone. His contempt pounded like blows from his tail. I shook, but dared not cower. Had I shown a rag end of fear or a flicker in self-command, had the stone been anything short of its legend, he would have devoured me. But I overmastered, and with loathing and reluctance the dragon turned aside and did my hest, carrying my brother's mangled body back to his swamp. And thus Adrikhedon became my slave: untrustworthy and disagreeable, but obedient.

In time, the girl my brother loved was also subdued. Women, it appears, are as difficult as dragons. I never knew if the first son she bore was mine, or if he was sired by my craven brother. The boy fled me as soon as he could run. No matter, he was one of twelve sons, each bigger and more powerful than the last. Together we scraped scars into Tuscany that would have made my father howl. Maimed and starving, his subjects begged for mercy. In the jaws of Adrikhedon's dragon army I ground up all that my father had done and spit it out, bloody and ruined, on his grave. Sweet redress for how little faith he had in me.

And then Yvess was revenged; my twelfth son was so brawny he slew my body soon after the first wisps of hair sprouted on his chin. But I am not so easily destroyed. What remained of my soul retreated into the gold that grips Yvess' jewel. My son was too frightened to use me, too greedy in his dotage to pass me on to his heir. So he hid me.

We are trapped now, the jewel and I, in a world that no longer believes in dragons. For eight hundred years I have waited, my hatred fettered, my fury impotent. Now is the hour to seize fate by the throat. She comes, a mere girl who cannot resist, the one destined to wield the Wyrmstone.

Chapter 1

The blade hit with enough force to jab zings through my head. I raised the hatchet in the pouring rain and hacked at the roots of Mom's dead fig tree, slamming blindly into the muddy hole, sure that my butter-loving heart would collapse. Barely visible in the filthy mess, the wood didn't even splinter.

Exhausted, my fingers let go. The blade dropped, driving several inches into the goo. Mom planted this fig, and she should have dug it out. It's absurd to plant a fig in the Pacific Northwest. It made hundreds of tiny green fruits that grew all winter long. They got fatter and fatter through the summer until you could almost taste how sweet they were going to be. Then, just as the first heavy rains began in September, they fell off. Thud. Dry and stringy with tough skins, coated with fine hairs, bitter. Not even the squirrels would eat them.

My mother grew up in Tuscany, the northern part of Italy, where I guess figs are friendlier. Maybe when she planted this tree she didn't know any better. But Mom was from the root-hog-or-die school of gardening. More erudite gardeners might give you a lecture on "the right plant for the right place." Mom never talked about it, she just ripped out anything that didn't thrive. Roses have blackspot? Yank them up by the roots. Columbine infested with caterpillars? Throw the whole wiggling mess into the clean green container. After years of intolerance she'd made a magnificent garden that admirers drove miles to visit. "How do you do it?" they'd ask. She wouldn't say. It was ruthless mass murder. She is, or rather *was*, a serial plant killer.

But not the fig. The fig could do no wrong. Green fruit beetles ate the leaves. Phomopsis canker killed branches. Nematodes knotted the roots. Mom battled these deformities as though the fig were a sacred trust. Diligently, Mom pruned, dug in worm compost, and swept away aborted fruit before we were overrun by ants. That repulsive fig took as much fussing as the whole rest of her third acre.

Then it died. Two weeks before her plane exploded, the trunk cracked and the black, dry remains of the cambium fell out of the gap like ash. It was left to me to finally dig the tree out. I put it off, and put it off, and put it off, inert with sorrow whenever I thought about pulling on her gloves and lifting her garden tools. Now here I was, unfit and unwilling.

I took off soaked gloves and wiped mud off my forehead. I hated sweaty tasks, and Mom and Dad left behind a lot of them. My brother, Justin, had more than enough muscle for this excavation, but he refused. Since our parents' funeral Justin made all of his decisions by throwing a twenty-sided die. In the case of the fig, Justin rolled a two, claimed the dead stump sat on "unhallowed ground," and avoided the courtyard, carefully entering and exiting by the driveway. Fantasy could be annoyingly convenient.

Justin is totally obsessed with the roll-playing game Age of Dragons. He advises me, "When all else fails, consult a dragon." No doubt a dragon could easily rip out Mom's dead fig stump, or even put a talon on why I chose to dig it up today, in the pouring rain. But dragons rarely ally with humans (Justin claims), and always for devious purposes, so good luck. That's probably for the best (Justin would warn), because dragons are risky business, cold hearted and cunning. They spend centuries lying in caves, plotting, and when they emerge they are formidable, outwitting even the sharpest hoard thieves and wyrm slayers. I guess that's why one waits until all else has failed. And there was another significant drawback: dragons don't exist. So, forget dragons. Since Justin's dice had instructed him not to help me, I was on my own.

Well, not quite. Because as fate arranged it, Mom and Dad left behind another opinionated kid, Nicholi, who won't listen to anyone but Didoo, his stuffed bear. Nicholi is only six; he can't hit with enough force to dent a daffodil. But Nicholi and Didoo are full of advice. They would cite Wikipedia: a hatchet has to have a head that weighs less than three pounds, or it isn't a hatchet. Three pounds was useless, they'd point out. This task needed one of Justin's Dwarven battleaxes. Lacking any magically forged weapons, I yanked the puny blade free and slung it aside. Wiping my filthy gloves down the front of Mom's raggedy garden coat, I went to find a pickax.

Mom's garden shed is just like Mom. *Was.* Just like she *was*: weird, but prepared. The dusty metal shelves were crammed to sagging with every strange thing she thought the family might need. A shed-full of her paranoia: her small hands bundling, sealing in baggies, wrapping together with wire, tucking things neatly into drawers as if someday our branch of the Sovrani family might be called upon to do something extraordinary. But all we ever needed were mundane things. That polished bamboo pole, honed to an impressive point and leaning beside the rake? Made for a squirrel nest high in the boiler chimney. That sledgehammer, handle thick as a troll's wrist and its head five pounds of deadly bludgeon? Used to pound in rebar for staking the dahlias. That mysterious clear tube of green liquid, sealed in a glass jar on the highest shelf? Instant bonding, indestructible, invisible drying glue for when Nicholi accidentally breaks Justin's Swamp Dragon miniature, which he isn't supposed to even look at much less play with, and Justin will be home in fifteen minutes and does she have anything that dries fast?

Since her death we rummage in here daily. Inside the doorway I stepped around the coiled Bonsai wire that Justin used yesterday to make a Skeletal Hand of Power. No doubt this was something to wield as his Age of Dragons friends rolled dice and leaned toward the center of the table, calculating hit points. This reminded me that said Hand still hung by the wrist, copper claws tightly flexed against the wall opposite Justin's bed, arched like a Tarantula about to spring. Mom and Dad didn't agree on much when it came to parenting, but about weapons they took a united stance; only Justin's Age of Dragons miniatures could brandish swords and hurl axes. No full-sized weapons, even homemade imaginary ones, in the house. For Mom's and Dad's sake, I'd have to do something about The Hand. Given the mood Justin had been in the last few days, the politics of removing The Hand were tricky. Something I wasn't looking forward to. I sucked in a deep breath of resignation and winter mold.

In the spring Mom's shed smelled like alfalfa pellets for the roses, and then WD40 in the fall for the pruning sheer hinges. Mom's odor changed too; you could tell her state of mind by her scent. On boisterous days she wore the sensuous Italian perfume Flora, filling the room with sweet, pollinating flowers. On bad days, when she folded into herself as quiet as a secret, she left behind whiffs of pungent, bittersweet Night Veil. Every morning the scent of her perfume hung over the coffee pot like news from afar. Despite all of my efforts, I'd never been able to wrap my head around her bizarre ways, her fears, not even her smell. No matter how heavy my regret, I would never understand.

I grabbed the worn handle of Mom's pickax. Mom had only been dead for two months, and already her pickax was nicked and stained with rust; one more thing that suffered without her. But it was still sharp—Mom asked Dad to keep her tools lethally sharp. And it was heavy. I hauled it out of the garden shed and attacked mud, roots, and sawed-off trunk indiscriminately, flinging crud ten feet in an effort to demolish something, anything, my misery.

At least I only had to contend with the stump. Our neighbor, Marty, who was deeply in love with his chain saw, sauntered over the day after the funeral and offered to cut the dead fig down. I guess this was his equivalent of bringing a casserole. At the time I was too numb and overwhelmed to think it through. Whistling and waving his blade, Marty sectioning the rotten tree, easy as slicing a Twinkie, then shoved the chunks into the belly of his covered pickup truck. He left a bare smudge right in the center of the courtyard where the tree's canopy had intimidated other plants. A mini wasteland in Mom's beautiful garden, with a hacked up root ball slimed in mud and an excavation hole rapidly filling with rain. And I stood in that hole, icy water rising over the top of Mom's steel-shank boots and pooling in my wrinkled socks. Gritting my teeth against the exercise, I raised the heavy pickaxe, cursed, shivered, and chopped.

I was about to give up when on my last weary swing, I heard a chink. Not the jarring crack of hitting a rock. Not the dampened thud of something organic. A metallic chink that quivered up my spine and made my ears ring with alarm. I froze, axe poised, breath held.

What the heck?

Cautiously, I stuck a gloved hand into the goo. A menacing heat diffused through my glove. Holy moly. I snatched back my hand. Dropping the pickax, I leaned above the pool of icy water, and peered into the slimy recess.

A small rectangular box lay wedged in the very heart of the roots, dented by their squeezing. Faint light seeped from box's seams, a milky glow that lit the roots, creeping onto my face. Warmth tingled through me, a glimmer of awe and fear. I felt a pull as binding as a rope, tied around my neck. This was it. This was what I'd been digging for.

That was ridiculous; I was here to dig the stump out.

I sat back on my heels and squinted into the hole. Mom

must have put this here; no one else dared to work in her garden. But what was it?

My heart leapt, puppyish with excitement. Calm down, Mimi. Hanging out with Justin and his Age of Dragons friends had warped my brain. This was not from Justin's *Book of Legendary Treasure.* The odd glow was an illusion of twilight, or my head, buzzing with that awful physical labor. I took a few deep breaths. Mom did mysterious things, but with ordinary objects. Given the ups and downs in Mom's stability, the box could hold anything from an umbilical cord to a gold brick. I could badly use a gold brick. Best case scenario: this would help pay the rent. Worst case scenario: the contents would be gross and senseless and I wouldn't be able to throw it away fast enough.

With semi-frozen hands, I clawed aside clay. The roots didn't yield to my tug, but hung on with a death grip. So I retrieved Mom's long-handled pruners from the shed. Straining and grunting, I snipped the roots one by one. They didn't spring back as I had expected; they curled around the box as though nothing short of chipping and shredding could destroy them. I had to pry off the fingers and snap them into little chunks at their knuckles.

Finally, I freed one face of the box. I wedged my hands around the metal sides and pulled. Hard. I braced myself with a foot and put my aching back into it. My grip slipped and I staggered backwards, falling to the bottom of the hole, wallowing, soaking wet in soggy boots.

Taking off a dripping glove, I shoved Mom's wool night watchman's cap out of my face. That fig was supernatural in its determination, as though it had a will of its own. But the box was mine. I could feel it yanking at my heart. I wanted it with a passion that overwhelmed common sense. So, despite a nagging thought that this was hella-stupid, I was going to free it.

I threw aside Mom's gloves and knelt in the muddy water. Wedging both hands into the cranny above the lid, I rammed my fingers through the tangle of roots and hooked the back of the box with my fingertips. Bracing my legs against a knot of wood, I groaned under my breath and heaved. Slowly the box moved. With creaks of protest the roots released their prisoner, scraping two deep gashes into the backs of my hands. I gasped from stinging pain as the container slid into my lap, heavy and warm as a living heart.

It was a stout, battered toolbox, six inches deep and one handbreadth square. A slender handle twisted, bent on the top. Dirt caked the seams and rust ate at the dents. The hinge pins were corroded, and the color had long ago chipped off the box's metal surface. In the front, a scruffy combination lock secured the tongue and loop of the catch. The numbers were long ago worn away and the dial was rusted. The box had the hopeful weight of gold bricks. I shifted it on my lap and its dense contents dragged from side to side.

I stood up, hefting my prize, cheeks so numb with cold that the drops barely stung. Rain trickled off my cap and into my open collar. The cuts on my hands burned, and my soaking wet jeans clung to my calves. I ached all the way to my soul. The loneliness of a funeral is nothing compared to what hits after the mourners leave. I had to bear this somehow, grow up fast for Justin and Nicholi. As Judge Burrows had reminded me at the custody hearing, I was only eighteen and couldn't afford to screw up. The court's supervisory stare was on me like a red laser dot trained on my forehead. One summer at the South Sound Culinary Institute didn't make me an adult. Partying with my boyfriend Duke was an education, but not in parenting. I'd had to leave college while I was still a dishpig, cleaning up after the master chefs. I'd better keep my head on straight or my two brothers wouldn't be in my custody for long. And as difficult as they were, I adored my brothers. They were not going to foster care. Not as long as I was alive.

I looked down at the damaged box. My mother buried this. I didn't know what it was or why she hid it. So much about her life, even her death, made no sense at all. But whatever was in this box was unmistakably mine. I knew it from the end of my frost-frozen nose to my feet, marinating in mud. Please, I begged, please—may it give me the strength to carry us through.

Chapter 2

I was dying to pull Dad's tools off the shelf and pry open the box, but Nicholi met me at the utility room door. He swiped at his tears in broad theatrical strokes, anxiously shifting from foot to foot.

"Didoo bearapulted into the bathtub, so Justin put-ted him in the dryer."

I flashed on Judge Burrows and my heart flipped. "Sweetie, you're too young to be in the tub without supervision, remember?"

"I was nevernot in the tub." He sounded annoyed that I'd doubted him. "Me and Didoo wanted to see if paper boats have floatitude."

"Do they?" I heaved my heavy box into the utility room sink and it settled with a rasping scrape, putting my teeth on edge. Behind me I could feel Nicholi's tense jitters. He must be hungry. I shouldn't have been outside so long.

"They float until they get wettish. Didoo's wet, too. He hateinates baths." Nicholi's voice inched towards more tears.

I glanced at him sideways. "He'll be okay, he has maxi-awesome-bearsomeness."

Nicholi cracked a smile. Word play was the domain of us kids. Dad, a United Nations translator who spoke six languages, corrected Nicholi's mangled creations and insisted that Nicholi "speak English." Poor Mom said nothing, probably uncertain what was in her Italian/English Dictionary and what was not.

I hurriedly stripped off my wet jeans and threw them in the wash. Nicholi stood rocking on one small, socked foot, the other foot pressed against his knee like a stork. His mouth shrunk to pinched and serious.

"But what if Didoo isn't dryofied by bedtime?"

"See, I'll turn up the dryer. He'll be dry in fifteen minutes."

I wanted to clean the burning scrapes on my hands. I wanted a hot shower and my soft, worn bathrobe. I glanced longingly at the box, wondering if there was any chance I could chisel it open quickly. But by then Nicholi would be so hungry he'd be flinging himself about on the floor, having what Justin called, "a rebelothon." I had to make dinner. I threw on sweats from the unfolded laundry pile. "How about something to eat?"

"No." He plopped down in front of the dryer, pressed little fingers to the glass, and watched his bear go round and round. "I looked it up on Wikipedia."

Wikipedia: when Didoo couldn't answer Nicholi's questions, he used his favorite online, user-edited source of truth and wisdom. In Nicholi's mind, if Didoo didn't know it, and it wasn't in Wikipedia, it didn't exist.

"There's no page on death." His voice wavered over the word death. "If you search, all you get is empty nothingness."

And there were our tears, brimming up, prickling and heavy, as if the accident were yesterday. Crouching beside him, I pushed wavy brown hair off his forehead. He looked like Dad, his wild eyebrows animated with emotion, megasweet blue eyes, and his widow's peak a dramatic gash dividing his face into a heart. We kids had bad timing for important business, falling apart when Mom and Dad were frazzled by the day's mishaps. They always stopped and kneeled down, a hundred pauses, a thousand interruptions, a million moments of patience.

I swallowed hard a few times before I could speak. "Maybe you could write the page on death. I'll help you."

"No. Mom and Dad are 'sposed to write it."

Nicholi's voice choked with bleak, unforgivable loss. Didoo thumped softly in the dryer, furry body falling, lifting to the top of the drum, then dropping helplessly down again. "Didoo says we're in uber trouble. I'm scared. I want Mom and Dad." Shimmery tears dripped onto Nicholi's T-shirt, running down the innocent face of Scooby-Doo. His little shoulders trembled as I hugged him to my chest. We wait, dinner waits, laundry waits, everything waits while Mom and Dad never come home again.

Justin was leaning into the open refrigerator when I came into the kitchen. He took out a Clementine orange, closed the fridge, and settled against the cabinet like a boulder. His eyes scrutinized everything as if it were dangerous. Pulling off a strip of peel with his bulky thumb, he watched me uncover the defrosted casserole sitting on the center island. I peeled back the plastic wrap and we both winced at the freezer-damaged noodles, deformed and mummified in pasty gravy.

We didn't get many post-funeral casseroles because Mom and Dad weren't popular. Until Dad quit working he traveled a lot, and Mom—well, her English was okay, but she failed miserably at being American. She was a smooth emulsion of old European elegance and Italian passion, with an aftertaste of dangerous mystery. Women were put off by her and men were tongue-tied. Therefore just a handful of casseroles, mostly from garden club acquaintances who'd seen Mom in her torn work coat with mud on her face. That made her a teaspoon more approachable. Still, something in her eyes kept them at arm's length. This bothered me more than it bothered Mom; I felt she needed friends, she didn't care. Now, looking at the disgusting mess in the china dish, I had a guilty flash of grateful thanks that there had been so few who sympathized.

"Where were you?" Justin popped half the Clementine into his mouth and chewed grimly.

I felt accused of neglect. "In the garden." I wadded the plastic wrap into a ball and didn't re-cover the casserole. Burning the yellow-sprinkles-that-might-be-cheese-on-top could only improve them.

He swallowed, looking disgusted. "So we're eating that?"

I opened the microwave and shoved the glop inside. "Sorry, I've been busy. I'll scrape the top off; the underneath won't be so bad." But it would be, I knew it, and so did Justin.

Justin scowled. At fourteen, he'd already mastered the fierce expressions of an epic warrior. His frown could slice air as clean as a sword blade. It separated with absolute certainty what was acceptable from what wasn't. This particular moment his scowl decapitated any thought of eating that casserole. Whack. Its imaginary head rolled into the gutter.

I took spinach from the crisper and began to rinse it in the sink.

"Pretend I'm the Night Hag. You have to steal from my table to keep from starving before you escape across the Desert of Snakes on your way back to—"

"Okay, okay! I'll eat it. It's just gross."

He turned away and went to sit at the table, sullenly chomping the orange, his hair falling over his eyes. Even from across the kitchen he looked enormous. He claimed he was half barbarian and half elf. The barbarian supplied the body, and the elf supplied the astute gray eyes and his shimmering cloak of brown woodland hair. His supposed heritage provided an excuse for not going to bed—elves never sleep. And for eating so much—barbarians love a good feast.

Yesterday at the custody hearing Justin and I stood side by side, my slight shoulder barely up to his armpit, his chest with the breadth and muscle of a linebacker.

"Mimi Jovel," said Judge Burrows, "it is only with grave doubts that I accede to your request to parent these boys. You look rather …." He didn't finish the sentence, because Nicholi broke away from our state appointed guardian and dashed across the floor, flinging himself into Justin's arms.

But in my mind I finished Judge Burrows sentence: light, fluffy, sweetened with corn syrup. Standing upright because I had a lot of air in me, like beaten egg white. A creampuff, waiting for some big bad wolf to gobble me down. My appearance is my worst asset.

Imitating Judge Burrow's grave authority, I had tried to make my voice weighty and confident. "My brothers will do fine, I promise." Now, looking at Justin brooding across the room, I wasn't so sure. He had dark rings under his eyes that troubled me.

I drained the spinach, chopped an apple and threw it in the bowl, then added a handful of almonds. Dang, there was no cheddar cheese in the refrigerator.

"Justin, what happened to the cheese?"

He swallowed his last hunk of orange and wiped both hands on his pants.

"What were you doing in the garden?"

An uncomfortable tingle of warning shot through my chest. I turned my back to him, staring into the safety of the fridge. Finding a buried box was so up his fantasy alley. But I didn't want to tell him. I had the uneasy feeling that that box might no longer be mine as soon as he saw it. And what if it contained something bizarre? With Mom, you never knew. We needed my rationality and not Justin's rampaging imagination to deal with Mom's creations.

"I was taking out the stump." True enough, I justified to myself. "What happened to the cheese?" I shoved aside containers on the shelves.

"Nicholi wanted cheesy crackers for lunch. Why don't you just leave that stump alone? Mom liked that tree."

"It's dead. It's making a mess of Mom's garden." With a deep breath, I turned around and faced him, square and unavoidable. "And a six-year-old didn't eat a pound of cheese."

Justin went still, like a little prayer of preparation. He'd done that frequently in the last few weeks, settled into himself as if readying for battle, some unnamed anguish flickering across his face. I wondered for a moment if he might finally say something about Mom and Dad's accident. Two months, and he'd said nothing.

Then, slowly, the corners of his elfin grin crept out from behind his hair. "I had to help him, didn't I? That's what brothers are for."

I stared at him. How does a sister console a grieving brother who's so burly and tough? He was a wall that I threw myself against, bruising on impact. I plunked the salad onto the table. "Here's your favorite salad, but you'll have to imagine the cheese." Justin's gaze dropped to the floor.

Nicholi came in, snuggling his warm, dry bear. He stood right in the middle of the narrow kitchen, placed so that I couldn't help but swerve around him on my way from the stove to the fridge, the fridge to the microwave, and the microwave to the table.

"Nicholi, set the table, please."

"But I'm hugging Didoo." Face stuffed deep in disheveled bear fur, Nicholi hummed the Scooby-Doo theme song, rocking side to side.

I veered by him with the hot pads, and then back around him with the tepid, musky smelling casserole. "Show Didoo how to set the table. He's old enough to learn."

Nicholi holds the world record for moving slowly. Super slo-mo replays on TV are nothing compared to Nicholi. I poured milk, made salad dressing, laid out napkins, sliced bread, lit candles, and dished out the God-awful casserole before he touched the first fork. I knew it did absolutely no good to say, even if I said it in my most patient voice, "Please set the table, Nicholi. We're waiting." He'd just say, in his most annoyed voice, "I *am* setting the table." He was setting the table for dinner in 2011. Unfortunately, we were hungry in 2010. So Justin and I sat watching noodles and gravy congeal as Nicholi arranged one piece of flatware at a time carefully in the center of each napkin.

And then came the hardest part of every surviving day. Worse than lying awake in my parents' empty room, worse than drying all of the tears Nicholi shed, or hoping for the tears Justin staunchly refused to shed, worse than the news that my parents' estate had been depleted when Dad quit work to care for Mom. Worse even than the demeaning mistrust of the custody court. We all reached around the table to hold hands.

This was when Dad always said, "May the circle be unbroken." With those words I used to see the net of our love crisscrossed on the back of my eyelids, supporting my whole world. Now, behind closed lids, all I saw was a YouTube clip of a tumbling ball of fire, emerging from a cloud of smoke, sharp with silver bits that were bent and mangled. A plane, carving spirals as it flipped head over tail, spinning down until it was swallowed by the dark waters of Puget Sound.

"May the circle be unbroken," I whispered. If my voice was too soft to hear, my brothers didn't ask me to repeat myself.

After dinner Nicholi set Didoo beside his plate of picked-over food and mashed his forehead onto Didoo's brow, as if they were melding minds. "Didoo is glad he didn't have to eat that gunkotard," he said.

Justin laughed. "Good word, dude. Gunkotard. I way hope that crud doesn't kill us."

I had a flash of guilt flambé: a culinary student feeding her family gunkotard. We'd been coddled, us kids, by a father who wished he was a gourmet chef, and by a mother who goaded him on. I would cook from now on—we couldn't eat another meal that bad.

Justin stood and found a twenty-sided die in his pocket. A devoted Age of Dragons player owns dozens of twenty-sided dice, each colored in its own unique way. Justin always had at least one, but usually four or five, in his pocket. When I did the laundry they wore holes through the fabric and banged around, denting the inside of the dryer. He rolled the die on his palm, glanced at the number, and then strolled toward the study leaving his dirty dishes on the table.

"Justin come back, it's your turn to do the dishes." It took an effort to be polite. I was exhausted, and seeping through the walls was the pull of the box. I wanted to pry it open, then collapse into bed.

Through the door I could see Justin sauntering across the obstacle course of the living room, avoiding scattered toys, teetering piles of books, and the balled-up socks that Nicholi left everywhere, threading his way to the Xbox.

"Justin, it's your turn. Come on," I called after him, no longer hiding my annoyance.

He stopped and turned about. I have no idea what kind of a look he gave me because hair veiled his eyes, but his body was loose with that casual confidence so intimidating in a big guy. He eased a hand into his pocket and took out another twenty-sided die. He ambled back and rolled the die on the table with an experienced snap of his wrist.

"Will to resist the command of the Night Hag," he said. He peered at the glittering rune and dot covered polygon. "Eighteen. Sorry about that." He really did look sorry—eyes crinkled with regret and shoulders slumped apologetically. He gathered up the die and walked out. The Xbox online zipped on and triumphant march music blared from the study, introducing *The Battle for the Universe.* I took ten deep breaths to keep from screaming. My insides churned, as chaotic as the messy kitchen, feeling trashed.

Justin had used dice for years in Age of Dragons, but now the dice rolled out-of-game, and with different rules. Over ten, he won. If the roll was nine or under, he lost. If it was exactly ten he could choose to use a 'luck point', of which he apparently got one a month. I, not a member of any Age of Dragons guild, didn't get any luck points. Wouldn't you know. All of this meant that Justin did what I asked fifty percent of the time. I suppose lots of people raising teens would be delighted with fifty-fifty odds. Justin went to school, he did his homework, and he loved his baby brother. In the bigger scope of things I should be grateful that so far, Justin's dice had not made any lethal choices. But at the moment I wanted to exterminate them. Hammer them to dust and flush them.

Still, I had no way to make a 220-pound half barbarian warrior do what he didn't want to do. Glad that Judge Burrows couldn't see me now, I bowed to bad luck and did the dishes. Then I folded laundry, made tomorrow's grocery list, checked the online want ads for a job (no luck points there, either), and drew a warm bath for Nicholi. He was in the study on Wikipedia and logged off in the record time of twenty minutes when I called him.

In the bathtub, Nicholi lay back against the white porcelain, sloshing warm water into tidal waves with his knees. He looked far too snug for a short bath. I sighed with exhaustion and tried to make myself comfortable on the heap of crumpled towels and paper boats on the floor.

"Bears are 'sposed to be self-helpful swimmers," he said. Nicholi's school has a pool, so I suspected that this was leading somewhere.

"Oh yeah?" I leaned forward and squeezed shampoo onto his hair, lathering it into thick spikes. Waves washed to his chin, rinsing away rivulets that trickled down his neck, foam bobbing at the rings around the tub that I hadn't had time to scrub.

"All bears swim, even black bears. That means Didoo has got to go to school and learnify how to swim."

Of course. For two months we'd been arguing about Didoo and school. Ms. Greer absolutely refused to allow stuffed animals in the first grade. Since Mom and Dad died, Nicholi furiously protested any separation from his bear. I couldn't decide who was more unreasonable, the six-year-old or the educator. Sometimes I was tempted to sew Didoo into a hidden pocket of Nicholi's coat, or put him in a brown paper bag and send him as lunch.

Not in the mood for a fight, I kept my mouth shut and

sculpted foamy ears that flopped on either side of Nicholi's head. Taking Mom's hand mirror from the bathroom drawer, I showed him his reflection. "See, now you're a bear."

He snarled at the mirror and then pushed it away. "But then Ms. Greer would make me stay home with Didoo."

"So we'll make you a stegosaurus instead." I swooped hair into a Mohawk crest. "I bet she doesn't have any rules about dinosaurs."

"No. I'm a boy." He dunked his head underwater and swung it back and forth, rinsing out suds. He held his breath for a long time, and when he came up his face glistened with stubbornness. "I need to take Didoo to school to learnify how to swim. Tell Ms. Greer."

"Why swimming?"

"'Cause Didoo gets toyitude when his head is wet."

I put aside the mirror and found a mostly clean towel. Hoping to ease Nicholi towards bed, I bent over the tub, holding the towel open. "Toyitude?"

"He's just a toy again, until he's dry." Nicholi's plump arms shot up, flailing in a frenzy, flinging spatters of suds into my face.

I drew back, blinking and wiping my eyes.

"And what if he sinks to the bottom and can't tell me where he is and I never find him? He couldn't self-help himself. He might be lost forever."

"Oh!" It was more a gasp than a word. I flashed on the YouTube image of Mom and Dad's fiery plunge into Puget Sound. It must rattle around inside Nicholi like a trapped wasp, stinging and stinging. His anxious little face made me ache with misery.

He scrambled out of the tub and I layered the towel around him, leaning to pat him dry, but he stepped back, obstinate in his cape of soft terrycloth.

"Bears live forty years."

"Wow." I ruffled his hair with my hand and then found a comb and cautiously tugged at the tangles.

"Didoo can't live forty years and not swim. Ms. Greer has to let him come to school."

"Can't he learn in the tub?"

"No! He needs something deepish. Ouch." He jerked the towel up over his head, pushing away my hand.

"Sorry." I tossed aside the comb, frustrated. There was too much about our lives that I couldn't control, including Ms. Greer.

"Bedtime. Go pick out a story."

As he dashed away, I gathered a heap of used towels and dropped them in the already full hamper. I heard the bed's squeaky complaint as Nicholi jumped in, then thrashing as he wormed his way to the bottom. "Didoo can't find me!" Covers muffled his yell.

I swooped Didoo off the bathroom floor. He always fell face down, the pink silk threads of his nose smashed by whatever surface Nicholi dropped him on. After years of abuse that pink was frayed, and the nose, like the neck where he was perpetually hugged, had lost its nappy fabric and was down to worn canvas.

I tucked the pudgy body under my arm and headed down the hall. Pausing in the doorway, I plotted a path across

Nicholi's floor. Nicholi's bed was an island, mountainous with blankets, in a dense sea of Legos. Suppressed giggles came from the heaving ridge at the bottom of the bed. Careful of my socked and vulnerable feet, I minced around sharp little plastic pieces and folded Didoo under the covers. Blankets writhed and scrambled, then Didoo's blue glass eyes and rounded ears appeared from under the bedspread.

"Didoo found you. What a bear." I sat on the bed and lifted covers off Nicholi's face. My heart flushed warm to see his smile. "What should I read to you, sweetie?"

He didn't hesitate. "*The Complete Book of Dragons.*" He heaved the book out from under his pillow.

Oh, no. This was Justin's book, and though he had at least thirty Age of Dragons volumes, he would not be thrilled with Nicholi borrowing it. Nicholi didn't mean to crunch miniatures or shred pages, but his dramatic gestures had a way of defeating things. "He pulpinates my stuff," Justin had complained. I glanced towards the door. *The Battle for the Universe* blasted from the study.

"Will you be careful?" I asked.

Nicholi nodded gravely. "Way careful."

"Well—okay." I set the book in my lap and immediately regretted it. The dragon on the cover was magnificently hideous. He had a buff, *Power Magazine* body with slime green muscles that rippled from spiked tail to shoulders, where the flesh thinned into vast wings. His scaly face was barbed at the snout with whiskers and protected on the forehead with horns, and his slit eyes glowed gold. He was colossal, slobbering over the cowering warrior he assaulted, about to deep-fry the poor man in a lethal blast of breath. This was going to give Nicholi nightmares.

"How about we read *Brave Ant*, or *Mille and the Alien*?" I asked.

He settled into his pillows and took a deep whiff of Didoo's fur, half closing his eyes. "Didoo wantinates this book."

I reluctantly opened the cover and leaned against the headboard, my arm around Nicholi's shoulders. Didoo sprawled across Nicholi's chest, his ragged face tranquil with whatever drowsy bears contemplate.

According to the Table of Contents, we could read about Lowland (swamp) dragons, Highland (mountain) dragons, the Legendary Dragon Wars, dragon magic, dragon anatomy and physiology, dragon hoards and how to steal them, or dragon reproduction, birth, and infancy. Infancy—that seemed least likely to terrify. How scary could baby dragons be? I found the page and started reading.

"Baby dragons, also called wyrmlings, are a foot tall and weigh six to eight pounds when they slash their way out of the egg. From their first moment of consciousness they are ravenous, a hunger they strive to fill for the rest of their long millennia. If you wonder why dragons are so nasty, you need look no further than their perpetual hunger. For both the aloof Highland dragons and the foul-tempered Lowland dragons, the hour of hatching is a fateful one; only one out of the brood will survive. Each hatchling will battle to the death against the survivor born before him, consuming or being consumed by the older brother or sister, with the winner lying in wait for the next egg to crack. If the eggshells were not impervious to

Lowland dragon acid and Highland dragon fire, the whole clutch would be devoured as eggs by the first born. Having gorged on their siblings, dominant hatchlings must be content for the next year with the less satisfying scorpions, tarantulas, snakes, and rats brought by their parents. Then the wyrmling is old enough to hunt."

Holy moly, this stuff gave me goose bumps. I glanced at Nicholi, but he seemed undisturbed. He took a pudgy finger and drew a soft, slow circle on his own cheek, then reached out and traced the baby dragon's triangular face. The wrymling had one eye wide open, the iris yellow and wary, guarding his life. The other eye squeezed closed in a grimace of unbridled malice. I felt grateful the critter was imaginary.

"Keep reading," whined Nicholi.

Without much enthusiasm, I turned the page.

"Dragons are so despicable that even their parents can't love them. The adults kill their young if the little feisters become annoying. Among Lowland dragons, squabbles over food or treasure are particularly common and often lead to an early death. Highland dragons are more circumspect. A wrymling who cannot tolerate his cravings and restrain his urge to steal the family hoard will be thrown to the mercy of Empress Yvess' Dragon Guard, where he either wrestles his greed into control or dies in the claws of his superiors. Dragon spawn survive because they are wily and calculating, not because their parents are particularly conscientious. If they live to learn the patience and fortitude their hunger demands, they are vicious, clever, little monsters."

I closed the book. "Nicholi, what do you say we read

something else? What would you like to hear?"

"This book."

Nicholi reached into my lap and wedged open the cover again. He studied the Table of Contents and turned to another chapter, careful not to crease his brother's pages. I sighed and glanced at the clock. Ten more minutes at the most, and then I could insist that he go to bed. I hoped he could sleep after this.

Instead of a tiny baby with razor sharp wings, this chapter featured a drawing of two Great Wyrms. One was a glittering blue, like ice. Her steely silver eyes glared with glacial hatred at the other, the ghastly green creature from the cover.

"Read this." Nicholi pointed to text under the dragons.

"The Legendary Wars between the Lowland dragons and the Highland dragons will forever make the two races enemies. Though dragons claim it is their basic natures that divide them, humans have long agreed that dragons are separated only by their mutual irrepressible greed.

"All dragons are naturally lazy and loathe to exert themselves, but there the similarity between the two races ends. Unlike the social Highland dragons, Lowland dragons are solitary, living alone in the foulest swamps, answering only to their king, Adrikhedon. With cruelty and cunning, they amass great heaps of magical objects which they swallow to increase their power. Over the centuries they have come together only when called to war. Their penchant for lies, betrayals, and shifting alliances make them a difficult army, and no other beast but Adrikhedon has been powerful enough hold their loyalty. No one doubts that Lowland dragons

would have won the dragon wars had Adrikhedon not abruptly and mysteriously withdrawn himself at the end of the year 1201, marshalling his army to aid the dreaded sorcerer Pancrizio, and then vanishing from historical record. Though the dragon wars dragged on for another three centuries, without Adrikhedon, stalemate was inevitable.

"Lowland dragons greatly prefer to be dragons, but if they consume enough magic they are capable of taking human form. Unlike Highland dragons who rarely, if ever, mate with humans, Lowland dragons crossbreed when they need minions, and the offspring of human/Lowland matings become slaves for—"

"Bedtime." I slammed closed the book and kissed Nicholi firmly on the head.

He wiggled with protest. "But you didn't finish."

"That's enough for tonight." I held my breath, hoping he was too tired for furious drama.

Nicholi frowned and half closed his eyes, not up for a rebelothon. I exhaled with relief. Tomorrow night I'd figure a way to read something different. Dragons were creepy.

"'Night, precious." I nuzzled his cheek and Didoo's nose and then rose to turn on the nightlight, leaving the door ajar. "Sleep well."

"'Night, Mimi." He said my name, soft as love.

Everyone calls me Mimi, but Nicholi says it so that my heart glows. My name is actually Massima. Mom claimed it was a lucky name, meaning "the great one" in Italian. Massima always sounded to me like enormous heaps, or some kind of hot cereal. Either way, it was a dumb thing to name an American child, and I insisted on Mimi instead. I always meant to ask my parents, "What were you thinking?" I guess now, unless I meet one of those gruesome all-knowing dragons, I'll never get to ask.

I went straight from Nicholi to the laundry room, where the mud-caked box sat drying in the utility sink. I closed the door and cautiously let my hand hover a few inches over its lid. No, I wasn't imaging things; it really did give off heat. Irresistible warmth, radiating promise. As if I had found a hunger that I had never known, and this was the sweet treat I craved. I yanked back my fingers and shuddered. What a bizarre thought. I needed to get a grip.

I hugged myself, studying the box. Light from the overhead bulb gave the tin a silvery radiance. Mom's hands would have been the last to touch this as she laid it in the ground. Then those hands, soft from moisturizing creams, had guided me again and again away from the fig tree.

How old was the fig tree? I couldn't remember when she'd planted it, but I must have been very young. I wasn't allowed to climb it, though its branches were spaced just right for my short limbs. No amount of arguing could convince Mom I would be safe in it. When I was around seven I felt the urge to move my tea party from the front porch to under its branches. I squatted in the dirt and tore up withered figs, arranging them on a maple leaf plate. My Barbies and I were halfway through our tea when Mom came flying out of the house, hands fluttering.

"*Fermati!*" In times of distress she always reverted to Italian. "Did you eat any?"

I could tell by the anguished twist of her mouth that the

only possible answer was 'no'. Dutifully I shook my head, swallowing a dry lump of bitter fruit as discreetly as I could. It burned all the way down.

"*Brava.*" She swept up the maple leaf, figs and all, and crushed it in one hand. She shoved the debris in her pocket and then lifted me out of the dirt.

"Come inside and have your *té*. We'll make cookies, Massima."

Cookies—a weighty bribe from my figure-conscious mom. And my imposing full name made it a command, not a request. I gathered up my Barbies and took her hand, feeling a little nauseated from the hard canker of fig in my stomach. Together we walked to the front door.

"You must leave that tree alone. *Hai capito?*" she had said for the hundredth time. When I nodded, contrite to have disobeyed, she kissed me on top of my head. Under our feet the roots of the fig had been growing around the box.

This box. Leaning into the sink, I wiped the dial of the padlock and examined the blank front where there had once been numbers, then I looked on the back for a sticker with a combination. No luck. The dial was gritty, stiff, and barely turned when I twisted. I whacked it on the edge of the sink, and then forced it around a half an inch. It screeched loudly but the shackle didn't pop open. I took the lock in my grip and yanked, hard, jolting the box's hasp. It thumped and grinded, but the hasp held. Finally I twisted the whole lock, grunting as I tried to bend the box's latch right off. Despite the rust, the metal held firm. Dang it, my hands just weren't strong enough. Okay, Miss-Hate-To-Sweat, time to get serious.

I opened the cupboard and pulled out Dad's toolbox.

As far as I knew, this was the first time any of us kids had ever touched Dad's toolbox. Dad wouldn't allow it. For Christmas, Father's Day, and birthdays he wrote down catalog numbers, and Mom mail ordered his tools from Snap On. They were stout-handled and sharp-bladed, expensive enough to warrant a gold bow. I had always imagined the pliers, screwdrivers, and chisels lying side by side in neat, sardine rows, as perfect as the day they arrived. So I was amazed when I opened the lid and saw them in a jumble, handles greasy, spattered with paint. This wasn't an idle collection, like my boyfriend Duke's plastic Pokémon figures. This was an extension of a practical man's hands, protected from us absentminded kids. Dad might forgive me for using them as long as I didn't leave them out in the rain.

I surveyed the hammer, chisel, screw driver, wire cutters, soldering iron—I had no clue what to pick. I was reaching for a hammer when I heard Justin lumbering down the hall at a run, fast approaching the utility room.

"Mimi?" he called.

I slammed closed the toolbox and shoved it back on the shelf. Frantically I looked around for something to hide Mom's box with. I heard the rattle of the doorknob and grabbed a pile of rags, throwing them into the sink. Then I whirled around, face flushed and heart pounding. As the door opened I snatched an unfolded shirt off the top of the dryer and shook out the wrinkles.

The door banged as it flew aside and Justin stepped in, chest still heaving from his run down the hall. He surveyed the room, gray elfin eyes methodical and piercing.

"What are you doing?"

"What does it look like?" I avoided his gaze, my shaky fingers folding a sleeve. There were piles everywhere in this room: piles of dirty clothes on the floor, piles of dry laundry on the drier, plies of muddy shoes and boots by the door. Let the pile in the sink just blend right in, I pleaded.

He shifted his feet out of fighting stance and took a deep breath. "What was all the banging and screeching?"

"The dryer door was stuck." I spit out the lie as fast as a snake, striking instinctively. So easy it shocked me. "Here," I hoisted an armful of dry laundry and pushed it against his chest, "fold this and put it away."

His long bangs were trapped behind both ears, exposing his expression. His worried frown dissolved into embarrassment. Holding the laundry against himself, he used his free hand to fumble in his pocket for dice.

"Enough with the dice, just fold the dang laundry. I'm sick of doing all of this stuff by myself."

He withdrew his hand, and for a moment he looked ashamed. "I'm sorry, but that's how it works," he said, "no dice, no action."

"Then get out of here and leave me alone." I turned my back to him. Trembling and confused, I grabbed up a matching pair of socks and stuffed them together.

There was a prolonged quiet, during which I could hear him breathing in, breathing out, in tense, short puffs. Finally he said, "Mimi, are you okay?"

I sucked in a quick gulp of air, holding back tears. No, I

wasn't okay. I wasn't myself, somehow, but I had no idea what was wrong.

"I'm exhausted, Justin, burnt crispy. The court hearing, the finances, I need to get a job. No matter how hard I try this house stays in total chaos." I turned around. "Can't you just help me? Do you have to roll those friggin' dice all the time?"

He set the pile of laundry on the floor and stuffed his hands deep into his pockets. His shoulders collapsed forward, the stoop creating an armor of shadow over his chest. He looked besieged and miserable. "Goodnight," he said, and he swiveled on his big sneakers and walked out.

Oh gees, what had I done? As if those dice were there to annoy me, and not Justin's bargain with overwhelming fate. I just should have let him roll.

"Justin?" I called after him as he clumped down the hall.

"Yeah?" He turned, his expression as worn as Didoo's fur.

"I'm sorry. Really. If you ever want to talk …."

"Yeah. Okay. No thanks." He plodded around the corner and I could hear him go down the hall and close the bathroom door. The buzz of an electric tooth brush, a toilet flush, a few moments of silence in front of the mirror. Somehow he had lived side by side with his grief for another day.

I closed the utility room door and sagged against it, trembling like a wretched blob of Jell-O. I had lied. Flat out lied to Justin, then attacked him and driven him out of the room. I couldn't remember a time when I'd ever been so awful. I swiped at tears with the back of my hand. I'd always been like Dad: considerate, honest. For Dad, the truth was the truth. Facing it taught more than evading it, and he spoke with straightforward kindness. But then, he traveled so much on his job that the truth only had to be told occasionally. Mom, who dealt more often with the dramas of growing children, was perfectly comfortable with rescuing a situation via little white lie. But I had a feeling this wasn't an insignificant fib; something important was in that box. I knew because Mom had lied about it for years, lied with her mouth shut and her eyes averted. Now I was lying, too.

I tossed aside the rags. The box hunkered in the sink, the mud smelling baked and earthy. I heaved it up and shook it with frustration. It rattled ominously, shedding dry flakes of dirt. Wrapping a few rags around the sides, I stuffed it in the closet under a nest of tangled extension cords. Tomorrow, when Justin was at school and couldn't hear my banging, I'd get that box open.

Chapter 3

Quartered in my dark prison, I wait. Patience and preparation are virtues I have mastered: a benefit of associating with dragons. I let my avatar drift from the box so that I might hover, murky as smoke, studying the mystifying things in this close little chamber. It appears to be a wash house, piled with fouled laundry and made hot by the odd devices that crowd against the wall. They whirl and thump and disgorge clean linen. The room smells of boys, an aggressive odor that has not changed over the centuries.

Tomorrow my prison opens and I can begin to make myself flesh. She has held me too long, the sorceress, and I am weary of being hollow, my grip without the density needed to crush. Despite her, I have divined the spell with which she closed the box. The lock was a brilliant weave of distraction and thew, invulnerable but for one flaw: of necessity the spell contains the name of the one allotted to break it. At great expense to myself, I have called this chosen youth. He will open the box and then dangle, useless: no wizardry, no skill with the sword, no talent that can stand against me. The sorceress' trust in him was a failing. I select my allies more wisely.

A cold draft blows under the door, announcing what I wait for. My useless film of a body wavers from nerves. I cannot afford to lose this skirmish. I have had to call repeatedly: to the girl, to the one who will open the box, and now to this unpleasant guest. It has used much of me, and I draw on the last gasps of my potency. I must claim the girl's strength, or perish. Thinning myself into a delicate haze, I mingle with the reflected moonlight that seeps through the window and stains the wall.

Of all the Eternals, the Doppelganger is the most despicable. Still, ghost that I am, I envy him his physical flesh as he slides under the door and reforms himself on the slippery floor. In this light I cannot see the pasty jaundice hue of his skin, but I can smell the medicinal scent of ether he exudes, as if he had gobbled an alchemist.

"I hear there is gain for me here." He wheezes like a leaking wine skin.

"Gain enough, if you are willing." I keep my voice low, so as not to alarm him.

He spies about, cautious, his gelatinous form melting and remodeling—a cat, a warrior, a sprite—not sure what nature of creature he opposes. It pleases me that he cannot find where I hide, that he must settle on the submissive form of a human boy.

"Show yourself, I don't do business with twilight," he hisses.

I laugh, a grating sound that he shudders at, and he backs towards the door.

"You're but an outline yourself, turnflesh." I soften my

voice to a seductive offer. "There is a human life I wish you to assume."

He expands into a troll, the biggest that can adjust to this tiny place. "Why would I bother?"

I let the silence build. I have hoarded strength for this moment, guarded every scrap of will to marshal Yvess' powers of illusion. He cannot know how weak I am, only how strong I am about to become.

I reveal myself suddenly. The glare of the Wyrmstone brightens his piggy troll eyes and he cringes. He reforms, shrinking back into a boy who shies away, gaping at the folds of red cape over my thick shoulders and the malicious sneer on my face, both made to appear solid in the dimness. He backs toward the door, skittish of what I pretend to be.

"I offer you a rich take." I keep my voice gentle but edged with command. "A wealthy youth with a pretty girl as a lover. It won't pain you to occupy his life or imitate his well-formed physique."

"What's in it for you?" His voice is steady but his body gutters like a harassed candle: nose melting, eyes fusing into one, hands shifting from claw to hoof to padded paw.

"A simple request. I want the girl subdued and brought to my mercy. Ill with womb fever would do me well. With luck she will become barren, like her mother."

He grins, and the boy's face reforms, perfect and handsome. "Weakened, not dead?"

"Not dead. And if you kill her I will feed you to dragons."

"Dragons?" He retreats another step. "You claim to master dragons?" Now he studies my face, and slowly recognition dawns. "There is only one who has ever commanded dragons. But legend has it that Sage Pancrizio Sovrani was murdered." He sniffs. "I do not smell the skin and blood of a sorcerer."

I would seize him with my hands if I could, but they would pass like mist through his neck. Instead I drift so that my face is but inches from his, the light of the Wyrmstone glowing. He blinks.

"For sorcerers," I snarl, "there is a frail thread between life and death. I can walk that thread like a bridge. Can you, Doppelganger? Shall we test you?"

He flinches and slides one more step, reaching the door. "And what do I get for my efforts with this girl?" He liquefies, dissolving back into the yellow ooze that would allow his escape.

Willing forward a few hard-won drops of Yvess' charisma, I coat and sweeten my words. "A simple spell that expands your ability to control minds. The families of those you kill and replace shall not recognize your theft so readily. And the girl will be easier to bid."

The ooze hesitates, surging now toward the door, now toward the seduction of my offer. A tentacle probes the doorsill and I curse myself for being powerless to stop him. Mustering all of my persuasion I say, "Pancrizio Sovrani has risen. A favor now could greatly improve your future, and a refusal could shorten it."

His muck thickens into a column that shoots upward, loathsome slime towering over me, lapping against the ceiling. His stench is stupefying; a man would feel groggy. The sleep before the clutch of death. The haze through which the turnflesh bites. This creature cannot claim me, but I fear he will strike through my avatar and discover how useless I am. Have I been unlucky enough to stumble across a Doppelganger with courage? I steel myself in the event that I must vanish, and the light of the Wyrmstone flairs with white fire, making the air crackle between us.

He wavers in the sizzling glow, forming a large set of teeth, which he snaps. I force forth the last vestiges of my power and steam with threat. He collapses.

"Cast your spell, then." He snivels, a puddle at my feet. "Tell me the name of this boy. Instruct me on the nature of what I'm to do."

Had I breath, I would sigh with satisfaction. They are slimy cowards, Doppelgangers, preying on the helpless. I smile at him.

"Hold still, shape shifter, so that I may cast."

This is it, then, the end of the strength sapped from the girl's mother. From now on I must soak from the girl as I press into her skin, borrow her dreams and her lips to work my spells. She is strong, made by the sorceress for just this task. And I am patient; I have studied the ways of dragons.

No sooner is the spell finished and my plan laid than the pale yellow slime slips back under the door.

Chapter 4

"*Diiidoooo.*" Nicholi's shrieks tore through the school halls, electrifying parents' scalps so that their hair stood on end, making other little first graders clutch, wide-eyed, for Mommy's hand. I backed away from the scene with Didoo scrunched under one arm, leaving Nicholi flailing on the floor. Every kick seemed to get me in the gut.

Ms. Greer stood over Nicholi, cool disapproval masking her other, less professional emotions.

"This will stop eventually." She brushed back her blonde pixie haircut with certainty. She looked rooted, legs exposed by her short wool plaid skirt, their slender length made even longer by a pair of red high heels.

What I wouldn't have given for just one teaspoonful of her faith. Her dogged self-confidence that she was always right. Mom wouldn't have nodded and backed out on brokenhearted Nicholi, wailing on the scuffed linoleum. But every morning for the last two months I'd backed helplessly away. I didn't know what else to do.

I still trembled when I got to Dad's Subaru, shaking so much that the key clicked and scraped against the lock before it finally slid in. I collapsed into the seat. At some point I wouldn't be able to stand Nicholi's suffering anymore. What could I do? Move him to a different school? I doubted that public schools granted transfer appeals based on stuffed bears. Plead with the principal? Slim chance that I could out-maneuver Ms. Greer. I had to figure something out. I waited until the quivering stopped before I took out my cell phone.

In this economy, there weren't many jobs for a dropout first-year culinary student with a specialty in pastry. I'd been looking for a month, living off the last of Dad's savings and feeling more and more desperate. According to the want ads I'd be lucky to serve coffee for minimum wage at a café, or slave for a pittance as sous-chef at some candles-and-wine-bucket restaurant: jobs that weren't going to support two kids. I picked this morning's paper off the Subaru passenger seat. The pages were soggy, the want ads blurred from lying in the rain on the front porch. I should just toss it before I was covered with bleeding ink. Then my eye was drawn to one dry square, right in the center of the page.

"Private chef needed. Experience, references, good wages. Call Eastman at ...."

My heart gave a little sauté of hope. Didoo was still wedged in my armpit, a fistful of my shirt twisted in his furry paw and tugging as if to restrain me. I pulled him free and lay him, plump and scruffy, across the steering wheel, then I rallied the courage to dial Mr. Eastman's number.

"Hello? Mr. Eastman? My name is Mimi Jovel. I'm calling about the chef posi—"

"Do you have experience?" His voice was clipped—a man

in a hurry, hustling as if this was one of many problems stuck in rush hour traffic, jammed tail to hood with a hundred others.

"No, but I studied a summer at the South Sound Culinar—"

"Come right away. Bring a CV and references." He rattled off an address on the twenty-seventh floor of the Welch Tower, downtown Bellevue, and hung up on me.

I didn't have a CV or a list of references, but I knew the difference between gourmet and gunkotard. If I could convince him to let me cook one meal, I knew I'd have a job.

I made it within twenty minutes to the sandstone art deco building and took the lushly-carpeted elevator up to the door that said Perris Eastman, JD. I borrowed a pencil from his secretary and copied the phone numbers of two favorite teachers onto a sticky note. Then, quaking with nervousness, I forced myself down the hall to his office.

"Come in."

Mr. Eastman glanced at me standing in the doorway, waved for me to close the door, then returned his attention to his phone conversation. Leaning back in his chair, he faced away as he barked into a headset. His hair was shoe polish black, but the back of his neck was deeply wrinkled and well past middle age. His confidence reminded me of Ms. Greer's: boldly claiming the terrain, stinking with poise as if it were eau de cologne. Beyond his huge picture window, Bellevue lay spread like a map. He hung up the phone and spun around.

"Where's your CV?" Spoken like a lawyer who'd spent forty of his sixty-five years browbeating juries.

I forced myself to stand firm under the assault of his glare. "I'm a culinary student, I don't have a CV. But here are some names for—"

"No CV?" He frowned with disapproval, as though his witness had just strayed off the agreed-upon testimony. "Are you sure you're not a middle school student? You look awfully young."

"I'm eighteen, Mr. Eastman."

I tried to look as confident as Ms. Greer. I held her in mind: one foot forward, coolly observing Nicholi's rebelothon, doling out Nicholi's options in tidy, compact bites. Make your choice, no second thoughts, no emotional mishmash. I stood as tall as my little frame allowed.

"I'm an excellent cook and a reliable person. My teachers can vouch for that." Aping Ms. Greer's steely calm, I dropped the sticky note on his desk.

"Hmm." He picked up the note and pondered the names, then scrutinized my face again, and I wondered if he was going to card me. Then his manicured fingers tossed my sticky note onto a pile of papers, the note assuming its place in the traffic jam of his problems.

"I'll call your references. Assuming they check out, you can start tomorrow. The pay is seven hundred dollars a week to prepare hot lunch on weekdays. Leave meals for the weekend in the freezer."

My heart bounded. Seven hundred dollars! This was luck I could use, for a change. I thought about how much closer I would come to paying the mortgage, keeping the electricity on, buying groceries.

"I'll take it. What foods do you—"

"It's not for me. It's for my client, Ms. Lizbeth Farr. I doubt you'll ever hear her complain about anything you cook."

He swung his chair around to face the window, leaving me to look at his thick, stress-hardened back bulging against his suit at the armpits. He tapped the phone on his ear, already on to the next pressing business. "My secretary can give you Ms. Farr's address, etcetera," he said to the view.

Etcetera turned out, in this case, to include a house key, an address in an exclusive Bellevue gated community, and a copy of Mr. Eastman's card with the office phone number on it. All of this the perky secretary had ready in an envelope on the corner of her desk before I could walk the ten feet between Mr. Eastman's office and reception. She gave me a smile sufficient enough to be friendly without wasting much energy at the corners of her mouth.

"Call me if you need anything. Don't bother Mr. Eastman," she said sweetly, handing me the neat packet.

"Yes, ma'am. And you are?"

"Eve Tavick."

I managed to walk like Ms. Greer most of the way to the car, but three floors beneath the Welch Tower the poised stride gave out. I dashed the last few yards and yanked open the rickety door of Dad's old Subaru as though I were Nicholi, sprinting out of school at three PM.

Didoo still lay against the steering wheel, patchy black fur and sapphire glass eyes indistinct in the dark corner parking space. I threw myself into the driver's seat and rested my forehead on his belly, letting his fat tummy cushion my collapse. Seven hundred dollars a week. If we didn't spend much my brothers might remain fed and housed, and I could keep that last few thousand of Dad's savings for emergencies. Hope flooded in, coloring my world from dark to sunny. And it had been so easy. Too easy, maybe. Was there some reason why Mr. Eastman couldn't fill this job?

My cell phone rang. I scrambled to wrest it from its case.

"Mimi Jovel, girl of my dreams."

"Hey, Duke." I grinned with happiness; I had a job, two lovable brothers that I could now support, and a cool, entertaining boyfriend that adored me. Things were going to be okay.

"What's up, Gorgeous?" Duke is a software engineer, but he has the sensual bass of a jazz singer.

"I just got a job!"

"Sweet!" His laugh was rich and buttery. "Something good?"

"Seven hundred a week to cook for some lady. I know that's not much, but it's cooking, and it pays my bills."

I felt a little embarrassed around Duke when it came to my poverty. Not that he cared. He dropped out of the University of Washington two years ago when he sold his first cipher for a million. He had enough business sense to sock money in the bank and live carefully until the next million fell into place. So at twenty-one years old he was rich, but still living like a college kid.

"Awesome. Let's celebrate. Guess who's playing at the Paramount tonight?" He sang a few bars of "White Midnight", his favorite Tin Dog hit.

Far off and faint, drums began pounding in my ears.

"Duke, it's a school night."

"Yeah, but …." His voice scratched to a stop. For two months he'd understood about nights making meals for the boys, early mornings to get them out the door, and weekends with a curfew, afraid to leave the boys alone all night. I worried that his patience was slow-cooking, and would be done any day now.

"But I didn't get to see you last week." No singing now, just straight talk. "It's only school, right? Not maximum security. Can't you cut a few ropes when the Lilliputians go to bed, come over for an hour?"

"I can't do that on a school night. I have to be at home if they need me." I didn't say I was sorry because my voice dripped with it. "I miss you."

Duke was silent. The beat in my ears dragged like a funeral march. Between the seats in Dad's car were old gum wrappers we kids had wadded up and dropped there, and I dug one out and nervously smoothed the creases.

"Can we go out Saturday night?" I asked, "Justin can watch Nicholi." I fished out another wrapper, flattened it, and pressed the two wrappers together.

"Not 'till Saturday? Dang, that's two more days, Mimi."

There was a painful pause, and I could picture his handsome profile as he stared off into the distance. I wanted to reach through the line and touch his shaved, warm jaw, feel him turn and slide his lips over my palm.

Far away, in the gloomy underground parking lot, someone slammed a car door, and the steel exit door beside my parking space trembled. I stared at the exit, reminded of the Portal of Doom featured on the cover of one of Justin's Age of Dragons texts: ashen gray, the metal dented out as though something fought to return from the other side.

"I'll tell Justin we'll be out late." I wished I could transform the Portal back into a simple door again. "Let me take you out this time."

"No, I make more in one day then you'll make in a paycheck." He recovered his cheerfulness. "Anyway, I have a surprise for you, so we're going somewhere special."

My heart dropped, the drums in my head booming frantically. I could guess the surprise.

The Portal of Doom swung open and a woman walked out, clicking across the parking lot in her posh boots and white cashmere coat. Could that be me, spending his money and hiring babysitters, swishing around free and easy, looking cute? It didn't feel like me, not on the inside, not on the outside. Duke waited for me to respond while I stared at the back of the woman's expensive coat.

"I'll get concert tickets. See you at five?" he said, finally.

I strained to keep my voice steady. "Okay. Love you."

"Love you, too." And he hung up.

I snapped closed the phone and looked at the gum wrappers. At some time during the conversation I had twisted them together, mangled, inseparable without damaging them. The last time we lay twined in his rumpled bed he had asked nosey questions about my preference for diamonds over rubies, white gold over yellow gold. He was going to propose. It was not that I didn't want to marry him; I did. It was just that when I stood in his bachelor-trashed apartment and considered all of his toys—two big screen TVs, four linked gaming consoles, walls of video games and heaps of sports car magazines—I realized that he was a piece from a different puzzle, from a picture of endless play and possibility. He wouldn't fit into this hole of a life fate had left me, no matter how hard we hammered. My heart rebelled when I admitted it, but he wasn't cut out to raise two handfuls of boys.

But you don't fall in love with someone and then give up because of jagged edges. Mom and Dad taught me that. They were like starlight and broad day, but somehow they made it work. Maybe Duke could move in for a while and see what our life was like. Then if he offered me a ring, I'd say yes.

I moved Didoo from the steering wheel to Nicholi's booster seat so Nicholi would find him waiting after school. Then I drove home.

I needed to sort white from dark laundry, change the sheets on Justin's and Nicholi's beds, and sweep shriveled vegetables out from under Nicholi's kitchen chair. But I ignored all of this and retrieved the metal box that waited in the utility sink. Hefting it onto one hip, I grabbed Dad's toolbox and carried them both outside.

Dad had two sawhorses with a sheet of plywood clamped across them, placed at the end of the driveway beside the garage. Throughout my childhood he stationed himself weekly at this improvised table, repainting a chair, feeding fresh string into the weed whacker, changing a bicycle tire. This table was where things too broken to serve their purpose were healed and sent back into the stream of life.

I opened the toolbox and stared at the jumble. I'd seen him fix a million things. His pudgy hands had short, sure fingers that pushed and twisted until things slid back into alignment. But I'd never known him to break anything. How would Dad have forced open this box?

Stumped, I improvised, grabbing a chisel and a hammer off the top of the pile. I steadied the tool box by leaning an elbow on the lid, then wedged the chisel against the hasp, raised the hammer, and whacked. The lock resisted like mithril, standing firm without a tremor. I struck again, whomping with all my force. No effect, not even a tiny dent. I turned the padlock, set the blade against the face of it, and bashed over and over, doing more damage to my wrist than the lock.

Sweating, I set down the hammer and shook my aching hand. This was just a stupid padlock, like Justin might put on his bicycle cable or Dad might put on the shed. It was true that I was a little wisp of a thing but still, I had to be stronger than a sixteenth of an inch of stainless steel. Seizing the chisel in my fist, I jammed it between the lock and the tongue of the catch, twisted it upright, and whacked a furious blow right into the metal of the box itself. The blade scraped with a screech, slipped, and jumped out of my hand.

"Whoa there! That's a good chisel!" yelled a voice.

I spun around. Anguish over a tool was so 'Dad', I half expected to see a ghost. But the voice was alive and my age, not a bit like Dad. He careened down my driveway carrying our battered garbage can, the can swinging as if he planned to hurl it and knock the chisel to safety. He halted a few feet away and dropped the can, standing easy in jeans and a worn canvas jacket. Short curls stuck out from under his battered gray fedora and corkscrewed over his heavy eyebrows.

"You'll ruin the cutting edge."

He retrieved the fallen chisel from the mud and wiped the blade clean with the fingers of his work gloves. Against the glove's leather I saw a deep nick, marring the pristine edge on the metal. My mouth dried shut, too mortified to speak. Using a thumb, he tested the defect and frowned. The sharp outline of his lips twitched, but he didn't comment. Dad would have turned purple trying to control his outrage.

The man laid the damaged tool in my palm. He set back his hat, and then, instead of giving me a well-deserved lecture, he flashed an ironic smile of straight, white teeth. He looked like he belonged in a spaghetti Western: half a day's stubble, nose a little off center, and shrewd eyes.

"I didn't know what else to use."

In my shame I sounded defensive. The box became every humiliating problem I'd faced since my parents died: using the wrong tools with inadequate strength, not knowing where to apply pressure.

He slid one hand out of his glove. Reaching into the sacrosanct haven of my father's toolbox, he lifted a pair of pliers. He gestured with the pliers tips toward the box.

"May I?" His hand fit the handle as if Dad's tools had always belonged to him. They just visited our house.

I hesitated, looking at Dad's precious pliers, snuggled in the stranger's muscled, rough hands. I had no reason to trust him with the pliers or my box.

None, except for the complete calm that settled over me. I nodded.

He discarded his other glove, picked up the box, and wedged his knees against the indentations in the tin. Using a fingernail, he scraped caked dirt off the hinges. Seizing a supporting wire that laced through the hinge, he knotted his muscles and pulled. The wires drew out one after the other, creaking and moaning. He tapped the box and the hinges sprung apart. He set down the pliers and dug out Dad's bolt cutter. With a steady squeeze he cut across the shackle of the padlock. It snapped and fell aside. Then, gripping with just his fingertips, he jimmied the rusty lid. I tingled as the lid let go.

"Here." He didn't look inside as he handed back the box.

For the briefest moment I met his gaze and the look electrified me all the way to the tread on my sneakers. Flustered, I put the box down and looked away, ignoring the scent of honest sweat and baked bread that he exuded. I was about to become engaged, and I didn't appreciate the way this man made me feel.

"Thank you," I said. But I felt more like saying, "Back off."

He cleared his throat. "I'm Anna Rossi's grandson, Carlo." Anna Rossi, our neighbor across the street who rarely came out of the house. Who knew she had such a grandson?

"Did you need something?"

I wanted him gone, anxious to examine my prize. Well, in truth, I also wanted to stop feeling like a bumbling idiot and a seduced fool.

"I found a garbage can in the ditch. Is it yours?" He waved a hand toward the heavy brown Rubbermaid, a row of calluses thickening his palm.

"Yes, thanks."

Neighborhood kids rolled them around in the streets if they were left out after garbage day. Garbage collection was Monday, and today was Thursday. It was a miracle that I got the garbage can to the curb; forget getting it back to the shed again.

"I'll put it by the shed." He slung it onto his shoulder as if it weighed nothing.

"No, I'll do it. Just leave it."

He put the can down, retrieved his gloves from the ground, and pulled them back on, all his movements as smooth and easy as finding the box's weakness. Then he raised his eyes and held my gaze. He reminded me of Mom's Italy: mellow red wines, pungent olives, sharp hard cheeses. He wasn't handsome exactly, with that wobble in his nose and the heaviness of his eyebrows. But still, he had an arresting face and a laid-back smile. It took every ounce of my fidelity to Duke to break our gaze and turn my back to him.

"See you later," I said. Now I felt triply embarrassed—caught being incompetent, disloyal, *and* rude.

Irritated with myself, I bent over the open box. A small package lay on the metal floor. It was the size and shape of a lamb's heart, trussed in a tight strip of oilcloth. A bizarre shimmer, writhing like burning liquor, poured over the surface: otherworldly light, too strange to grasp. I looked away and looked back, but the shimmer was still there, filling me with dread. My hand hovered over the packet, reluctant to touch it. A confusing babble flooded my thoughts.

It's yours child, take the pretty thing.

Don't touch it, Massima!

Choose well, tiny human, there's no going back.

I stood, immobilized. I could close the box and never know this gift. It was enough, probably, if I managed to pay the bills and keep my brothers alive until they could fend for themselves. Mom and Dad wouldn't fault me that I'd made such a mess of things, as long as we all survived. But I wanted more. For me. I was too young to wither into an exhausted, overwhelmed drudge. Something vague flittered in the corner of my vision, too swift to snatch up and examine. An elusive wisp of hope. Hope that I was more than I'd ever imagined. I would have this one, small yearning for myself.

Reaching over the edge of no return, I closed my hand around the object. It felt warm and surprisingly light, nothing like the weight I had carried from the laundry room. A pleasure in my hand, sending tingles of exhilaration through my chest. In a hurry now, I lifted the package and tugged at the wrapping. The oilcloth unwound easily, slick and flexible. Underneath lay newspaper, *The Seattle Times*, folded over something dense and feverish.

Breathing suspended, I unfolded the paper.

My heart lurched, thrilled with wonder: a gemstone, splendid enough to be a crown jewel. An amethyst, purple as royalty, gripped in a magnificent setting of tangled golden roots. Slender tendrils of gold reached from the sides to trap the stone, the gem's color writhing into swirls wherever the icy metal touched. The six facets of the stone reflected so brilliantly that misty light radiated from its face. Sparks flashed in its depth, explosive with power and possibility.

I loved it instantly. Dropping the paper, I pressed hot stone and frigid gold into the skin of my palm. Confidence and robust vigor surged through me. This was as I was meant to be, not ground down by chores and overwhelmed by bad luck.

I felt a flash of anger at Mom for having hidden this. Dad, with all of his rational ideas, wouldn't have understood. He'd have locked the gem up to keep it from being stolen. But Mom—the beauty of this stone would have gripped her soul. Perhaps she hadn't wanted to share it, as I didn't.

I flipped the stone over. Fine root hairs curled from the golden setting, creeping over the flat back as if alive. In the very center of the gold was a smooth indent, a thumbprint-sized oval. At the top, someone had soldered a golden loop to the edge with clumsy fingers, marring the fine work. Strung through the loop was a strip of brown leather, making a necklace. Where did Mom ever find such a jewel?

With my free hand I grabbed up the newspaper. The date on the page was March 1st, 1992: the day I was born.

The weight of the date fell on me, heavy and ominous. Soon after my birth, Mom had wrapped up a gem worth a fortune, protected it in a layer of oilcloth, and locked it in a metal box. Then she had buried it. Had my birth somehow forced her to do this?

No, I wouldn't even consider that. I'd been a baby, born as innocent and unremarkable as the next. There was another explanation, there had to be. I scanned the newsprint. The city of Sea-Tac had been renamed SeaTac. The county won a grant to house the homeless. Parents lobbied for a new Ballard High School. It was just another day in the news. Nothing pertained to a gemstone, buried by an eccentric Italian. The box could have been buried any day, the date on the paper pure coincidence. But even as I told myself this, my heart thrashed around for reassurance.

Laying aside the paper, I examined the oilcloth. It was just shiny fabric. The only thing remarkable about it was how well preserved it was, given that it was at least eighteen years old. Ordinary cloth and paper. There must be a common sense explanation.

"Why did you bury this, Mom?" I murmured to myself.

"It was a pain in the butt to liberate," said Carlo. "Be careful."

Shocked that he was still there, I whirled around.

"What do you mean?" I squeezed the gem in my fist and pressed it to my belly, squaring off against him as if he might snatch it.

He opened and closed a gloved hand. "I saw you digging it up last night. Someone broke a sweat trying to make it inaccessible. I'm sure they had a reason."

I looked away, not willing to accept the logic of this or any other argument that meant the stone was not perfect.

"Jewelry can't hurt you." I turned back to the gem, cupping it in my hand, reluctant to put it down. The leather dangled between my fingers, cool and soft. On impulse, I slipped the cord over my head and let the gold lie cold and light, tingling against my skin. It swung under my shirt, making a soft whisper as it brushed against fabric. I stuffed the oilcloth into the battered box and closed the lid.

Carlo considered me as I folded the scrap of *Seattle Times*. When I looked up and defiantly met his gaze, he shrugged.

An eloquent, collectable, Italian shrug.

My father was a connoisseur of shrugs, especially Italian shrugs. That's why, he used to say, he fell for my mother. Hugh Jovel leaned over the bread basket at one of my grandfather's spectacular dinners to ask Vedette Sovrani for the butter, and she shrugged. He swears the shrug said, "Ask-me-on-a-date-and-I'll-pass-it-to- you." Mom laughed whenever he told this story, but she didn't contradict him.

Dad could reproduce many varieties of shrugs gathered over his lifetime. He had us all in stitches, dinner around the kitchen table, when he mimed everything from "Don't-argue-with-your-father," to "Justin-you're-hogging-the-muffins." Puffing up his tubby torso, deforming his elastic face, and skewing his head tilt said it all.

My father would have collected Carlo's shrug. It managed to say, "Just-a-friendly-warning" with the consoling spread of his hands, "Can't-blame-a-man-for-trying" with the upward thrust of his shoulders, and, "Find-me-if-you-need-me" in the deepest black of his eyes. Carlo, cheeks ruddy from the cold and fedora tilted over one eye, was an annoyingly appealing man.

Then he turned and walked away. I should say ambled away. He moved so effortlessly he hardly seemed to be shifting solid weight. With a pang of regret I watched him all the way down the driveway, getting smaller and smaller until he disappeared behind Ms. Rossi's laurel hedge.

I looked down at Dad's toolbox. Carlo had nested the pliers, bolt cutter, chisel, and hammer among the other tools. The handles now neatly accommodated each other like married couples do, finding ways to interlock so that everyone had enough space. It was an odd thing to think: tools, married in a toolbox, and I wondered again how Duke would fit into my brothers' lives.

And I was thinking about marriage when I should be leaving to pick up Nicholi and Justin from school. Reluctantly taking my hand off the gem, I gathered up the newsprint and empty box. The box was light when I lifted it, just flimsy tin. Baffling, how insubstantial it had become. In a hurry, I rushed to stow the battered toolbox, oilcloth, and newsprint on the shelf by my parents' bed, where I slept now that Nicholi had my old room. That way I could look at it again if I wanted. Grabbing two popsicles from the freezer I ran for the car, feeling the gold swing across my upper chest.

Justin waited at the corner by the elementary school, a rock in a stream of children, rushing and leaping towards home. Nicholi jittered beside him, hopping from foot to foot. The din of escaping students roared through the open car door.

"Climb in, guys. Don't sit on the popsicles," I said.

"Didoo!" Like every day after school, Nicholi threw himself on his booster seat and smothered his bear with neck-breaking hugs and Eskimo kisses. Justin fastened his and Nicholi's seatbelts, then opened a melting popsicle, laying the other one on his lap. As I pulled away from the curb Justin finished his popsicle in three bites. In the rearview mirror I saw him opening the other one.

"One of those is for Nicholi, Justin."

"He doesn't care. He just wants his bear."

"Di*doo*, Di*doo*, Di*doo*," chanted Nicholi, fleshy human nose pressed against pink, embroidered nose. His chanting crept under my skin: the aching rhythm of sadness we all suffered. I don't know how he endured listening to himself.

"Ask him."

Justin rolled his eyes. "Nicholi?" His sigh betrayed how ridiculous he thought this was. "Do you want this popsicle?"

"No. Di*doo*, Di*doo* ...." All the way home Nicholi chanted. All the way home, every day, for eight weeks. Justin never complained that it was annoying, never told Nicholi to shut up. He just ate his snack and brooded out the window.

Times like that helped me control my temper when I felt ready to strangle Justin. At home, Justin disappeared to do homework and Nicholi dragged Didoo around by an arm, staying under my feet where I could trip over him.

"Didoo was born the same day I was," said Nicholi.

"Hmm."

I turned on the oven, then stripped baked chicken off a carcass. In Dad's kitchen, a good chicken pot pie starts with homemade broth. I put aside the meat and threw the carcass in a pressure cooker.

Dad taught me to use a pressure cooker: snuggling the finicky lid against the rubber seal, flicking loose a stuck pressure valve, judging the water level so food didn't burn to the bottom or boil to soggy. These were my first, cherished, cooking lessons.

Nicholi fiddled with the creases in my jeans, wrapping loose fabric around Didoo's chubby arm. "Mom made Didoo for me 'cause she knew I wouldn't be hugeish, like Justin."

"Ah!"

I chopped an onion and peeled a carrot. In fact, Didoo had been Mom's as a child. It was a miracle he had endured two childhoods without being loved into dust. She took Didoo off her own bed the day she and Nicholi came home from the hospital. Ignoring warnings about stuffed animals and Sudden Infant Death, she propped him against newborn Nicholi in the crib.

"*Bene*, you are safe now, *figlio mio*," she had said. You're safe, my son. From what? By twelve I was used to Mom's eccentric ways, so at the time I thought nothing of it. Now, feeling the slight weight of my jewel and looking at the back of Didoo's head as he was dragged across the dirty floor, I wondered if there might be more to it than I understood. No, crazy thought. I dumped vegetables into the pot.

Sock-footed, Nicholi followed me as I stepped out into the November rain into the kitchen garden to collect thyme, oregano, and the frost-burnt remains of Dad's lovage.

"Can Didoo tell you a story?" he yelled across the yard.

"Sure."

Back in the kitchen I threw the herbs into the pressure cooker, then set it on the stove. Nicholi leaned heavily on my legs, almost pushing me over, wet socks leaving footprints wherever he stepped.

"It's about a little girl who was a sorceress, and a trashinator named Pan—cri—zi—o." He bounced Didoo four times on my foot, emphasizing each syllable.

I absorbed the thumps, trying to keep my hands steady as I sifted flour for crust. "What's a trashinator?" I asked.

"A bad guy who likes to trash things." Resting against my thighs, he shivered with appropriate drama, shimmying from shoulders to knees, causing me to scatter loose flour on the floor as I rolled a circle of dough. I leaned down to wipe up the mess. "The trashinator followed her around but she ignorinated him."

"Ah!"

I yawned, the long, exhausting day thickening my mind like a roux.

"Then she got older and couldn't have babies so she asked for the trashinator's help."

"Oh?"

Nicholi spent too much time building Legos under Justin's Age of Dragons game table; he overheard things that were way over his head. I sliced shallots, wiping onion tears from my eyes with the back of my hand, wishing I could just sit down and put my feet up.

"The trashinator made her promisify that he could have her first born, and she could have the next borns."

I needed to get the child play dates with kids his own age. I scraped shallots into the fry pan and inhaled deeply as a sharp burst of perfume exploded from the hot oil. Dad loved that smell.

"But she was trickolish. She went to the Highland dragon empress …."

I half listened, my mind mostly on caramelizing onions. Nicholi chattered on, a confusingly wild tale about the sorceress making a pact with the Highland dragon empress, and a huge fight between the trashinator and the sorceress, which the sorceress wins, imprisoning him. And then the sorceress' first born is left alone to kill the trashinator. Honest to God, between inheriting my mother's imagination and hanging with teen fantasy gamers, Nicholi wasn't fit company for other children.

Twenty minutes later I maneuvered around him to set the whistling pressure cooker in the sink. With a wooden spoon I pressed the valve and steam billowed from the top.

Nicholi stood on tiptoe and held Didoo up to see the curling vapor. "Didoo says a pressure cooker can wabbit a wizard's whizzle."

"Wabbit?" I asked, though I was equally confused about whizzles.

"Weakify, silly." Nicholi collapsed at my feet and lay sprawled with his tongue lolling, terminally wabbitted, his bear flopped over him in sorrow. Then he sat up. "But that's not how Trimble's gonna find the trashinator. Trimble's gonna use gunpowder."

The word walloped me out of my semi-attentive daze, jerking my attention off the pie dough. "Gunpowder?"

"Justin said so when he con-fer-ence-in-ated with Trimble on Skype." Nicholi snuggled his face into Didoo's scruffy belly. "How do you find a bad guy with gunpowder?" he mumbled through fur.

"I have no idea."

So this was the plot of an Age of Dragons campaign. Thank God. I should have guessed Justin and his wizard pal Trimble were designing some pretend hell to fight evil in. Relieved to have sorted fantasy from reality, I opened the pressure cooker. As I poured the pungent liquid through a sieve, I imagined the satisfaction on Dad's jovial face, missing him as I strained mushy bones and fragments of herbs from the amber broth. As I stepped around Nicholi to get the fry pan, he chattered on about gunpowder and how it is made of potassium nitrate which, according to Wikipedia, is contained in cow manure.

"Exploding poop! BOOM!" Nicholi flung Didoo and the bear bounced off the ceiling and plummeted toward the stove. I jerked out an elbow to divert Didoo to the floor.

Suck in deep breaths, force out controlled exhales.

Grit my teeth. Dad never yelled, no matter how annoying we kids were. Sometimes he grimaced with the effort, but he always kept his voice at room temperature. I turned to Nicholi. "Why don't you and Didoo build Legos under the kitchen table?"

"No." Nicholi giggled. "Didoo and I want to see exploding poop."

"No poop in this kitchen. But we're going to be eating gunkotard again if I can't cook."

Nicholi bumped his tummy over and over with Didoo's head. "Gunkotard is worse than poop," he said gravely.

I leaned down and kissed his forehead, just below his spike of widow's peak. Then I turned around, added flour to melted butter and whisked in broth, thickening it into gravy. I opened a spice bottle and smelled the parched snap of curry. Stirring slowly, I enjoyed the scent and a few seconds of silence.

"Didoo and I can't play with gunpowder." Nicholi sounded both awed and disappointed.

"That's right," I said, striving for a tone with authoritative clout. I heaved the heavy pan, pouring gravy over chicken meat and shallots, struggling to control the pan's weight.

The doorbell rang and Nicholi danced off to answer it, leaving me a few unmolested minutes to line a deep casserole with pie dough, pour in filling, and fit the top crust. I was cutting a heart pattern on the pie when Case prowled in.

Justin picks friends for what they bring to an Age of Dragons campaign. Elusive, wiry, girl-chasing Case was popular because he brought trouble. He had lush, engaging eyes, and until I came to know him well, his eyes were all I could remember of his face; the rest of his features slunk away. I had the feeling that those eyes took note of valuables, dark corners, and escape routes. But he was a slyfoot in the Age of Dragons game; if he wanted someone to like him, they liked him. He had what Justin laughingly referred to as "charisma poisoning."

"Yo, Mama Mimi, what's cookin'?" His thrilled tone made me feel that I was the best thing about his day.

"Hey, Case. Justin's finishing homework in his room."

Case sniffed the pie. "Oh, dude. This is fantastic."

Faint wisps of steam rolled off his shiny head. For as long as I'd known Case, he'd shaved his head, bald and oval as an egg. His eyebrow color shifted, hinting sometimes at the black of a faded photo, sometimes at murky brown liquid. But he was the first of Justin's friends to show signs of needing to shave. In another few months his upper lip might betray his true hair color.

"May I?" He flashed the appeal that attracted clusters of blushing teen girls.

"Yes, you may stay for dinner, if you can talk Justin into doing the dishes. I'm sick of this dice business."

He backed away, hands up, "No way. The Case doesn't interfere with The Dice. You're stomping on sacred ground there, Mama."

I sighed and shoved pie into the oven, slamming the door more forcefully than I intended. After Case's mom died of a faulty heart valve he practically grew up at our house, so I'd been his "Mama Mimi" since I baked him his first batch of cookies. I knew he respected me more than the numerous women who eased in and out of his Dad's life, but that didn't make him any less of a challenge when it came to negotiations.

Nicholi crawled in on hands and knees and wrapped his arms around my legs, squeezing tight. "I'm an alligator," he growled and bit my pant leg, tenting the fabric with his teeth.

Case's slippery scrutiny took in the defeated look of me: kitchen a mess, Nicholi on my leg, the floury knife clutched in my hand. He gave a conciliatory waggle of his elusive eyebrows. "We'll clear everything off the table."

"And empty the dishwasher?"

"Ah ... no." He sidled up to me and twinkled, hazel eyes full of promises to be a good boy. "But I'll eat all the pie so you don't have to put away leftovers."

I snorted. "You're no help." I stepped around him dragging the alligator that clung to my leg, and opened the refrigerator. I reached into the crisper.

"Would you cut up broccoli?"

"Broccoli? Will you make that incredible dressing for it?"

"Asian dressing doesn't go with chicken pot pie."

"I don't care, it's awesome." He smiled, dazzling as sunshine steaming off rain.

I couldn't help but laugh; he looked so full of enthusiasm. "Okay, if you want." I handed him the broccoli. "You can use this cutting board. Nicholi, I need to be able to walk so I can finish making dinner." I tried to pry Nicholi's grip off my calf, with no success. "Why don't you ask Didoo to tell you another story?"

"I'm an alligator, and I'm hungry." He bit again, this time a little closer to the flesh.

Dad, where did you find all of your unfailing patience? Stiff-legged, I hauled Nicholi to the toaster. "Okay little alligator, let's make peanut butter on toast."

"I'm the greatbig-inest alligator."

"Then I'll put lots of peanut butter on the toast."

Nicholi clung to me while the toast crisped, while I spread the nut butter, and as I hobbled to the table. Then he scrambled into his chair and chomped a reptile-sized bite, mashing sticky bread against his nose. Giving a peanut butter muffled growl, he flung wide his arms, knocking the plate skidding across the table. I snatched at the plate and caught it, forcing in another deep breath, carrying the china to the safety of the sink. I felt light without him on my legs, as if more than just his fifty pounds had been shed. The kitchen became grand and spacious without him underfoot.

Diced shallots, red chili sauce, sugar, lemon juice, soy sauce, mashed garlic, hazelnut oil … I threw them all in the dressing bottle and looked in the cupboard for sherry vinegar.

My mother claimed that she married my father because, when she opened his kitchen cupboard in Sienna, she found eight varieties of vinegar. My mother hesitated to marry an American, she claimed, because they eat soybeans—which should only be fed to cows—and because Americans eat in five minutes while standing up, or even worse, while driving. When she saw the white balsamic next to the raspberry balsamic, the red wine vinegar, sherry vinegar, apple vinegar, and rice vinegar imported from Japan, she knew that Hugh Jovel was, by her standards, civilized. Which was a good thing, she said, because she'd fallen in love with him when she first saw him at that fateful dinner. She had been heartbreakingly disappointed when she'd heard his American English and realized that he came from the land where "fast" food was considered a good thing.

She didn't mind that he had no aristocratic surname, grounded to the land for centuries like her family. Sovrani, she had once confided, was associated with as much wickedness as it was nobility, and she was glad to be rid of it. Another thing I'd never get to ask her about. She didn't object to Dad's middle class job as a UN translator, for like most people of old wealth she took pride in her disdain for money. She was concerned, like any good Italian woman, with what Dad ate.

My father, for his part, kept up his end of the bargain by stocking his kitchen with an ever widening array of vinegars. He also filled a four-foot cupboard door rack with spices, and collected a library of cookbooks any chef would envy.

Hence, we had sherry vinegar, which is lightly woody, more sour than a good red balsamic, and mixes wonderfully with lemon juice. The bottle was almost empty, and on seven hundred dollars a week with two kids to support I couldn't afford to buy another one. Unless, of course, I married Duke.

Instinctively, my hand reached for my jewel.

Icy gold chilled my chest and the hot stone heated my fingers. Mom and Dad married young, and they married for love. It would devastate my romantic mother to think that I might marry for money. I wouldn't, of course. I couldn't imagine being that desperate. And I loved Duke, didn't I?

I poured our last three tablespoons of sherry vinegar into the dressing jar and shook the vinaigrette vigorously.

At the cutting board, Case slit broccoli throats with cunning knife work.

"Bow to the Master of the Blade," he advised the rendered vegetables, staring with fascination as florets rolled under his knife. In Age of Dragons, Case's character had reached the "Death Shadow" skill level in sleight of hand, escape arts, thievery, and assassination. Which made him more than a match for broccoli.

Justin emerged from his room just as Case and I put it all on the table: pie bubbling and smelling like rich comfort, broccoli still a little crisp and stained red by dressing, and cold milk to the brims of the glasses.

We sat down, held hands, and silence settled over our table. Smells of my father's kitchen wafted over us: vinegar, chicken gravy, hot pie crust. Dad's dinner prayer rose in my throat, echoing in my head, his voice clear and alive. More than anything on Earth, I wanted him to say his blessing again, feel that safety and love. We were so lost without him. Something dark crept into me, threatening to swallow this warm kitchen. My heart thumped, frightened under the gold of my mother's amethyst. I tried to speak but my throat closed tight. I gripped Justin's fingers on one side and Nicholi's on the other. I couldn't hold this broken circle together. Even with Dad's toolbox. Even knowing how to use a pressure cooker. Even with seven hundred dollars a week and everything in Mom's garden shed. Even with Mom's magnificent gem.

"Excuse me, I … I … I'm sorry," I whispered. And I fled to my room.

Chapter 5

There was a time when surveillance from my tower gave view to rolling hills of sunflowers, a murky swamp in the eastern lowlands, and the distant smoking stone of sacked villages. Tattered refugees from Adrikhedon's fury sheltered in my domain, and I could see their bent spines as they toiled in my olive groves and hauled rock to fortify my walls. The wind was hot and smelled of iron in the sand. Now, looking out over what eight hundred years has contrived, I am almost sorry to have pounded so much of the old world to dust.

This modern town is majestic, but men have starved their souls, leaving little for those of us who come to ruin them. The city's borders spread to a vast horizon, pricked with heaven's lights. Its people slump with greed, both hands gripping all they have while their eyes measure their neighbors' good fortune. Wonders of glass stack upon each other as if the inhabitants lived in hives. Their frail towers glisten and reflect like ice melting. Everything is pleasant to rest the eyes upon, too beautiful to leave standing.

This wet city blazing in flames; that will be intoxicating. Small Tuscan villages roared, crackled, and screamed, but the sound could only be faint compared to vast Seattle burning. Groveling peasants have so little to lose, only so much is gained by snatching it away.

My pulse leaps and beads of sweat wet my forehead when I think on Adrikhedon's dragons, unleashing pent-up wrath upon this rich city. Acid, claw, and razor wing scything these affluent insects to the ground, vomiting down hell upon their magnificent nest. The ripe flavor of terror, the screech and bellow of the dying will course through my fractured soul like heady wine.

There was a time I did this to punish you, father, but that was long, long ago. After centuries as a pale avatar, I find I have developed a simple, all-devouring craving for destruction.

Chapter 6

"Adrikhedon! Wake, scaly glutton. You thought to be rid of me, didn't you? You breathed a few breaths without me, that is all. Crawl out from the mud where you are sulking. I conjure my forces, keen for war. We will drive dragons before us like a windstorm. Wake. Soon we summon the teeth and jaws of our army."

Far off in the moonlight the waters of a brackish swamp tremble into rings. A spiny back thrusts upward, massive, filling the mire, water retreating off scale and hideous strength. The moon flees behind clouds. The wind, empowered by darkness, begins to moan.

"Proch mandatum niss calx sna rů gethrix …."

~

I woke with a start, my teeth clenched hard against the rasping words. The image didn't fade as a dream should. A tower remained, impossibly tall, teetering over me as if it might collapse and crush me. A man stood at the broken peak of it, a big man wrapped in a cloak as red as a massacre, his thick arms reaching for the distant heaving swamp. Dreadful light streamed from one hand, obscuring his face. The other hand was so dark as to be invisible. And his voice, gravel and hot tar, scraped the air as if to draw blood, my echo of his words lost in a pleading whisper. Together we chanted a language that I had never heard, my voice faltering and hair rising on my scalp as I understood.

By the power of the stone I command you ….

I trembled with fright, trying to shove the words out of my mind, block them from escaping my dust-dry throat. My heart raced like running feet, frantic to elude him.

This man would kill me. Or perhaps worse. Far, far worse. My limbs iced up with that frozen kind of terror that makes a dreamer unable to run. Only my eyes moved, jerking over the tan bookshelves, the braided rug, the wicker reading chair. There was nothing in my parent's bland, suburban bedroom with which I could protect myself.

In the dim light, my gaze latched onto my parents' wedding photo, their faces vague outlines on the opposite wall. My real problems rushed forward: Justin's dice, Nicholi's bear, the chaotic house, the bills and mortgage. I collapsed into my pillow with relief. How real the nightmare had seemed, not the usual partially-cooked silliness. And here I thought *The Complete Book of Dragons* was going to frighten Nicholi! I laughed, giddy from my escape.

As if reality wasn't scary enough.

My gaze wandered to the white ceiling where shadows from the tree outside the window swayed back and forth. The remains of the night's rain dripped off the gutters with a steady *plink plink.* I sat up and turned on the lamp.

Beside my parents' photo the familiar painting of a Tuscan castle became visible: a landscape with a stark gray cylinder of tower that time had half toppled. Sleep had distorted it into something horrific. I would never look at it again without breaking a sweat.

I propped myself on pillows and drew the amethyst's leather string from beneath my nightgown. The stone was murky with drifting shades of purple, bright sparkles folded into the mist. Its beauty pulled at my soul, a hunger to hold all of Earth's precious riches. The wise splendor of objects that shine and hang heavy, graceful with power. The purple seemed to whisper: I pressed the warm stone to my ear. The murmur was too soft, meant for another world. I closed my eyes against the prickling strangeness, reminding myself that a jewel, no matter how superb, was just a stone.

Had Mom felt this same aching desire when she looked into the gem? About four months before her death Mom had one of her dazed mornings when she wore Night Veil, that scent that imposed thick silence on us all. It was right before I left for summer session at the culinary institute. I was boxing my things so Nicholi could move out of Justin's room and into my old one. I found Mom standing in the living room, catatonically still. She had put on every necklace she owned, every ring, every bracelet. Not my gemstone, of course, which was imprisoned under the fig, but everything else: cloisonné and cameos armored her chest; diamond and mother of pearl earrings swung from her ears; jade and coral bands clamped up her arms; and silver, gold, and turquoise gloved her fingers.

Tearful with panic, I ran to find Dad, who was fiddling with a spent smoke detector at his driveway work table. He took her to see Dr. Harvey, and we worried for three days while she recovered in the hospital. That was when Dad began unpaid leave from his United Nations job and started living off savings, staying close to her, keeping her in sight.

Perhaps that's why she had chosen, long before, to bury the gem under that hideous fig. There was something about the stone's beauty that disturbed reasoning, and for all her vivacious Italian exterior, Mom teetered on that blurred edge between reality and illusion. I longed to offer her the healthy stockpile of common sense that I had inherited from Dad. What I wouldn't have given to gift that to her.

I turned the necklace over and studied the point where the loop had been added to the back. It had been broken and soldered back together at some time. The repair work showed traces of uneven melt and scorching, as though a child played at goldsmithing. There was a soldering iron in my father's toolbox. I could check the tip for gold, but I suspected I wouldn't find any. It would have been too long ago and anyway, my skillful father would never have done such a sloppy job.

Then I saw the inscription. How odd that I hadn't noticed it before, written with a swooping hand in the smooth oval thumbprint on the back. The words were tiny but deeply carved and unmistakable. I squinted at them, holding the gold to the light, finally getting Dad's magnifying glass off the bedside table.

> *Natus, semines quae terram efficiunt,*
> *Sanguis qui ullum marem transit.*
> *Tribuete natus huic mulieri,*
> *Omnis eorum maior quam posterum,*
> *Quoad uterus centum reges foras ederit.*

Latin? Dad read Latin. "The only dead language still alive," he'd joked. I could pick out a few words. *Sanguis*: blood. *Terram*: similar to Italian for soil. *Uterus*: that was easy. *Centum reges*: a hundred kings. Blood, soil, uterus, a hundred kings. Made about as much sense as my nightmare. What was the name of that multilingual translation website Mom liked? I couldn't remember. Nicholi would know; he used to sit on her lap while she translated our report cards.

I turned the stone over and looked into its velvety depths. It made me ache, want, and shiver. Too bizarre. I should take the necklace off, re-bury it, and forget it. But that would be stupid. I slipped the jewel back under my nightgown and snapped off the light.

Outside, rain pattered against the window, soothing as kisses, gentle with comfort. On the back of my closed lids I saw Carlo's dark eyes, steady and intimate. I lay transfixed, awash in the warmth of him, the long gravel driveway extending beyond us until it met the impenetrable wall of laurel around Ms. Rossi's house. Slender trickles of desire prodded me toward him.

I abruptly opened my eyes to the shadowy ceiling. He had surprised me at a vulnerable moment; that explained why I was drawn to him. His hand fit around Dad's pliers; that must be why his presence comforted me. And he had given me advice—beware. Absurd advice, despite the attractiveness of the giver. As if I were blind to my problems. But the warning was touching, oddly romantic.

My heart grabbed for Duke, playful, faithful Duke, and hung on with the grip of guilt. If only I could talk to my beautiful mother. Being Italian, Vedette had no hesitation about displaying her allure to its best effect, so she must have handled innumerable temptations. Despite Vedette's beauty, she was unwavering in her loyalty. If only I could ask her, woman to woman.

I remembered visiting Tuscany when I was Justin's age, for my grandfather's funeral. I barely knew my mother's family, so I occupied myself during the dull hours of the service studying the Sovrani women. It was awe inspiring, bordering on magical, the way they stayed so attractive. As though their bosoms were bewitched into lifting, and their charmed lipstick wouldn't stray beyond the vermillion borders of their lips.

Over time I divined Mom's secrets. She maintained her hourglass by ruthless diet. She rejected any fabric that didn't perfectly accentuate her eyes, skin, and hair. She bought only a few, breathtakingly expensive clothes, cut specifically for her figure. She wasn't adverse to bras that pushed, carved, and rearranged, and used very high heels so her shapely calves moved gracefully as she walked. And at least once, perhaps more like twice an hour, she did a discreet ritual: tuck clothes, pin up hair, pull back shoulders, and check makeup. She did it so quickly and naturally that onlookers missed it if they blinked. Unless Mom was in the garden she looked gorgeous, her perfectly made-up eyes searching the room for Dad. And it was those mysterious eyes, more than her tempting appearance, that told the truth: whoever challenged Vedette's fidelity was swept aside, easily, by one smile from Dad.

I realized after two weeks of trying to copy Mom's beauty that I just didn't care enough. I flossed the oatmeal out from between my teeth, passed a brush a few times though my straight, dark hair, threw on whatever clothes appealed at the moment, and then forget my looks for the rest of the day. No one would catch me in clothing that I couldn't lean over or take a deep breath in. Only when I dressed for Duke did my appearance suddenly matter. For dates with him I painstakingly recreated my best imitation of Vedette's charm.

And Duke appreciated me: his eyes stayed on me when we dated, and his heart overflowed with roses, kisses, and compliments. It was shameful not to show him the same devotion that he showed me. If my mother could be faithful, then I could, too. My future with Duke may be tied in complicated knots, but I was not about to abandon it for Carlo.

I rolled over, punched my pillow, and tried to sink into the soft blur of sleep. I lay there, my pulse slow in my ears, aware of every creak and shift in the house. This was hopeless. Thank God the alarm clock went off. Friday, four-thirty AM. I tapped the button to stop the noise. One last school day, then Nicholi could hug his bear all weekend.

Groggy and wrung out, I swung my feet over the side of the bed. I'd set an early alarm so I'd have time to make flan for Justin's Spanish class. A Spanish flan has to be cooked on the stove for an hour to condense the milk, and then it's baked for another forty-five minutes. I wished he'd offered to bring tortillas instead.

I was digging in my drawer for bra and panties when I heard myself mutter, "*Sublach kossўova maneth ....*"

Rise hideous fist ....

I felt a flicker of fear, and then every cell in my body bristled. I'd already had the stuffing scared out of me, and once a day was all I'd put up with. Pressing my mouth closed, I forced the phrase aside. But when my attention wandered to finding socks I caught ghostly words slipping out again. Get a grip, Mimi. I yanked on jeans and a sweatshirt. Nightmares were bad enough; I refused to have insane days as well.

I fought the absurd urge to whisper as I whipped eggs and milk, and as I set the finished flan on the counter to cool. I resisted again when I woke my brothers, and as I folded laundry. But the intrusions vanished when Justin came tearing into the laundry room, towel wrapped around his waist, long hair dripping wet, eyes wide with panic.

"Did you put The Hand in the pudding?"

"What?" I put down the shirt I was folding. "What hand?"

"The Skeletal Hand of Power." He clutched the towel in tight fists. "I put the flan on my bed with my school stuff so I wouldn't forget it. When I came back from my shower The Hand was in it."

"*In the flan?*" He had to be joking.

I followed him into his bedroom. On rumpled blankets at the foot of his bed were his knapsack, school books, sack lunch, and the flan. The white china casserole dish was still covered with the plastic wrap I'd stretched across it. The Skeletal Hand of Power lay in the flan, woven wire claws pierced through the plastic and sunk deep into the warm pudding. Oxidation from the copper wire leaked into the custard, staining the golden crust a poisonous green.

I was speechless.

"If I'd been in the bed it would have gotten me." My barbarian giant of a brother was in a cold sweat.

"Justin, it was a freak accident. It fell into the flan."

"No friggin' way. I nailed it to the wall. It didn't happen to come un-nailed and *fall* all the way across the room. It was aiming for me."

"An inanimate piece of wire can't *aim*." That was true, wasn't it? Of course it was.

He yanked a ruler out of his knapsack and poked cautiously at the wrist stump. "That's what it's made to do—attack heat. It clamps on, the hotter the object, the more deadly the grip." The hand didn't respond to his prodding, so Justin put the ruler down. "The question is, who animated it?"

That was a creepy thought. But when it came to reality, I stood firmly with my father. "Gravity," I said. Still, I couldn't help but fumble for the warm stone, glowing under my shirt, its delicate weight suddenly a target in the middle of my chest. "Well, in any case, the flan is ruined," I said. "Dang. It was good too. I licked the spoon."

Justin swore under his breath, tucked his towel in place, then using his pillow as a hot pad he picked up the clawed flan. Still wet from his shower, he carried the pudding out of the room. I heard the front door open, then slam.

I was in the kitchen making oatmeal when he came to find me ten minutes later. He was goose bumped from the cold and looked grim. He put the empty casserole dish on the counter.

"Where's The Hand?" I asked.

"It's history." I pictured the wire mangled into a ball by his huge hands and tossed in the garbage can. One problem solved, and without argument, too. Maybe that was worth the sacrifice of a flan. "That was half my Spanish grade," he added.

"I can't make another Spanish flan *now*. You'll be late for school, and my new job starts this morning."

He shoved his veil of wet hair aside and pleaded with gray elfin eyes. "But I need it or I'll fail Spanish."

I stared at my sopping wet hulk of a brother. Everything about his posture mourned for all we'd lost: his weighted sloping shoulders, his shivering hands clenched in his armpits, his hair that dripped as relentlessly as the rain. Dad may not have believed in the lethal power of bent wire hands, but he would have moved heaven and earth, or in this case milk and eggs, to help our family. I grabbed the *Joy of Cooking* off Dad's shelf and rifled through the index. Justin leaned over my shoulder, his hair brushing water onto the pages.

"Do you think your teacher can tell the difference between a Spanish flan and a French flan?"

He shrugged the classic, "I-don't-know."

"Well, we'll risk it. Go dry off and get dressed."

Oven at 325, boil water, whisk eggs, heat milk, add vanilla, caramelize sugar. I plopped a dozen pudding cups in the water bath and opened the oven. With small cups the flan would be done in 40 minutes; we'd leave just ten minutes late for school. Fastest flan in the west. French flan, however.

I closed the oven door and turned around, gazing at the mess. After I'd left last night, Justin and Case had piled up the dishes. They didn't rinse them, blissfully unaware, or perhaps unconcerned, that chicken pot pie gravy dries into glue. Plates, glasses, and pots occupied both sinks, and the refuse from two flans littered the kitchen island. I should have been annoyed, but compared to everything else this morning it was manageable. Nicholi was suspiciously absent from under my feet. I went to see what he was up to.

In his bedroom, Nicholi stood in his sea of Legos and struggled to pull another sweatshirt over the ones that he already wore, an odd camel hump under his layer of hoods.

"What are you doing, sweetie?"

His startled gaze jerked toward the door. "Nothing."

"Nothing" can have as many meanings as one of Dad's shrugs, and this "nothing" was not the bored, reassuring kind. It was the any-adult-with-two-eyes-in-her-head-would-have-the-sense-to-investigate kind. I swept Legos aside with one foot and edged closer for a better look. The lump between his shoulder blades was squishy, and suspiciously Didoo-like.

"Let me see, sweetie."

Nicholi hunched into his clothes. "It's *nothing*," he snapped. When in doubt, get loud, fluff out your feathers and fan your crest, rattle your tail. That had been Nicholi's way since before he could walk.

"Nicholi, we have to leave for school soon. Let's make sure

Didoo gets breakfast before we go, okay?" I cautiously reached to peel off one sweatshirt.

He jerked away, flinging himself onto his bed. "Didoo isn't hungry."

"Well, he will be, as soon as you leave for school. He'll be really hungry."

"*No!*" screamed Nicholi, kicking his feet. "*No! No! No! No! No! No!*"

And he was off. During Nicholi's rebelothons Justin and his Age of Dragons friends referred to him as The Berserkidude. They invented this character type for Nicholi: a frenzied sprite, incapable of dying while he tantrums, howling through a battle and ripping apart whatever stood in his way. There had to be a strategy for controlling Berserkidudes, but I wasn't educated enough in Age of Dragons to know.

If only Mom were here. She was the one who handled Nicholi's rebelothons. With the opening refrains of Nicholi's screaming, she'd settle into a comfortable chair, enjoying the drama as it unfolded, as confident of the ending as a script writer. Nicholi shrieked and writhed, swept into each performance, desperate to, if only once, rewrite the ill-fated ending. When the last firework exploded and the fur was done flying, Mom would repeat in her sensuously accented English whatever request had caused the eruption. Nicholi, exhausted, would comply.

It never worked that way for anyone else, including me.

Nicholi spread his arms and legs snow angel style and grabbed onto the edges of the mattress with both hands, shrieking as if to bring down the sky. I stood over Nicholi's bed, wondering how he could kick and thrash on his back with that lumpy hump underneath him.

I glanced at my watch. For Mom, the show usually lasted ten minutes. But for me, the record was 30 minutes. I didn't have 30 minutes right now. What did Mom think about while Nicholi screamed? Had she noticed the miraculous creases at the corners of his eyes? Creases that accordion together in smooth, rosy folds when he cries, the skin still so new and beautiful. Or was she like me, a knot of impatience inside, seven fifteen and already running late?

The kitchen timer rang. If the flan overheated it would congeal like rotten milk. I abandoned Nicholi and went to put cool water in the bath under the cups.

Justin came into the kitchen and scooped four heaps of oatmeal into a mixing bowl. Standing at the kitchen island, he dumped in milk and brown sugar then shoveled up a bite.

"Sit down while you eat, please, Justin. You know Mom never allowed us to eat standing up."

He peered at me through his long bangs. I could tell he was trying to decide if this was worth throwing dice over. I turned my back and found a bowl in the cupboard. Maybe it no longer mattered if we sat while we ate. Maybe we were one hundred percent American now; the voluptuous, mysterious Italian, gone. I set my bowl of oatmeal on the table and pulled up a chair.

Nicholi came in as I took my first bite, face flushed and wet from crying. "I wanna hugolate my Didooster." He tugged at his layers of sweatshirts.

"I'll help you."

We peeled off six sweatshirts, one layer at a time. Underneath the last was a tangle of duct tape wrapped around his chest, the sticky white side folded over the slick sliver side. Nicholi had managed to plaster Didoo into the shallow hollow between his shoulder blades.

"Were you trying to take Didoo to school?"

"No." Nicholi sucked in a shaky breath. "I hid him from the trashinator."

"Why?" I picked at the tape. The sticky side had fused flat to Nicholi's skin, refusing to let go.

"Because he might kill him with gunpowder, silly!"

His voice mewed with indignation, as if he knew I hadn't believed a word he'd said in the kitchen the other day. I kept my embarrassed mouth shut and didn't probe further. Instead I tugged at Didoo, hoping to pull enough tape loose around his chubby middle to get some leverage, or make a narrow gap for scissors.

Justin stood at the kitchen island wolfing down the last of his oatmeal. He studied me with intense concentration as I worked at the stubborn tape, and I wondered if he was thinking about how Dad might have fixed this. How clumsy my efforts were in comparison. When I had a good flap, I pinched it firmly and yanked. Nicholi shrieked as tape peeled back. A deep pink swath glistened where the top layer of skin had ripped off.

"Owwww … Owwww …."

I reached for him. "Oh! Nicholi! Oh my God—"

Shrieking, he backed away from me. "Owwww … Owwww."

"Oh Nicholi, I'm so sorry." I tried to gather him in my

arms, but he skuttled backwards. Smack, the back of his head thumped into the kitchen island.

"*OWWWW* …." His hand flew up to the injury. Then he collapsed onto the floor, howling.

I knelt and lifted him but he was a limp weight, flopping out of my arms and onto the floor again.

"I'm so sorry, I'm so sorry." Desperate to make it better, I stroked his face, caressing the furious tears.

Justin threw his oatmeal bowl into the sink and strode into the study. Through Nicholi's sobs I could hear him tapping away at the computer keyboard. Then he was on the phone. I tried to comfort Nicholi for a few miserable, helpless minutes, then Justin came back with rubbing alcohol and gauze pads. He squatted beside me.

"What are you doing?" I asked.

Staying away from the raw spot, Justin dabbed alcohol on the duct tape with gauze, dissolving the glue. Impressively calm and focused, he eased tape off Nicholi's ribs. Nicholi stopped crying and watched Justin's big hands at work. I tentatively explored the back of Nicholi's head, searching for bleeding gashes: none, thank God. Within a few minutes Justin had removed the tape, leaving crisscrossed filaments of dirty glue and a 4x3 inch patch of raw flesh on Nicholi's shoulder blade. Nicholi sat up as Justin turned his attention to wrestling tape off of Didoo. The tape pulled out a fair amount of Didoo's fur, which clung to the sticky side in thick, disturbing clumps. Nicholi took his bear and scrutinized every remaining tuft of Didoo's pelt, and then buried his face into the familiar frayed nose.

"How did you figure that out?" I asked.

Justin shrugged off my admiration. It was a shrug straight out of Dad's collection: his eyes shy and proud, an annoyed lunge forward with his shoulders, and a dismissive wave of his hands. "Poison Control."

"Poison Control? What made you think of them?"

Justin stood and shoved his hands into his pockets. "Case uses it sometimes."

"For what?" I did my best to keep my tone light.

"Umm, well … " His hands hid deeper, " … he *is* a slyfoot you know."

"What does a slyfoot need Poison Control for?"

"Umm, nothing." And he pivoted on a heel and left.

That "nothing" was a whole, long conversation, I could tell. One that made my already exhausted insides sink and quiver. But it was two minutes to eight and we had to get out the door. I stood up and helped Nicholi to his feet.

"Come on, sweetie, let's go cover your cut."

"I'm hungry."

"Hmm. Would you like some Cheerios?" I herded him into the bathroom, where I fashioned a bandage out of two oversized Band-Aids. "We'll put a little Neosporin on … like this—"

He shied away. "Is it going to hurt?"

"No. Then we'll cover it up … see, all better."

He wrapped both arms around his bear and hung on, rocking back and forth. The kitchen timer announced that the flan was done.

"I have an idea," I said as I guided Nicholi back to the

kitchen. "Let's have a special treat, a picnic in the car on the way to school."

"*Eat* in the *car*?" Nicholi gawked in fear and awe, as if he could hear Mom's peppery tirade of Italian, scolding from her grave.

Enough already, Mom, this was a frigging emergency.

"Sure, why not? We'll put Cheerios in a baggie and you can eat them in the back seat." That was novel enough, and naughty enough, that Nicholi didn't even put up his usual fight about getting out the door. I dropped Justin in front of Eastlake High juggling books and a tray of flans, and then drove around the corner to the elementary building.

Nicholi threw open the car door. "I want to show Ms. Greer that I ate in the car."

"Good idea."

He pressed the almost empty bag of cereal to his chest and danced into the building. I wondered if Ms. Greer fed her kids, assuming she had any, in the car. Probably: it was a Greer-efficient thing to do.

"Bye Nicholi," I called. Then it struck me; Didoo still sat in the car seat. I couldn't believe it was going to be this easy. Maybe I wouldn't even arrive late for work. For one, brief second, I had hope that the worst might be over.

Chapter 7

The address that Eve Tavick provided was a gated community at Bellevue's city limit, surrounded by hundred-foot evergreens, dense salal, and human-sized sword ferns. The uniformed gatekeeper had my name on his list and buzzed me in.

"Here's a map," he mumbled between chews of his gum. "Watch for Ms. Farr's mailbox, you can't see the house through the trees."

I took the map, grateful for Eve Tavick's efficiency. It would be dicey, but I might make it before my new employer began to wonder.

I wandered around the maze of lanes until I found the mailbox, then pulled off onto a long gravel road, expecting a grand mansion with a circular drive. Instead I found an eerie, one-story house, low to the ground, giving the impression of having fallen together from wind-toppled cedars. Angular beams jutted into the sky, suspending four large windows in the front. I gazed at the tangled architecture with awe and doubt. Not a light was on. The windows were darker than the forest around it. Maybe no one was home and my tardiness would go unnoticed.

Not seeing a garage or carport, I left the Subaru in the driveway and hurried to the entry. Three feet from the door I had the creepy feeling that I'd been noticed. Not the neck-tingling warning that someone was watching. More an eerie perception, seeping through my skin, that I had been recognized and allowed to pass. I paused, peering over my shoulder for a watchdog, checking dark windows for a weirdo with a shotgun: nothing, no one. Cautiously I inched forward.

In the dirt before the door was a scratched pentagon filled with triangles, the whole thing as wide as a stop sign. I froze, deeply uneasy. By the worn look of it, the symbol had been cut a long time ago, too deep in the soil for weeds to hide. I couldn't imagine why anyone would carve such a thing. Seven hundred dollars a week, I reminded myself, and you're late for your first day. I knew it was silly, but I decided to step over, rather than on, the scratches.

A note hung taped to the front door. Spindly looping letters informed me that the door was unlocked, that "I" had gone out on errands, and that "you" should let yourself in. "I" would be back shortly. The message was unsigned. What great luck: tardy, and no employer at home to catch me.

I turned the handle and entered directly into the living room—no hall, no chance to prepare for the shock. An awful smell stuffed up my nose: a thick breath-full of mud with faint undertones of rotten. I choked and would have backed away, but I couldn't take my eyes off the room.

The front bank of windows was probably only fifteen feet tall, but they framed an overwhelming view, as though I stood inside a huge eye, gazing at the wild Northwest woods. The windows formed the wide end of a cone, with walls and ceiling shrinking toward the back, where the cone narrowed to only seven feet. There, windows watched over a beaver pond. Ignoring the smell, I crept further inside.

A catwalk created a ledge all the way around the room. Below this narrow walkway, the room dropped half a story, creating a sunken cavern. The depression was filled with soft couches and expensive Persian rugs, all shabby and scuffed.

Above the catwalk were floor-to-ceiling shelves, ending where the ceiling arched. The shelves were crowded with bizarre things: an African spear, Grecian pots, a Japanese doll in a glass case, a bronze mask, an inlaid knife, a fertility statue. The oddest thing I could see was a huge animal bone, massive enough to be a woolly mammoth's, decorated with carving. There must have been hundreds and hundreds of objects, disappearing off into the far reaches of this private museum, millions of dollars' worth of priceless artifacts.

I stood blinking, adjusting to the gray light filtered through the trees, stunned by the beauty and strangeness. So many splendors, so much myth and legend, woven, forged, and carved. I inhaled deeply, as though to suck the magnificence into my heart. The muddy odor faded, replaced by the scent of history: old silk, burnished metal, wood polish, raw wool … all confined by an earthy closeness. What an amazing place. Sinister though; I couldn't help but worry about the underlying rot.

I crept downstairs into the sunken living room, scanning the walls for a door. I couldn't see any. I picked my way around the couch and chairs, and then saw steps leading up the other side. At the top step, a break in the bookshelves marked a semi-hidden door, flush with the wall. There was no handle so I pushed gently. The door swung in.

I peered into a narrow bedroom with a small bed. At the far end, the high back of an upholstered armchair hid all but the top of a person's head.

"Oh! I … I'm so sorry, Ms. Farr," I stammered. "I didn't think anyone was home."

She didn't move.

"Excuse me, Ms. Farr?"

Her chair faced a glass alcove with a 180-degree view of the pond. Beaver had taken down trees and dammed a small stream, bringing the water level to within twelve feet of the house. Gnawed trees rested at all angles. Crumbling stalks of cattails, withered flag iris, and the blackened nubs of water lilies gave texture to the thick mud at the edges. The pond covered at least a third acre, and I had the uneasy impression that the bedroom leaned toward it.

I advanced across the rug, expecting her to turn so I could give a nervous apology. But it was as though I wasn't there.

Anyone who has seen an emu would recognize Ms. Farr: a wrinkled, diamond-shaped face on a long neck, round, glossy eyes, and an upper lip that hung over the lower one. She sat bolt upright, eyes fixed on the pond, wispy and skinny enough to pass for a starved bird.

"Ms. Farr?" I said softly, standing beside her chair.

Slowly she turned, looked at me, tilted her head all the way to one side so her left eye aligned above the right one, and then swiveled around and lost herself in observing the pond again.

I waited, baffled. A kingfisher lit on the branch of a felled tree, inspecting the water's shadows. The wind roughed the surface of the pond into dark spines.

Ms. Farr didn't speak or move.

I stood torn between brushing frizzles of hair from her eyes, and backing away from her strangeness.

"Well," I said finally, "I guess I'll go find the kitchen."

Her erect frame stayed still, long neck poking out of her bathrobe, wide eyes surveying the pond. Not knowing what else to do, I turned away. I was beginning to understand why this job might be vacant.

Across the room, two flat rectangles that passed for doors led out of the room. I walked around the lumpy bed mounded with a checkered brown comforter and pushed at one handleless door. A bathroom. The other door led to the kitchen.

The kitchen was L shaped with a band of windows at eye level, views everywhere except where the door led to the bedroom. In a rectangle between bedroom and kitchen, windows looked out on an ancient cedar. In the only attempt at gardening I'd seen so far, someone had trimmed the lowest limbs, leaving stubs from which they'd hung birdfeeders. But instead of seed the feeders were filled with dirt. A bright orange salamander sat on the feeder tray, and it jerked its head when it saw me, pumping up and down nervously on its front legs. Then it scuttled into the feeder and disappeared in the dirt. That probably eliminated half the candidates for this job, right there.

The kitchen was barren. Not a flour tin, fry pan, or pepper grinder on the steel counters. The stove was pristine; the stainless expanse of the sink wasn't marred by so much as a sponge. I put my purse on the counter and started opening cupboards. Thank God there were pots, casserole dishes, and even a wok. But only two cutting boards. Dad always said that any meal worth making required at least four. I searched for the pantry and found it behind two large cupboard doors. The shelves were bare except for a few boxes of Earl Gray tea and some dry cereal. I opened the refrigerator: milk, eggs, and Jell-O pudding cups.

The door behind me swung open with a bang. I wheeled around, hand instinctively grabbing for my gemstone, my heart in my throat. A tall, sinewy man slouched in the doorway. Everything about him gave the impression of indolent laxity. His joints were so loose that his feet splayed out, and his oily, jet black hair drooped in strings to his shoulders. His acne-pocked face was skeletal, eerie, with a quiet malevolence that made me want to back up, out of range. He slung two bags of groceries onto the counter. From six feet away I could smell rot, sucked in with each of my shallow gulps, raising goose bumps on my skin.

"Are you what he sent me?" His right eye was green and his left eye so pale a blue as to show the red reflex, shining behind it. He gawked at me, an arrogant, hungry stare.

Buzzing with adrenaline, I closed the refrigerator door and inched away. "I'm Mimi Jovel, and yes, I'm the cook." I kept both eyes on him, feeling like a little bird that fluffs out its feathers to look bigger.

His gaze slithered from my face to my feet, and then centered on my chest where it practically burned a hole through

the hidden gemstone. "Well at least you're worth looking at."
Jaw dangling, he managed an open mouthed smirk. "I bought
groceries." He eased around the counter and turned his back
to me, heading for the door.

"Wait! Who are you?"

He rotated just his head, sneering back over his shoulder.
"Steve. But it hardly matters, you won't be around long
enough to need names."

Against my better judgment, I pursued him through the
door and into Ms. Farr's bedroom. "Hold on, Steve, I have
questions."

He stopped. "What?" The word dripped with contempt.
All of these years I'd been listening to Justin's Age of Dragons
group talk about *loathsome*—a *loathsome* Banshee, a *loathsome* Wercat—and I'd thought the word was silly. What in
real life is ever, truly *loathsome?* Now I knew.

Drawing on my disgust, I kept my voice rock steady.
"What does Ms. Farr like to eat?"

"*Phhhh,* how should I know?" He narrowed his eyes, making even his bored expression threatening.

Behind him, Ms. Farr still stared at the view as though it
were a TV, apparently unaware that we were there. I had a
bottomless wave of compassion for her, stuck here with this
creep. Seven hundred dollars a week, I reminded myself. Feed
my brothers, pay the mortgage, keep the lights on. I gagged
down my revulsion.

"I need to know what to cook."

"Cook anything you want." He gawked at me again. It
made me feel naked. I wanted to put on one of Dad's big

overcoats and pull a ski hat down over my face.

"Italian, French, Greek … ?"

Steve dropped onto Ms. Farr's bed and sat there in a brooding slouch. His mismatched eyes wandered over me, settling again in the center of my chest. My hand flew up to cover myself, and my fingers pressed against the amethyst. It was burning hot, and a bolt of vehement fury shot through me.

Steve's attention glided to his pale hands and his abnormally long, filthy fingernails. He heaved a sigh—the most energetic thing I'd seen him do so far—and patted the bed beside him. "Come here," he said, leering.

I didn't move.

Power welled, a pressure bigger than my chest, bigger than the room. I found his eyes and locked on. His green eye glowed gold at the center, cruel and piercing, and his blue eye was hidden in haze. I felt as though I were expanding, huge wings bursting from my shoulders, claws sprouting from my nails. A terrifying savagery fought to explode inside me. I swear, in that moment, if he'd touched me I would have ripped his neck open.

Smooth as silt, his gaze slipped away. He folded pale fingers in his lap and contemplated the squares on Ms. Farr's checkered bedspread. I stood shaking violently, as afraid of myself as I was of him. Deep breaths, calm down, Mimi. This isn't you; you don't attack people. Bad morning, not enough sleep, too many problems: not a winnable defense in a murder trial.

"Ms. Farr doesn't eat much of anything." His voice was nonchalant, as though he hadn't noticed my near abandon of rational control. "I don't even know why my uncle insists on hiring a cook. She hasn't spoken in—I don't know—ten years? Most of the time she won't even acknowledge that you're in the room." He got up. "Cook whatever you want. You're the expert." He retreated to the door leading to the living room. Without turning around, he jeered, "I give you two weeks."

Two weeks around him would be an eternity. "Your uncle is Mr. Eastman?" I said to the closing door.

"Yep, that's me, Steve Eastman." He let the door bang shut behind him.

I resisted the urge to dash screaming to Dad's Subaru. I should have figured the salary was too good to be true. They don't pay $30,000 a year to cooks who dropped out of culinary school, then let them work in pleasant, friendly places. But face it, I was desperate. And for all his slimy bullying, Steve had run from me. A temporary retreat only, I suspected. I didn't trust him a whiff. Then there was poor Ms. Farr—I could barely see the top of her pink scalp, shiny under her frazzled hair, poking up from behind the armchair. I hated to abandon her. I prodded myself back to the kitchen to inspect Steve's groceries.

The two bags held a carton of orange drink that was only half juice, two green bananas, a loaf of cheap white bread, canned spaghetti sauce, sliced American cheese, several chicken flavored Bowl O' Soups, dry pasta, and a bag of carrots. I couldn't cook with this. I left it all spread out on the counter and went back to Ms. Farr's room.

I knelt, my knees in the shaggy carpet. "Ms. Farr?"

Outside, under her captured gaze, light rain fell on the pond, washing the already saturated landscape.

I took her hand. It was icy cold. I rubbed her fingers to warm them. After a minute she shifted her gaze to me. "Hi," I said.

Her round, large eyes blinked twice.

I squeezed her hand. "I want to make something you'd really like to eat. What should I make you?"

For a moment I thought I saw a flicker of recognition, a slight lean forward, a tentative smile. Then she withdrew her hand and riveted her attention back on the swampy wildscape. I couldn't tell if she thought about, or even saw, the choppy waves she stared at, or if she felt the chill on her skin. Had she lived this way for ten years? I couldn't help wondering if her life was peaceful, or torture.

I stood and searched for a sweater. There was no dresser or closet, only a large wooden chest at the end of her bed. I opened the lid: a set of summer pajamas, a light robe, underwear, and socks lay on top. I pushed them aside, feeling for a sweater underneath. All I could find were books and papers. I rearranged the clothing, then closed the chest. The best I could offer was the comforter. It was bulky, but when I put it around her shoulders she grabbed with both hands and tugged it close. Tea. If nothing else, I could make her tea.

When the tea was ready, I carried the pot in on a cutting board because I couldn't find a tray. There was nowhere to put it but on the floor, so I set it down and decided to brave an encounter with Steve to find a table.

In the living room, Steve reclined on the couch, his shoes

on the tan upholstery and his black hair shedding on the cushion he used as a pillow. He appeared to be reading, and as far as I could tell, my rummaging around didn't disturb his concentration. Either that or he pointedly ignored me as I hefted a small coffee table up the stairs and through the door. It was no surprise that he didn't offer to help.

When I placed the warm mug in her hands, her fingers closed around it and she smiled but made no effort to drink. I left her alone and went to plan a menu.

Of the things Steve bought, the carrots were of use. The rest I put away in the pantry and refrigerator. Steve's purchases gravitated toward Italian, so I decided on lasagna and marinated beet salad. No pressure cooker. No beets without a pressure cooker. We'd have spinach salad, and I'd steam carrots. For future meals I'd have to cart a pressure cooker back and forth from home, but that was manageable. Ms. Farr's evident dementia was manageable. I wasn't so sure that Steve would be manageable, but I was buoyed by the feeling that I had won round one, even though I'd done it at peril of hysteria.

Steve was asleep when I returned to the living room, spread across the couch like a dirty smear of gum. I screwed up my courage and nudged his foot with my shoe. "Wake up, please."

He snapped awake, eyes slits, mouth hanging open. "Whaaa?"

I assumed Ms. Greer's one-foot-forward-no-nonsense stance. "Is there a budget?"

"A who?" He propped himself on bony elbows.

"Budget. How do I buy groceries?"

He flopped back down and closed his eyes. "I already bought groceries." He sounded incredulous, as though I demanded that he repaint the house.

I cleared dry nervousness from my throat. "I have to do my own shopping."

He didn't answer, and I wondered if he'd gone back to sleep. Did I dare nudge him again? "Steve?" I waited, and he opened just his green eye. "I'm a cook. A good one. I'm going shopping now so I can do my job. How do I pay for it?"

Glaring at me with that murky green gaze, he reached into his pocket and pulled out a QFC gift card. He flew it at me, sideways, as though it were a Frisbee. I snatched the card out of the air. He rolled over and was snoring before I closed the front door.

The helpful guard at the gate directed me towards the nearest QFC grocery. I bought enough to make a large pan of lasagna, thinking that it freezes well for the weekends. And I bought two cutting boards. When I returned forty-five minutes later Steve hadn't moved. I was beginning to wonder just what his job was, aside from being nephew to Mr. Eastman.

In the kitchen I relaxed into making Dad's lasagna. My father loved Italian food, because Italian food meant Italians with their dramatic, uninhibited shrugs. Arms flung wide, shoulders pulled to the tops of the ears, and the inevitable puttering, blowing, and whistling accompaniment. All over Italy people shrugged eloquently, and my father went to worship like a pilgrim.

Grinding nutmeg for the béchamel, I remembered him making lasagna. Light on his feet for a pudgy man, he trotted around the kitchen, whisking white sauce, draining steamed spinach, pouring cabernet into the pot of bubbling skinned tomatoes, and dumping browned beef on top. "Tonight, Mimi, we will eat and shrug like the Romans."

Dad at the head of the table, entertaining us. Nicholi, giggling so hard that he fell under his chair. Justin, jumping up to see if he, too, could imitate that shrug. Mom in tears from laughing, trying to catch her breath enough to say, *"Bravo, amore mio!"* Bravo, my love. Then the multiple layers in the lasagna exposed with a cut of Dad's spatula: all of the ingredients of my family's happiness snuggled one on top of the other, deliciously thick with care and devotion.

I made the lasagna in ten layers the way Dad did. And when I took it, bubbling and crusty out of the oven, the smell filled the kitchen, wandered through Ms. Farr's room, and woke Steve from the dead.

He arrived and stood with his back slumped against the kitchen door, one foot facing east and one facing west, watching me stack the dirty pans. "That … uh … really smells good." He drew a greedy breath and rubbed his hand across his mouth, wary as a snake. I was pleased to hear a tiny pinch of respect in his voice.

"There's plenty if you want some. It'll be better if you let it sit for twenty minutes." Uneasy about turning my back to him, I kept an eye out as I washed the spinach.

"So, uh … where'd you learn to cook?"

"My father, mostly. But I've had a summer in culinary

school." I broke wispy little stalks off the delicate winter leaves. "Does Ms. Farr walk?"

"Sure." He sucked on his teeth, ogling the lasagna.

"Why don't you set the kitchen table? We'll have lunch in here."

Both eyes—green and blue—streaked to my face, and if *loathsome* can look surprised, he nailed it. "Together?"

"Why not?" I gripped the colander with spinach flopping over the sides, steeled for another showdown. "Bring your enemies to the table," my United Nations Dad was fond of saying. "Meals are better than battlefields."

Steve shrugged! A reanimated corpse of the spirit of Italy. As Dad always said, "There's good in everyone." I suspected that I had just seen the whole of Steve's good side.

But he did set the table, even clumsily folded paper towels for napkins. Then he left and returned leading Ms. Farr, who struggled to free her hand from his. Ms. Farr picked each foot up carefully, her head turning left and right but eyes not appearing to register. He guided her to one end of the table and she sat, hugging herself when he let go. I knew exactly how she must feel, being touched by him.

I sliced hard-boiled eggs, crunched bacon onto the spinach, whisked a touch of brown sugar into oil and red wine vinegar, and dressed the salad.

"What do you want to drink, Ms. Farr?"

She fingered folds of her paper towel as if she wasn't sure what it was.

"Give her water," said Steve.

I didn't like his imperious tone, but I didn't have any milk and she'd already had tea. Dad's voice echoed in my head, "Pick your battles, Mimi." I added ice to her glass and filled it. Cutting the lasagna, I remembered Dad serving the family, holding the spatula as competently as he held all tools. We came to Dad's table with our wires all tangled and our wheels flat; we left whole.

Steve ate three huge slabs of lasagna, two cups of carrots, and three-quarters of the bowl of salad. Ms. Farr ate two bites of lasagna and a leaf of spinach. She drank her glass of water. Then she passed into an unconsciousness that I assumed was sleep, eyes closed with her pointy chin digging into her thin chest.

As I rose to clean up, Steve pushed back his chair and slid forward on the seat, making more room for his lanky legs. With the tine of his fork, he picked a shred of spinach out of his teeth.

"What do you do around here?" I asked as I stacked the plates.

"Mmm … stuff." He leaned forward, cut a corner off the remaining lasagna, and forked it into his mouth.

Stuff? Stuff himself? Sleep on the stuffed couch?

Steve stood up. "Back to your room," he said to Ms. Farr, as though putting a pet in a cage. She woke, shuddered, and tried to draw away as he pulled her out of her chair. He guided her through the door, and I wondered if she felt terribly lonely. If she even knew he lived here, sleeping on her couch. Hopefully her dementia was blind oblivion.

I finished the dishes. Steve was back reclining on the couch with a magazine as I passed though the living room.

"There's lasagna in the Tupperware, and more in the freezer. Two minutes in the microwave, add a little milk if it gets dry. I'll be back Monday."

"Uh," he grunted. He held the magazine so that instead of his face I saw an Egyptian mask. An Archeology magazine: what a surprise. He seemed so narcissistic that I couldn't imagine him interested in anything other than Steve Eastman. I closed the door behind me with relief.

Picking my way through ferns, I turned back to look at the windows. They looked like the eye of a cone-shaped telescope, dropped in the mud, looking down into some dark underworld instead of up to the stars.

Chapter 8

"Highland (mountain) dragons live above the tree line in Alpinthrix—what humans call the Italian Dolomites. Unlike Lowland (swamp) dragons, who must consume enchanted items for their magical powers, Highland dragons are born spellcasters, especially skilled in creating illusion. It is said that Empress Yvess can make illusions so powerful that they are capable of existing, reproducing, and dying like living things. Some argue that her son, the formidable Vasborya, is nothing but an imagined dream, and that Yvess' mate, the dreaded Emperor Carrach, (killed by the legendary sword Deathwish in the hundredth year of the dragon wars), was never, in fact, true flesh."

I snuck a peek at Nicholi to see if he was asleep yet. He had one eye open like a baby dragon, and he trained it on me when I stopped reading, clearly expecting me to go on. I had sworn to myself that I was done reading *The Complete Book of Dragons*, but Nicholi threatened full-fledged Bezerkidudeitude when I opened *Mille and the Alien*, so I relented. Pick you battles, Mimi.

That's what I'd been doing all day, it seemed. I was so glad it was Friday night and my worst battles were over.

"Highland dragons are partial to beauty, and revere anything that pleases their artistic eye—natural, human made, elfin charmed, dwarf forged, or dragon dreamed. Unlike Lowland dragons, they are loathe to take human mates, mainly because few humans meet their exalted expectations. Throughout the centuries, however, the occasional sorceress of exceptional beauty has succeeded in seducing a Highland male, making offspring of remarkable—"

I read ahead silently, skipping beyond the paragraph on Highland dragon/human matings and the half human creatures they created. No need to give Nicholi more fodder for his confused imagination.

"Highland dragons amass treasure for pleasure only, and their art, gems, and artifacts are fiercely guarded and rarely stolen. Most slyfoot, rangers, and wizards who aspire to steal from dragons target Lowland hoards because, though dragon robbers lose their lives in droves, at least if a sneak succeeds he can be certain his pilfered riches are not an illusion that will grow teeth and claws. The legendary slyfoot Snick is the only dragon robber known to have lifted a prize of tremendous value from a Highland dragon (and survived beyond their gates, that is). In approximately 782, Snick absconded with a priceless enchanted amethyst belonging to Yvess, one that had been cut by the dwarf king Gendrad Stormhammer such that the six facets magnified Yvess' power, and though Yvess hunted Snick down and slaughtered him for the theft, the gem was never found. Pity the poor human or dragon who hides this precious jewel in his hoard."

Nicholi gave a sleepy sigh, and Didoo slipped from his

grasp. I tucked the bear under the covers so that their faces were nose to nose.

"Hey sweetie, do you remember the name of that website Mom used for translating?"

"Garblenot." He closed his eyes.

"Goodnight, little heart," I whispered. My lips on Nicholi's widow's peak, I breathed in his scent of strawberry shampoo and peanut butter. Mashed against Didoo, Nicholi smiled.

In the study, I booted up the computer and pulled the necklace from under my shirt. I could see why Age of Dragons had dreamed up a legend about an amethyst; staring into the velvety gem washed me in the extraordinary. I clicked on Latin/English, and then typed the gold's inscription into Garblenot's translator.

Sons, seed when to set in place earth, blood when cross any billow. To give out this woman sons, each large how then, until her womb beating to join a hundred kings.

Garblenot wasn't living up to its name. I fingered the tiny scratches of inscription. The necklace was old but the engraving was sharp and perfect, like the vermillion border of Mom's lips. Words to protect childbirth? A prayer to make a son a king? I Googled the price of hiring a Latin scholar: I could pay him, or buy two weeks' worth of groceries. I sighed with frustration. No-way-no-how could I chose Latin over groceries.

Sons, seed when to set in place earth, blood when cross any billow. That made no sense at all. Did Dad translate the words for Mom? Mom had found enough meaning in the necklace to bury it, practically irretrievably. Face it, Mimi, she was crazy. My throat tightened and my eyes welled up. I'd felt so frightened and embarrassed when Mom exposed glimpses of her confused, internal struggles. Now I wish she'd told me more. Maybe I could have understood, even helped her. I needed to put this aside before I dissolved into tears. I logged out and went to bed.

~

Saturday night I sat at Mom's vanity, dressing for Duke. I lifted her hand mirror, seeing my eyes, that icy blue four shades paler than Dad's, almost silver.

"Where did you get those dazzling eyes?" he used to tease, as if he didn't know he was the blue-eyed parent. My forehead was long and my face narrow; I would never be as beautiful as my mother. But tonight I'd give it my best shot. If Duke offered an engagement ring, this was one of the most important nights of my life. Who knows, hidden under all of Duke's other talents—humor, business, programming, picking a great place for a romantic date—there might also be some parenting skills. That was my idea of a wonderful fantasy: Duke would move in, we'd have our old closeness back, and my brothers would grow to love him.

I angled the mirror to see my hair. Mom would have appreciated the neat arrangement of pins that held up my twist, too thick to stay in her golden comb all night, but it would give a great first impression. I rose and checked that the hook and eye on her wool miniskirt was closed. Being Italian, Mom never objected to skirts cut as short as curves would allow.

And her carved jade beads draped nicely over the front of her blouse, snuggling in the soft swoops of cream-colored satin, hiding my amethyst underneath. Mom would have approved of how fabulous I look. Putting down the mirror, I slipped into her black four-inch heels.

As I reached to turn off the closet light I heard myself whisper. "*Arahm maneth eirstatu ss ...* " A rushing sound, soft as pebbles, poured from my mouth, landing on my chest so that I could hardly breathe, " *... usst.*" The last word was hacked from the back of my throat.

Let the hand that seeks me ... burn.

I trembled in the dark closet, wobbling on Mom's high heels, the room stifling with the sudden taste of dust and iron.

"*Arahm badrá leln ss ...* "

Let the spirit that knows me ... I would not say it. Never. By force of will I clenched closed my throat, snapping down on the atrocity that possessed me, frantic to withhold the final words ... *know death.* It burned in my head ... *leln morrtarr ... leln morrtarr ...* like the fire that consumed my parents. Hot, dry, full of hatred, raging like a storm. *Know death.* My hands covered my mouth and squeezed with all my might. I would not say it. I would not say it.

My ears rung in the silence. Gradually my throat relaxed. I realized that I had stopped breathing and I gasped in a lung-full of air. Was the urge to whisper gone? I peeked out, rolling my gaze up, down, into the dark corners where Mom's dresses hung and Dad's shoes made indistinct shapes. Nothing moved, breathed, or blinked.

My pulse surged, fierce as blows from a pickax. Something

was terribly wrong. Maybe I should go see Dr. Harvey. But what about the custody court? If Dad hadn't been there, would they have taken us away from Mom? I had to deal with this; no one could know. I ran from the closet and slammed the door.

The doorbell rang and Justin clomped across the living room to answer it. I could hear a deep voice; Duke was here. My hair had fallen from its pins and comb, and my blouse lay askew. I yanked out the pins and let the thick mass fall free. With a few quick pats I smoothed the creamy satin. Facing the closet door, I backed away, one cautious step at a time. By the time I'd reached the hall I felt foolish. No voices in my throat. Nothing followed me. I'd been under a lot of pressure lately. I hadn't slept well. I was like my father, not my mother. I was not going to drift out of reality. One last swat at my hair, align my skirt, and straighten the necklace that concealed the bulge of the amethyst. I needed to stop trembling toes to scalp, and get ready to give Duke that wonderful night we both deserved.

Duke leaned against the doorframe of the study, watching Justin play *The Battle for the Universe*. Nicholi snuggled in Justin's lap with his eyes almost closed, pulling at the sticky white glue still clumped around Didoo's middle.

When Duke saw me he raked back his wavy, whiskey colored hair.

"Ready, Mimi?"

Duke always looked striking—that slender, muscular build and those playful hazel eyes—but tonight he was decked out in pressed chinos, with a white dress shirt under his leather jacket, and he looked like a successful photo shoot for *Gentleman's Image* magazine. He leaned to kiss me on the cheek and I could smell a waft of cologne, unusual for him; he must be as nervous about his upcoming marriage proposal as I.

I steadied my still shaking insides and forced a bright smile. "Yup." I turned to Justin. "There's leftover chicken pot pie in the fridge. Salad's in the blue Tupperware. Drink milk, okay? Not root beer."

"Uh-huh." Justin raised his eyes and contemplated Duke, his thumbs flying his Galactic Fighter low over the ground without need of vision, taking out Republic supply bases with impressive precision.

"Nicholi your bedtime is no later than nine. You get cranky if you stay up late, so listen to Justin and go to bed. Justin, do yourself a favor and put him to bed on time."

"Uh-huh." He continued to analyze Duke, gauging him like an opponent that he might take a sledgehammer to. I flushed with embarrassment and took Duke's hand, hoping Duke, who gazed at me, hadn't noticed.

"Doctor Harvey's phone number is on the fridge, remember?"

"Uh-huh." Justin caught Duke's eye and Duke looked away.

Of all the nights for Justin to decide that he didn't like Duke. What was Justin so upset about? It was not as if Nicholi would be any trouble.

"And Justin?"

Republic forces dropped out of the sky and blasted Justin's fighter to smithereens. The shards expanded across the screen in a blaze of fire, rolling like Mom and Dad's airplane. Fragments scattered into smoke. Justin stared at the screen for a second, and then set the controller on the couch. With a sharp intake of breath he arched his back and laced his fingers behind his head. Elbows jutting into the room, he glared straight ahead.

Nothing was right in Justin's world, I reminded myself. If only he would grieve out loud, just once, let all that sorrow go. But sometimes he was more formidable than a dragon.

"Justin?"

He looked at me, then he glanced at Duke, squinted, and looked away. He was in a foul humor.

"Thanks for babysitting."

A faint smile, more elfin than barbarian, lit his face, mysterious and clever, as baffling as his bad mood.

"Bye Nicholi, bye Justin. I have my cell phone on." I slipped my arm through Duke's, walking cautiously in Mom's spiked heels.

"You look hot, babe." Duke's lips brushed my neck below my ear. He took my coat from the closet and held it open.

I flushed with embarrassed pleasure. Duke wasn't usually this aggressive, even when I dressed in my Italian mother's clothes. His eyes savored me. His hands slid over my skin and raised the hair on my arms as he helped me on with my coat. I liked his new cologne: the scent of clean leather and exotic spices, slightly medicinal, like sweet ether. I leaned my cheek against his shoulder as we walked to the car.

A Lotus! I froze, dumb with surprise. Duke had never driven anything but his old MG, the cloth top ripped and duct tape sealing the back window.

"What did you buy?" I pulled away so I could see his face, my jaw dangling with amazement.

"You like it?" He grinned ear to ear.

"Yeah, but … the expense … what changed your mind?"

He raked his hair back again; such an odd, vain gesture for unassuming Duke. I didn't remember seeing him do that before.

"I'm sick of living poor. I'm not a starving artist, I'm cutting edge."

Then he leaned forward and kissed me, enfolding both my lips in his and drawing me in, the passion practically knocking me over. He'd never put so much ache and bite into his desire before. It absolutely melted me. One kiss and I was ready to go home with him, forget the dinner. Who was this man?

He held open the door, watching my skirt ride up as I folded to fit in the front seat. Unlike his bachelor-trashed apartment, his new car was immaculate. Pikachu in a clear rubber ball had been glued to the dash of the old MG. Now a top of the line GPS ruled the dashboard.

"Where's Pikachu?" I couldn't imagine Duke's car without the little Pokémon inside his rubber ball, fat arms out in a wide embrace, delighted with everyone.

"Mmm … things change." He tossed this out offhandedly, preoccupied with finding which pocket had his car keys.

I didn't know what to say. Pikachu was his good luck talisman. Duke had claimed that he made his first fortune because of that rubber Pokémon ball; it gave him the idea for his antiviral cipher. He explained once—in confusing detail—how his cipher finds patterns in the viral's defense, " … making the shell invisible so that the shape of the virus inside could be accurately decoded."

"Did you throw the ball away?" I asked, incredulous.

Duke eased into his seat, and closed the door. "No, I just didn't want to gum up my new dashboard." He rested a hand on my knee. A clean, uncallused hand that never did anything to put dirt under his nails. His little Lotus was roomy enough inside that he could lean over and give me another long, comfortable kiss, making my head swim, sliding his hand further up my leg.

"God I missed you," he breathed.

"Not as much as I missed you. I've been buried under a pile of laundry. I'm sorry, Duke."

"No, don't be. Life's too short to be sorry." He put his key in the ignition and the Lotus purred. "Tonight—" His voice had gravelly undertones, and he paused for dramatic effect. "Tonight, even the legendary chef Mimi Jovel will be awestruck. I swear this to you, exalted Mimi, or I will eat my air freshener."

I laughed, then reached over and lay a hand on the back of his neck, gently kneading the knots.

He relaxed into my hand. "I have reservations at Tripoli's. I hope you're seriously hungry."

I gave his neck a happy squeeze. "I'd go if I was stuffed."

Tripoli's was one of the restaurants that *did* cook better than I. Way better than I. Way out of my price range.

Duke's eyes lingered on my face, watching my pleasure.

Then he rested his fingertip on my lips. "Say no more. To Redmond." He slammed the Lotus into reverse and tested the theory that the Lotus can go from zero to sixty in 4.9 seconds.

The MG had been sporty, but with the Lotus pushing seventy-five on the highway, Duke seemed to have found his element. I closed my eyes, frightened as his testosterone-powered reflexes zipped the car around corners. He turned up the music and sang along to Tin Dog in his resonant bass, filling the car with a beat that overpowered any sensible, dependable thoughts.

Dad used to joke, "The good thing about marriage is that you always get more than you bargained for." Six months had seemed like enough to know Duke, what he wanted (his career, me), who he was (good-natured, responsible). But now there was this new side of him: the fun with a more dangerous edge, the desire for me a little wilder. It seemed like more than just engagement ring jitters. Or was it? What did I know about how he felt, asking me to marry him? Maybe after the last two months he was scared he was losing me. I turned and studied his profile: the sensuous line of his mouth, open as he sang, his honey blonde eyebrow a confident, strong arch. Give the man a break, Mimi, you've held him at bay for too long.

I wiggled to get comfortable in the hard little seat. With guilty relief, I closed my eyes and let myself relax, my hand snuggling into the soft hairs on the back of his neck. I had been thrown into adulthood by an explosion. Held there by love. Bound by a responsibility that sometimes felt so heavy and impossible I thought I would be crushed. Tonight belonged to me and Duke; let my troubles blow out the Lotus Elise's windows.

Sitting at a table graced with candles and roses, Duke reached across and slipped his fingers over mine as though taking possession. I turned my hand palm up to his smooth skin. The waiter served salad: white and green asparagus with soy/truffle vinaigrette.

"Try this, it's beast with the salad dressing." Duke nudged his wine glass across the table.

I had flipped my glass cup-down to save me the embarrassment of revealing that I was underage, so I surreptitiously sipped from his glass, and then took a bite of salad. A white from Chile, slightly musty to complement the asparagus and rice vinegar, so light against the truffle oil.

"An amazing choice with rice vinegar," I said.

Duke laughed. "Isn't it? Have some more, I ordered a different wine for dinner." He topped off the glass and slid it toward me again. "How do you tell one vinegar from another?"

I gave him a quizzical smile. He knew that. We'd laughed over Dad and Mom's vinegar story a million times. "Dad, of course."

Duke raised his glass. "Here's to Mimi Jovel, vinegar queen, and the hottest date in Seattle. And to Tin Dog, the world's best band." He clinked his wine against my water glass and took a sip. "This is going to be one raging concert tonight. Let me show you the play list from Thursday's show—"

I was grateful that there was no vinegar in the herb-encrusted lamb roast, the tarragon infused beets, or the pine nut polenta, because by the third glass of wine I would have been hard pressed to tell apple cider from balsamic. The hazel of Duke's eyes looked softer and richer with each new glass. I forgot all about gluey stuffed bears and annoying dice. I leaned into the spice-and-oiled-leather smell of him, embracing his balmy attention as he poured the last few drops of a Merlot into his glass and pushed it my way.

By the time dessert came—a lemon curd pie—I was giddy.

"Making lemon curd officially counts as upper body exercise." Even to me, my voice sounded slurred.

"Why's that?" Duke brushed loose hair off my forehead and steadied my chin with his silky fingers.

"Because you have to stir nonstop for fifteen minutes. Then, just when your arm is about to fall off, you slowly blend in two sticks of butter cut into one-quarter-inch pieces. Lemon curd will give you forearms of steel."

"You," said Duke, eyes glowing, "are so funny." Then he leaned forward and kissed me so long that people at nearby tables stared.

"I won a contract with MNF," he said, as we pulled back from the kiss. The collar of his shirt hung open a few buttons and I could see his strong neck as it connected to the muscles of his chest. He reached for my hand, his skin melding into mine. "A half million dollars to upgrade their product. Not bad for a geek who dropped out of college." He gave me a smile, lopsided, with just the left corner of his mouth enjoying the irony. "That reminds me, I have something—" He dug with his free hand in his pocket.

Under his fingers my hand began to sweat. It had been such a confusing evening, muddled by wine and his intoxicating cologne, spun in circles by his odd behavior and the seduction of his kisses. And now he was going to propose.

Should I say yes, should I say maybe? What kind of answer was "maybe" to a marriage proposal? I laughed, a twinge frightened, head too foggy to think. I fell in love with a tender genius who'd made a fortune, but as he said, "Things change." Had things really changed that much? I was too drunk to think about it. His fist came out of his pocket and he set the contents on the tablecloth next to the roses.

Concert tickets.

I felt blank, empty, wiped clean as a countertop.

"Is that the surprise?"

"Surprise?" He stared at me. For a second he blurred, his skin melting into yellow goo, his eyes shifting on his face—cat-like, hawk-like, wolf-like. My neck prickled with fear and my pulse leaped. I blinked, almost screamed, but then the hallucination vanished and he was Duke again, smiling softly, love in his eyes. I swallowed against fear and nausea. I shouldn't have drunk the wine. I wasn't used to alcohol, and I'd had these little hiccups in reality lately.

"Yes, the surprise." Duke grinned. "Concert tickets, the best in the house, front row center for you and me, Mimi."

"Oh!" was all I could force out.

I should be relieved; deep down, in the common sense core I'd been denying all night, I knew I wasn't ready for marriage. But instead my heart ached with disappointment. I was losing him. Even as his need for me seemed more intense than ever, somehow I felt he was gone. Then he leaned forward and kissed me again, his tenderness so possessive that I forgot everything but his heat, skin, and scent.

Before the concert we went back to his apartment and threw the mixture of clean and dirty laundry off the bed. I stood in the middle of his bachelor chaos as he ran his hands down my sides, gently squeezed my waist, and then unzipped my miniskirt.

"Take off the bra but leave on the satin blouse," he whispered. His hand caressed the sides of my breasts, avoiding the gemstone that burned hot enough to hurt. Duke was a skilled and playful lover, but never, ever, had he made love to me with such passion.

I was sobering up on his bed, my hazy brain trying to grasp what worried me, when my cell phone rang. I found it on the sixth ring.

"Hello? This is the Kirkland police. Am I talking to Mimi Jovel?"

"Yes!" I sat bolt upright, tangled sheets and crumpled clothes whirling in my vision. "What's the matter?"

"Well, ma'am, there's been a fire." A surge of adrenaline shot up my neck and vibrated in my tipsy head. "Everyone is okay, but you need to come home. Now."

"Oh my God. I'll be right there."

I slammed the phone into its case. "Duke, come on, we have to go. My house caught on fire." I dug through blankets for my skirt.

Duke wandered out of the bathroom, looking God-like in

his boxer shorts. "Say what?"

"A fire!"

He cocked his head as if this didn't register. "Where?"

"My house." I threw his chinos at him. "Come on."

I zipped my skirt and yanked on my nylons, ripping a wide run from my toe to my thigh. Stuffing Mom's jade beads into my purse, I broke a fingernail against the folded note Justin had brought home yesterday afternoon, requesting a student-parent-teacher conference on Monday. I buttoned my coat with trembling fingers, wondering if Justin would be alive to have a student-parent-teacher conference. I shouldn't have left the boys alone. They were my responsibility now; whatever happened, it was always my fault. I didn't bother to brush my hair. Instead, I stood fidgeting by the door.

Duke searched the rack in the closet for the right shirt.

"Come *on*, Duke."

What was the matter with him? I suppressed a few of Mom's Italian swear words.

"Sorry, I'm coming. The first time in history a woman has to wait for a man to dress, and you get all impatient." He laughed at his joke, his eyes on the clothes rack.

Holy moly. I stared at him. Was he drunk? No, he nimbly buttoned his shirt then sat down, steady and calm, to tie his shoes. Something had warped inside him. Death by too much money? Now was not the moment grieve, or to figure it out. I snatched up his car keys and staggered out the door, trying to stay atop Mom's high heels. He came out a minute later, hair combed into place, and took the driver's seat.

"Hey, so … are your brothers okay?" he asked as we pulled

away from his condo. His voice cooed with concern, but I couldn't bring myself to look at him.

"I don't know, the policeman didn't say much." I kept my eyes on the road, ignoring the stew of anger and sadness that bubbled inside. Later, I told myself. Right now, Nicholi and Justin need me.

The rest of the drive home was silent and took forever. Every stoplight seemed fifteen minutes long, familiar landmarks passed at an agonizing crawl. Nicholi and Justin are alive, I kept telling myself. Waves of panic near to drowned me, and I clung to those words like a scrap of timber. They are alive: the policeman would have told me if they were dead. When we turned the final corner I saw three fire trucks, their strobe lights a madness of white and red flashes. I jumped out the door before Duke brought the car to a full stop.

"Justin! Nicholi!"

I shoved aside the wooden police barrier and wobbled down the street in Mom's heels, tripping over fire hoses, yelling frantically. Activity bustled at the end of our driveway, where black smoke curled from Ms. Rossi's hedge. I fought down another ripple of panic. As I stumbled closer I saw, thank God, that our home was intact. But Ms. Rossi's laurel was devastated—a crispy, charred hole where fire had eaten a ten-foot-wide swath. The grass was black were flames had tried to get to Ms. Rossi's house, which was also, thank God, intact. Two firemen manned a hose, snuffing out the last embers.

I grabbed a firemen's arm. "Where are my brothers?"

The fireman jerked away. Hands full of fire hose, he gestured with his chin, yelling to be heard over the commotion. "Stay behind the barrier."

A short, hefty policeman hurried up beside me. "You Mimi Jovel?" he hollered in my ear.

"Yes. Where are my brothers?" I stood on tiptoe, scanning over his head for a wavy little mop of hair and some broad barbarian shoulders among the throng of medical and fire personnel.

He waved me toward my driveway, calm as directing traffic. "Let's move aside. Your brothers are okay. The little one's in the ambulance."

My head snapped to the waiting aid car, my pulse racing wildly. "What's wrong with him?" I craned to see into the back of the ambulance but the inside was too dark.

"The paramedics have it under control." He took me by the elbow and tugged me across the street, half holding me up as Mom's shoes slipped on the muddy asphalt. "The older one's in the squad car. We'll take him in for questioning. His friends scattered."

"What friends?" I could barely see Justin's bulky profile behind the bars on the squad car window.

The policeman pulled steadily, guiding me down my driveway to where we could hear without yelling.

"Well, it seems there was an accident." He took off his cap and scratched his head, considering me with a sharp-edged gaze. "Do you know anything about gun powder?"

"Gunpowder?" I blinked at him. Nicholi! What had the boys done? This didn't seem the right moment for stories about exploding poop and a trashinator.

"Did you know that some teens had a party at your home tonight?"

"A party?" My stomach flipped over. I don't know if it was the wine, the rich food, or the shock, but suddenly five courses of incredible cuisine came back up. It retched out of my stomach in painful heaves, causing the policeman to leap aside. When I was done and panting he edged back, leaning forward into my breath.

"Miss, have you been drinking?"

I jerked my head up and stared blankly at his tough, weathered face. Don't breath test me, Oh God don't test me, I prayed. My temples started to throb, as though Judge Burrows' gavel pounded on my head. What a total idiot I'd been, going out and leaving the boys alone, drinking underage, letting Duke seduce me while the boys did God-knows-what with gunpowder. I'd megablown it; one breathalyzer and my custody was over. For three seconds the policeman and I were eye to eye at the crossroads, and my heart stood still.

Thank God for the paramedic, a skinny chipmunk of a guy who scurried over from the ambulance and bounced in front of us like he'd had too much coffee.

"We're taking the little one in. Is this the responsible adult?"

The policeman hesitated, focusing on my torn stockings, disheveled hair, and practically nonexistent miniskirt. "I guess you could say that," he said.

"Can she come with us, or do you need her at the station?"

The policeman hesitated again, as though chasing questions that slipped and slid about.

"Miss Jovel, when I asked your brother, Justin, why he put gunpowder in a milk carton and lit it, he claimed it was the dice's decision. Like—you know, gaming dice. Does he have some sort of psychiatric problem?"

He seemed to think this was a yes/no question.

"It's … ah … difficult to explain." I ran a few fingers through my hair, hit a large knot, and gave up.

The policeman cocked his head, smile steady, eyebrows up like he stood ready to listen.

I took a deep breath, reluctant to advance onto the mysterious ground of Justin's grief.

"He plays a fantasy game called Age of Dragons with twenty-sided dice. After my parents died he decided that fate was in charge of his life, so whenever he has a decision to make he rolls a die—"

The policeman grimaced as if I was unhinged. I gave up and stood there, my fingers on my temples where Judge Burrows' gavel pounded with a vengeance.

The policeman didn't speak until it was clear that my feeble explanation was finished. "Well, in any case … " he drawled his words, giving me a second chance to interrupt if I had more to say. Finally he added, "We'll just hold him in juvy until you're free."

With tremendous relief, I hurried after the nervous paramedic to where the ambulance idled. One back door gaped open, a little lump of Nicholi inside, hidden under blankets on a stretcher.

"Nicholi!" I lifted a foot to slip off my heels, frantic to climb into the back.

The paramedic thrust a hand out to restrain me. "I'm glad you're here. Your little brother was … uncooperative … until we gave him back his bear. He seems to have calmed down now." The paramedic shot me a quick, sideways glance. "Look kid, I don't have any children, so maybe I'm speaking out of turn here, but your brother ran into a wall of fire to retrieve a stuffed animal. The boy was dragged out, flaming all over. Even his shoes were burnt. It's a miracle that he wasn't crisped head to toe."

The paramedic rushed on, speech rapid and wet with a spray of spittle. "I told him never to do anything that stupid again, and do you know what he said?" The guy took a breath, but didn't give me time to answer. "He said, 'Don't worry, mister, Didoo won't let me die.' Your brother needs help. Imaginary friends are one thing, but this—this is over the top." He glared at me with beady quick eyes. I was the adult responsible for this child's faults.

My mind had stalled at *dragged out, flaming all over*, the image paralyzing. A rolling ball of fire, dropping into Puget Sound. Fate pursued us, determined, relentless. Not fate, who? Who stalked us so cruelly?

Let the hand that seeks me, burn. Let the spirit that knows me, know death. That was crazy, Mimi. Paranoid. No one was trying to kill your family. The Age of Dragons game got out of hand because no adult was there to supervise. Don't try to blame this on anyone but yourself.

Nicholi curled on the white stretcher, wrapped in a little ball around Didoo, trembling and naked under two cotton blankets. What remained of his charred clothes lay in a plastic bag by his bed. When I lay my hand on his shoulder he twitched and opened his eyes.

"Mimi!" He started to cry, soft little heartbreaking sobs. "Mimi. Mimi." He clung to me. "Didoo got pusherdragged into the fire. He almost died."

I held my brother as close as the narrow, high stretcher would allow, tears streaming down my cheeks.

"It's okay now. He's okay. We'll go to the hospital and then we'll go home."

I kissed Nicholi's hair, smelling burnt polyester, fur and sweat. Tasting the nauseating lingering seduction of Duke's cologne.

The paramedic made me follow in the Subaru, unwilling to abide by protocol and let me ride in the ambulance. I grabbed some clothes for Nicholi, then drove very carefully, making sure I didn't weave in my lane. At the hospital they sent Nicholi into a pediatric exam room and me into a windowless box of concrete they called "the private conference room."

After about an hour of pacing the twelve-by-twelve floor and anxiously kicking my feet against plastic chairs, a disheveled social worker showed up. Her clothing was untucked and mismatched, as though she'd been dragged out of bed. We must have looked quite the pair. She pulled her chair a little too close to mine and smiled a broad, sugary smile. I could smell her Patchouli Oil perfume. I hoped she couldn't smell my alcohol.

"Miss Jovel, I'm Tamara Whitting. I work for Child Protective Services."

She set a medical chart on her knee and fiddled with the paper tab marked 'Nicholi Jovel'. "I understand that your parents recently died? I'm sorry to hear that. How are you doing?"

How was I doing? I pictured my response in a file on Judge Burrows' desk. I was exhausted, my stomach flipped now and then, and my head throbbed. One brother was in the hospital and one was in the police station. I was totally confused about Duke, and, when I wasn't looking, voices, visions, and nightmares crept up on me. And something dreadful had happened tonight to Ms. Rossi's laurel hedge, the details of which, I suspected, were going to be a lot worse than I could imagine. *How was I doing?* I didn't dare tell this solicitous, ratty-looking middle aged woman my long, miserable story. No part could be told without all of the rest spewing out, like juices spurting from a hot pie when you break the crust.

"I'm … " I swallowed, " … okay I guess."

Her sugary smile faded. She leaned forward, her solid *hausfrau* torso pushing into my space. "Were you aware that the paramedics found a nasty wound on Nicholi's back?"

My heart rate sped up and I shrunk away. "No, I mean, yes, I knew it was there, but the paramedics didn't say anything."

"Can you tell me, please, your version of how it got there?" Her wide-set eyes focused on me over her the flattened bridge of her nose.

My version? Was that why Nicholi and I were separated, so they could grill him about *his* version? My heart clutched: he might invent some wild and garbled embellishment, some story Didoo told him.

"He taped his bear to his back with duct tape."

She nodded once, curtly, as though she'd predicted what I might say. "The same bear that he dove into a burning hedge to save?"

"Yes. Since my parents died, he refuses to be separated from it."

She crossed her thick legs, her green polyester pants riding up her shins to show white socks and Birkenstocks. "So I understand. And in taking the duct tape off, his skin tore?"

"Yes. Justin called Poison Control and they told him how to take the rest off with rubbing alcohol. What's this all about?"

She studied me, her square chunk of a face looking tired. "The burns on his chest are very odd."

"Burns? They didn't tell me—"

"He *is* burned."

She leaned back, tapping her pencil on her thick palm. "Given what supposedly happened, the doctor said he should have third degree burns everywhere, no hair, skin blistering like paint. But all he has are a few flash burns on his chest." The intensity in her eyes pinned me to my chair. "The burns are symmetric, and seem to make some kind of symbol. The doctor has never seen anything like it. Do you have any idea *how* those burns got there?"

It took me a moment to find the breath to answer.

"No," I whispered.

"I'm wondering if the burns were there *before* the hedge fire, and if the story of him running into the fire isn't quite the truth."

Under her intense gaze I started trembling. She was working up to a full-fledged accusation; I could see it in the grim clench of her jaw. I didn't know how to head her off, how to defend myself.

"Were you aware that abusive parents have been known to tie children up with duct tape?"

"*What?*" I found myself standing, my voice shrill and panicky. "I didn't abuse my little brother Ms. White … or … whatever your name is. He put the tape on himself."

"And the burns?"

"I didn't burn him, really, I didn't." I couldn't believe she would think me capable of this.

"And you brother, Justin?"

"No! He would *never*—"

She shoved back her chair and stood, an inch or two taller than me even though I wore heels and she wore sandals. "There will be an investigation, Miss Jovel. There's nothing to worry about if you've done nothing wrong." Oily anger seeped from her words.

"Can I please see Nicholi?"

"As soon as the doctor clears him." Her glare was hard, authoritative. "Your brother has an unhealthy attachment to that toy. I recommend some counseling."

I swear, it was a conspiracy. I appeared to be the only one in the world who thought that Nicholi's love for Didoo was a rock in all of this swirling insanity. I waited until she left before I cried, quietly, trying not to swell up my face so everyone in the emergency room would know. Then I opened my cell phone and called Duke, desperate for someone who believed in me.

It took him ten rings to answer. The Tin Dog concert blasted in the background. "Hello?" he hollered over the din.

"Duke, they took Justin to the police station, and they think I'm abusing Nicholi." Tears rose in my throat, strangling my voice.

"What? Mimi, I can't hear you." Giggling, cheering, and off-key female singing reverberated in the background. "Can I call you tomorrow?"

This was the last straw. He'd been such a solid, generous guy when I fell for him. Now he was more convoluted than my nightmares. I hung up and dissolved into uncontrollable sobbing.

When I could cry no more, I straightened my clothes and went to the triage desk. The triage nurse pointed me towards cubical seven. "They're ready to discharge him. Are you a relative?"

"I'm his sister, and I have guardianship." Well, for now. If I could keep my problems under Judge Burrows' radar.

"Sign here, please, and … here." She held out forms. "You have an adorable, bright little sweetie there, Miss Jovel." I felt a rush of love for Nicholi, and I choked up again as I signed my name.

Nicholi sat on a white cot, surrounded by a curtain through which I could hear every conversation around us. I presumed that ours could be overheard as well. "Ready to go home?" I felt self-consciously cheerful, as if the social worker might be hiding in the next cubical, taking notes.

Nicholi brushed his lower lip back and forth across Didoo's

dirty ear. "Little alligators hateinate hospitals," he whimpered. I choked up again, and gave him a trembling smile.

The doctor arrived, his stiff military bearing at odds with his stained white coat. "Are you Miss Jovel?"

I nodded, searching his bland face for signs that he, too, suspected me. He looked away as though to avoid conflict.

"I'm Dr. Peters." His handshake was short and gentle. "Nicholi is fine. He breathed a lot of smoke and may have asthma for a few weeks. I want him to use an inhaler if he starts to cough." His hands, splotched with betadine, handed me a prescription stapled to several pages of written instructions.

"These are the burns."

Nicholi scowled as Dr. Peters pulled up his shirt front, but he didn't resist. "They are too superficial to blister …."

I didn't hear the rest, because the burns took my breath away. A pink, flushed, heart shape mid-chest, with jagged lightening streaks radiating from the center. A rune. I'd seen similar drawings lying around the house after an Age of Dragons game.

"Nicholi," I interrupted the doctor, and his detailed instructions faltered, then politely stopped. "Tell me what this is." I pointed to the burn.

Nicholi yanked down his shirt and squirmed, squeezing his bear against his chest. "I don't know. It was there after the man pulled me from the fire."

"Who pulled you out, Nicholi?" Beside me I could sense the doctor's interest, silently taking note.

Nicholi's beautiful eyes, cornflower blue like Dad's,

opened wide enough to let in the whole world, generously accepting it all. "The man who saved Didoo."

"You don't know who he was?"

"Uh-uh." Nicholi pushed his face into Didoo's belly and kissed him.

Dr. Peters caught my eye. "Amazing isn't it? Like the miracle of the sacred heart." He stared at me, clean military crew cut showing the embarrassed flush on his ears. He nervously cleared his throat. "You've seen the social worker?"

"Yes. I didn't burn him, Dr. Peters, and neither did Justin."

He looked away. "We'll let social work sort that out."

He took a canister of white salve and dipped in a Q-tip, then raised Nicholi's shirt and spread the cream on the burn. Nicholi watched him with intense interest but didn't resist. Dr. Peters let the cream air dry for a minute, then lifted the back of Nicholi's shirt and showed the freshly bandaged tape wound on his shoulder blade.

"Put triple antibiotic on this twice a day," he handed me another prescription, "and call your doctor if it looks infected. You do have a doctor, don't you?" His precise gaze flicked to my face; not having a doctor might be more evidence of abuse.

"Yes. Dr. Harvey, at Eastside Primary Care." At least I'd done something right in this mess.

"Doctor Harvey?" He looked relieved. "Oh, well, no problem then. I'll send my notes to him. Follow up with him on Tuesday. Do you know what an infection looks like?"

"Yes." Sort of. But I couldn't bear to admit to any more stupidity tonight.

"Miss Jovel—" he paused, his gaze taking in my skirt, shredded stockings, and wild hair as though fully appreciating them for the first time. "Your little brother has very poor judgment and an overactive imagination. These are normal at his age, but he requires closer supervision than your fourteen-year-old brother can provide. If you can't watch him, find an adult who can."

If he had been angry, accusatory, threatening, then I would have had an excuse to be angry in kind. But he lectured me gently, as though all I needed to correct my parenting was a tablespoon more information. My face flushed hot. Nicholi's poor judgment, which seemed so obvious in the glaring light of the curtained-off hospital cubical, had zoomed right past me. I'd spent two months doubting my ability to provide for and discipline my brothers, and now I hadn't appropriately supervised them either.

I dropped my gaze to the linoleum floor, fighting to hide my shame. "Yes, Doctor, I'll watch him from now on. Thank you."

Sick with dread and sure that we were headed for another disaster, I packed Nicholi and Didoo into the Subaru and drove to the police station. Nicholi fell asleep in his car seat, so I carried him into the station, staggering on those frigging high heels, his fifty pounds a dead weight, asleep across my shoulder. A female police officer took pity and brought a blanket for him to curl up in. He lay at my feet, pressed against Didoo, and slept through the grilling Officer Dray gave Justin. Grilling, well, *I* felt grilled. Justin didn't seem to mind at all.

In his tiny office, Officer Dray stood behind his desk, palms on the wood, glaring down at Justin's low chair. "Tell me what happened tonight, from the party to the fire. Every detail." He was enormously fat with two rows of buttons straining his uniform, and his salt-and-pepper hair was tinted blue by the fluorescent light.

Justin fished a green twenty-sided die from his pocket, rolled a three, and said, "No."

I closed my eyes and leaned against the wall. Numb prickles crept from my cramped toes to my knees, making my legs quiver. Don't do this, Justin, I prayed silently, it's too risky. When I opened them again, Officer Dray's complexion was bright pink, like he'd been walloped in the gut.

"What do you mean, *no*?" He slammed a hand flat on his desk and I jumped.

Justin didn't. He sat cool as a breeze, turning dice slowly in his fingers, elfin eyes hidden behind his hair.

"Look, you little jerk, you wanna spend a night in jail?"

I had to intervene. I groped for courage, trying to think how Ms. Greer might handle this. I came up empty; nothing I'd done all night even remotely resembled her self-possession.

"He won't tell you officer," I whispered. "Nothing will make him go against the dice. I'm sorry."

Officer Dray stared at me. He stared at Justin's Zen-like calm. He tented his fingers on the desk and leaned way over, practically touching Justin nose to nose. "How old are you, Justin?"

Justin didn't answer. The dice revolved in a leisurely circle on his palm. Fate had decided that Officer Dray was not to know the story. Who was Justin to fly in the face of fate?

"He's fourteen," I said.

"Shit, just a kid." Officer Dray spun a circle, paced two feet to the wall, and then wheeled about again, veins bulging over his graying temples. "Listen to me, boy, you're headed for trouble. I've got no witnesses so I've got no case, but I'm smart enough to put two and two together." Big wet rings formed under Officer Dray's armpits, and his forehead dripped. "I'm sending you home in your sister's custody. If the owner of the hedge presses charges for destruction of property, I suggest you get a good lawyer." Thumbs hooked over his wide belt, he rocked up on his toes and shouted down onto Justin's bowed head. "I'll be watching you, young man. If you so much as litter, you'll feel the full force of the law."

Justin didn't even blink.

He slept in the car all the way home. Grateful to be out of there, I spent the ride home breathing: in, out, in, out, not enough strength left to think. Home. The door was unlocked and the lights on. Mom and Dad's folding party table stood in the middle of the living room, littered with root beer bottles, candy wrappers, Age of Dragons miniatures, books, dice, and character sheets. The kitchen was a mess from rampant snacking, and the Xbox, television, and stereo all blasted as though the party had dispersed fast. Other than the mess, the house was blessedly intact.

I put Nicholi to bed fully clothed and snuggled covers over him and Didoo.

Justin stood in the kitchen, drinking a glass of milk. I tried to be calm.

"Help me clean this mess up."

He took out his dice. If he had rolled under a ten my parenting days would have been over. I would have strangled him on the spot, and spent the next twenty years in jail. But he rolled a fourteen. Fate had decided that I was to raise this boy instead of killing him.

It took only an hour to throw the bottles in recycling, put away the table, arrange the books, dice, miniatures, and papers on Justin's bookshelf, and vacuum the living room floor. Justin put dirty dishes in the dishwasher and wiped counters. When I handed him a broom he swept the kitchen floor. As he lumbered off to the bathroom, I called after him, "Justin, I want to know what happened tonight."

He pivoted slowly, taking dice out of his pocket.

It took every bit of restraint I had not to whack the dice from his hand.

"Don't you dare roll those dice. You tell me what went on. You owe it to me."

"No dice, no action. That's the rule." Unruffled, he turned and walked away, closing the bathroom door behind him.

"You punk!"

I stomped into his room, swearing under my breath, and grabbed the character sheets off his bookshelf. According to the sheets, Case the slyfoot, Trimble the wizard, Larry the dwarf fighter, Paul the halfling cleric, and someone I didn't know, Elina, a female elf ranger, had been at the party. Justin, as always, played the barbarian warrior. I knew how to make them talk. Tomorrow they'd tell me everything. I knew that for certain, because I was the best pastry chef in my culinary class.

Chapter 9

The secret to good molasses cookies is a pinch of black pepper stirred into the flour, and they are baked just enough to leave the centers yielding and soft. Buttermilk makes incredible chocolate cake, and the peanut butter icing should be creamy enough to lift little chocolate jimmies up on peaks. The best brownies are baked in cupcake pans, a chewy caramel pushed into the center of each one. Lemon bars require fresh lemons, and sifting and resifting the confectioner's sugar until it drifts across the tangy top like fairy dust. None of this was gourmet pastry, but it was what I needed.

Every time I'd fallen asleep I'd had visions of Nicholi, burning all over, dragged from the fire. By three in the morning I'd given up any hope of rest, so I calmed myself by baking.

It was five hours before the boys were up. Nicholi woke first, wandering into the kitchen still dressed in his smoky clothes, dragging Didoo by one arm.

"What are you making?" He pulled a chair up to the island and climbed onto the seat. When he saw the feast he dropped Didoo, leaped off the chair, and dashed for Justin's room.

"Justin! Justin! Mimi's baking!" He sounded like a robin chortling over the sunrise.

"Huh?" Justin was still groggy. "What's she baking?"

"Everything. Cookies and cakes and stuff. Tons of stuff."

Ten minutes later I heard Justin make a phone call. Then he came out, unshowered and hurriedly dressed in last night's clothes. He dragged another chair to the island and watched me take things out of the oven.

Case arrived quickly, within a half an hour of Justin's call. Paul, Larry, and Trimble were there within the hour. Pretty soon I had seven gazes, arranged in an arc before the island, studying my every move: Case wary, Justin Zen-like, Larry fearless, Trimble thoughtful, Paul nervous, and little Nicholi's eyes wide with wonder. Nicholi held Didoo so that his sapphire glass eyes, bubbled by the fire, barely showed over the island counter. When I placed the last piece of peppermint candy on the white cake and set the cake in the middle of the banquet there was a soft, collective sigh.

I let the tension build. Arms crossed over my chest, I waited until I was sure they were listening.

"You have a choice." My voice was as icy as the Night Hag's. "You can tell me what happened. Every detail, blow by blow, or—" I looked deeply, one by one, into each pair of transfixed eyes, "—you can sacrifice all of this," I waved a hand over the loot, "to the food bank."

It would have taken Fiendkiller's Flail to bludgeon through the silence. "Here are the rules," I continued in my deadliest rasp. "Number one: no names. Refer to everyone as 'somebody'. Number two: no lying. If I find out that one of you lied to me I will never bake that person so much as another biscuit. Number three: one at a time you will answer all my questions. The decision to take the feast has to be unanimous: either you all speak, or the feast goes."

The boy's expressions retreated into shadow, their thoughts impenetrable, even by wizard's light.

"Justin, you are excluded from this decision. I won't have the dice interfering." Justin nodded, eyes down, stewing in some hidden emotion.

Paul tentatively raised a hand. "Excuse me, Mimi?"

If Paul makes it out of adolescence unscarred by his shyness, he will be an attractive young man. He's certainly handsome enough with his red hair and beach-boy freckles. But timidity rules his life, makes his steps falter, and demands an explanation for his very existence. Only a deeply challenged Paul would force himself to speak at such a tense moment.

My eyes met his.

His gaze scurried away and hid among the hills of frosting on the cupcakes. "Can the party talk together for a few minutes, privately?" His words were barely audible.

"Of course."

The grim group rose from their chairs like a regiment of zombies and retreated out of earshot into Justin's room. Nicholi tiptoed after them, flattening Didoo onto his chest with the force of his worried squeezing.

Ha! They were snared, and I knew it. Now, like the Night Hag with a catch in her net, I would haul them in.

I ate a brownie, then a molasses cookie, and had a glass of milk, slowly washing every bite around in my mouth, savoring the scrumptious flavor. I wiped crumbs off my smiling lips as they returned.

Larry, the vanguard fighter, stepped in front of the group, too short to completely shield his friends, but thick enough to absorb the first blows. His stumpy fingertips rubbed at his bulb of a nose. "Will you tell the police what we say?" he asked.

"No. Never. I swear."

I'd known Larry for six years: Larry preferred situations he could fight his way out of to ones where he had to negotiate. His forehead wrinkled with a frown, a fold thick enough to bash down a wall without damage. Damage to Larry, that is. He gave a brief, "all clear" nod, and the boys sat down. Then they rotated in unison toward Trimble.

Trimble is another of Justin's friends who has the charisma to get away with anything. At some point Trimble must have decided that he veered so far off the path of his high school peers he may as well finish himself off. He adopted the habit of wearing fabrics from his ancestors in Africa: intense reds, golds, and greens printed in delicate geometric patterns with overlapping bold swirls. Someone (his mother?) fashioned these fantastic textiles into lose fitting shirts, which he wore, draped to his ankles, over black jeans. On any other high school boy the clothes would have been a death warrant. On unflappable Trimble, the three-wise-men robe and his beaded corn row braids demanded shocked respect.

Trimble's face reflected a mage's calm. "Justin called—"

"*Somebody* called. No names, please," I said.

"*Somebody* called a meeting about ... " he paused, rolled his deep brown eyes up as though doing some internal editing, then recommenced with confidence, " … a potentially lethal situation. We conferenced from five-thirty until eight-thirty, had pizza, then Jus—*somebody* rolled dice about casting a Reveal Evil spell. The answer was yes. Somebody got the gunpowder out of his room, and I cast the spell. Things didn't … take the turns we expected, so we managed the best we could, then retreated when the police came."

I'm certain that Trimble is headed for a career in law; he has such factual calm and assumed innocence. I wasn't counting on getting much out of judicious, regal Trimble.

"Next?" I said, looking at Paul. The boys leaned forward protectively as Paul worked himself up to answer.

"I … I … I don't have anything to add," he stammered, brushing a hand nervously over his mouth.

"Where did the gunpowder come from?"

Paul drew an anxious breath. "Somebody's father packs his own bullets and has a tin of gunpowder in his garage."

Case's father, no doubt, working all night and sleeping all day while his kid heated up trouble. "And somebody took it?"

"Some of it."

I suppressed the urge to shriek and bite off a few heads. "Did somebody's father know about this?"

In unison, the group shook their heads: no.

"So, this gunpowder has been in somebody's room for … how long?"

Paul cringed and snuck a peek at Justin, as though asking permission to go on. Justin stared straight ahead, his fate already sealed. So Paul studied the floor, and I could see the perfectly straight part through the red bristles of his crew cut.

"Four days."

Four days. Nicholi, my ear-to-the-ground little brother, had tried to warn me in his roundabout way. That was the problem—the roundabout way; I could never sift fact from fantasy, game from reality.

"I assume somebody was waiting until I was out of the house to, ah, let somebody else cast a spell with this gunpowder?"

Paul nodded weakly.

Frustrated, I sucked in a lung-full of air. But really, what did I expect? They spent hours playing a game they win by deceiving dragons—the shrewdest creatures to ever plot and scheme. Sneaking by me must be hilariously easy.

Justin sat next in line. I passed over him with a scowl and rested my inquisitor's gaze on Larry.

"Why wasn't Nicholi in bed when the gunpowder was lit?"

Larry, a big brother with ten siblings, rolled his eyes to the ceiling and shook his head. "It was only eight-thirty and Nicholi refused to go to bed. I told them it was a dumb idea to do anything before he fell asleep, but they went ahead anyway."

"Didoo had to help," said Nicholi.

"It's not for little kids," said Larry in his experienced big brother voice. I should have left Nicholi with Larry instead of Justin.

Nicholi tugged on Didoo's ear, distorting his bear's head, then let the soft cloth snap back into place again. "Didoo says magic fires are tricky."

Larry shook his head again. "That's *why* it's not for little kids." Then he turned his gaze to the peppermint cake.

In Age of Dragons, Larry's dwarven axe can single-handedly clear a battlefield. Though he is the smallest of Justin's friends, I suspected that when it came time to devour the feast, he would end up getting the biggest cut. Others have learned to scramble out of his way.

I turned to Case. "So, tell me about the fire. What happened?" My eyes locked on his to remind him that future meals from Mama Mimi were at stake.

Case's gaze slunk away into the dark shadows. Like all slyfoot, Case played by different rules. To become a slyfoot you have to steal all manuals and tools from the store—a pay-in-advance system whereby you actually own all your books and equipment, but can't have them unless you sneak them by store security. Case had won possession of a small library and a large bag of tricks.

"Mimi, you should have seen it. I know—it kind of caused trouble—but it was *awesome*." Case leaned forward, warming to his tale. I think he may have a few levels of bard in his personality as well. "We put three inches in the bottom of one of those square paper half-gallon milk cartons. Trim—uh, somebody prepared a spell to flush forth evil while somebody else did a charm of protection."

"Protection?" I asked. Paul, no doubt, the halfling cleric who healed with herbs and spells. His skills kept him out of the peril of battle, and because he had the power to shelter and revive other players, everyone was motivated to keep him alive.

"Yeah, uh … somebody thought you might be in trouble, so he asked somebody else to use part of the flash to shield you."

"You were playing with gunpowder and worried about *me*?" Boy logic eluded me.

"Yeah. Anyway, we dropped the match and—Dude! It blasted straight up, roaring like a rocket engine. There was a foot of air between the top of the carton and the flame, and then a six-foot pillar of *fire from hell*." He grinned, blazing with delight. "This awesomely wicked Basilisk appeared—"

"Basilisk?"

"Yeah, you know, flaming salamanders, the ones known for their love of torture. Seven feet tall, human torso, serpentine tail, burning spines—the usual. And he was *pissed*. He backhanded the milk carton with his spear. Didoo was sitting on the ground—"

"He was trying to help," said Nicholi.

"—and the carton spun fire in a circle *this* big," Case held out his arms like a bragging fisherman, "then it swept up Didoo and shot twenty feet down the driveway, into the bushes, pushing Didoo like a bulldozer. Nicholi starts screaming and runs into the flames. The Basilisk raises his tail to slap us, but this guy, I swear to God, he leaps out of nowhere. Like he fell from the sky or something. He's wielding a rake like it's a bow staff. The Basilisk takes one look at him and vanishes. The guy bounds into the fire, grabs Nicholi, who's burning like a human torch, and heaves him up on his shoulder, hauls him out of the flames, and rolls him in his coat. Then he uses the rake to pull Didoo free, stomps on the bear a few times to put out the sparks, shakes him, and hands him to Nicholi. We're all standing there, blown away, except for Pau—somebody, who runs down the driveway, sucks this humongous draft of healing from the fire, and slaps it on Nicholi's chest. So he's just finished restoring Nicholi when the—".

"Wait—chest?"

"Yeah, somebody wouldn't let anybody die in battle. He's not a noob, you know. Then the police sirens start howling. We all ran, except for Justin, I mean, except for somebody, 'cause he would never leave Nicholi." He paused, obviously overcome with wonder. "It really was sweet, Mama Mimi! You should have been there."

My eyes closed involuntarily as the word *sweet* bounced off the image of Nicholi *burning like a human torch*. One thing for certain: Case would never babysit Nicholi.

I wanted to scream, "*Are you out of your frickin' minds?*" But I took a few breaths, and between clenched teeth I forced out a more sensible question: "So, no one burned Nicholi's chest before the explosion?"

Case's jaw dropped and he stared at me, a horrified cringe around his eyes. "Heck no," he said. "He's our Little Dude, why would we hurt Nicholi? We do know right from wrong, you know."

Yes, they did. But they didn't seem to know truth from fantasy, so I still had no idea what had really happened. At least there might be other, less imaginative witnesses. Ones the social worker might believe. "Who was the man with the rake?"

They all looked at each other.

"I don't know. Somebody," said Case, and he gave one of his charming grins.

Everyone found this humorous except me. "Yeah, *some-*

body," they repeated, snickering and jostling each other. But the social worker and I had no sense of humor when it came to flaming six-year-olds.

"And who is Elina?" In my anger, I could no longer keep my voice at room temperature.

Paul, Larry, Case, and Trimble all turned in unison to ponder Justin. Justin, the coolest cucumber in the refrigerator, blushed as red as a tomato. Oh my God, my brother has a girlfriend, and she was here with him, unsupervised for hours.

I flashed on the condom lecture Mom gave me when I turned sixteen, sliding the slippery yellow tube over her fingers and saying in her quaint English, "It must fit over the man like this ... Never put on olive oil or cream for the skin. That would make *un piccolo foro*, a little hole that ...." At the time, I almost died of embarrassment. I couldn't imagine that this steamy, humiliating lecture could ever apply to me. I planned to avoid sex until I married. Then I met Duke and, fortunately, he seemed to already know what to do with a condom. So I left all of the messy details to him.

It seemed cruel beyond torture that fate now expected me to give Mom's condom lecture to fourteen-year-old Justin. To interrupt the awkward silence I stood and rearranged brownies on the plate, pushing around chocolaty crumbs. Maybe Case would tell him. No, something this important couldn't be left to Case. Talking to Justin about Elina was a river that I would have to cross alone, like all of the other raging rapids Mom and Dad had left me.

"Are we done yet?" asked Larry, eyeing a scrap of brownie that had fallen off the plate and lay, rich and spongy, just within reach.

"Almost. Can anyone explain to me *what* you were trying to *do*?"

There was a profound silence, all eyes on the feast, all mouths zipped shut.

Finally Justin took a die from his pocket and tossed it on the wood of the island. It skittered to a stop an inch from the molasses cookies. A thirteen. He brushed aside his veil of hair and looked up, eyes welling with such darkness that my heart stood still.

"Evil pursues our family," he said. "All the portents point to approaching war. Someone stalks us, but I can't find him, pin him down. I don't know who we're fighting, but I do know that we're losing. I'm sorry, Mimi. I thought perhaps Trimble's spell would show us the face of the master. But we only saw some dragon's servant before the enemy turned our spell against us. Between the four of us we barely had the skill to survive. I don't know how we have any hope of winning."

Holy moly. My heartbeat lurched from zero to one hundred and fluttered in my ears. We had slipped into collective insanity, sliding down the muddy slope of Mom's schizophrenia into a world of nightmares and paranoia. Thank God the dice had silenced Justin in Officer Dray's office.

"Justin," I said, holding his tortured gaze, "there is reality—safe, here, our family, our house—and there is your game, treacherous and complicated. We have to keep them separated in our minds or the court will *take you away from me.* Do you understand how important this is?"

"Yup, I do."

He can be very matter-of-fact, my brother. Then he frowned, and his gaze sought Trimble. Trimble looked at Case, Case looked at Larry, and Paul looked at Justin. All the boys nodded knowingly, leaving me clueless.

"Don't worry, Mama Mimi," said Case with that smarmy persuasiveness that occasionally annoys me, "Justin has reality covered. Maybe even better than you do."

I wasn't at all sure that was true, but what were my options? Trust some unknown psychiatrist? Notify nasty Ms. Social Worker? *No, no, no, no, no* screamed my insides, as panicked as one of Nicholi's tantrums. I'd figure out a way to help Justin without risking custody. Our family was grieving. With luck, with enough patience, this would pass for both of us.

"Okay, the questions are over. The feast is yours. But before you eat, there is someone you owe an apology to."

Justin, with Dad's sense of fairness, knew immediately what I meant. "Her house is cursed," he said.

"Sure is," said Larry. "Trimble's spell revealed a—"

"Forget the curse." I leaned over the feast. "Who is going to apologize to Ms. Rossi for what somebody did?"

They sat, seemingly at a loss for words. Surprisingly enough, Paul finally spoke for the group. "We'll go over and say we're sorry, I guess." He squirmed in his chair as though the mere thought of it might kill him.

"Can Didoo and me come, too?" asked Nicholi.

Being where-the-action-is around this household was rough on Nicholi. I have no idea how Mom and Dad spread their umbrella of protection so easily over him, covering his little head from the cold rain and falling debris of living with a teen. When Mom and Dad were still alive, Nicholi didn't try to grow up too fast.

Justin reached for his little brother and pulled him into his lap. "No, Nicholi, this isn't your fault. You don't have to apologize."

Nicholi snuggled his cheek into the rumpled, dirty fabric of Justin's shirt.

"I want to be somebody, too."

"You are somebody. You're Nicholi Jovel, my best ever uberbro." And Justin kissed him on top of his smoke-grimed head.

In that moment, I forgave Justin everything.

I retreated then, to let them eat what I'd baked. No doubt they would devour every last, sticky glob. Thank God they were fourteen and able to eat like trolls or it would probably have killed them.

While they munched and verbally replayed the *awesome* destruction of the milk carton, I grabbed cinnamon sugar, nuts, a napkin, and one of Dad's fanciest china platters, and disappeared into the utility room. Reaching in the closet, I moved aside towels and retrieved a pastry I hadn't offered them: a cinnamon roll with homemade caramel on the sugary mounds of dough. I eased the soft buns out of the pan and onto the platter. Through the open door came the boys' excited chatter, muffled by overlarge bites of pastry and generous slurps of milk.

"Mumble mumble explosion," laughed Justin.

"Mumble mumble a one hit K.O.," declared Larry.

"Mumble mumble kick-ass way for mumble mumble," snickered Case.

"Mumble mumble probably dead before I knew what hit me but I'd risk it just to mumble mumble," vowed Trimble.

It made the hair on my skin rise up and try to crawl away. They were fearless to the point of idiocy—well, all except for Paul, of course. They were grim and pale-faced about some "master" they couldn't see, but the fire that had raged practically on top of them? They crowed about it, as though they lived to light it again! What would Dad say? "Steady, Mimi, truth can be hard to get a grip on. Don't let the hard facts drift away."

I pressed pecans into caramel, arranging nuts in a pattern of swirls. What were the hard facts? Bad dreams, a compulsion to whisper, a wire hand in a pudding, a fantastic yarn about a Basilisk, a burn in the shape of a heart on Nicholi's chest—hardly facts that would hold up in Judge Burrows' court. And what they did suggest was not in my favor. Lately, I'd felt shaken and tossed, like one of Justin's dice. I had to land face up, facing the real dangers. At least I had my amethyst to give me strength.

I dusted with cinnamon sugar, watching crystals fall randomly on the sticky caramel. It was coincidence, it had to be, my vision of the man in the tower and Justin's "master," our mutual feeling of impending ruin. *All the portents point to approaching war.* Was it true that the best we could do was survive? No, our side had courage, cunning, raw strength, and an untapped well of power. He was going to get a battle he hadn't counted on. But his dragon—now he was seriously devious. That was their way, swamp dragons—they made you feel that the fight was in your favor, or at least dead even. But then the filthy *bechmukk* showed their teeth ....

My hand froze, suspended over the decorated pastry.

The thoughts had escaped, sneaked from a place so well hidden within me that I immediately felt lost, unable to turn back and trace the trail. The vision was faint, but I knew dragons, sure as I knew my own cinnamon rolls. Was it years of listening to the boys talk? No. *Bechmukk.* Beastmuck. The boys didn't speak a dragon's tongue. I squeezed closed my eyes and leaned against the wall, trying to get my bearings. A path led from somewhere. I could feel it, as if a draft wafted from its passage. I strained to see what lay just out of sight. Nothing, blank, the way sealed over.

But in the darkness behind my lids, two worlds shifted: background leapt into the foreground, foreground faded to background. Two alternate films of my life played on top of each other. I couldn't reconcile both worlds, like double vision or broken 3-D glasses.

I yanked the amethyst out from under my shirt: hot stone, icy gold. My fingers sought the heat, pressing against the mysterious gem, avoiding the cloying gold. A rush of calm flowed through me. I breathed in slow and deep. It was time to stop asking, "Am I crazy?" and to start asking, "Whose advice should I trust?" Dad's? Mom's? Justin's? I pressed the stone to my reeling forehead, shivering, afraid.

Then I realized: it didn't matter—reality, insanity, collision of two worlds. I had one, and only one, goal: raise my brothers. I'd have to deal, one smack at a time, with any fact hard enough to whack me. I opened my eyes. The room looked as I'd left it: chaotic piles of dirty and clean laundry, and a cinnamon roll smelling like Dad's Sunday breakfast. Dad had anchored Mom, I could see that now, but she didn't have her head in the clouds. She'd sunk her polished nails into the belly of a nightmare. Was it truly a nightmare? Maybe. God, how I wished they were both beside me.

I flicked open the napkin and it fluttered over the rolls. The frail paper edges stuck precariously to caramel on the lip of the plate. My life was falling apart because of dice, fires, bears, bills, laundry, and mostly because of grief. That was my line, if anyone asked. The rest I'd keep my mouth shut about until I had the facts sharply in focus.

I put on sneakers and coerced my feet into marching down the gravel driveway, past the charred laurel, to Ms. Rossi's porch. The wind swatted a few black, curling leaves against my shoes, and the smell of burnt sap clung to the damp morning air. Brushing the dusting of flour off my shirt, I straightened the napkin over the pastry and composed my face before I rang the doorbell. Then I waited, mouth dry, fingers trembling.

Mom sometimes visited Ms. Rossi, but hadn't said a word about her. Ms. Rossi never came out of her house, not once that I knew of, and she'd lived here for over ten years. She might forgive the boys, but then again, she might be furious and press charges. My stomach fluttered as I fantasized Judge Burrows presiding over the case. Through the slender window parallel to the door, I saw Ms. Rossi's bent form shuffle forward. I stared at the new white paint on the boards of her porch, embarrassed and frightened.

She opened the door. "Yes? Who is it?"

Her faded blue eyes looked right at me. It's impossible to say how tall Ms. Rossi used to be, but now she stood to almost four feet. If standing was the word. Her back was so curved that her moment-to-moment view was of her stomach, and she had to twist her neck into a painful-looking 'S' to see me. Around her bone-thin shoulders hung the crocheted sweater of a much bigger woman, overwhelming her housedress. Someone had tied a lace ribbon, neat and perfect, in the thin white braid that remained of her hair.

"It's your neighbor, Mimi Jovel. May I come in?"

Her wrinkled face made a cranny of a smile. "Yes, yes, of course." She tottered sideways so I could pass.

"I brought you a cinnamon roll, Ms. Rossi. I just wanted to say—" For a moment the apology was harder than giving Justin a condom lecture, and my courage floundered. How could I have been so irresponsible? That fire might have reached her house!

I took a breath and blurted out, "I'm very sorry about what my brother and his friends did to your laurel."

"My laurel?" She peered at me, eyes clouded and squinting. "Here, I'm forgetting my manners. Please, come in and have a seat. Should I get a few plates for the roll?"

I felt so ashamed I could hardly speak. "Oo … okay," I stammered. If those boys didn't apologize to this helpless, sweet, old woman I was going to—to what? The only hold I had on them was the flimsy grip of their respect for me. And their gluttony.

She led me to her white corduroy couch. The whole room was white, not stark, but soft, reminiscent of clean fluffy towels. Fresh pink roses in a glass jar decorated the coffee table. They complemented the only other thing with color in the room: the pink ceiling. It certainly didn't look like a house cursed by evil. Maybe that piece of the boys' story could be safely classified as fantasy. But then, what did I know about curses?

A few minutes later she hobbled back from the kitchen, two tea cups rattling on an unsteady silver tray. She had cut slices from the roll and arranged them in a fan on Dad's china platter. There was tea with sugar and cream, and tiny spoons to stir with. I watched her withered hands pour tea as I agonized over how to proceed without stumbling into the "facts."

"Now, dear, let's taste this roll." She served me a slice on a china plate strewn with painted roses, then eased herself onto the couch next to me.

"Ms. Rossi—"

"Call me Anna, dear."

"Anna, my brothers accidentally set fire to your laurel hedge last night." I held my breath.

"Oh, did they?"

Bent over, she sipped her tea. After a moment's thought she said, "I wondered about all of the commotion, firemen knocking at the door, sirens blaring. So much falderal and oo-la-la, I couldn't make heads nor tails of it."

She took another sip of tea, and then a slow smile spread across her face. "You must thank them for me. I hated that hedge."

I exhaled with a violent cough. Everything I had planned to say flew out her lace-curtained windows. To cover my confusion I snatched up my teacup.

"Laurel is very ugly, don't you think? It's really intended to be a tree, and we hack at it, like naughty children who take scissors to their hair, and after awhile it grows back so thick that it walls us in. I much prefer azalea, or lilac. Though lilac doesn't grow as well as it should in this climate." She put down her cup and peeked up at me with intense interest. "Don't you think?"

I gulped my tea, warm as her gaze. "Well … um … lilac needs alkaline soil, so I suspect it's the soil and not the climate."

"So like something your charming mother would say," she answered, and I wondered just how well she'd known my charming mother.

"You're not angry about the hedge, then?"

"Heavens, no. This morning the house had so much light! I should have had Carlo replace it long ago."

Melting into her couch with relief, I watched her take another bite of the cinnamon roll and struggle to manage the nuts with her dentures. When she had finally ingested her bite, she said, "Have you met my grandson, Carlo?"

"Ah—yes." And, I added silently to myself, I'd prefer not to talk about him. Carlo, with his exhilarating eyes, made me think of my relationship with Duke, and Duke was yet another raging rapid with rocky shoals that I had to swim sooner or later. Later. I looked for a way to change the subject, picked up the teapot, and offered her more tea. But she was not deterred.

"Carlo's been living here this last year." She held out her cup so that I could pour. "He's such a great help. I'll send him over to see if there's anything he can do for you."

"You're very sweet, but no thank you. We're managing fine, and I'm sure Carlo is busy." I said this firmly—a clear line in the sand. "What do you think you'll plant?"

"Plant?" She stirred her tea, staring vaguely into the cup. "Oh, yes, the hedge. Azalea, I think. But what color? I'm partial to pink, but there are so many wonderful colors." She smiled sadly. "Your mother made a beautiful garden. I was very, very sorry to hear about your mother and father."

I must have received sympathy from a hundred people by now, but each time my pain was as fresh as the first time, forcing tears from my eyes without consulting me, my sadness a sinking rock in my chest.

Her thin, cool hand rested on mine. "There is nothing like a loss to change our world, is there?" The empathy in her voice was comforting, and I felt, for one moment, less alone. The grandfather clock ticked, two sparrows argued outside her window, a car drove by. I could say nothing through my grief. In silence, we both sipped our tea.

Finally I said, "My brother and his friends will come by to say they're sorry for burning down your hedge. Please don't thank them."

She craned to look at me. "Why not?"

"My little brother almost died in the fire. I don't want them getting praise for playing with gunpowder."

"Oh my!" Tea sloshed over the rim as her cup wobbled,

the trembling liquid almost filling the saucer. "Is he all right?"

"Yes, he's fine. Some stranger pulled him out. You didn't happen to see the man, did you?"

"No, I hardly see at all. Just light and shadows." She set the messy cup down. "Thank goodness your brother survived. Well, what should I say to the boys, then?"

"Please have them pay for a new hedge. It's the least they can do." I stood to go.

Her fists sunk into the couch cushions and she pushed herself unsteadily to her feet. "I'll have Carlo estimate what a hedge of azaleas costs." She shuffled down the hall to let me out. "Do drop by again. I enjoy your company. And thank you for the cinnamon bun. Did you make it?"

"Yes." I felt so relieved and grateful I wanted to bake her a million more. Only next time I'd leave off the nuts.

"You're quite the baker." Her voice dropped to a whisper. "I'll have to hide it from Carlo so I can eat it all myself." Then she giggled, impishly cute.

I suppressed the rush of warmth that made me want to throw my arms around her, and I squeezed her hand instead.

Heading down the driveway to home, I no longer worried that Ms. Rossi would press charges and the boys would go to jail. I worried that, after talking to her, they'd be inspired to blow up the rest of her hedge.

When I walked in, the house was unnervingly quiet. Over-fed boys lounged sleepily in Justin's room, murmuring to each other and thumbing through Age of Dragons texts. I searched for Nicholi and found him in the study at the computer, consulting Wikipedia, Didoo in his lap.

"What are you searching?" I tried not to sound paranoid.

"Fire."

I lay a protective hand on his head. "Oh?"

Nicholi swung his legs in the too-tall chair, causing Didoo's chin to bump against the keyboard. "Do you think the hedge was hot like a Bun-sen-bur-ner, or hot like a blow torch? One is 2,900 degrees and one is 2,300 degrees." He sounded more fascinated than frightened.

I pulled back his dirty hair, combing through knots with my fingers, exposing his beautiful widow's peak. He smelled like smoke. "Both of them could have killed you."

"The fire wanted Didoo, not me."

He said this with confidence, as though he and the fire had had a heart-to-heart. Snuggled in Nicholi's lap, Didoo faced the computer screen, pink nose now filthy gray, belly and ears singed, worn neck with a small hole where the canvas had finally torn through. Only Ms. Greer, through rock-ribbed persistence, had been able to stretch the distance between Nicholi and Didoo. But like two ends of the same rubber band they always snapped back together again.

"The next time Justin or any of his friends mention gunpowder, you need to tell me. Do you understand, Nicholi?" I strove for Dad's behave-or-else tone.

"I told you. You just don't listen." He pouted, managing to look both endearing and impossibly stubborn with the same puckered lips.

"Could you say, 'Mimi, you need to listen now,' when I'm not listening?"

"Maybe." He clicked out of Wikipedia, and turned off the computer. "Didoo says you're a worryobot who stressinates about the wrong things."

I picked up the bear. His glass eyes had tiny melted holes like bubbles in a blue sky. Dirt caked what little fur he had left. He was a stuffed disaster. "What should I be worrying about?"

"Only saying what you mean, not castifying for other people." Nicholi snatched his bear back and hopped off the chair.

Dumbfounded, I watched him wiggle side to side as he untucked his T-shirt. Even when I tried to listen, only Nicholi's words, not their meaning, penetrated. "Castifying?"

"Spells, like what wizards do, but you're not a wizard."

With that little gem of gobbledygook, he stuffed Didoo up his shirt and wedged him through the neckline, so that a bear appeared to grow from Nicholi's chest. Then he waltzed out of the room. I thought about my whispering. It was an eerie thought, that I might unknowingly cast spells. Clearly more fantasy than fact. So much for my plan to heed Nicholi's warnings.

"Wait." I caught up with Nicholi and, fingertips on his shoulders, steered him toward the bathroom. "Bath or shower?"

"Showers are for school days, silly."

"Bath, then, and Didoo needs to be put through the wash."

"No. Don't wash Didoo. He doesn't like it." But we were headed away from the washing machine, so Nicholi didn't resist.

As I ran bathwater, Nicholi dawdled over the multiple

knots he'd tied in his shoelaces, then turned his pants inside out and made the pockets flap like puppy ears as he danced them back and forth across the room.

While Mom was in the hospital, Dad put Nicholi to bed, brushing his teeth for him when the delays exceeded Dad's patience, sometimes carrying a wiggling Nicholi under one arm and dumping him into bed. Nicholi didn't tantrum or fuss for Dad; he knew it was a game lost before the opening move. Dad had limits, like an egg timer. He cooked in a predictable three minutes. When time was up, Dad walked away. If Nicholi wanted a bedtime story or a back scratch, he used time wisely.

Mom relished Nicholi's spontaneity and let him wander toward bed, twisting hand towels into turbans, sketching soapy alligators on the mirror, and gliding in wet circles on the bathroom floor. "Life isn't long enough to hurry," she said. And hers wasn't.

So, I waited for at least ten minutes, feeling guilty for not enjoying Nicholi's antics as much as Mom would have. Finally at my limit, I kneeled down and lifted Nicholi's shirt over his head, dropping Didoo onto the floor. "Okay, into the bath. I have a big mess in the kitchen to clean up this morning, and lots of laund—"

The scorch in the center of Nicholi's chest was gone. Healed. Completely. Not a scar or hint of pink where the red heart had been, and the jagged zaps radiating from his sternum had evaporated.

"Your burn!" I gasped at his clear, innocent skin.

"Mm-hm." Nicholi jerked away and splashed into the

bathtub, sloshing water over the edge.

"What happened?"

"Nothing." He leaned out, grabbed a toy duck off the floor, and balanced it on the turbulent waves. "Why does this floatinate better than paper boats?"

Fed up with the word 'nothing', I hardened my tone. "Really, Nicholi, I need to know. Tell me about the burn."

"I don't remember anythingamajigs, okay? I just remember Didoo screaming and when I touched him it was all darkish and then I woke up with some man stare-raking at me." He dragged the duck underwater, let go, and watched it pop to the surface.

"Do you know why the burn is gone?"

"Maybe." He swatted the duck's tail and it skittered over waves, banging beak-first into the wall of the tub.

I reached in and plucked up the duck. Nicholi's eyes met mine. "Tell me, please," I said.

"No." He reached for my hand but I hid the duck behind my back.

Striving for measure of calm, I took a few slow breaths. "Tell me."

"No!" He took a deep inhale and plunged underwater. I could see his bulging cheeks and wide open eyes staring like a blowfish, hair swirling. When he came up he spit a spray of water, hitting my free hand draped over the edge of the tub. I wiped my fingers on my jeans. "You're not understandish, so why bother?" He rolled onto his tummy and dove again.

I sighed with frustration and dropped the duck on the floor. Leaning back on my hands, I watched roiling bubbles pour from the sides of Nicholi's mouth.

When he surfaced I said, "They think I burned your chest, or that Justin did. They don't believe it was the fire."

He reached over the edge of the tub and snatched the duck, and with a satisfied smile he tossed it hand to hand. "I know. The crankodile must have asked me ten kazillion times if it was you."

"The crankodile? Do you mean the social worker?"

"I don't know who she was. She said her job was to protectify me. That's stupid, she's not a cleric. That's why I told Didoo to *whoosh* Paul's protectify heart. Since Didoo's supposed to keep me safe he didn't want to, but I made him, 'cause I don't want crankodiles getting you in trouble."

I stared at him, speechless.

"Little alligators are smarter than crankodiles," he added, then he sunk his teeth into the rubber duck and glided underwater, scowling on the bottom, still and dangerous.

Holy moly—these were the things that passed for facts in my screwed up world. I watched my little brother pop his head out of water, grab the shampoo bottle, and squeeze way too much soap into his hair. Could any piece of his story be true? Nicholi made a massive lump of gray suds, standing out from his scalp like swollen, dirty popcorn. With flat palms he slapped the sides of his head, spattering foam onto the walls and floor. Then he dove underwater again, sending melting globs of suds to the surface.

Let's pretend Didoo actually does protect Nicholi, and not just in some psychological way. In which case, Paul could possibly heal whole-body burns. Which would mean that Justin might indeed be hunting an enemy who is about to start a war. My spine stiffened. All of this pointed to the man in the tower, too ominous to ignore.

And in the quiet of that moment, I felt him. He looked down from the tower's height: distant, invincible. I could feel the weight of his gaze, swept clean of compassion, the flat stones of his eyes harder than diamonds. Gold seared into my skin, spreading ice through my chest. Shivers shook my torso, and stinging pins crawled toward my fingers. I wanted to be my father's child, believe that Dr. Peters' salve had healed Nicholi's wound. Seeing reality as Mom must have seen it was terrifying.

Calm down, Mimi, no one had his hand on our throats, yet. To steady my trembling, I tugged a towel off the rack. When Nicholi surfaced, I held it out, willing my voice to be firm. "Time to get out, little alligator."

"*Raaaar!*" he yelled, and he dove under again.

It took most of the day to shop for groceries and do the chores that could no longer wait: scrub the neglected bathroom, and mop away food scraps stuck to the kitchen floor. I didn't have enough time to dust and vacuum.

I almost called Duke—I held my cell phone, finger poised over the numbers—but then I snapped it closed. He should be calling me, asking about my brothers, offering help. His silence rang like a slammed door, the ominous Portal of Doom, bent and unyielding, desperation pounding, unheard, on the other side. I didn't call him. I waited to see if he would do the right thing. He didn't. So I scoured the bathtub with the fury of a Banshee. By bedtime I felt depressed and exhausted.

Late that night, when Nicholi was asleep, I exhumed an old condom package from the bottom of my purse and cautiously approached the study.

Justin sprawled on the couch, the Xbox booming.

Mom did this and so can I, I advised myself, clearing my dry throat.

"Justin, can we talk?"

His thumb pressed the 'A' button and the Shuttle he piloted froze in midair. "What?"

"Are you and Elina serious about each other?" The words seemed louder than necessary, more of a challenge than I intended.

He swept aside his hair, a wary tilt to his head. "What?" The hair fell back and immediately covered his eyes again.

"Look I ... I don't want you having sex. You're too young and—"

"God, Mimi, this is totally cheese-monkey." He threw down the controller. "I'm not having *sex*." The 'sex' became several syllables, smeared around as if this conversation completely disgusted him.

"Good." Heart racing, I threw myself into the treacherous rapids of Mom's lecture. "Look, this is a condom—" I opened my hand, and the tattered paper pouch with the flying saucer roll of rubber lay limp and damp with sweat.

"No way." Justin was on his feet, looming over me. He dug out a die, tossed it on his palm, glanced at the number, then said, "I'm outta here." Face red, he marched out of the room, the die clutched in his balled-up fist.

I sagged to the couch, miserable and embarrassed, wondering if my brother would ever speak to me again. This was a job for Dad. Where in the hell was Dad? He'd left me to do his dirty work: talk about condoms, take guff from social workers, work a crappy job to pay the mortgage. Not to mention determining the frigging facts that kept us face forward in reality.

I surged to my feet, stomped to the front hall, and yanked on Mom's steelshank boots. I threw her old work coat over my bathrobe and snatched up her gardening gloves. Shivering with cold, I found the pickax and lantern in the garden shed. The stump lay just as I'd left it, muddy and stubborn as ever, dead useless. At ten o'clock at night in the pouring November rain, I hefted the pickax and slammed at the roots. Over and over, until I could no longer lift my arms, my face splattered with filth and dripping with sweat. It had given up its prize and decayed into slimy splinters, but the stump still refused to budge.

Chapter 10

In my dream the dragon crouched, a mountain of scaly bones backlit by roasting sun. His green hide reeked of rotted flesh and malice glared from his slits of eyes. I overflowed with dread, feeling the poisonous corrosion that seeped from his heart, sensing how much he wanted to rip me apart.

He panted and sniffed me, his breath a sour, hot steam, and I was too petrified to tremble, too far beyond panic to even shift my eyes. With every cell I pleaded, "Wake up!"

"You are an unlikely master."

Orosiss he called me—master—and the 'ss' of his guttural language bubbled, like the acid dripping from his lower jaw.

He slithered his armored whip of a neck so that his spiked snout was in my face. His barbed whiskers could slit my throat with a toss of his head. Two horns thrust beyond his skeletal jaws, penning me within reach of his teeth. One eye opened wide and the golden pupil dilated, the glow of his red reflex pushing into my thoughts, groping at my impulses, savoring my despair. Far down the path to my soul, hidden in my inner landscape, a pathetic scrap of myself resisted. His layered eyelids blinked, but he didn't look away.

"You are no match for him. He will rip through you like a soft underbelly. What was she thinking, your foolish mother? Tread lightly, *plo vitthrik,* when he learns how weak you are we will both be lost."

Plo vitthrik. Tiny human.

He rose from his crouch and the gold coins encrusting his belly scraped together and creaked. He gave one last sniff at my head, as though inhaling a pie he longed to eat, and then launched heavily off the ground. Wings snapped, fanning gusts of foul air into my face as he lifted over my head. Only when he flew high enough that his wings became smudges of murky gray, only then was I released from the suffocating panic of his presence. I wilted, collapsed onto the sand.

～

I sat bolt upright, awake, racked with chills, amazed to be alive. The dark room stank of sweaty terror. I threw off the damp covers and launched out of bed, running barefoot down the hall. My fingers rattled against Nicholi's doorknob, but fortunately he sleeps hard. I didn't care that the Legos poked and bruised the soles of my feet. I hurried across the room and, in the dim glow of the nightlight, found *The Complete Book of Dragons.*

Back in bed, I turned on the light and opened the book to the Table of Contents: Lowland (swamp) dragons, Highland (mountain) dragons, the Legendary Dragon Wars, dragon magic, dragon anatomy and physiology, dragon hoards and how to steal them, or dragon reproduction, birth, and infancy.

I found the section on swamp dragons and examined a close-up of his face: a horned, cadaverous lizard, covered with dark green spikes and scales, eyes cruel and hungry. Under the detail of an eight inch incisor it said,

"Creatures of sump and quagmire, they breathe underwater and lie in ambush in the deep slime waiting for unwary deer, ducks, and men. Enjoying fermented meat, they leave a fresh kill uneaten for weeks, and their swamps smell of decayed bodies mixed with the acid stench of their breath.

"Neither swamp nor mountain dragons engage in a fair fight if they can avoid it. Unlike mountain dragons, who are endlessly polite while plotting to eat you, swamp dragons have no pretence of manners. If they do not like you and your raiding party (and you can assume that this is the case) they take to the sky in apparent retreat, only to suddenly appear from the marsh under foot, or from storm clouds overhead. Before you can mount a defense they snap you up in massive jaws and gloat over your dying. Only when cornered, or to protect something exceptionally precious, will swamp dragons engage in open face to face battle. Then they are vicious: goring and skewering with lethal spikes, crushing opponents with massive bodies, and spitting acid with remarkable aim. It is no accident that they are the pinnacle of the food chain and prey on whomever they choose."

With trembling fingers I lay the book flat in my lap. Such a beast had called me master. *Orosiss.* Imagine harnessing a dragon. What kind of soul could seize such reins? I searched my darkest corners for some hint that I was his master. No, it was cruel joke, or a case of mistaken identity. Maybe he thought I was the man in the tower. But he referred to my mother—my *foolish* mother. Vedette had done something he didn't approve of. What a woman to have dared defy dragons! I felt a flush of awe and pride, mixed with longing. He might be able to tell me more about her, if I could bring myself to ask.

I thumbed through the book.

"Dragons have four inner eyelids to protect their sight in bog, blizzard, sandstorm, or poisonous fog, and to prevent spellcasters from reading their thoughts. Blindsense is their strongest asset, allowing a dragon to locate what they seek— enemy, treasure, or escape route—even in the pitch black."

If only I had the nerve to ask who he thought I was, and exactly how *we will both be lost.* What could threaten such a beast? I swiped perspiration off my forehead with a corner of the blanket, and then tucked the covers tighter around me. I felt chilled to the marrow and achy all over. Ignoring my feverish misery, I kept searching, rifling pages, skimming chapter after chapter. All of this detail about dragons, and nothing to help me speak with one.

"Ten thousand dragons died in the dragon wars. Since dragons mate every hundred years, their population has had a glacial recovery. As of 1860 it was estimated that there are only forty dragons left in the world: twenty in secret mountain lairs, and twenty asleep in underwater caves."

Forty dragons on the whole frigging Earth and I had to attract the attention of one of them. Did fate hate me, or what? I chucked the book onto the bed and it fell open to this:

"So you want to talk to dragons? Then you are a suicidal bonehead."

I picked the book back up.

"Be sure that you are a powerful bonehead, a well-informed idiot, before you speak your first word of Draconic. From the moment of conception dragons are conscious, learning dragon ways while still in the egg. But a human must study Draconic—"

I skipped ahead. Draconic didn't seem to be my problem, no doubt thanks to Dad's language-loving genes. A few pages later I found this: *"Rules for conversation with dragons:*

"Number 1: Never show fear to a dragon. The submissive-cower position triggers the instinct to attack. Be sure that you are capable of standing upright, back straight, eye contact. Be certain. Absolutely certain, or you can kiss your bony head goodbye."

Holy moly. My terror had kept me standing, saved my sorry butt. I shuddered, fear and fever egging each other on.

"Number 2: Dragons lie. Always. Except when a partial truth suits their plan better. Some say dragons are genetically incapable of telling the whole truth. Sort carefully through everything they say. Don't ask, 'What should I believe?' ask, 'What does this liar want me to believe?' and act accordingly."

I thought back over what the dragon said, searching for lies. Was I strong in some mysterious way and he feared me, hoped to dominate? Or was I as weak as he claimed, but against our common enemy my frailty was somehow to his advantage and therefore to be gloated over? I assumed we had a common enemy. Perhaps the lie was our implied allegiance, and he was laying plans to double cross me. My gut instinct was that he wanted to cower me and then swallow me whole.

But I could see no profit in that; surely he had better things to eat.

So, I had stood against him, and he had retreated. In which case, I could expect him to lie in ambush. Justin would know, but I had no intention of telling Justin. He and his band of fanatics would pick up war hammer, staff, and axe, and dash off to die in glory. I planned to raise my brothers, not sacrifice them to dragons. They admitted that we were in over our heads, but that didn't stop them from delighting in their *fire from hell*. This was rip-roaring fun to them, and they trusted Paul to keep them breathing. Could Paul keep me breathing? I pictured his pretty, peachy complexion, shy smile, and pale freckles. One cringe and he was a dragon snack. No, if this monster wanted something of me, he'd have to deal with me. I wouldn't put the boys in harm's way.

I picked up the book and read the last rule:

"Number 3: Dragons are notoriously persuasive and might convince you that they are an ally. You must NEVER forget: no dragon is EVER your friend. Mountain dragons are true only to their kin, and swamp dragons are true only to themselves. If they save you from the jaws of death, it is because they have horrible things in store for you."

Well, that settled one question. Why did he come, then, and interrupt my dreams? Then it hit me; of course! Talk about being boneheaded, the answer was so obvious only a total noob could miss it.

I reached a hand down my neckline. The leather cord felt sticky and soft. I pulled out the gemstone and lamplight struck its face. A hundred flickers of light streamed across the ceiling, a luminescent bloom sparkling on the plaster. It took my breath away. He couldn't have it. It called to everything good in me, bursting with all of the beauty of life. I would die fighting for it with every ounce of my strength. This was mine.

I tucked away the gemstone, snapped off the light, and lay down, headachy and nauseated. I'd watch for him, my semi-delirious mind promised, in the puddles under my feet, in the gloom overhead. He wouldn't take me unaware.

Chapter 11

Half asleep the next morning, I sensed a vague shape wavering overhead. Its touchless fingers drifted across my brow as if testing for fever, causing a wracking chill. My eyes flew open but it was gone. I lay with racing heart until I realized that, whatever it was, it was far too ethereal to be a dragon. I didn't *really* expect a dragon to ambush me from a puddle in my yard, did I? Maybe. Yes, maybe I did. What a strange and feverish night.

I felt too lousy for a fight with Nicholi, so after dropping Justin at the high school I pulled into the elementary school parking lot, jumped out of the car, and swept Didoo out of Nicholi's hands. Nicholi scrambled out after me.

"Look," I said, leaning back into the car and strapping the bear into Nicholi's car seat, "Didoo wants to wait right here. He'll save your car seat for you while you're gone." Then I heaved fifty pound Nicholi onto my hip for the second time that week, and slung his knapsack over the other shoulder. "Wave goodbye so he's not lonely."

Nicholi began to whimper, "Di*doo*, Di*doo*," as I dashed for the school doors. It was a matter of seconds before the whimper became a wail, so I crashed forward, queasy from effort, practically knocking over little kids in my way.

By the time we got to Ms. Greer's room Nicholi was screaming, but at least I didn't have to forcibly pry the bear from the gaping hole in his heart. I set Nicholi on a hallway chair, and he immediately flopped onto the floor in a howling tantrum.

Ms. Greer appeared at her classroom door.

"You *carried* him in here?"

The question was so full of scorn that I almost cracked. I opened my mouth, less than an inch away from yelling, "Let a grieving boy have his bear!"

Then I snapped my mouth closed, a heartbeat short of giving nasty Ms. Social Worker more evidence of my failings.

Ms. Greer pursed perfectly made up lips, glaring as though she fantasized rapping my knuckles with a ruler. Then, with professional iciness, she forced a smile.

Barely in control of my anger, I turned away and kissed writhing Nicholi on his head. With effort I made it down the hall, sweating, dizzy. When the social worker called Nicholi's teacher, what would Ms. Greer say about me? Given my luck, there was some law against scowling.

Still flushed from hauling Nicholi, I drove back to Justin's school for his student-parent-teacher conference. I could guess what this meeting was about: Justin wasn't happy, he'd pulled into himself, and he needed counseling. Boy, was I wrong.

Justin's academic advisor, Mr. Masters, was a grizzly of a man whose voice, I'm sure, carried to classrooms several doors down the hall. Bearded and gruff, he dwarfed the mild-mannered principal into a mouse. His muscle squeezed Justin on one side, and the principal on the other, flat against the bookshelves in the principal's office.

"Were you aware that Justin has been handing in only fifty percent of his school work?" Mr. Masters boomed.

Surprised, I glanced at Justin, who stared passively straight ahead. "He does his homework," I said.

"Well, I gather that he rolls dice, and depending on the outcome he either hands in his work, or throws it away." Mr. Masters' thick eyebrows snapped down with disapproval.

Those dice were getting to be way too much trouble. "How long has this been going on?" A stupid question; I knew the answer. Mr. Masters' pause for recollection gave me time to fight a wave of wooziness.

"Two months. Everything he hands in is excellent. The papers I've managed to retrieve from the trash are also A+ work."

There was a painful silence, during which the two educators in the room appeared to ponder A+ homework, casually thrown away, while I contemplated my blithe promise that my brothers *would be fine, Judge Burrows, don't worry.*

The principal cleared his throat, a squeaky, ineffective little sound.

"Justin, you are one of the brightest boys in ninth grade. You're in junior level math and English, and your standardized test scores are exceptional. Why are you doing this to yourself?" His voice sounded strangled, tight as his small tie.

Justin turned cool, gray eyes on the two educators who

perspired before him. "It's not up to me." He sighed and slumped, squinting at the dingy linoleum, obviously ready for this to be over.

I glanced at the clock, then at the door, wishing I could just grab his hand and run.

"What do you mean it's not up to you?" The grizzly flushed around his collar. "*You* decide to roll the dice and submit to the outcome. *You* decide, Justin."

Justin's elbows rested on his knees, his head hung forward and shoulders curved, his hands folded softly as though he might be asleep.

"I want a commitment from you that you'll hand in your work from now on," said Mr. Masters.

Justin's back expanded and contracted with deep, slow breaths.

"Justin?" the big man insisted.

Slowly Justin straightened. His hand slipped into his pocket and he drew it out in a fist. Casually he dropped a twenty-sided die. It rolled to Mr. Masters' shoe and bumped against the toe, flipped over once, and lay still. Justin stretched forward to pick up the green plastic focus of everyone's attention. A ten.

"Sorry." He looked genuinely grieved. "Fate wasn't with you."

Panic rose in my throat. "Couldn't you use November's luck point?"

"What are you talking about, '*luck points*'?" Mr. Masters was on his feet, filling practically the whole office. He flung out his hand, palm up. "Give me that die."

Justin raised his head. He unfolded out of the chair, his hefty size no match for the even more barrel-chested Mr. Masters, but then, Justin trained to fight dragons. They faced off, the kid serene and centered, the man growling and gnashing. Justin squeezed his right fist. For a horrendous moment, I feared a wrecking ball was about to fall on my world: Justin was going to hit Mr. Masters.

I tilted on the edge of my seat, ready to leap on my brother.

But Justin opened his fist and dropped the die onto his left palm. A three. I practically fainted with relief. He handed the die to Mr. Masters. The teacher was deluded if he thought my brother was handing over his fate.

Under dark whiskers, Mr. Masters' face glowed pink with fury. "If I ever see you roll dice again in this school you are suspended, do you understand? You are to hand your homework *in*. *Hand it in.* Have I made myself clear?"

"I understand what you are saying to me, Mr. Masters."

And Justin's voice made its final drop, the last sweet piping of childhood, gone. A shadow where his beard would grow stained his clenched jaw. Mr. Masters didn't push it any further. He nodded and left the conference.

Justin took a weary step toward the door. "Are we done now?"

"No … er … not yet."

The principal, whose name I hadn't caught, snuffed in a few quick inhales, as though his lungs had been waiting for Mr. Masters to leave.

"Sit down, Justin. Thank you." He wrested his chair away from its cramped position against the wall. "I know your parents recently died—the middle of September wasn't it? Yes, well … is there anything I can do?"

The question hung heavy in the silence. Justin stared at the principal, his face compressed with concentration, as if trying to fathom how anyone could do anything about our parents' death.

"No," he said finally. "There's nothing you can do."

"Well … er … if you would like to talk, my door is always open."

Justin stood. "Can I go now?"

"Yes. About the dice—I will back Mr. Masters up, Justin."

Justin shoved one hand deep into his pocket, fingering his remaining store of dice, and stood a moment as if considering a reply. Then he left.

I rose to escape.

"Wait a minute." The principal touched my arm, a tentative, skittering brush over my sleeve. "Your brother is very troubled. May I suggest some counseling?"

I was so relieved to be back on familiar ground, it was hard not to laugh.

"Thank you, Mr.—?"

"Peppercain. Jerry Peppercain."

"I'll give it some thought."

It was nine AM by the time I nosed Dad's Subaru into traffic, toward the grocery and Ms. Farr's. The traffic on I-405 was heavy, giving me plenty of time to *give it some thought*. Not about counseling (which would be as well received as a condom lecture) but about homework. Justin wasn't done with his dice, of that I was certain, and he'd just demonstrated his talent for acting in secret. I suspected that from now on homework would be thrown away before he arrived at school, and the dice, when rolled, would never roll under the nose of Mr. Masters. Which meant that his grades would drop from A+ to a C or C-, depending on fate. To the authorities who scrutinized us this would be more evidence of my failure. I wondered what other decisions Justin left to chance. I wondered if he had handed in the second flan I'd practically killed myself to make, or if a dice roll had relegated it to the garbage. Then I thought of dice, Elina, sex, and condoms, and my heart clenched. My thruway exit saved me from agonizing further over this.

At Ms. Farr's, Steve reclined on the couch, his blue eye closed. His green eye scrutinized every shift, push, and pull as I manhandled groceries through the door.

"What's for dinner?" he asked.

"I'm roasting Chicken." I hauled bags downstairs, nauseated from a fresh waft of the house's stench. "How's Ms. Farr?"

"She's always fine." He didn't reach for the heavy bags, he just watched me struggle. "Will you make another spinach salad?"

"No, I'm going to marinate beets." Something was different about the living room: a vague sense of absence. In my achy, spent state I couldn't quite put my finger on it.

"Beets?" Steve made a disgusted grimace.

"You'll love them, trust me."

His green eye squinted, clearly dubious about trust.

I scanned the room. It was the bone, that's what was missing. The massive, carved bone that once lay between the bronze mask and the inlaid knife. Its absence made a hollow in the cluttered shelves.

"Where's the bone?"

"Bone?"

I raised a finger toward the gap.

"Oh, that." Steve sunk deeper into his grimy cushions. "I sold it."

"You *sold* Ms. Farr's carved bone?"

He closed his eyes with bored indifference. "Don't get all huffy, that's my job. How do you think she pays for all this?"

"You're an artifacts dealer?" I didn't believe it.

"Yeah. Did you bring dessert?" His eyes snapped open and he leered at the grocery bags, tired of Jell-O and Bowl O' Soup, no doubt. I bet the lasagna in the freezer had been defrosted and devoured within hours of my leaving.

"I'll make cookies if you'll go to the store for flour. Who buys Ms. Farr's artifacts?"

"Museums."

How awful that she had to sell her amazing collection. I wasn't at all sure Steve was the best person for the job, but I suspected that, as far as Mr. Eastman was concerned, this was a problem solved. I collected several bag handles onto one hand, and left the other bags on the floor. "Help me carry this stuff, will you?"

"Yeah, all right." But he continued lounging. His glance flicked down and both eyes—green and pale blue—rested right on my hidden amethyst. I hoisted groceries and walked away, glad that my flannel shirt was buttoned to the neck.

Ms. Farr sat sentinel over a foggy view, head flopped sideways, blanket held tightly, as if the last two days had never passed.

"Ms. Farr? Good morning."

Her gaze skimmed over me without any sign of recognition, then swiveled back to the drifting mist and subtle waves. From out of a grocery bag I pulled Mom's green cashmere cardigan, the one Dad bought in Berlin on a trip to perfect his German. One night when I was around ten, Justin, Mom, Dad, and I drove home from the movies. Snuggled in the back, I fell asleep with that sweater around me. It was like sleeping on a purring cat.

I had to pry at Ms. Farr's fingers, but with effort I wrestled off the blanket and tugged on the sweater. As the softness enveloped her, she clutched the two front halves of the sweater and leaned forward to lay her cheek on the fuzzy fabric draped over her knees.

"Ms. Farr, did you know that Steve sold your carved bone?"

She closed her eyes and breathed steadily, face in the sweater's fuzz. No hint of expression revealed her secrets.

The bone must be a dinosaur's, given its length and thickness. What shaman had carved it, knob and shaft, with crosshatched lines and tiny circles, praying for a good hunt? She could tell me if she still remembered, if she could speak. I kissed her softly on her frizzy head, hoping she felt at peace.

The kitchen was bare with its usual scrubbed cleanliness, cold and sterile, in contrast to the salamanders who ate the slugs crawling on the feeder. I made tea and Ms. Farr opened her eyes when I set my cutting board tray on the coffee table in her room. She sat folded, head on her knees, eyes following me around as I maneuvered a kitchen chair into place beside her. She sat up when I offered her a cup, then swung her gaze to the pond, tea cradled in both hands. The tea was hot, sweet, and strong.

"It's nasty out there," I said.

Fog settled over mud and water, ghostly. Through the white I could barely glimpse angular stems of broken cattails. Vague dark shapes formed and vanished, like huge bodies rolling in the gloom. A duck quacked, a muffled, startled cry that went abruptly quiet. I thought about dragons lying in ambush, and shuddered at my strange delirium the night before. And to think she stared at this dreary pond, hour after hour.

"Ms. Farr, I wonder what you think about, sitting here. It must be lonely."

Using both hands, she brought her tea cup to her mouth and sipped. It was hard to know, but maybe she heard me.

"I feel alone, too. I have my brothers, but I really miss my parents. They died a few months ago."

There was something gentle and serene about her. The skin over her cheekbones crinkled with concentration, and her eyes rarely blinked, deep in a meditative trance.

"I wish I knew what you need to get well," I said.

Unexpectedly, inexplicably, she turned to me, her eyes on mine with recognition and intelligence. She reached a boney hand and rested it on my cheek, something my mother might do. Then she set her tea cup on the coffee table, pressed her palms together, and stared without blinking at the eerie water. I finished my tea looking back and forth from her face to the pond; both were equally impossible to fathom.

Tea finished, I went to the kitchen. With the oven preheating, I washed a chicken, dried it, and rubbed the skin with lemon, garlic, and sage. I peeled and cut celeriac, parsnips, and potatoes, and was tossing them in oil when Steve crept in. He dumped the remains of the groceries on the counter, then stood at a respectful distance, head thrust forward like a vulture.

"Do you need anything besides flour?"

Just his presence made my neck prickle. I gave the oiled vegetables a toss with my fingers. "I don't know. What kind of cookies do you want?"

"What kind?" He sounded baffled.

"Ginger snaps, butter cookies, peanut butter?"

Slit-eyed and lower lip sagging, Steve contemplated the world beyond store-bought chocolate chip. "Can you make macaroons?"

"Sure. I won't even need flour. I'll give you a list."

His pulled up his shoulders as though he had wings that might flap with happiness. "Macaroons!"

I turned my back, afraid he might see me laugh and think I was laughing at him. He was an unsavory pile of bones, but his enthusiasm for food pleased the chef in me, the girl Dad raised. I tore paper off a bag and jotted down a shopping list.

"Pay attention when you choose the coconut, the bag should be heavy and the coconut moist. If you bring me dried up flakes your macaroons won't be half as good." I handed him the scrap of paper and he pinched it between long, filthy fingernails. "How about ... three dozen?"

"Yeah! I'll be right back." He jammed the scrap in his back pocket and practically flew out of the room.

"Real vanilla now, not artificial," I called after him.

"Whatever." The kitchen door slammed, then Ms. Farr's door slammed, then the front door slammed. I doubted that anyone could be Steve's friend, but maybe, stuffed with enough cookies, he would be bearable.

Roasting chicken with roots takes twenty minutes per pound, so I had a good hour once I set it in the oven. Ms. Farr was absorbed in her vigil so I went to the living room and studied the objects on her shelves. I lingered, touching fabric, metal, and wood, marveling at the craftsmanship and strangeness. She had collected everything, from exotic head-dresses fashioned of butterfly wings, to miniature twelfth century portraits of knights and ladies. Who had she been, when she was sharp-witted enough to choose these objects?

Finally I came to the gap where the bone once lay, and I lifted its neighbor, an eight inch stone knife. The man carved on the handle crouched, knees up, hands forward in prayer. Inlaid turquoise, gold, and shell spread a fan on his ribs and drew intricate squares down his limbs. Holding the heavy knife, I tested the blade against my thumb—sharp.

Steve returned with a bang of the front door. "What are you doing?" He hurried over.

"What's this?" I asked, opening my hand.

He shifted groceries from hand to hand, as if preparing to snatch. "A thirteenth century Aztec dagger, made to perform human sacrifice."

Holy moly, the pretty little guy was a murderer. I set the

deadly blade down so fast I practically dropped it. "Where'd she get all of this?"

"She was an anthropologist." He waited for me to jump off the catwalk, and then brushed past me, headed for the kitchen.

I followed. "What happened to her?"

"I don't know. I'm not a doctor." He dropped the grocery bags on the counter. "Stay away from her stuff." His voice was soft, but nasty doesn't need volume.

He crossed thin arms over his chest and slouched in the doorframe, a sourpuss who definitely needed cookies. With scavenger patience, he watched me find a bowl and baking sheet. There was no parchment paper, so under his oppressive glare I greased the sheet with a little butter, and then took condensed milk and vanilla out of the grocery sack. He couldn't have chosen an easier cookie—stir, drop, bake, and eat. The only secret to these was good ingredients. The coconut looked fresh and soft. He left when I put cookies in the oven.

Ten minutes later he was back, supporting himself against the doorway as though it might become his permanent roost. "Is lunch ready?"

"Just about." I lifted the pressure cooker off the stove and did Dad's quick release of steam in the sink.

"You're good with that thing," he said.

"We all need our weapons." I laughed at my joke, but Steve didn't. He closed his green eye, and just the blue eye studied the pressure cooker as I drained the beets, the palest of rose glowing through his pupil.

"Will you help Ms. Farr to the table?"

Macaroons came out of the oven, golden and smelling like heaven. He left with reluctance, but he complied.

Ms. Farr came in with high, precise steps, as though she was stepping over breakable things. Steve set the table without being asked and poured Ms. Farr's water. He ate half the chicken, two large heaps of roasted root vegetables, and even managed a third of the beets. Ms. Farr pushed her food around with a fork, ate four bites, and then drank her water. After lunch Steve helped her back to her room and then disappeared into the living room with two dozen macaroons on a plate.

Kitchen clean, I brought a macaroon to Ms. Farr. She stroked the surface of the cookie, her fingers exploring protrusions of coconut in the sticky surface.

"Are you comfortable?" I asked.

Without altering her fixation on the pond, she reached for my hand. Her fingers were warm, closing around mine tenderly, then she let go.

"I'll be back tomorrow," I said.

She didn't turn, but the loose skin on her chin lifted as she smiled.

Steve slept, sprawled on the couch as though he'd been dumped there. On the floor beside his flaccid hand lay the empty cookie plate, and an open anthropology textbook with a photo of the Aztec knife. I tiptoed over and stooped to read. One thousand human sacrifices a week to the god Huitzilopochtli. The carved human drove the blade before him as though the knife directed the thrusting, and the living executioner was merely an accessory to the knife's bloodlust. A magnificent work of art that had killed one thousand people a week.

I stood up and backed away. What would give a priest the conviction to raise a knife and kill thousands? It must be terrible to take on such a burden of souls, frightening to believe in such a bloodthirsty god. And how powerful is the knife, that mediates between heaven and earth.

A pulse of awe surged through me. I had the inexplicable feeling that Ms. Farr's artifacts had come here to rest, retire from enslavement to human need. The weighty meanings and gruesome tasks humans gave them were forgotten. A knife that killed thousands slept in peace beside a goddess who protected childbirth. A mask that frightened spirits lay beside a spear that subdued lions. All of these objects could finally become stone, bone, and metal again. She knew their meanings and their past, and she accepted them. She had gathered them in a graveyard for things of power. Like a priestess, she had guarded them. Now she watched outward instead of in, and they were being sent back into the world again. Whose hands would they fall into?

I glanced down at sleeping Steve, but he wasn't asleep. He was still except for a slight heave and fall of his chest, and through barely slitted eyes he studied me. Lazy, malicious, calculating as a predator. He made my skin crawl.

I backed up the stairs, all the way to the door, too scared to put my back to him. Who knows what he understood about Ms. Farr's artifacts, but he was going to sell them, and no one was going to stop him.

~

All the way home Nicholi's "Di*doo, Di*doo" pounded like a sledgehammer, but I endured it as stoically as Justin. As I turned the corner I saw empty garbage cans lining the street, and realized that it was Monday. Shoot, I'd forgotten to put out the cans again. By Thursday I'd have white plastic trash bags stacked against the garden shed, torn apart by dogs. Two months now, and I still couldn't get the routine. Then I saw our cans—recycling and garbage—waiting empty at the end of our driveway.

"Justin, did you put out the trash?" I tried to express delight rather than dumbfounded amazement.

He gave me a perplexed frown. "No."

Dang, here I'd hoped he was spontaneously doing chores. "Would you do me a favor and bring in the empty ones?"

He pulled a die out of his pocket and rolled it in his lap. I couldn't see the result in the rearview mirror. As I pulled to a stop he jumped out, slammed the door, and skulked toward the cans.

There was a note taped to the front door, the 'Mimi' written in Duke's small, tight script. I pulled it off with my teeth, struggled the door open, and dumped knapsacks, lunch boxes, and sweatshirts in a heap in the hall.

"Hey, Mimi," the note read, "your cell phone was off so I came looking for your smile. Dinner Saturday night? Duke."

He had to be kidding. No phone call all day Sunday, and then *I came looking for your smile.* "Things change," he'd said.

Well, he was about to find out just how new-and-improved things were.

I crumpled the note and was about to toss it when I realized: he'd put out the garbage! It was a little toe wedged in the closing Portal of Doom, but a toe nonetheless. Maybe I would listen to him plead his case Saturday night, rather than text a flaming goodbye to his cell phone.

I used the last of Dad's expensive Kalamata olives to make spaghetti puttanesca. Soon we'd be eating cheap. Justin won the roll over the dishes again, so I cleaned the whole frigging kitchen alone. I should have told Mr. Masters about all of the dice in Justin's pockets, drawers, and miniature boxes: rid myself of the little plastic tyrants. I felt ill and achy by the time I finished tucking Nicholi in, but I went to Justin's room. Piles of Age of Dragons books hemmed in his bed, a fortress of fantasy. Sitting cross-legged on the floor, I tried to cut a deal.

"Justin, roll against me. If I win, you give me all of your homework."

He didn't look up. "Why would I do that?" He lay on his tummy with his elbows on his pillow, the back of his hands supporting his chin, his nose in *A Handbook of Weapons: the Brutal, Subtle, and Enchanted.*

"So Judge Burrows doesn't think I'm a total dork and take you away."

He scowled that barbarian frown that could cleave ideas in two. "What do I get out of this?"

"You get to live in your own house instead of in foster care! Work with me, Justin, we're going under."

I'd felt lousy most of the day, but now in my anger the vague warmth became fever, and the nausea became pelvic cramps. I really needed to go to bed.

"What do you want in return, Justin?"

He studied the bare wall ahead of him, hopes and dreams hidden in the elfin depths of his gray eyes. "I'll name it later."

"What? You mean after I roll?"

"Yeah." I could tell by the flat barricade of his voice that he wasn't in the mood for compromise. What could he want that I'd never agree to? He could ask for no more chores, and I'd essentially be his maid. He could refuse to go to school. He could ask that I not interfere with Elina. The stakes were too high.

"No, you need to tell me your side of the deal before the roll."

"Then, no roll."

"Justin, that's not fair!"

He turned his head and scraped aside thick, brown strands of hair. "'Don't ask life for justice, ask for mercy.' Isn't that what Dad used to say?" His eyes were dark with misery.

I sputtered with exasperation. "How are you going to get into college with C or C- grades?"

"Who says I'm going to college?"

"Mom and Dad did. You're too smart to flip burgers for a living."

Justin tossed aside his book, stretched arms toward the wall, then collapsed into his puffy white pillow. If only I could disappear into something soft and ignore our future! My cramps became heavier and heavier, making me lightheaded.

Then my flow started. I was midcycle; I shouldn't be having a period. Could I have missed a pill? Was I miscarrying? I had a wave of anxious fear. I pulled my knees to my chest and cringed against pain.

Justin glanced over and must have thought I was reacting to our fight. "If it means that much to you, just roll the dice and pay the price."

"Good night." I stood and staggered into the bathroom, looking for a hot water bottle and a sanitary napkin. Three Ibuprofen later I was finally able to fall asleep, the amethyst clutched in my hand.

Chapter 12

A green kite, drifting in the sky, looping up, tail trailing, spiraling down, triangular body sleek. It's starting to snow. White flakes whirl in its wake. Not a kite, a dragon. Lazy, powerful muscles gleam as he drifts closer, soaring over the decayed tower, winter on the land below. The man, who had appeared so large in other dreams, could fit in the dragon's mouth and bulge down his throat without choking him. But the man watches calmly from the hole torn in the tower, his red cloak whipping up fallen snow.

"You sleep underwater, twenty massive bodies, sunk deep in the mud, dreaming of storm, blood, and fire."

The man's voice rasps, pulled through my lungs, stealing my air, sapping my strength. I burn with fever, toss and thrash, but I'm too weak to shove him off my chest.

"Outer eyelids sealed against icy muck, inner lids pressed in layers against malevolent eyes. Centuries of listening for the stealthy thief have sharpened your hearing, and every scuttle and tread on the shore echoes in the holes of your ears. Ripples of water tickle your blindsense. The scent of man rests on your tongues, clings to your nostril slits, promising satis-

faction. You are beautiful in your hideous power. My children, my army."

His right hand raises a staff, dark as a dying star. He lifts his left hand and all is brilliance. My stone, he holds my gemstone! Burning, hot as my head. I struggle to stand, to shout with fury. He glances down and flicks his staff. The blow hits me with a crack. Stunned, I fall on the frozen ground, throbbing, depleted.

"Proch mandatum niss calx sna rů gethrix … "

By the power of the stone I command you …

" … flrr rŭss auchen aurum."

… open your golden eyes.

~

Tuesday morning I woke too early, the winter night still pressing heavily on the windows. Wide-eyed and exhausted, I stared at ferns of frost crawling inward on the glass, only a small, dark center still transparent. I had to break free, now, before ice enveloped me. I sat up in a panic and cold air hit my chest, wet from its roasting sweat. Racking chills chattered my teeth.

I dragged myself out of bed and staggered, shivering, to the painting of the tower. Yes, that was the stronghold from my nightmares: a gaping hole instead of a roof, rolling hills of Tuscany sunflowers melting into the smoking edges of battered little towns. I lifted the painting off its hook and flipped it over. On the back was the Sovrani family crest, stamped in gold with the conviction of eight hundred years of wealth and privilege. *Torre dello Stregone Pancrizio*—Tower of the Sorcerer Pancrizio.

Tingling dread raised hair on my arms. Pancrizio. *It's about a little girl who was a sorceress, and a trashinator named Pan … cri … zi … o.* Didoo's story! Nicholi tried to tell me, but as usual he spoke in impossible riddles. Who was the little girl? *Then she got older and couldn't have babies so she asked for the trashinator's help.*

I set the painting down and backed away. In a dark frame I saw another picture, dragged from memory, forgotten for years. "I'm pregnant, *amore mio.*" My beautiful mother, face radiant, calling across the house to my father. Joy illuminated her suffering, her infertility a dark beast, dragged from the underground and thrown into sunshine. Oh Mamma, I built a sad, crazy mannequin of you, and set it in your place. What did you pay to have me, then Justin, then finally twelve years later, Nicholi? How little I understood.

Then it hit me: he could have her first born, and she could have the next borns.

I breathed in the hostile shadows. Every hair lifted on end, and my heart stilled. A sacrifice. I felt the blade on my neck. Mom had not abandoned me at her death; she'd abandoned me at my birth.

I yanked the amethyst out from under my nightgown and held it, trapped in my shaking grip. I should be furious, but with my throat under the knife I was reduced to terror. I knew without a doubt what hovered, poised to take possession. But I couldn't believe she would allow it. She had loved me. I knew it. From the gentle way she'd pushed hair out of my eyes, from the strength of her arms when I'd run to her, crying. It was an accident that she'd left me a mortgage, a necklace, and two boys the raise. It must also be an accident that she'd left me to Pancrizio. *He could have her first born.* No, I couldn't believe it. Didoo must be wrong.

I squeezed the stone, feeling icy gold drive into my palm. She had left me this necklace. No, wrong. *You must leave that tree alone. Hai capito?* She tried to keep it out of my hands. But the jewel was my beauty, my passion, all that I was and never knew. In my tight fist, the pits and snags of the poorly soldered loop dug into my flesh. She once jerked on the leather cord; I felt it. Wrenched so hard the loop had broken. Why reject such splendor? But then she had resoldered it, a sloppy repair, done in haste by inexperienced hands. Gift or curse? She didn't know, couldn't decide. It was a gift, Mom, a gift. Why couldn't you see that?

She was trickolish, Nicholi had said. Didoo's story: the Highland dragon empress made a pact with my mother. *Mountain dragons are true only to their kin, and swamp dragons are true only to themselves.* Mom believed that Yvess would keep a promise. Was this why the dragon called her a fool? *Dragons are never your ally. If they save you from the jaws of death, it is because they have horrible things in store for you.*

I didn't understand: Mom didn't explain anything.

I sank to the floor, eyes open, the room prickling with points of light like enemy campfires. I wanted to turn on the bedside lamp, see all that loomed around me, but I couldn't force my legs to rise. How many enemies did my family have?

Pancrizio, a marsh-full of dragons, and now the Empress of Illusion herself. And that wasn't counting reality: Judge Burrows and the crankodile—why could I never remember her name?—Officer Dray, Mr. Masters, and Ms. Greer ... Crap, we were doomed.

Sitting in stillness, I waited for my life to end. Breath wheezed in and out, sweat slicked my shivering skin, my abdomen ached and cramped. It didn't matter how hard we fought. Justin was right, there was no way to win. If Mom's sacrifice to Pancrizio had at least saved my brothers it would have been worth it. But he would take whatever he wanted. We were more than outnumbered, we were just potatoes, waiting to be mashed into dinner.

Freezing, I was freezing, trembling with shakes I couldn't stop. The only warm bit on me was the stripe of tender heat across my fingertips, soothed where I pressed the face of my gem. I opened my hand: the jewel glowed brilliant in the dim light, as if trying to burst from its setting. I was an idiot, blithely pickaxing a hole too deep to climb out of. *All the portents point to approaching war.* Twenty dragons, rising from the marsh: what a way to die.

I began to laugh hysterically. Now I knew I'd completely lost it; I wanted to fight. I didn't have to just roll over and let Pancrizio trashinate. *Orosiss* the dragon had called me, master, as if I could lead him on a string. Perhaps it was a dragon lie, but maybe I was capable of great things. The thought lifted me into giddy hope. Could it be true? The dragons knew. Just don't let Judge Burrows or the crankodile catch me asking.

I threw off my sweat-soaked nightgown and went to stand in the shower, necklace dangling, warm water washing my quaking bones.

~

In the morning it took another three Ibuprofens to get me out of the house, and I ached as if I'd been beaten all over. Trying my best to ignore it, I dropped Justin at school. On the way to Nicholi's appointment with Dr. Harvey, I studied my brother in the rearview mirror. He looked delighted to have extra time holding his bear. He sat in his car seat with his nose pressed to Didoo's grimy snout, murmuring an intimate sing-song of love.

"Didoo, Didoo …."

"Nicholi, could Didoo tell me another story?"

"Mm-hm." He kissed Didoo's cheek. "If you promise to use your listening ears." His eyes flicked to mine, two sky blue gems sparkling over Didoo's singed fur.

I nodded. "I promise."

Nicholi flipped Didoo around so that he faced me. The bear's grimy smile curled at the corners, and his left cheek bulged where stuffing had shifted. "Didoo says that before he was born, Agata lived in his stuffofied body."

"Agata? Stuffofied?" He'd lost me already. But then, what did I expect, *Winnie the Pooh?*

"You're supposed to listen!"

"Sorry," I said quickly.

"Agata was born into Mom's bear toy when Mom was

eight. Mom needed Agata because she found a Wyrmstone in Grandpa Tito's safe and she stoleborrowed it."

A Wyrmstone. My gem had a name—assuming stuffed bears were reliable narrators. I blinked at the yellow lines, whizzing by on the highway. Didoo's stories zoomed out of left field, spun me around and tore off, leaving me dizzy. "Be careful what you believe," Dad would say. "We make our own reality." Hush, Dad, I need to listen.

"The trashinator started bugging her. He couldn't hurt her 'cause he was just an either-real avatar, but she didn't like it."

Either-real? Ethereal? And I had no idea what an avatar was, but I didn't dare interrupt.

"She took the smell of Grandpa Tito's sunflowers and castified Agata. Grandpa Tito was mad 'cause his sunflowers wiltinated, but he got over it and now Agata guarded Mom."

So according to Didoo, Mom started fighting Pancrizio when she was just a child. A child with the skill to conjure a guardian. Wow. Then I remembered her betrayal and felt a jab of anger: she wasn't so powerful if she had to bargain me away.

"Did anyone else know about Agata?"

Nicholi bit Didoo's burnt ear, his voice muffled with fur. "Nope."

"Did anyone know about Pancrizio?"

"Nope."

"Did they know Mom was a sorceress?"

"Nope." Nicholi spit out the ear and scowled. "You're asking, not listening!"

"Sorry." I made a contrite shrug. I knew so little it was nerve racking.

Nicholi smoothed his spittle off Didoo's fur, then rested a cheek on his bear's head. "Didoo says no one never knew nothing, and when Grandpa Tito died and they opened the safe, Mom liefooled them and said she'd never seen any stone. Then she moved here with Dad and Agata died, so Mom borned Didoo and you know the rest."

The rest? I didn't know anything! Like, how did Agata die? But that wasn't the best question, given Nicholi's fears. I pulled into Dr. Harvey's parking lot and turned off the car. Unfortunately, Nicholi stayed quiet. After a few moments, I ventured, "Why is it called the Wyrmstone?"

Nicholi rotated his bear to face him, mumbled in a singed ear, then turned Didoo back around. "He says to be carefulness, Mom couldn't control it."

My lily-livered insides dropped and fluttered. Whatever the necklace was, Mom failed against it. All of those days in a haze of Night Veil, so desperate she'd made a pact with Yvess, and even then she couldn't keep the fig alive or the stone buried. I cleared my throat but only managed a whisper. "What was the bargain she made with the empress?"

Nicholi snapped off his seatbelt and shoved Didoo into a chokehold under one arm. "Who knows? Moms and dragons are good at keeping secrets."

I'll say they are.

Nicholi bounced out of the car and zigzagged across the lot, stomping ice on frozen puddles. I hurried after him. He threw open the door and blasted into Dr. Harvey's office.

"Wikipedia says machines started making tree paper in 1844," he announced to Becky, the pleasant young women who ran Dr. Harvey's front desk. She smiled as if Nicholi brightened her day. "Were you there when paper was raggedy instead of woodish?" he asked.

"Definitely before my time. Did you want something to draw on?"

"Yes, please." He plopped Didoo on the desk and Becky handed him paper and crayons. "I'm going to draw Mimi killing the trashinator with the Wyrmstone."

Becky and I both blinked a few times. Little boys sure didn't keep secrets as well as moms and dragons. Thank God judges, social workers, and receptionists didn't understand a word they said.

Before Nicholi put crayon to paper, Marcella, the nurse, poked her head into the waiting room. "Dr. Harvey will see you now, Nicholi."

The story goes that Dr. Harvey delivered me as a baby. Apparently, right after my birth, I grabbed a fistful of surgical gown, yanked his face down into mine, and socked him in the chin. At least that's what my mother swears I did. I was newborn so I don't remember. Mom told the story with great drama, clenching a hand over her head in mock fury, and swinging the other arm so wildly it's amazing that I managed to hit anything. Dr. Harvey, an upright Englishman, apparently tucked in his chin and drew back, saying "Brittan and Italy signed a peace treaty in 1947, little one. Your mother should teach you more history."

Mom told and retold the story, imitating his wounded dignity, laughing so hard tears rolled down her cheeks. But from then on she, and by extension our family, saw no other doctor. It was he who diagnosed each of Mom's longed for pregnancies and brought us safe across the battlefield of birth. His hands gave us every vaccination and took Justin's appendix at four AM one Sunday morning in July. Those hands were close to seventy now, but they were still strong enough to hold the confidence my family placed in them.

Nicholi was as irreverent as I'd once been, racing into the exam room and throwing his arms around Dr. Harvey's leg, knocking the doctor backwards with affection. I found a chair by the exam table and lowered myself into it, grateful to be off my unsteady feet.

"Did we bring our bear?" Dr. Harvey accepted the hug, and then squatted down. "Let's see, then."

Nicholi handed over Didoo and gravely pointed out belly burns and ear singes, then dirty tape glue crisscrossing Didoo's stomach.

"Had a rough week, have we?" Dr. Harvey ran his hands over charred patches, and fingered sticky mats of fur. "Nothing that a good bath can't put right." He handed the bear back. "Have your sister wash him with a little hot water. He won't be perfect, mind you, but we all get a few scars as we grow up."

"Didoo doesn't like baths."

Dr. Harvey reached out and lifted Didoo's chin. "You're a tough old bear, aren't you? You'll survive a bath."

Nicholi made a face but didn't argue. He put his bear on a chair and scrambled onto the exam table. Without being asked, he yanked up his shirt front. "See? Gone. The man with the rake was faster than fire."

The doctor's eyebrows shot up. "Well, well." He ran his fingers over Nicholi's sternum. "This is quite the thing, then, isn't it? Healed already. You're lucky there are clever men with rakes. And your cut?"

Nicholi pointed over his shoulder at the bandage. "I was trying to save Didoo."

"I see. Brave boy." Dr. Harvey tore open an alcohol rubbing pad and slid an edge under the silk tape, dissolving the adhesive. "Tell me about it."

Nicholi teared up and his lower lip quivered. "The trashinator's trying to kill Didoo, so I have to protectify him."

Oh my God, all of those fights with Ms. Greer! Was it true that Didoo wasn't safe without Nicholi? Just in case, I'd have to guard him. I'd keep this caretaking responsibility to myself, in the event that Judge Burrows didn't consider me capable of mothering of a stuffed bear.

Dr. Harvey's eyes flicked to Nicholi's face, gauging his distress. "Your bear must be grateful to have such a boy." Nicholi basked in the warm gaze, laying his head against Dr. Harvey's side. Under Dr. Harvey's gentle hands the bandage came off painlessly. He lightly prodded the wound. "Are you better now?"

Nicholi scratched his nose. "Mm—hm."

Dr. Harvey checked a few of the redder wound edges with a lighted magnifier. "Does it hurt?" He set the magnifier down.

"No."

"Good. I'll have Marcella put some cream on for you."

Nicholi looked disappointed. "You do it. I want you to do it."

Dr. Harvey hesitated, his features sharp compared to his soft, white hair. "Right. It would be better if I did it, wouldn't it?"

He left the room and came back with Silvadene. His hands deftly fashioned a bandage out of gauze and silk tape, then dressed the wound. "There you go, right as rain."

Nicholi jumped off the exam table and grabbed bear, paper, and crayons. "I want a sticker!"

"You've earned it. Go find Marcella." He waited until Nicholi closed the door before he sat down. Hands resting in his white coat pockets, he crossed one ankle over his knee, gaze wandering the room as though procrastinating. Finally his eyes met mine. "CPS rang, Mimi. They wanted to know if I thought you capable of abusing Nicholi."

I don't know if it was illness or fear, but my heartbeat felt irregular and weak. "What did you tell them?"

"I said," he leaned back and closed his eyes, "I said that Mother Theresa would beat orphans in India before you would lay a hand on Nicholi."

Tears sprang into my eyes. I wanted to say thank you, but instead I pitched forward and put my head between my legs. With an undignified moan, I watched the floor buzz and darken, wondering if I would pass out.

Dr. Harvey stood over me, his grip keeping me from falling. With his free hand, he pressed cool fingertips to the back of my neck. "How high has your fever been?"

"I don't know," I mumbled. "I didn't take it."

"What are the rest of your symptoms?" He found my wrist and pressed on my pulse.

"I've had terrible cramps."

"Stomach?" He wrapped a blood pressure cuff around my arm.

"No, it's—" How embarrassing. Only the fact that I'd known him all my life allowed me to go on. "I'm bleeding, but my period's not due for a week."

Stethoscope in his ears, he listened as the cuff hissed and flattened. "Are you pregnant?" The question was straight forward, as though pregnancy was a part of every conversation.

"I don't think I forgot any pills." The wave of dizziness passed and I leaned back, clammy and panting.

"I'll send Marcella to help you onto the exam table."

Marcella, the only women I ever knew as beautiful as Mom. I was too young to remember the brouhaha over Marilyn Monroe, but Mom wasn't. Mom was born around the time of Marilyn's death, and grew up admiring the American icon, as soft as a Renoir at a time when most European girls wanted to be twiggy French *gamines*. "She knew what it was to be sexy," Mom had said with mild hostility, unable to come to terms with the fact that the world's idol was Californian, not Italian. *Marie Claire* magazine's September 2000 edition on Marilyn Monroe still lay by Mom's bedside.

Marcella didn't look like the feisty movie star who died so mysteriously, but looked instead as Marilyn Monroe might have, had she made it to sixty. Her waist was small, and her chest was a bank of motherliness. Her sweetheart face was framed by flipped up waves of silver. Mom couldn't have missed the resemblance. Perhaps that was another reason she insisted on this doctor's office.

Who knows what Marilyn's personality was like, but Marcella excelled in soothing suffering. "There, Mimi. Get up on the table so we can examine you." She guided me, her touch settling my spinning insides. She had, after twenty-five years as Dr. Harvey's nurse, picked up the habit of referring to both Dr. Harvey and herself as "we."

She cleverly negotiated the ties on a hospital gown and arranged a paper drape over my lap. I closed my eyes to rattling instruments on a tray. Dr. Harvey returned and seated himself at the business end of the table. After a few minutes he rose and helped me sit up, then handed Marcella the culture tubes he'd collected.

Marcella's gaze travelled his deeply lined face, and it occurred to me for the first time to wonder about their relationship. I'd grown up coming to this office, but I'd never noticed that, besides being doctor and nurse, they were also man and woman. There was something about their eye contact that shared love as well as a professional burden.

Marcella helped me into my clothes, fussing protectively. "We want a urine sample. Are you strong enough to walk?" They'd been a couple a long time, I realized, as I followed her instructions in the bathroom. Why had they never married?

Back in the exam room I waited, lightheaded, clutching my abdomen against cramps. Dr. Harvey came back looking even older, as though weighed down by my test results. "Well, no pregnancy at least, which I assume is a good thing. Tell me about your boyfriend, Mimi."

I stared at him, confused. "Duke? He's a programmer, why?"

"Is he faithful to you?"

I inhaled a whiff of panic. "Of course. What's the matter?"

"You have a pelvic infection, a serious one, enough that in some circumstances I might hospitalize you. Is there anyone who could care for your brothers if I put you in the hospital?"

"No. What does this have to do with Duke?"

I've had moments when I wished I could go back, undo one act, change one split second. Dr. Harvey looked as though he was having one of those moments: regretting, blaming himself, eyes pained. "This is not necessarily Duke's fault." He pressed his palms together and rested them in his lap. "Women get a variety of infections, many of them not sexually transmitted. The test results will clarify all that. But," his fingers twisted into a clasp, "did you remember what I told you? You must always use condoms. Always. You kept your promise to me?"

"Yes." At least I thought so. In fact, I'd been a bit tipsy Saturday night, and I didn't remember noticing one way or another. But Duke wouldn't … I mean … he knew how I felt. We'd laughed when I dramatized Mom's lecture, but he knew that I was serious about condoms. "If he isn't seeing anyone else, he couldn't give me anything, could he?"

"One partner, no infections." He frowned, clearly hoping I would give this further thought. But Duke, for all of his faults, was not a philanderer. No possible way.

Dr. Harvey found a prescription pad in his pocket. "Marcella will draw blood and give you a shot of antibiotics. I want you to take this prescription." The page, tearing off his pad, sounded loud to my feverish brain. "Start the medication tonight. We need to see you back Thursday." He handed me the small square of paper. "Does insurance cover your prescriptions?"

"I'm not sure, it was Dad's insurance."

"Right. Have Becky check your card. If needed, she'll find you some samples. You're to be home in bed, resting."

This was terrible timing; two days on the job and calling in sick. "I have to work."

"Not until Thursday you don't. Who's your employer?"

"Mr. Eastman, but—" I pictured Mr. Eastman, surveying Bellevue's budding skyline, scowling about my absence. I pictured Ms. Farr, eating Jell-O and rehydrated Bowl O' Soup, or maybe Steve would just give her water. I shouldn't feel guilty. It wasn't my fault.

"No buts. Leave his number with Becky and I'll make arrangements. With luck, you'll be on your feet by Thursday." I stated to rise, but he reached out and touched my hand. "Your mother—" he began, and then abruptly stopped.

A zing of excitement coursed through me. Yes, I thought, go on, what is it? But he looked away and cleared his throat. "This infection could sterilize you if you don't take care. Do as I say. Agreed?"

Sterilized. Of course, he knew about Mom's infertility! I leaned forward, heart pounding. "I found a necklace, buried under Mom's fig tree. It was wrapped in newspaper from March 1st, 1992—my birthday."

His British composure dissolved, and he inhaled a few flustered breaths. Eyes fixed on the wall, he said, "The Wyrmstone."

My pulse raced so fast I felt giddy. "You know about it?"

"I know of it." He looked up, grazed my stare, and then looked away.

"Tell me what you know."

He pulled his eyebrows together and swallowed several times. "I can never repeat what your parents told me in confidence. That's the medical code of ethics, Mimi, and I've abided by that code for forty-five years."

"But they're dead!"

"I know." He wiped his brow. "I was only privy to fragments of the story. Your mother said she would tell you, when you were old enough."

"Old enough? I'm raising two brothers, paying adult sized bills, and making, God help me, life altering decisions. I'm old enough."

"This was up to your parents, not me." His voice was muted but resolved.

"But they're *dead!*" This was ridiculous.

"I cannot repeat what they told me not to repeat. Not as long as I wear a white coat and carry a medical license. It's not just the law, it's a matter of principle."

I stood gaping at Dr. Harvey, his skinny face perspiring, his white hair whipped up as though he'd been in a fight. I could tell him about Pancrizio, about dragons waking in the mud, tell him Mom was a sorceress, and that a dragon empress was coming for me. But look at him; he was as rational and scientific as his medical journals. He'd put me in the hospital, like he did Mom. I needed to find another path.

"What was wrong with my mother?"

"Health records, including mental health records, are strictly confidential." A sad smile turned up his mouth. "I suppose you were right to punch me that first time we met."

With a snort of frustration I whirled to go. It felt adolescent, but I pointedly slammed the exam room door behind me.

Nicholi was parked at the front desk, playing Pokémon on Becky's computer. "Didoo and I are staying here," he announced.

With a deep breath, I squelched a grumpy response. One hand on my cramping abdomen, I dug in my purse with the other, searching for an insurance card. Becky took the card with a placid smile and disappeared to call my insurance company. "This card expires at the end of the month," she said when she returned. "Until then, prescriptions are covered."

Thank God for tiny blessings. I wondered how a request for health insurance for myself and two brothers would go over, after two days on the job.

Well, no, in fact I didn't wonder—it didn't have a prayer.

"I have to be off work until Thursday."

I wrote Eve Tavick's phone number on a sticky tab for Becky. Then I stared at my stubborn little brother, fused to the computer screen. "Come on Nicholi, time to go."

Nicholi scowled. But rather than have a fit in front of a waiting room full of people, he elected to crawl, Didoo in his mouth, all the way around the room and then, ever-so-slowly, hop out the door. Much better than a tantrum.

All the way to school I wondered how I would find the strength to separate Nicholi from Didoo. It was a struggle to keep my feverish eyes on the road and my aching arms lifted to the steering wheel. I'd have to promise to keep Didoo safe, but what kind of guarantee could I give that would convince both of us? I had no idea *what* might come for Didoo, or when. Assuming, of course, that the danger wasn't straight out of Nicholi's imagination. I couldn't carry fifty-pound Nicholi in today: that, at least, would please Ms. Greer. In the parking lot I opened Nicholi's door and knelt down.

"Nicholi, please do me a favor."

"What?" He held Didoo against his cheek, his round face cherubic except for the devilish widow's peak.

"I'm sick today, and loud noises hurt my head. Could you say goodbye to Didoo quietly? I'll keep him safe, I promise." My voice wavered on the promise, and his eyes flicked to mine. Dad would never have made a pledge he might not be able to keep. Mom, too, was more wary about promises than she was about lies. In fact, I don't remember her ever promising us anything. But she was there, day after day, a silent, living commitment. More powerful, perhaps, than the vows she made to Yvess and Pancrizio?

Tears beaded up on the rims of Nicholi's lower lids. "No."

"Please?" Down-on-my-knees was not an admirable parenting technique, but it was all I had the strength for.

"No." He buried his face in his bear.

"How about this, would you let Didoo take care of me, so I don't feel so awful? Please?"

Nicholi held Didoo at arm's length and studied the scuffed-up face. Then he pushed the bear into my hands. "He says it's okay. Just for today." He still cried when he got to

Ms. Greer's door, but I had the feeling the tears were more to drive home a message to Ms. Greer rather than the usual desperation.

It was ten thirty by the time I arrived home. My hip throbbed where Marcella had forced in the shot, and I doubled over when waves of cramps caused dizziness. I stopped to get the mail and leaned against the mailbox, head down, afraid I would pass out. It took a few minutes to find the strength to collect the letters—mostly bills—and then drive into the driveway. I made it as far as the couch before I collapsed, curled around Didoo.

Around noon the doorbell rang, waking me from a heavy sleep. I tugged open the door to see Carlo with a covered pan in his hands. The Spaghetti Western cowboy who had so valiantly defended Dad's chisel, arriving again when I was at my worst.

"My grandma sent this over." He opened the lid. Beef barley. Homemade soup looks different than canned soup, the vegetables still crisp at the edges and the chunks of tomato still intact. It looked delicious. Carlo gave a sweet smile. Attractive men can be so overwhelming when they direct all of that macho at one target. Duke could have done that, with his looks and money. He wouldn't, though. Duke had a good heart.

"Tell her thanks. She's so nice, your grandma."

"Are you okay? I saw you by the mailbox. You didn't look so hot."

"I have the flu or something. I need to go lie down."

He held out the pan. "Are your brothers all right? I mean, I could drive them home from school if you needed." He had a husky voice, not radio quality, like Duke's, but gentle when he wanted it to be. Right now, he obviously wanted it to be.

"I'll go get them. I'm not that sick."

"No offense, but you look awful. I'd be happy to help."

What was with this man? Mr. Johnny-on-the-spot. Didn't he have anything better to do than to come over here and make me feel incompetent? I took the pan, anxious to shut the door. "I appreciate the offer, but I'll be all right, really I will." I put a hand on the door handle, not sure how much longer I could stand without leaning on something.

"If you say so." He backed off a few steps. "Well, if you need anything, I'm over at Anna's. See you, Massima." He turned to go.

"No one calls me that." The words flew out involuntarily, my tone hostile. But, in fact, Carlo's earthy voice made 'Massima' sound charming.

He stopped on the front stoop and stuffed calloused hands in his pockets.

"Sorry, that's what your mom always called you when she visited Grandma."

"Yes, well, you know Italians. Everyone calls me Mimi."

Carlo smiled faintly. "I'm stuck with an Italian name, too—way too long."

I was intrigued. "What is it?"

The tanned skin of his wonderful cheeks and jaw flushed warm. "My name is Giancarlo Alberto Ettore Rinaldo Rossi."

I burst out laughing. Carlo grinned and shrugged a sheepish, inward curl of embarrassment, classic and touching. Dad couldn't have done it better.

"Long," I agreed. Our eyes met, suffering together over our shared heritage. Then a wave of nausea hit me and cold air brushed my feverish skin. "I'd better go. Bye, Carlo." I shut the door and braced against it, chilled and trembling. I put the soup in the fridge, set the oven alarm for three PM, and then crumpled back into a ball on the couch, squeezing Didoo.

When I woke at three I was damp, weak, and exhausted. Despite Carlo's doubts, I made it to school safely. On the way home, freezing rain hammered the car and Nicholi relentlessly chanted his Di*doo* mantra. I slumped in my seat while Justin ran in to buy milk and pick up my prescription. If Justin had rolled below a ten he would have gone without milk, because I barely made it through toasting cheese sandwiches and heating soup before I had to go to bed. Justin rolled a twelve and the dishes sat in the sink.

Sometime in the night Nicholi crawled into bed with me, and I woke to see his face, pushed about and distorted by the pillow. Bright blue eyes peered at me. He'd wedged Didoo against my side, between us. The bear's love spread like a blanket. My amethyst had slipped from my nightgown and lay exposed on the pillow. I quickly tucked it under my gown, hoping Nicholi hadn't noticed.

"You okay, Mimi?" he whispered.

I stroked his mop of curls. "Yes sweetie, I'm okay." In my fingers, the hair of the widow's peak felt silky. Dad was pleased that Nicholi inherited his dramatic hairline. "Only good feature I have," he'd joked. "Hopefully he'll get the rest from his mom." My dad, who wanted to repair and guard the world. Now he had left all of that tenderness to his little son.

The next morning when I dropped Nicholi at school, he kissed Didoo and then shoved him into my hands. "He says you need him today." I hugged Didoo to my chest, warm with gratitude. I slept all of Wednesday, wrapped around Didoo, barely waking in time to pick up my brothers.

~

Thursday my fever was gone.

I'm not, typically, a sneaky person, but while Justin showered I rummaged through his trash can and pulled out three pages of algebra, which I hid in my purse. There were no homework papers in any other can, so I hurried back to the kitchen to make French toast.

Nicholi must have decided that I was well, because he screamed all the way down the hall, threw himself in front of Ms. Greer's door, and wrapped his body around Didoo in a death grip. Ten minutes later his voice, and grasp, still hadn't given out.

Ms. Greer stood in the doorway, preventing the bouncing popcorns who were her students from spilling into the hall. Her slender legs were covered in plaid wool pants, and she wore a white turtleneck to match. A pair of lovely gold and pearl earrings dangled among the blonde strands of her hair. My mother would have approved.

Ms. Greer stooped down, so as to be closer to Nicholi's ear. "Nicholi, you have a choice. You can give your bear to Mimi to take home, or I will give it to the principal."

It! She called Didoo "it." I wondered what it felt like to be so confident, that you never knew when you were dead wrong.

"Noooooooo." Nicholi's body contracted into a tiny, tight ball. I had to give Nicholi credit; he really knew how to prolong a fight. If he ever decided to become a social activist, the world would change.

"Nicholi, on the count of three, Mimi is leaving. If you don't give her your bear, it will spend the day in the principal's office."

"*NOOOOOOO!*"

"One … two … three." Ms. Greer pointed me towards the door.

I gritted my teeth, wondering what the principal would do if Pancrizio showed up to claim Didoo. Couldn't be much worse than what Judge Burrows would do if he heard I'd fought a teacher over a toy bear.

I was three-quarters of the way down the hall before Nicholi caught up with me. Tears streaming down his face, he shoved Didoo into my hands. "Make sure you protect him," he wailed.

I hugged Nicholi close, overwhelmed with love. "All day long. I won't let him out of my sight."

"All day?" His wide gaze pleaded. "Promise?"

Oh boy. I could see filthy, battered Didoo in Ms. Farr's kitchen, perched on the immaculate steel counter while I cooked. That wasn't exactly the professional impression I'd hoped for. But what the heck, Ms. Farr wouldn't care, and Steve could keep his comments to his grimy self. "Yes, everywhere I go."

"Love you, Mimi." He backed away as Ms. Greer's heels clicked toward us. He waited until she was inescapably close, then dragged himself in his best super slo-mo toward the classroom, making Ms. Greer wait, toe tapping, as he plodded.

On the way to Dr. Harvey's office I drove by Justin's high school, pulled over, and parked. The halls were deserted, everyone in class. Determined not to run into Mr. Peppercain, or worse yet, Mr. Masters, I peeked around each corner as I navigated the maze of wings. Anyone watching would have thought I was a student, sneaking off for a smoke. I made it to the administrative secretary's office without a run-in.

The secretary was too busy for curiosity. "Can I help you?" She hardly looked up from the envelopes she stuffed.

"Yes, I'm Justin Jovel's sister, Mimi. Could I have a list of Justin's teachers?"

"Of course, Miss Jovel. Just a minute." She put aside her work and opened a computer file, printed off a sheet, and handed it to me. "Will there be anything else?" Her hands were already reaching for un-stuffed envelopes.

"Where are the faculty mailboxes?"

She pointed down the hall. "In the faculty lounge. You're not allowed in there. Is there something I can do for you?"

"No, not today, maybe later. Thanks."

Down the hall, I turned to make sure the secretary's door was closed, then cautiously cracked the door of the faculty lounge. Who knows what I'd say if anyone was inside—something lame. Thank God the room was empty. I slipped through the door. Rifling through my purse, I found the math pages and matched the name of Justin's teacher to a slot in the letter cabinet. In a flash, I'd shoved Justin's math assignment into a cubby and was back out the door. With Ms. Greer's don't-give-me-no-grief walk, I cruised back to the parking lot, where I collapsed in the car, relieved that no one had questioned me.

I'd better start thinking up good excuses, because it was only a matter of time before someone began to wonder what I was doing, day after day, lingering outside of the faculty lounge. If I mailed his homework, the teachers would really think it odd. As it was, they might ask Justin why he left homework in their mailboxes. This wasn't going to work, I knew it. I'd miss papers, hand in the wrong things, and Justin would get wind of it. But I didn't know what else to do, and in the meantime, perhaps I could at least help him earn a B.

Becky gave me a big smile when I walked through the door. "You look better! Dr. Harvey's running a little behind. You'll have to wait."

"Okay." I picked up a magazine but didn't read. I'd almost drifted off to sleep, my spine digging into the hard wooden chair, when Marcella called me.

She weighed, squeezed, and poked with various pieces of equipment, then scrutinized my color. "Your test results are in. Dr. Harvey will review them with you." From the motherly concern on her face, I knew something was wrong. She reached into a cabinet and took out a small, square package. "We're going to teach you how to use a condom." She tore off an edge of the package.

I laughed with disbelief. "I know how to use a condom."

I don't know how Marilyn Monroe looked when she was angry, but Marcella lost that sweet blonde-appeal and suddenly become grounded, like a lightning rod. Her voice dropped an octave. "No you don't, or you wouldn't be in this mess. Now listen—"

Her lecture wasn't embarrassing—she definitely had the condom talk down pat—and without Mom's pidgin English it wasn't comical. Marcella included a list of Consumer Reports recommended brands, and her graphic demonstration using two fingers left no doubt as to how the thing was placed and removed safely.

"Any questions?" she asked when it was over.

"No. That was ... perfect. Marcella, would you do me a favor?"

"What?"

"If I bring Justin in, would you say all of that to him?"

Marcella's gaze opened wide. "He's fourteen, Mimi. Is he into this already?"

"No, at least, I don't think so. I hope not." I covered my face with my hands and leaned, elbows on my knees. From the darkness behind my closed lids I could almost bear to tell her. Almost. Justin storming out of the room, Elina, gunpowder, CPS, Judge Burrows, Nicholi's burnt chest, Didoo, Pancrizio, swamp dragons, the awful date with Duke: all of it knocking at the door, asking to be let out. But I couldn't speak. Not even to Marcella.

I felt her arm around my shoulder. "It's okay. Bring Justin in, we'll see to it."

Thank God Dr. Harvey returned and saved me from crying. Crying is the kind of thing I prefer to do alone.

With brisk British courage, Dr. Harvey sent Marcella out of the room and sat down, steeling himself with a few deep breaths. "Mimi, you have Chlamydia."

"What?"

"Chlamydia. A sexually transferred infection. I presume transferred from Duke?"

"Duke gave me something?"

Dr. Harvey nodded.

Duke was unfaithful to me. It sounded flat, impossible. The man I knew, the one I gave my heart to, was faithful.

But maybe I didn't know Duke. Perhaps I'd imagined knowing a brilliant, goodhearted geek, and I'd overlooked something very important about him. He had become, in fact, a mystery. A big, appalling mystery.

I should be furious: the deceived lover. Instead I felt oddly light, as though a massive uneasiness suddenly dissolved. The Portal of Doom opened, but I wasn't falling into The Black Abyss of No Return. It was Duke who tumbled, spiraling downward into the bottomless hole, achieving the depths no human can measure, too deep to ever crawl out again.

"The bastard," I whispered.

Dr. Harvey didn't move a facial muscle, not a twitch. Meeting his stoic gaze I wondered, to how many women had he told this kind of ugly news? Mom was fond of saying that throughout history the English faced down the Romans, Picts, Danes, Saxons, Huns, Visigoths, French, Spanish, and Germans, only to go on and pick fights in Africa, China, Australia, America, and any other land they could sail a frigate to.

They were bred, she claimed, to be lean and tough under their well-tailored suits.

"Did he give me anything else?"

Dr. Harvey exhaled—he'd been holding his breath. "Fortunately not. We tested for the whole panel: Gonorrhea, Hepatitis B and C, Herpes, HIV, syphilis, HPV … You carry nothing."

Duke was now a tiny speck of white, pulsing like a star, light years away, too distant to ever reach. Then he fell from sight, leaving a burning sting in the remains of my heart. I stood alone in the cursed portal that I'd dreaded and avoided. No one was left to lighten my burden.

"Massima?"

I glanced at his sad, strained face and didn't correct him. Calling me Massima was the privilege of a man who knew more about my family than we knew about each other.

"You are a bright, courageous, and very loving young woman. In all of your dealings with men, never forget that. You deserve respect."

As though I were alone, I began to cry.

Chapter 13

Steve leapt from the couch, black shirt tails flapping, when I walked through Ms. Farr's door on Thursday morning. His arms dangled at awkward angles, and pink tinted his gray complexion. "You're here!"

I was stunned; this was the creep who had bet I'd be gone in two weeks.

His next comment was, "I figured you for dead. What's for dinner?"

Well, that put my importance in perspective.

"Scallops and lemon confit."

"Mmm, can't wait." He watched me cross the room and stagger upstairs with the groceries, then he flopped onto the couch, making dust and hair rise in disgusting puffs.

Ms. Farr sat exactly where I expected. "Good morning. How are you?" I set the groceries behind her and touched her arm. She lifted a hand and took mine with a warm grip, eyes staring at the view.

Winter whipped the pond. Powdery frost coated the dead vegetation. Delicate teeth of ice whitened the edges of mud. Waves were frozen into crests on the surface, like monstrous dark backbones. It was chilling, eerily like a dream.

Then suddenly I realized; I'd left Didoo unprotected! He was in Nicholi's car seat. I'd even forgotten him during my doctor's visit. I dashed out of the house, startling Steve off the couch. Peering through the car window I could see a furry black body folded nose to toes in the seat. Weak with relief, I threw open the door and snatched him by a droopy arm. I hurried back into the house, hugging his pudginess to my chest. It was hard to believe this little rag was a threat to Pancrizio, and God knows what I'd do if the sorcerer came after him, but there you have it: we protect whatever fate drops in our laps.

Steve's mismatched eyes narrowed, tense and hostile as they followed us to Ms. Farr's bedroom door. "What's that?" he demanded.

"A toy."

He snorted, blowing dark mistrust into his exhale.

I ignored him and closed Ms. Farr's bedroom door behind me. "Here." I set the shabby little bear in her lap, grimy against my mother's plush sweater. "This is Didoo. He wanted to meet you."

Still looking at the pond, Ms. Farr found and fingered the bear. She started at his head, feeling each feature carefully. Slowly she worked her way down to the fat belly, and then curled her hands, one around each leg. Didoo slumped, face on her knees as she clung on. He looked safe, settled in her lap, her grip as tight as Nicholi's, so I patted her boney hand and hauled groceries to the kitchen.

I suspect that I chose lemon confit because it takes three

hours to make. Three hours to think about Duke while lemon slices baked from bright yellow, the pulpy under-skin a cottony white, to a delicate, evasive amber, the pulp now transparent.

I sliced lemons as thinly as Ms. Farr's dull knives would allow, imagining various scenarios for confronting Duke. I considered sending him a letter. No, I wanted to see his expression. He had deceived me, and I didn't understand how. When I saw him again, would I feel dishonesty in his compliments, hear shallow undertones in his rich bass? I was curious to know, now that I had the truth, if his game would be obvious even to foolish me.

Finding a glass baking dish, I floated lemon slices in sugar syrup, poaching in sweet to balance the bitter and sour. Perhaps Duke had changed. Perhaps I'd loved one man, and then missed his metamorphosis into another, harsher creature.

While the oven heated I washed and peeled parsnips, then prepared fruit for a cinnamon apple crisp. The crisp was to keep Steve civil. Ms. Farr probably wouldn't eat more than a taste of it.

I didn't want to confront Duke in his apartment. His forty-eight-inch TV played explosion-and-car-chase movies, boxer shorts lay about, and his kitchen smelled of coffee and pizza. Surrounded by his things, I was just another form of entertainment. And I couldn't very well say what I had to say in public: "Excuse me, waiter, may I have some ice water? And by-the-way, this jerk gave me Chlamydia."

I mixed topping for the apple crisp and slid dessert into the oven next to the lemons. I would find a babysitter for

Nicholi, and send Justin to a friend's house. Alone in my own home—that was my safe place, the place from which I'd confront Duke.

Wiping clean the steel counter, I swiped across the distorted reflection of my face. Vague shadows of dark and light were all I could see of myself. I had fallen in love, utterly misunderstanding the man I had such strong feelings for. A love like my beautiful amethyst: misty and secretive, full of desire and longing. Incomprehensible.

When I brought in tea, Ms. Farr was not in her chair. My heart clenched and I searched around in a panic. I checked the bathroom: empty, so I dashed into the living room.

Steve snored on the couch, oblivious. Ms. Farr balanced, light as a sparrow, on the catwalk surrounding the sunken living room. Didoo was wedged under an arm. Methodically, her hands felt objects on the shelves. She lifted a beaten bronze mask, stuck her fingers through the eyeholes, and then put it down. She fingered a fat-bellied fertility goddess, stroking knobs carved on its head. Moving along the shelf, she tested object after object, touching, always rejecting, until she came to a folded blanket.

When she shook it out, it was shaped like a shawl: a half circle with a long, cream-colored fringe. A double border of black and yellow surrounded a white bear's face, staring fiercely from the center, teeth bared. She wrapped the blanket around Didoo's small shoulders. Its richness gave dignity to Didoo's scruffy face. His small, distorted head and round ears rose regally above the long, elegant fringe. He was transformed into a wise and compassionate bear: glass eyes pocked by all he had seen, fur singed from his noble trials. Tucking trailing ends of the blanket around him, Ms. Farr handed the heavy bundle to me. The fabric was rough and smelled of oily wool. She laid her hands over my grasp and patted my fingers. I had the impression that she gave the blanket to Didoo.

"No. It's beautiful, thank you—" I took Didoo by the ear, "—but he can't accept it." I tugged Didoo free and handed the blanket back.

With a dreamy smile, Ms. Farr stepped forward and wrapped the shawl around me. Weight and oily scent draped over my worn shirt and jeans, hiding the little bear I cradled in my arms. Inside the folds I felt shielded, protected from all that assailed me inside and out. I felt, for once, at peace.

With her high, precise steps, Ms. Farr walked the border of the sunken living room and disappeared through her bedroom door. I stood watching her go, too washed in tranquility to call after her.

"You can't keep that." Steve sat bolt upright, glaring over the couch, green eye and blue eye fully open. He looked more energetic than I would have thought possible.

"I know." It annoyed me that he presumed to make Ms. Farr's decisions for her.

"It is a Chilkat robe, and worth more money than you'll ever make, from now until you die."

He swung long, gangly legs over the couch and strode to where I stood on the wooden walkway.

I narrowed my eyes at his aggressive stance. "What's a Chilkat robe?"

"Tlingit Indians, from Alaska. This is an original, made from mountain goat hair and cedar bark sometime in the 1800's." With unexpected swiftness he leaped onto the catwalk. "This is a particularly rare blanket, because it shows the white spirit bear of the Tsimshian people. Not a common subject for a Tlingit blanket."

Perhaps he was an artifacts dealer after all.

Looming over me, he grabbed the blanket edges and peeled the heavy flaps apart. I could smell the randy bite of his sweat, foul as swamp water, and feel damp heat seeping off his shirt. As his filthy fingers unwrapped my chest, his gaze riveted on the hollow at the base of my throat.

I shuddered and stepped back, letting the shawl fall into his grasp. "I'll go check my lemon confit."

Ms. Farr was back in her chair when I passed through her room, and the confit, as I suspected, was not anywhere near done. I propped Didoo on the counter and busied myself sectioning grapefruit and caramelizing pecans for the salad. I didn't know what to do about Steve's sliminess, that animal power that stalked me from the bushes, despite my best efforts to treat him like a human. He was a feral creature who took food from my hand, but who knew what he was thinking? Unfortunately, there was more than seven hundred dollars a week to keep me here now. There was Ms. Farr.

So, as the brown sugar bubbled and melted over the pecans, I thrust Steve out of my mind and pondered Didoo. I had no idea what the Tsimshian believed about spirit bears, but it wouldn't surprise me if Didoo was one. Could a sorceress conjure a spirit bear? Since my parents died, he'd done more for Nicholi than any of us. Anyone who could keep a child standing after such a lethal blow must have compelling magic.

I boiled water for a new pot of tea. Ms. Farr opened her eyes when I set the pot down. I lifted Didoo off my cutting board tray and put him on the floor facing the pond. We sat side by side in silence, watching sparkles of sun on frost whenever the clouds parted. Melting ice and mud steamed like our tea. Ice cracked and moved as though bodies twitched underneath.

"Next week is Thanksgiving. Did your family have a Thanksgiving ritual?" I watched her lost and staring eyes for a response, wishing she could answer. "Thanksgiving is the most important holiday for the Jovels. My father used to cook for twelve hours. We teased him that one day he'd fall asleep in his gravy."

Ms. Farr turned from the pond. Tea cup snuggled in her lap, she studied me as I went on.

"It's all about being grateful for what you have, that's what Dad said. But I never really *felt* grateful. He'd say his Thanksgiving bit before we ate, and I'd think, 'Yeah, yeah, that's great Dad, but I want to get out and enjoy myself before I become old and thankful.'" I took a sip of warm tea, and felt it slide down my throat, sweet and comforting. "I think Dad was grateful because he had so many people to love, despite their flaws, maybe even because of their flaws. So many people who loved him in return."

I emptied my tea cup and put it on the table. "How do you know?" I asked Ms. Farr. "How do you know when you love someone for who they are, and not for what you imagine them to be?"

Sun broke through the clouds, and a sliver of light fell across Ms. Farr's throat. She shuddered, then stood and went to her wooden chest. Throwing aside clothes, she dug to the bottom and pulled out a package wrapped in white paper. Lifting each foot high in her odd walk, she returned to her arm chair. It took a while to wrestle off the paper, but underneath was a 5 x 7 framed photo. She brushed away dust and handed the photo to me.

It was taken in Egypt, a monstrous stone sphinx crouching in the background. The couple in the photo were not posing in front of the sphinx, however. The man was tanned to dark walnut and dressed in jeans and shirt so dusty you couldn't tell their color. In the center of the frame, he lunged for a woman. She had a devilish laugh on her face as she jumped out of his grasp. Her rusty red braids swung toward the man like arms, reaching for him, and her army boots, up in the air a few inches off the sand, seemed light enough to fly. Despite her efforts, he was about to catch her in midair. I recognized the woman's triangular face, fuller and softer on her long neck. The life in her eyes was magnetic. By their graying hair, I could tell the lovers were not young. The smile on his lined face said that he adored her.

With gentle reverence, I set the photo on the table. "He looks like a wonderful man."

For the first time since I'd known her, Ms. Farr nodded. "What happened to him?"

Ms. Farr's head drifted slowly down as her cupped hands

drifted up, and when they met, she cradled her face cautiously, as though she didn't recognize it. She let out an anguished gasp, a cry so sad it could have come from a grave. Sinking her face firmly into her hands she began to sob, squeaks and guttural groans that were almost inhuman. It brought tears to my eyes to see her in such pain.

I reached for her and she lay her forehead on my cheek. Together we leaned into the triangle of our troubles, hoping we'd hold up. I knew there was nothing I could say; what fate takes away, we mourn forever. She calmed after a while, laid her head in my lap, and closed her eyes. I stroked frizzy gray hair off her wet face.

"I'm so, so sorry," I whispered. She quivered once, and an exhausted peace settled over her.

Outside, two mallards dropped from the sky, skidded to a stop on the floating ice, ruffled their wings, and then squawked and flew away. Clouds fled overhead. I looked again at the photo of the couple in Egypt. I would be grateful to have such a love, even knowing it was a love that I could lose.

~

After school Nicholi dashed past Justin, propelled himself into his car seat, and squeezed Didoo to his chest. "Did Didoo stay with you the wholefull day?"

I pretended not to hear, thinking over my options. Having missed an hour, it was really more the whole-*ish* day, rather than the whole-*full* day. But, in fact, Didoo was fine, so technically I had protected him. I suspected that technically wasn't good enough, though, when it came to love.

"Di*doo*, Di*doo*, Di*doo* … " For once the chanting was a relief. In the rearview mirror I could see Justin, lost in his own thoughts, glazed eyes on the passing traffic. Unfortunately, five minutes later Nicholi asked again, "Mimi, did you watch Didoo like you promised?"

I wished I'd taken a class in child psychology instead of Pastry Shells 101. Dad or Mom, truth or lie? Given a choice, I'd much rather be Dad. "Well … I … forgot for just a few minutes. But he's okay, right?"

The car became eerily quiet. I couldn't have hurt Nicholi more if I'd slapped him. "You promised." There were no tears yet, but they were coming, I could tell by the indignant quiver in his voice.

"I'm sorry, it was just a few minutes." I met his betrayed eyes in the rearview mirror. No, there was nothing technical about Nicholi's love. It was an all-encompassing rainbow of devotion, arched over his whole world.

Justin came out of his daydream and glanced back and forth between us, then extended a shielding hand across the back of Nicholi's car seat. "What's up, Uber-bro?" he asked.

"The trashinator in the stone." Nicholi's words were strangled. Tears oozed from his tightly squeezed lids and dripped down his pink cheeks.

Justin squinted. "Stone?" Every cell in his elfin brain must have leapt to alert. He studied Nicholi with half closed eyes, practically drilling a hole in the little widow-peaked forehead.

I tightened my grip on the steering wheel. Dang, Nicholi had noticed my amethyst. Of course it couldn't stay hidden forever. I probably should have shown it to Justin a long time ago, asked for his advice. But I didn't want a fight over it, one I was likely to lose.

Then it hit me: *trashinator in the stone.* What was Nicholi talking about? Pancrizio wasn't *in* my gemstone. Who knew what the Wyrmstone could do, but if Justin believed it was a threat, he would definitely take it away from me. Pulling up to a stoplight, I pleaded silently that Nicholi could, for once, keep a secret.

"The trashinator's going to kill Didoo." He sobbed so heavily that he gasped to breathe, small shoulders collapsing inward as though he were trying to disappear into his own chest.

Guilty, heart aching, I maneuvered through traffic, looking for a place to pull over. Selfish to worry about my gem in the face of Nicholi's pain. Careless to have forgotten Didoo in the car. Stupid to make promises when I was so fallibly human. Where were Mom and Dad? I couldn't think of a living person I trusted for advice on how to handle this.

Justin, God bless him, unsnapped Nicholi's car seat buckle and pulled his little brother into his lap. Folding his arms around Nicholi's trembling body, he snuggled Nicholi's face, slimy with tears and snot, into his neck. Together they rocked back and forth.

I found an exit off the highway and pulled into a filling station. Ignoring the 'no parking' sign, I stopped by an air tank and stepped into the icy sleet. There was no room inside with the car seat and Justin, so I knelt on half frozen concrete, slushy rain falling on my head. Not knowing what else to do, I reached through the open back door and put my arms around both my brothers.

Nicholi's sobs came farther and farther apart, until, finally, he stopped crying. Justin kissed him on the cheek. I sat back on my heels, shivering in the cold.

Justin bent into the cuddle of his embrace. "Nicholi, have you asked Didoo?"

"What?" The word was muffled by the thick shell of Justin's arms.

"How we protect him?"

Sniff. "No."

"Would you ask him?"

Another sniff. Nicholi snuggled his chin into Didoo's nose. After a minute he said, "Didoo wantinates the Chilkat robe."

I took a deep breath and blew it out slowly. Dang. Can't Nicholi and Didoo ever ask for anything easy?

"It doesn't belong to Didoo, it belongs to Ms. Farr."

Justin's gaze jerked to mine. "What's the Chilkat robe?"

"You have to let him wear it," Nicholi whined.

I adopted Dad's end-of-argument tone. "No, it's not mine to give away." Then I said to Justin, "It's an antique blanket in Ms. Farr's archeology collection, worth a fortune."

Justin raised an eyebrow. "Case could get it. He can steal anything."

"No way! Don't even *think* about it!" Stealing from Ms. Farr. Unthinkable. And that was all we needed—burglary charges for Judge Burrows to slam his gavel down on.

"Chill, Mimi, I was kidding. Gees, you have no sense of humor anymore. Nicholi, is Didoo safe in the robe?"

Nicholi sniffed, and then nodded.

Using his sleeve, Justin wiped tears off Nicholi's cheeks. "If Mimi wraps him in the robe while you're at school, would that be enough?"

"I guess so."

Justin's gray elfin eyes were calm as a king's. It amazed me that someone so wise would roll dice, light gunpowder, and toss A+ homework.

"Will you do that, Mimi?"

More promises. Steve wasn't going to like this. He was going to snarl with his yellow teeth and loom over me like the specter of death. But it wasn't Steve's robe, it was Ms. Farr's, and she'd made it clear that Didoo was welcome to wear it, so Steve could take a frigging hike. Maybe he'd cross Ms. Greer's path while he was hiking and they could commiserate about stubborn boys and stuffed bears.

"Okay, I'll wrap him in the robe."

Nicholi breathed a few quiet puffs. "You promise for reality this time?"

"Yes, for reality." And a very strange reality it was, too.

A tiny smile curved Nicholi's lips. "Mimi, you're all smearoozled with mud."

That's because I'm a parent, I thought, but I kept this complaint to myself. Standing up, I wiped slush off my sore knees.

Justin extended a flat hand. "Give me five." Nicholi

slapped Justin's palm, then climbed back into his car seat.

The rest of the ride was quiet: no chanting, no crying, just each alone with their thoughts. I thought about promises: Duke's broken one, Dr. Harvey's infuriating one, Nicholi's ironclad one, and Mom's silent one. We promise based on what we believe, but we're wrong, all of us, about how the world will challenge us. Perhaps this was an impossible world to make promises in, but because of love, I would keep trying.

Chapter 14

I creep on dirt, packed by the centuries at the tower's base. Above me the sky hangs heavy with storm. I sneak furtive glances up, praying that I am hidden by the sloping angle of the wall. I can't see them but I can hear their voices: the dragon's steady leak of steam, and Pancrizio's grating response, shredding the Draconic as if he hates it.

"So remove her, snake, I lose patience with your delays." Pancrizio uses the words *dedoz mortar—finger of death*—for 'remove', and I shiver at the cruel implications.

Dragon claws scrape on stone, knocking free bits of rock that hop and tumble down the tower, grazing my shoulder as I flatten against the wall. The tower groans as he shifts his weight. "Remove her yourself, if the task is so easy. I find her uncommonly stubborn and hard to break."

Dear God, don't let this argument be about me. I bend and hunt desperately through the grass that sticks up in tufts, hands combing the prickly blades. I need to find what I came for and get out of here, but I have no idea what I seek.

"She is just an old woman!" says Pancrizio, and I tingle with relief.

The dragon snorts, and a flock of crows rise, shrieking from the frozen fields beyond the tower. "And you are just an old man." He flaps his wings one whomp, blowing foul air which raises the dust around me. "She is strong beyond even your powers, great spellcaster, because her hoard loves her." For 'great', he smears the word *gruss* with drawn out S's to imply bloated.

"Then take her hoard, isn't that what dragons do best?" The sorcerer's voice is sharp with impatience, but there is no bristle of wounded pride. He must not know enough Draconic to catch the insult. "I want my army free. They grow restless in the borderlands."

"Dragons are never restless, human."

The tower wall beside me rocks as the dragon lifts off, stones trembling, sand streaming from cracking mortar. I hear the slap of his wings against his sides as he hovers. "Patience, *Orosiss*, I chew her thinner and thinner." With thumping gusts of air, he flies away.

Frantically I search. Grass hisses and rustles, dry dust rising gritty in my nose. I stumble forward and trip, falling painfully to hands and knees, crumbs of hard turf digging into my palms. The amethyst slips from under my shirt, dangling exposed on its strap before my nose. The winter sun breaks through the clouds and hits the gem's facets. Bruised purple swirls like liquid. My heart reaches for the beauty. Words flow slippery and bitter from my mouth, easy as spittle: *"Proch mandatum niss calx sna rŭ gethrix."* *By the power of the stone I command you.* Above me, Pancrizio shouts a brief, furious, howl. In the grass, my searching fingers close on something slick and metal. Sharp. I gasp as it cuts.

In the reflected face of my jewel I see Pancrizio in the tower above. Face bare to the wind, he studies the distant hills, intent on the danger but confused about the direction. His expression is cold, features punished like eroded rock, not an ounce of mercy left clinging in the crevices.

I grab the blade at my fingertips and it slices me again, blood making it slippery. I stumble to my feet and find the handle. The grip, wound with a cord of braided hair, fits my hand like my father's chisel never could. Holding the heavy sword before me, I run.

I woke with my fists clenched so tight fingernail lines pressed into my palms, the memory of the sword's cut searing.

I snapped on the light and examined my hand: intact. No sword beside me, no blood on the sheets. Collapsing into the pillow with relief, I listened for the usual sounds of the house: refrigerator hum, furnace click and bang, creaks from the roof. I was accumulating objects I didn't know how to use: a Wyrmstone, a sword. I must ask for Justin's help, he really did show remarkable maturity. But he was fourteen and in love with danger. I couldn't risk it, not with so many snooping adults who noted every mistake and calamity. Somehow I must understand before I got us all killed.

I reached to my bedside and picked up the scrap with the Latin inscription.

> *Natus, semines quae terram efficiunt,*
> *Sanguis qui ullum marem transit.*
> *Tribuete natus huic mulieri,*

Omnis eorum maior quam posterum,
Quoad uterus centum reges foras ederit.

Ms. Farr might know Latin. Was she the old woman Pancrizio cursed for keeping his dragons at bay? I only knew two old women—her and Ms. Rossi—and neither of them looked up to restraining dragons. *Her hoard loves her.* Dragons have hoards. Perhaps the woman in question was a dragon. I rolled over and put the pillow over my head. If only I could ask. Even dragon lies had to be better than ignorance. In any case, I'd take the Latin with me, see if Ms. Farr could help.

~

That morning Child Protective Services called.

"Ms. Jovel? This is Tamara Whitting. I'll be making a home visit today at two-thirty."

"Oh!" In my surprise, I almost knocked bubbling Cream of Wheat off the stove. I stuck the phone in the cradle of my shoulder, hanging on with my chin and grabbing onto the pot. "I thought Dr. Harvey said—I mean, why are you coming?"

"With injuries as serious as Nicholi's, and with Justin's police record, it's customary to make a home visit."

Her tone made it sound dreadful, as though Nicholi was mortally damaged, and Justin was hell bent toward doing hard time. Still cradling the phone between ear and shoulder, I lifted two bowls off the stack in the cupboard and poured Cream of Wheat, accidentally dumping the boiling cereal over my thumb.

"Ow! … Ouch … Oooo …." I set the hot pan down and stuck my thumb in my mouth, trying to keep the sucking sound inaudible. The phone slipped and crashed to the floor just as Nicholi came streaking out of his morning shower, shivering and naked.

"Mimi, there's no towels!" he said petulantly.

"In the laundry room. I haven't had time to fold them. Just take one from the basket." I spoke as calmly as I could, aware that Ms. Social Worker could hear me.

Nicholi dashed out of the kitchen, leaving slippery, wet footprints.

I picked up the phone with my right hand and shook my still stinging left thumb.

"Sorry," I wedged the phone back under my ear. "Look, Ms. White—"

"Whitting, Tamara Whitting."

"Sorry, Ms. Whitting. Look, I work, and the boys get out of school at three. Two-thirty is an awful time. Could you come this evening, maybe at four, or after dinner?"

There was a sullen silence, then, "I have another case at four-thirty and I don't usually work after six. Especially not on Friday night. Are you available now?"

"No! I mean, I'm sorry, but I have to make breakfast, pack lunches, wash another load of laundry, and get the boys to school, then I have to go to work—"

Was she totally clueless?

"Mimi? Mimi?" Nicholi stood before me, soggy dark hair in his eyes and wrinkled towel pulled tight around his shoulders. "Where's Didoo?"

I covered the phone with one hand, in case my answer caused Nicholi to erupt in a rebelothon. "He needed a bath, Nicholi. He's in the washer. I'll put him in the drier as soon as I'm off the phone. Go get dressed, now, sweetie. I left clean clothes on your bed."

Nicholi's lower lip stuck out in a 'V', mirroring the 'V' of his widow's peak. "He didn't wantinate a bath," he growled through clamped teeth.

No tantrum, please, not now. "Hold on, Nicholi—" I put my hand on Nicholi's wet head. "Ms …. ah … Whitting, could I call you right back?"

"You can't avoid this, Ms. Jovel. I am going to make a home visit."

"Fine. Make a visit then." Her insinuations were poking through my patience. "I'll be here after four. I have to go take care of my brothers now. So if you'll excuse me … " Maybe it was a stupid thing to do—and I did feel guilty about it—but I hung up on her.

I took a breath to calm my trembling insides. "Yes, Nicholi?"

"No baths for Didoo." He exaggerated his adorable pout, stretching his face into a long, sad mask with two rascally blue eyes peering out. Definitely better than a tantrum.

"Dr. Harvey recommended we wash him, remember? Let's go see if he's clean." I guided Nicholi's damp little shoulders towards the laundry room.

Didoo lay flattened against the central spinner of the washer, tangled in clothes, nose and belly into the hard plastic. I extricated him from the arms of my blouse and plumped him up with three forceful squeezes.

"See? He looks great."

Actually, he looked like a rag, the noble Tsimshian spirit faded in the wash. But he smelled better. I popped him in the dryer and cranked it to high. "Go get dressed, now, it's time for breakfast."

Nicholi plopped in front of the dryer, watching his bear tumble.

"What do you want on your Cream of Wheat?" I asked.

"Brown sugar and milk, plus butter." He sounded so disinterested I was surprised he answered.

"Come show me how much."

Nicholi guarded his bear with rapt attention, giving no hint of an effort to stand. Some things move too slowly to notice in a lifetime: continental drift, the erosion of mountains, and Nicholi, obeying an undesirable request. Capitulating to the forces of nature, I went back to the kitchen, poured milk and brown sugar on Nicholi's cereal, added a small pat of butter, and brought him the bowl.

"Here." I handed him the cereal to eat, naked, on the floor.

At that moment I had an image of cake batter, spinning in a bowl; the longer it spun, the further away from the center it drifted, until finally it whirled into an unrecognizable, insipid layer, smeared up the sides of the bowl. Ms. Whitting would see how thinly I was spread. How I struggled. She would see that I was losing it.

I could not allow her to take my brothers away.

I handed Nicholi a spoon and went to call Justin out of the shower.

Nicholi's hair still had a few wet tufts when I dropped him at Ms. Greer's room. Kneeling in front of the door, I took his small, hot hands in mine.

"Should Didoo to go to Ms. Farr's?" I asked, and then I held my breath.

"Yep." He shoved the clean, fat body against my chest. "Wrapolated in the robe, right?" Children streamed around us in the hall, making so much noise that we had to put our heads together to hear.

I exhaled slowly. "Promise." Even picturing Steve's snarl, my voice didn't waver.

With a quick, brave nod, Nicholi released his bear and turned to Ms. Greer's door. "Bye, Mimi," he called over his shoulder, and he darted into her room.

I stayed on my knees before Ms. Greer's cheerfully decorated door, her paper Thanksgiving turkey jiggling in the breeze of running children. "Thank you, Justin. I owe you one. I won't forget it," I whispered to myself.

I looked up to see Ms. Greer a few feet away, arms crossed, observing me coolly. Her sleeveless burgundy wool jumper accentuated her cool-headedness, and her toned biceps bulged a little where her hands slid under them. She clicked over to me on black high heels.

"Amazing what behavior modification can do, isn't it?" She offered me a hand up.

"Behavior modification?" I stood without her help and brushed off my dusty pant legs.

"Nicholi and I made a star chart last week. He gets a star for every morning he comes to school without crying. Looks like we're off to a good start." Her smile spread broadly, beaming with triumph.

"Yes, well, he does seem to be better."

I had no intention of telling Ms. Greer that Nicholi's new confidence had to do with a 19th century Tlingit Indian ceremonial robe belonging to an archeologist who hadn't spoken in ten years.

"You haven't signed up for a parent-teacher conference yet." She pointed to the signup sheet on her door, hanging over the turkey's head. "I still have time open this afternoon."

"Oh. I wasn't aware—"

"It's routine at the end of the first semester. Just a time to talk about Nicholi's progress."

She glanced at the scruffy bear stuffed under my arm, and a moment of displeasure flashed across her face. It occurred to me that if she could get away with *not* talking about Didoo she would consider the conference a success.

"This afternoon I have another appointment," I said. An appointment with a big woman in neon polyester and Birkenstocks who hoped to prove me an unfit parent. There was so much about Nicholi's life that whizzed by Ms. Greer. Nicholi's problems as big as trucks on the highway, and she sat, back to the windows at the truck stop, oblivious to the roar.

"How about we meet on Monday, after school?" she asked.

"Fine." I caught myself discreetly tucking in my wrinkled shirt and touching my unbrushed hair, performing my mother's ritual to right myself in the face of Ms. Greer's fashion perfection. With a gracious smile she turned away and traipsed into her classroom, leaving me buffeted by the onslaught of children who hustled to class as the bell rang.

Now I had three meetings to dread: Ms. Whitting, Duke, and Ms. Greer. Oh yes, and Steve. I walked to the parking lot, wondering which would be the worst of the four. If only I could send Ms. Whitting to investigate Duke, and solicit Ms. Greer to handle Ms. Whitting. Maybe united they could subdue Steve.

I continued to fret as I successfully sneaked Justin's homework into faculty mailboxes, then agonized more as I pinched garlic buds for firmness at the grocery store. I longed to be ruthless, cool, and composed at these mêlées. I was none of these things. Honest to God, I felt *guilty* about hanging up on a woman who accused me of abusing my little brother. Only in the safety of my parent's house could I tell Duke that he was a bastard. And, faced with Ms. Greer, I was as floppy as the pink salmon filet I bought for Ms. Farr's dinner. The dragon was right: I was a soft-bellied human, no match for Pancrizio. With or without magical weapons, I was hopeless.

Later, hauling groceries down Ms. Farr's driveway, I paused to get a better grip on the handles and looked up at Ms. Farr's house. Sinking into the pond, merging into forest undergrowth, it slipped away like Ms. Farr's consciousness. Perhaps Ms. Farr wasn't lonely. Perhaps it was heaven to be so undisturbed, to be absorbed into Earth like a fallen tree.

No, it couldn't be heaven to be so alone. I'd do anything for the love in Nicholi's goodnight kisses, or for the privilege of watching Justin and his friends grow into men. If miserable confrontations and glaring humiliation were the price, I'd find the courage to pay.

Steve was awake when I arrived, flipping through his anthropology text, feet on the couch. He stretched his arms over his head with a casual, sluggish yawn, his green eye wandering to Didoo—whose head stuck out of a paper bag—as his blue eye closed.

"What's for dinner?"

"Salmon." The groceries were too heavy to haul across the room in one trip. Setting them at the bottom of the steps, I gathered a more manageable handful.

He scratched his ribs, his gaze never leaving Didoo's singed face. "I don't like salmon. It's too bland."

"Do you like spicy food?"

"Yeah. The hotter the better." He sat up straight and I instinctively backed away. "Can you cook Mexican? I *love* refries, tortillas, stuff like that." Apparently *love* didn't begin to express his appetite for south-of-the-border cuisine. *Love*, as he said it, made hair prickle on the back of my neck.

"I can cook Mexican, but tonight we're having Cajun. How's Ms. Farr?"

"Okay." He picked up his anthropology textbook and went back to reading.

She did, indeed, look "okay" as I passed through her room to the kitchen. When I came back a few minutes later she hadn't moved.

"Hi. It's Mimi." I stood next to her chair. Gradually her head turned, a smile spreading as slowly as honey drips. Eye contact, a pat on the hand, and she gazed at me for a full minute before turning back to the pond. I took that to be a warm hello. I plopped Didoo in her lap, then steeled myself with three deep breaths before I went to get the Chilkat robe.

My pulse sped up and my spine tingled as I pushed open the living room door and climbed onto the catwalk. I could feel Steve's stare, hot as magnified light, glaring on my back. "What are you doing?" he asked.

I kept walking. My shaking fingers seized the oily wool. When I spun around, the blanket heavy and rough in my hands, Steve was on his feet.

"What the hell?" he whispered—more a curse than a question. His green eye seeped poisonous fury; his blue eye was as icy as death.

Don't cower, Mimi. Head up, shoulders loose, let him know that if it comes to a fight, you're committed. My gemstone pulsed over my quivering heart, the beat rushing into my blood, into my head. I squeezed the blanket hard to keep my will from wavering. He moved between me and Ms. Farr's bedroom door, upper lip curled, teeth showing. I kept walking. Protect Didoo, keep my promises. Get out of my way, scumball.

I drew close enough to feel his damp heat, his breath sour and nasty. I locked my gaze on those unblinking, hooded eyes. *Proch mandatum niss calx sna rŭ gethrix. By the power of the stone I command you.* The words swirled in my head. My lips moved, silently. *Get out of my way.* He wasn't moving. In the depths of his eyes burned the seething core of him, rigid with the impulse to attack, teetering on the edge of striking.

"Proch mandatum niss calx sna rů gethrix."

My whisper shook us both, rocking the ground under our feet. But he stood, and I kept coming. I was a foot away now and he towered over me. With the next step I would slam into his chest. Don't hesitate, Mimi. I lifted my foot, and he stepped aside.

Without looking back I walked past him, up the stairs to Ms. Farr's room. My hands were shaking so hard I could barely wrap Didoo in the blanket. I snuggled him into Ms. Farr's lap and then escaped into the kitchen. Leaning on the steel counter, I panted with fear. I could feel Steve in the living room, pacing like an animal. I closed my eyes and watched him make furious circles. After awhile he calmed and lay on the couch. We breathed together, breathing in the shift in our relationship, breathing out our next strategic next moves. He'd make a good ally, if managed properly. He was knowledgeable; maybe he could read Latin. And unlike Ms. Farr, he could speak.

Bring your enemies to the table, Mimi, meals are better than battlefields.

I miss you, Dad. Reaching for the groceries, I pulled out the salmon.

Basic Cajun vegetables are onions, green pepper, and celery, cooked in a little butter until they are clear and soft. Basic Cajun spices are hot: black pepper, red pepper, white pepper, dry mustard, and garlic. Herbs like sage, thyme, bay, basil, and oregano remind the Cajun that they have French ancestors. Together they make a flavor that lifts the tongue and sends it dancing wildly down the street.

As smells filled the kitchen, Steve appeared. He seemed to have mastered his fury over our showdown. Sidling over to the table, he sat with his Anthropology text and made a pretext of reading, all the while surreptitiously watching me stir together and spoon out macaroon batter.

Finally, apparently unable to stand the suspense any longer, he said, "Are you making those Macaroons for me?"

"Yes."

He folded his fingers over his text book, set his chin on his hands and stared worshipfully at the oven. "All of them?" As amiable as he looked, I didn't trust him an inch.

"If you tell me something." I put cookies in the oven.

"What?"

"Where can I get Latin translated?"

His blue eye blinked.

I took the folded inscription out of my pocket and angled it over the table so he could see.

He scooted his chair forward and peered at the script.

"Yeah, it's Vulgar Latin. Given the cadence, I'd say it was written by a native speaker, so it had to be written before 1600."

Steve was clearly more intelligent than he let on. "Let me see." He reached for the scrap. Reluctantly, I let it go. He scanned the lines several times before I pulled the paper from his grasp. He watched me shove it in my pocket, eyes narrowed to thoughtful slits. After a long pause, he said, "It's written on your amulet, isn't it?"

I sucked in a breath, taken aback. But given the way he stared at my chest, it should be no surprise that he'd noticed. I nodded cautiously.

"I'll give you $100,000 for that necklace," he said.

I stood breathless. That was *a lot* of money. That would solve *a lot* of problems. I turned my back on him and poured soaked rice into a sieve, still unable to inhale. Struggling to regain my composure, I gave the dripping rice a shake.

"Tell me why it's worth so much." I kept my back to him as I poured rice into the cooker, afraid my face might reveal how badly I needed money. Afraid to admit to myself that I was unwilling to part with my stone at any price.

"I have a use for it." His voice was neutral, noncommittal.

"What can the necklace do?" With trembling fingers, I added chicken broth to spiced vegetables in the skillet, buried a few bay leaves in the broth, then put on the lid so it would simmer. Steve hadn't answered, so I turned around.

The look on his face brought dread, rising from the ash colored floor where I stood, seeping into the bones of my ankles, and streaking up to my heart.

"You can't understand. Take the money and get rid of the gem, before someone dies." His voice was a hiss, his lips pulled tight into a sneer.

I swallowed. "What's to understand?"

"Give me the amulet and I'll get a translation."

I wanted to turn my back, stop staring, but I didn't dare.

He'd been angry over the robe, but I realized now that I had barely brushed the skin of his strength. He'd backed down, let me win. But the Wyrmstone was clearly worth drawing blood over.

"No." A whisper was the best I could manage.

He stood up and sauntered towards me. He was larger

than I remembered, his gangly limbs invigorated with power.

"At least have the sense to stop wearing it," he said. "It's very—" he stepped nearer, "—very," he stepped even closer, "dangerous," he loomed over me, snarling into my face as if I were a bite of dinner, "to toy with dragons."

Then he slid past me, out of the kitchen, and was gone.

I stood backed against the stainless steel island, gripping the cold metal behind me, my whole body fighting the urge to run. Who was this man? A lot more than just Mr. Eastman's nephew. It took ten deep breaths to clear my mind enough to think, and three more deep breaths before I realized that the vegetables in broth were boiling over.

I leaped to turn off the stove. As the popping, sputtering sauce calmed down, I breathed in short little gasps. My love for the Wyrmstone was irrational. Problems in two crazy realities had mounted like piles of trash since I had put it on. I should sell the stone and move on, get another job. Justin, Nicholi, and Didoo would be safer. There was one, major, insurmountable hitch: Ms. Farr.

I reached for the slab of salmon, steadying my hands on the familiar thick softness of the fish. Was there any chance Mr. Eastman could be persuaded to replace Steve? Unlikely. I took the wobbly cut of flesh to the sink and rinsed it, then patted it dry in nervous dabs with a paper towel. I couldn't leave her with him; I'd felt that since the beginning. Though he never seemed to threaten her, I couldn't stand the thought of Ms. Farr abandoned to his care in this bizarre house. I hated it even more than the thought of my magnificent gem in his hands.

As I rubbed the salmon with Cajun spices, I decided that I would stick it out. For Ms. Farr, and for my gemstone.

I took Macaroons out of the oven and cranked up the temperature to 550 degrees. Spreading tinfoil to line a baking pan, I wondered why it was so important not to wear the necklace. Apparently it allowed me to *toy with dragons*, which was something I had no intention of doing. *Orosiss*—master. But to *master* is as different from *toy with,* as *live* is from *die.*

It wasn't clear to me how Steve knew so much about my gem. Maybe the Wyrmstone was in one of his anthropology texts. Worth investigating, and best of all, an anthropology text contained reliable facts. Steve, Dr. Harvey, Didoo, Ms. Farr—not the easiest sources of information. And dragons never seemed to be around when I needed to ask them. It made me sick with dread, but I might be forced to ask Justin. No, I couldn't risk losing my stone to him, or sending him off to war. There had to be a right way, a right time, to involve him. Right now, however, I had to bake salmon and call Steve and Ms. Farr to lunch.

Ms. Farr ate her whole piece of salmon and a quarter cup of Cajun vegetables. From now on I'd cook spicy for her. Steve devoured the hot food as though ravenous. Sullen and silent, his mismatched eyes deliberated my every move as he gobbled. Then he disappeared to his couch with two dozen macaroons. I just knew that he'd leave crumbs and flecks of coconut stuck to the old hair on the cushions.

When it was time to go, I went to collect Didoo. He leaned against Ms. Farr's chest, cozy in the robe, glass eyes gazing at the pond, white fringe flowing over Ms. Farr's knees. Dark clouds rolled overhead and sleet hammered the choppy water, pounding the last remnants of floating ice.

When she felt my touch she jumped, her arm stiff under the fabric of Mom's soft sweater. Her overhanging upper lip pressed so tight against her lower one that her mouth disappeared in the crease. Her frightened eyes pleaded. I knelt beside her with concern. She held out her left fist, offering what her fingers hid. I gently opened her grip.

In her hand lay Mom's Night Veil perfume bottle.

No way.

Blood drained from my head, leaving me lightheaded. I tingled with fear. I stared at the tiny vial, trying to remember when I'd seen it last. Maybe the week before Mom left for Italy, on her vanity, the round, fat base on a square of Italian lace, its slender neck outclassing her other perfume bottles. There was the stopper, jammed deep into the cinnabar mouth, but now sealed with black wax. Curious: Mom never kept it sealed. But it was her bottle without doubt; I recognized the pattern of creeping hairline cracks.

No, wait—the dresser *wasn't* the last place I'd seen her vial. She had taken it to Italy for the trip that killed her. I could picture it lying on a silk scarf in her suitcase. The bottle swam before my eyes. It was impossible that Ms. Farr could have Mom's Night Veil; it burned with the airplane.

I peered into Ms Farr's large, round eyes. "Where did you get this?"

All I saw was fear. She slid the vial into my hand and closed my fingers over it. Then she raised my hand to her lips and kissed my knuckles. She had befriended the trinkets we grip for luck, the human forms we worship as sacred, the bright, reflective objects we stare into to see ourselves. And somehow, miraculously, she had rescued Mom's Night Veil.

"Please tell me how you got this."

If only she would speak.

She pushed my fist into my pocket, patting through the cloth as if to remind me to keep it hidden. Then, eyes closed, she leaned against her armchair with an exhausted sigh.

I folded the Chilkat robe and returned it to the living room shelf, Steve glaring at me. His anthropology text lay by the couch, but I didn't dare approach it. As I walked out the door I felt the vial in my pocket, oddly reassuring, like holding a rabbit foot while charging into an ambush.

I picked up the boys and was driving in a trance, lost in thought about the Wyrmstone, Latin, and Mom's Night Veil, when Justin abruptly said, "Mr. Samosa wants to know why my math homework was in his mailbox."

There are lots of movies about people who try to cheat fate, and their stories always end badly. I wasn't really expecting to fare much better, but I'd hoped to hold out longer than a week.

"What did you tell him?" I asked.

"I said my sister probably put it there." In the rearview mirror I could see Justin glowering. After a minute he said, "So, Samosa wanted to know *why* you put math homework in the gym teacher's mailbox."

Dang. I'd been so worried about being caught, I'd shoved it in the wrong mail box. Stupid. Stupid.

"And you said—?"

Framed in the rectangular metal of the mirror, Justin gave a victorious smirk. "I told him he'd have to ask you. I gave him your cell phone number."

Great. My first instinct was to reach down and click off my phone. If Mr. Samosa wanted to harass me, he'd have to stand in line behind Ms. Whitting, Duke, Judge Burrows, Steve, and Ms. Greer. Wait his turn behind a dragon army and that rock-faced trashinator named Pancrizio.

I stopped at a stoplight, and over the hum of the motor Justin spoke again.

"You have no right to interfere, Mimi." He bristled with that insulted tone, familiar from my attempted condom lecture.

"I'm not going to let you fail out of school."

"I made you an offer."

How dare he be so indignant? I was trying to help.

"Some offer—roll against you, not knowing what I have to lose."

He looked sullenly at his lap. All the way home I kept expecting him to speak again, but he didn't.

At home I helped Nicholi make a collage of magazine cuttings for Ms. Greer's fruits-and-vegetables-are-good-for-you project. Then I made Justin roll dice to clean his room, and finally folded the thigh high pile of laundry.

Unfortunately, there wasn't time to search the net for anthropology websites, because at six o'clock I opened the door and there stood Ms. Whitting. A stale puff of fading Patchouli Oil blew in with the November rain. Her bloated orange parka hid her from head to midcalf, the color and style appropriate for an arctic expedition. She tossed back her hood and glowered as though I had conjured the freezing downpour specifically to annoy her.

She pushed past me before I had time to step aside. "Someone rude enough to hang up on me *would* leave me standing in the sleet." She unzipped her dripping coat, tugged it off, and slung it on the door handle of the closet.

"Well," she wheezed, as she stalked into the living room.

The sounds of Justin's perpetual battle against the Republic blasted from the Xbox in the study. I hadn't dusted in a month, and it was all I could do to keep dirty clothes off the floor. I'd given up on toys, junk mail, crayons, Legos, plastic turkeys from the first grade Thanksgiving assembly, and Nicholi's single, balled-up socks. Justin's Age of Dragons group had left plastic miniatures engaged in vicious battle on the coffee table, and manuals of monsters, magic, and the arcane teetered two feet high on the couch. The laundry I'd folded but not yet put away leaned in top-heavy stacks against the legs of the armchair. The house looked like a cross between a ransacked toy store and a crowded Laundromat.

"Have a seat." I swept Nicholi's drawings into a pile to clear a place in Dad's armchair.

She sat reluctantly, as though dust might ruin her polyester pants. "Where are your brothers?"

"Justin's playing Xbox. Nicholi's in the kitchen working on his Lego castle."

"I see." With theatrical severity she pulled—I couldn't believe it—a little black notebook from her pocket. "There were a few questions left unanswered from the investigation, and of course, I needed to see all of this ….” Her hand swept the room as though it were damning evidence.

“What are your questions?”

“Do you have legal custody of your brothers, Miss Jovel?”

“Well, no. I’m not twenty-one, so their legal guardian is a court appointed lawyer.” She must have known that—it would have been clear from Judge Burrows’ custody ruling.

“How old are you, exactly?” She looked up sharply and caught my eye, as though I might lie. She knew my age; she was asking questions she knew the answers to.

“Eighteen and a half. I’ll be twenty-one in two and one-half years.”

“I can count, Miss Jovel.” She made a few notes in her book. “I understand from Ms. Greer that Nicholi has had severe behavioral problems in school over the last few months.”

I flushed with annoyance. “I—I wouldn’t call them severe.”

“And Justin, according to Mr. Peppercain, has gone from an A+ student to a B- student, and his grades continue to fall.” Her tone was as monotonous as peeling potatoes, as if, somehow, this made her professional.

“That’s true, but it’s not that he doesn’t do the work, he just doesn’t hand it in.”

“That makes no difference as far as his teachers are concerned. Mr. Peppercain says Justin bases his decisions on a *dice rolling game*?” She breathed vigorous disapproval into those last three words.

Oh boy. We were way beyond Ms. Whitting’s depth here. Even if I wanted her to understand, no words could bridge the canyon between Ms. Whitting's Birkenstocks and Justin's barbarian boots.

"Is this the same dice rolling game that caused the fire last week?" she persisted.

I just looked at her, my head looted of thoughts like a tomb.

"Mimi, teenagers need structure and discipline. They need to know who is in charge. Take the dice away. Tell Justin he can't watch TV or go out with his friends if you catch him using them. You need to take control, Mimi."

As if Justin's dice were a mere squabble between us mortals, and not some kind of crazy signpost in this impossible world. His pact with destiny. I said nothing.

"Are either of your brothers in counseling yet?"

"No, I haven't had time to set that up. I have a new job."

"I see." Which, when she sneered it, sounded more like "icy." She crossed her legs and one Birkenstock slipped half off her foot, exposing the arch of her wet, white sock. "And what is this job?"

Now I knew how Justin felt. In the face of this interrogation I wanted to pick up one of his dice, roll it, and give fate a chance. A nine or less and I could have the pleasure of passively watching her mouth move. Seeing her get angrier and angrier until she left (finally—thank God) in a huff. An eleven or more and I could do my duty, answer her stupid questions as fate required, and get on with my life. She and her intrusive will could no longer bear down on me. It was brilliant. Why didn't more people decide with dice?

Because they could lose people they loved.

"I work as a private cook."

"You work, *and* take care of two brothers? Rather over-whelming to be a single mom at your age, isn't it?" She leaned forward and formed one of her sugary smiles, only this time it was an invitation to confess, rather than to confide. "Do *you* think you are doing an adequate job parenting your brothers?"

A pained and furious silence descended on the living room. My thoughts screamed so loud I was afraid she might hear them. No. No, I didn't do an adequate job. From the morning bowl of cereal Nicholi ate naked on the floor, to the dice roll that put Justin to bed at night, I doubted everything.

I stared blankly at the mature woman who sat, thick legs crossed and sandal dangling, in my father's reading chair. I hated the experienced gray streaks in her hair. I resented the way she poised her pencil over her little black book, as if I, too, should listen well and take notes. I sat still as a rabbit on pavement, Ms. Whitting's headlights bearing down on me, and darkness all around. Which way to run?

Then it occurred to me. If she had the authority to take my brothers away, if she had all of the damning evidence she needed, she would have already taken them. She didn't like being dragged out of bed at midnight and being kept at work after six. She was making absolutely sure that Nicholi, Justin, and I never set foot in her emergency room again. She was here to bully me.

I leaned forward, bringing our noses closer together. "There is one thing that I never doubt. I love my brothers, and I would do anything for them. Right now, that will have to be enough."

Her breath smelled of peanuts, which for a brief moment overwhelmed the scent of Patchouli Oil. "Love is not enough. As you get older you'll discover that you need skills as well." Not wavering in her glare, she ripped a page from her book. "Here, sign up for my parenting class. And try to stay out of trouble. I'd better not hear about so much as a seatbelt infraction." She handed me her phone number and rose, brushing off her pants. "I'll see myself out the door."

Nicholi came in when the door slammed, and flopped into my lap. "At night, alligator eyes glow green for little alligators, and red for big ones."

I turned my dazed attention to him. "Oh?"

"Crocodiles have fangs that stick out, but alligators keep theirs hidden."

I absentmindedly combed fingers through his hair. "How about crankodiles?"

Nicholi raised his upper lip to show his teeth. "Crankodiles had better go back to salty water where they belong, and stay out of little alligator's houses."

I sighed. As much as I would love to sick Nicholi on Ms. Whitting, tooth dents in her leg wouldn't help our case. "Someone's on the phone," Nicholi added.

I sat up. "Who?" Engrossed in my confrontation with Ms. Whitting, I hadn't even heard it ring.

"I don't know. Some mom." Nicholi climbed onto my back and I carried him to the kitchen, his legs squeezing my ribs.

"Hi, it's Beth, Tank's mother." Other moms always managed to sound so cheerful and relaxed. "You called about having Nicholi on Saturday? I'm sorry, but we have a family engagement. I hope you find someone."

"Thanks for calling, Beth."

This was the third mom to call about tomorrow. Case's dad could have Justin over, no problem, but so far no one could take Nicholi. If my last hope, Amy Brennet's mom, said no, I could either cancel with Duke, or tell him he's a cheating bastard in front of Nicholi.

I hung up the phone. "Come on, little alligator, let's go brush those incisors." I shifted his weight so I could walk without staggering.

With Nicholi asleep, it was time to test the waters of asking for Justin's help. Just one toe in, to see how he'd respond. So I carried the *The Complete Book of Dragons* to the living room, Mom's Night Veil poking me through my pocket.

Justin hunched, glowering on the couch like a gargoyle, every Age of Dragons book he owned open and overlapping on the coffee table. He pointedly ignored me, alternating between taking notes and tapping the eraser of his chewed pencil against his hand. Miniatures rested on his knees: an army of dragons of various sizes, all looking mean and determined.

I collapsed into Dad's armchair and winced at the faint whiff of Patchouli Oil. For a moment I considered how best to approach my brooding barbarian with the elfin intelligence. Then Justin glanced up and saw his book.

"Where was that? I've been looking for it." He sounded hostile enough for two complaints: stealing his book *and* interfering with fate's plan for his homework.

Not wanting to incriminate Nicholi, I chose one of Mom's white lies. "In my room."

"I need it back." He leaned forward and grabbed the book, then returned to rolling dice and calculating attack and defense points as though I didn't exist.

"Justin?" He didn't answer. What would Dad have done? Say something funny, make Justin laugh despite himself. Those were easier days.

"Justin?"

Sullen silence.

"Look up a minute."

His head jerked up impatiently.

"You're going to Case's Saturday night. I have a meeting with Duke."

"A meeting? What, the jerk doesn't date you anymore?" His vehemence surprised me.

I cleared my throat. I'd rehearsed the words silently, but it was so much sadder out loud. "I'm breaking up with him."

"Finally. Good riddance." Justin picked up a die, tossed it, and wrote a number on his graph paper.

So I'd been right about Justin's feelings. "You never said you didn't like Duke."

Justin snorted. "You never asked."

True. It hadn't occurred to me to ask Justin's advice on my love life. "Why don't you like him?"

He met my gaze, brother to sister, we're-all-in-this-together, the chance to dis Duke tempting him away from his fury. He filled his chest, paused for a second, and blew out a puff of disgust. "Do we have to talk about this?"

"I'm just curious."

"So you tell me." He gave an antagonistic scowl before he put his head down and hair fell over his eyes. "Why are you breaking up with him?"

A flush crept up my neck, heating my face and making my scalp burn. I pulled off my sweater and threw it over the armchair, half trying to cool off, half hoping to delay until I could think of something. Nothing came to me but Dad's bare truth.

"He … he gave me … Chlamydia." The last word was barely audible.

"It figures." He threw dice again and wrote numbers.

"Do you know what Chlamydia is?"

"Yeah, I took health class." He frowned over his work for a moment and then he looked up, eyes mischievous with a spark of Dad's humor. "I should tell him about condoms."

I burst out laughing. I savored the image of slicked-back, ultra-cool Duke getting a verbal thrashing about his incompetent use of condoms. I liked the idea of Justin having to give that embarrassing lecture, too.

"Awesome idea," I said.

"Are you okay alone with him? Maybe I shouldn't go to Case's." So willing, my man-child brother, to throw himself into a fight. I could picture monstrous Justin, heaving Duke out the door, Duke's perfectly formed limbs and wavy curls flying. Sweet. But perhaps too delicious for Judge Burrows and Ms. Whitting.

"Thanks Justin, but I have to do this myself." I watched him erase a number, then toss his dice again. "You didn't tell me why you don't like him."

Justin fingered his dice. "He wasn't so bad when he was just an irresponsible playboy, but he's been eaten by a Doppelganger."

I squinted, confused. "What?"

Justin grabbed the *Manual of Eternals*, flipped through it, and held the book out, pointing to a blob of yellow slime, puddled on a dungeon floor.

"You're kidding!" I laughed, incredulous. But there was the color that fleeted across my drunken vision, Duke's face melting, fusing, then reappearing. It was the alcohol; this idea was absurd.

Justin read the text under the drawing: "*An unsurpassed imitator, the Doppelganger steals the appearance of anyone or anything. Selfish and solitary, it transforms itself to deceive, trap, and then kill with a combination of sedating ether and vicious teeth. The victim is eaten, and the Doppelganger lives the victim's life until it grows bored or is unmasked by a spell of True Sight.*"

Justin leaned forward, gentle as a counselor. "He's dead, Mimi. I'm sorry. I never liked him, but it's not a nice way to go, even for an immature jerk."

All I could do was blink and stare. Dead? No. I handed my brother his manual. "That's ridiculous. No one replaced Duke. He's just a bastard." A bastard who, unfortunately, was lots of fun.

Justin shrugged off my denial with Dad's expert hunch of one shoulder. "The question is, what did the Doppelganger want? He clearly wasn't trying to kill you, or you'd be already dead."

"You've completely lost me."

Justin nodded his head knowingly. "Thank God someone around here has a scroll of True Sight."

I stared at him; not one word stepped forward to express my amazement. And to think I was about to ask Justin's help sorting my confused realities.

The doorbell and the phone rang simultaneously. I jumped for the door and Justin lumbered to the phone.

Carlo stood on the front porch. He extended a plate with rain soaked fingers. "Thanks for the cinnamon bun." Dad's favorite china platter, painted with everyday apples and garlands: a welcome relief after listening to Justin's absurd ideas.

"Come in." I stood aside so Carlo could pass.

He shook his soaked jeans jacket and hung his fedora on the same doorknob where Ms. Whitting had hung her coat.

"I have leftover cherry pie," I said.

"For real?" His eyebrows were very black when they were wet, giving his face a serious expression.

"Do you want some?"

He took in a deep breath. "Is that a trick question?"

We laughed, and I decided that I really did like this man. But then, I'd liked Duke, too. I turned abruptly away.

Carlo moseyed into the living room. A five o'clock shadow made his features look particularly square, and I wondered if he'd been too busy doing something for his grandmother to shave. He walked toward the armchair that had my pink sweater thrown over the back, glanced at the sweater, then moved the *Manual of Eternals*, and sat on the couch.

I retreated to Dad's kitchen to heat a piece of pie. Dad

preferred Montmorency cherries, fresh off Mom's tree in the back yard and dripping with sour yellow juice. He froze the cherries in pie-sized amounts. This pie had just enough sugar to keep the eater from puckering. It tasted fantastic with a dollop of vanilla ice cream.

When I brought in the pie à la mode and milk, Justin sat next to Carlo on the couch, passing Carlo his miniatures.

"This is a Pitiless Cat," Justin said, holding out a purple panther with fangs.

"Ugly," said Carlo. "Maybe he could eat the rats in Grandma's attic. It doesn't matter what I do, we just get more of them."

"Yeah," Justin laughed, "except that a Pitiless is nine feet long and weighs 500 pounds."

"Hmm, that's overkill." Carlo passed the miniature back.

"Rats are part of the curse," said Justin.

Carlo's eyebrows shot up. "Curse?"

I cringed; that's all we needed, to strengthen the neighborhood impression that our family harbored crazies.

"Yeah. Haven't you noticed? Your house is slipping into chaos."

"I guess I have. The electrical wiring shorts, the plumbing stops up, the appliances break. I just figured the house was old."

Justin smiled, a wise elf. "Trimble could help. He's good with curses."

Anxious to interrupt this conversation, I leaned over Carlo, holding out pie and milk. I could see the blunt cut of his fingernails and smell the scent of warm bread coming from his flannel shirt. Carlo reached for his pie, brushing my fingers as he took it, and I drew back. He gave me a honeyed smile, as though he hadn't noticed my withdrawal, and turned back to Justin. "Trimble can lift a curse?"

Justin nodded, "Oh yeah."

Carlo took a bite of pie and closed his eyes. "Unbelievable," he murmured, perhaps about my pie, perhaps about Trimble and curses. Either way, the sharp, strong lines of his mouth lifted into sweet, irresistible curves.

I turned away, not wanting to feel so tender. Why trust my judgment about any man? I went to the armchair and snatched up my sweater, self-consciously putting it on and working closed the buttons. When I sat down the feeling had gone and he was simply Carlo again—the rough cut, casual neighbor who seemed to come around at all the wrong times. Like when Justin decided to resurrect Duke.

"Speaking of curses, somebody's mom called—she can't take Nicholi tomorrow night for your *meeting*," said Justin.

"Why not?"

"She didn't say."

Dang. I fiddled with buttons on my sweater, feeling smooth shell against fuzzy angora as I tried to think of options.

"I could stay home and watch Nicholi, and you and Duke could go out," said Justin.

"Thanks Justin, but—" One more trip to the emergency room and Ms. Whitting would have us *all* in foster care.

Justin grinned. "Maybe you could dump the creep after Nicholi goes to bed. Better yet, don't even let him in the house. Make him stand in the rain when you dump him."

"Justin!" I tried to shut my brother up with a stare.

Carlo looked back and forth between us, obviously curious but too polite to ask. To cover my embarrassment, I looked out the picture window at the puddle of mud surrounding the partly uprooted fig, the mess scarring Mom's beautiful court-yard. Carlo's eyes followed mine and examined the fig as well, no doubt wondering why I hadn't dug it out. Duke and that stubborn fig: two more of my messy problems unrolling in front of Carlo.

"I have an idea—" said Justin.

"Let's talk about this later," I said.

"Just tell him on the phone. The bastard doesn't deserve to see you again."

"*Later*, Justin." I tried to make the tone, and the glare, fi-nal.

"Whatever." Justin turned back to his miniatures and graph paper.

There was an unpleasant minute during which the only conversation was the patter of dice skittering across an Age of Dragons book, and the scraping of Carlo's fork. Then Carlo plunked his fork down and stood up. He took the plate to the kitchen and came back with his fedora and coat.

"You should open a restaurant." There was more than support for my cooking in his smile, there was an awkward apology for what he'd overheard.

"Bye," I said inelegantly, too humiliated to meet his eye.

"Yeah." He turned to go, and then changed his mind. "Anna loves to babysit, if you ever need it." He shrugged, this one a common, uncollectible rising of his shoulders to emphasize that this was a casual afterthought.

Great. He'd unlocked the Wyrmstone's box, brought soup when I could hardly stand, and now offered a babysitter so I could break up with Duke. It was almost as though his strings were tangled hopelessly with mine; I couldn't make a clumsy mistake without yanking him in to rescue me.

He opened the front door, letting in the splashing sound of icy sleet. It fell all night long: freezing, relentless rain.

Chapter 15

Above the tree line, mountains reached for the abundant sky, nothing to hide the peaks that glared white with glaciers. I balanced on a slope of scree, one bare foot on slippery ice and the other in unstable rock. A valley, veiled with patchy clouds, spread thousands of feet below me, and my stomach clutched as vertigo spun the basin in slow, spiraling circles. I couldn't see a road through the trees below me, no hut, not even a cow path. How did I get here in my summer shift, my hair blown around by high mountain winds? I shivered and clutched my bare arms, at a loss for where I was and how to get home.

"You are not as wise as your mother, nor a fraction as stunning." The watery voice rushed like a stream downhill.

I startled, twisting to see behind me. I lost my balance and staggered into a crouch, shards cutting my feet.

A stone's throw up the slope, she, too, crouched, gleaming and terrible. Her huge blue thighs settled over the rocks, and silvery eyes sparkled as though I amused her. She was as beautiful as the swamp dragon was ugly, a magnificence that exerted a kind of tyranny; anything that couldn't match her was worthless. I struggled not to cower, forcing myself upright against panic.

"What do you want?" I whispered, my Draconic almost lost in gasping.

She yawned lazily, and I stared into her gaping maw of ice-sharp teeth, shuddering at their elegance, before she abruptly snapped them closed. "It is not what *I* want, it is what *you* want. You wished to consult a dragon?"

There had been questions, yes, in some far-off world that my frightened brain couldn't recall. But looking at her—the sun shimmering in a blue halo over her fine scales, the as-new perfection of her muscles, the superb points on her silver claws—I couldn't imagine a single problem, not even a broad topic, worth bothering her about. So I was reduced to the obvious.

"W—who are you?" I stammered.

She snorted, and far below us an avalanche of rock shifted with a dull rumble, gathered into a roar, and tore down the mountain, flattening trees with deafening cracks.

She waited until the din faded.

"It is a sad world you live in, where I am not known on sight." Her eyelids closed to half slits. "Perhaps it's for the best if Adrikhedon prevails, and razes your ignorant cities to the ground." She rose to all fours and her shadow cast over me, spreading down the mountainside. I stood paralyzed in her massive shade.

"But then he would get this—" She crept forward and reached one sickle of a claw, hooking the leather cord around my neck. Delicate as a barber's razor, she plucked the

Wyrmstone out from under my shift, leaving only the faintest scratch across my throat. The jewel dangled from her curved talon, purples swirling in mad ecstasy. Her lithe neck wove forward, thrusting her triangular head into my face. Her breath steamed with the hot sweet of East Indian spices.

"We cannot allow this to fall to scum dragons. It must stay with the breed, mustn't it, child?" She used the word *castaz* for breed, meaning family, clan, or race. Also meaning, 'Ones we eat with mild regret.' She unhooked her claw and the stone fell back against my chest, swinging in rhythm with my wildly pounding heart.

"So—" she looked to the sky, nostrils flaring as they tested the cold mountain air. "You will keep your mother's promise to me, yes?" She turned her head and gazed into my eyes, the silver blue of her pupils hard as mithril, and I realized—her eye color exactly matched my own.

"I don't know what she promised," I whispered. Whatever Mom's covenant, I was clearly dead if I violated it.

"How careless of Vedette." She wagged her head, staring into my transfixed gaze. "You will return the stone to its virgin beauty, which means, of course, that you will destroy the gold Pancrizio bound to it."

I swallowed hard against my dry throat. "And then hand the stone to you?"

"What do you think, child?" When a mountain dragon smiles, it has more menace than her teeth.

My insides tangled into knots. "I—I don't know how to do that."

"Your mother didn't have much fortitude, but she was

clever. She devised a method. Pity that Adrikhedon killed her before she told you. But you'll figure a way, I'm sure. After all, I have your mother's word."

Her lavender tongue slipped out of her mouth, touching me in the smallest kiss on my cheek, leaving behind a delicate burn.

"Goodbye, child. I will come to you when the stone is relieved of its cage."

She lifted with great, easy flaps, buffeting me in gusts of wind as she soared up the mountainside. Under her sparkling belly the glacier shook. Ice rattled free, sliding toward me in a rumbling wave, gathering boulders as it came, crashing and rolling, unstoppable. I screamed and tried to run, falling over jagged hunks of rock, the ground slicing my bare feet. The avalanche scraped over me within seconds, weight crushing me to the mountain.

"Help!" I yelled. "Yvess, help me!" The world was nothing but silver blue ice.

~

I woke fighting tangled blankets, my pillow flying across the room and slamming into my parents' wedding portrait, knocking the photo from the wall.

"*Schpart ss!*" I yelled into the quiet of the house, *save me!* I tumbled out of bed, free of the covers, and lay panting on the floor.

Alive. Breathing. Oh God. I curled into a tight ball, sobs wracking my chest, deep gasps of air sucked between my whimpers.

I could no longer face this alone. I had to have help. Mom, Dad where were you? Killed by a dragon, Yvess said, spiraling in flames into the water while he soared lazy circles overhead. Adrikhedon. I hated him. If I could master any dragon it would be him, command him to throw himself onto my sword. Lop off his head and spike it on the end of my mother's garden hoe.

I struggled to my feet, still blubbering. Wrapping my bathrobe around me, I staggered down the hall. By the time I'd reached the computer my crying had stopped. *Wyrmstone*, I searched, *Anthropology: mastery of dragons, artifact and dragons, Yvess' stone, Pancrizio's stone.* There was nothing. Not a single hit. It must be somewhere in one of Justin's heaps of Age of Dragons texts. Dang. No other choice now, it was Justin, or nothing.

I waited until breakfast was over and Nicholi played in Wikipedia. Justin was in his room with the door closed.

I knocked on the door. "May I come in?"

He grunted. He hunched at his desk doing homework, three pages of mathematical solutions written in his fine, precise hand.

"Justin, I need help."

He bowed over his work, semi-ignoring me.

"You can be pissed at me about your homework later, but for just a few minutes, listen to me." My pleading drifted, light as powdered sugar, off his mansized shoulders. He turned the page of his Algebra text and ran his finger under the next problem.

I reached for the Wyrmstone, then decided against it, and

instead dug in my pocket and placed the curvaceous Night Veil bottle on the page of his open textbook.

Justin's gaze found the vial. "Holy shit," he whispered. He pinched the round belly of it in his thumb and forefinger and turned it over and over, studying each detail in awed silence.

"Holy shit," he said again. With one hand he swept clean a space on his desk, with the other he set the vial down so gently his big fingers shook. Then he flattened his palms on the wood, bent down, chin to the table, and examined the wax that sealed the stopper. "Where'd you get it?"

"Ms. Farr, the lady I work for."

His elfin eyes snapped wide open, and then narrowed to gray half moons. "How did *she* get it?"

"I don't know."

"You don't know." He sounded annoyed, impatient. He stood and circled the room, bare feet slapping the hardwood floor, contemplating his hairy toes, each go-around making me more anxious. After the third circle, he pointed at me.

"Sit down." He pointed to the chair.

With as much dignity as I could muster, I sat.

"Stay right there. I'm calling the guys."

He stalked out the door, a young warrior with the enemy in his sights, off to gather his comrades.

I slumped in the chair and put my head in my hands. I shouldn't be doing this. I should be the heroine, striding with confidence, making the rules, shouldering lonely responsibility. Isn't that what judges, teachers, and social workers expected? Their advice was as overwhelming as too much salt. The boys might look like men, but they were teens: reckless with invincible bravado and overactive imaginations. But, unlike adults, boys knew it wasn't stuffed bears, dice, or lack of discipline that threatened our family. In the end it was obvious; if these boys couldn't guide me, all was lost.

Paul arrived first, but everyone else came soon after, car doors slamming, parents calling goodbye, and bike brakes squeaking. They clamored into Justin's room saying, "What's up?" and, "Hey, dude." Stopping in an arc around his desk. One by one they fell silent as their gazes found the Night Veil.

Nicholi padded in in his pajamas and squeezed between their legs, holding onto Justin's knee with one small hand.

"So," said Justin, his voice cutting through soft sounds of breathing, "tell us."

I cleared my throat. "Tell you what?"

Justin stared at me. He glanced up at the white ceiling, looked down at his picked-ragged fingernails, took a breath that filled his chest, and then launched.

"Mimi, you've got to talk to us. All of this crap is coming down and you never *say* anything. I hear you yelling and thrashing in your sleep and I don't know what-in-the-heck is going on. A Doppelganger stalks you, a Basilisk attacked us, the front garden is unhallowed ground, there's a curse on the neighbor's house, and now you show up with Mom's cinnabar vial that should be ashes under several hundred feet of water in Puget Sound." His voice rose to a barbarian bellow. "You are so friggin' difficult to get through to—"

He broke off, halted by my open mouthed amazement.

"But," I protested, "you're the one who's said *nothing* since Mom and Dad died."

"No." He spun around so that his back was to me and his face was to the alert, quiet boys. "It's not about Mom and Dad. We—" his arm swept across the arc of his friends, "—have been worried sick about *you*. We spend half our time casting spells of protection, preparing weapons, seeking ways to unmask the enemy, while you—" he spun back to face me, arms up, entreating the sky, "—fold the friggin' laundry. Tell us what you know. All of it. *Now*."

Stunned by this furious blast, I sat blinking, taking in their worried faces: Trimble's deep wells of eyes, Larry's wrinkled forehead, Paul's blanched cheeks, Case's fingers tapping nervously on his thigh, and little Nicholi, now hiding under the desk, his gaze like two swimming saucers, the tears almost ready to fall. Trust them, Mimi.

Trembling, I reached down my shirt. "I guess it all starts with this …." With a gentle tug, I exposed the Wyrmstone.

There was a moment of profound quiet then, "Yo!" breathed Larry.

"Hella-epic," murmured Trimble.

"Oh, crap, there *is* a stone." Justin dropped his hands to his sides. "How long have you had that?" He stepped forward, not giving me time to answer. "Dang! Have you been just wearing it, like it was a stupid locket or something?"

He kept on coming, backing me against the desk.

"Hold on." Paul scooted between us, holding Justin off with a fingertip. "Let me see it." He extended a hand.

With a great reluctance, I slipped off the necklace. Paul held it by the leather, letting light from the desk lamp flash off the facets, turning purple prisms on the walls. In collective awe we watched the jewel flicker and writhe, misty fog seeping off the stone and curling around the dancing reflections. Then, avoiding any contact with the stone, Paul laid it reverently on the desk.

"Trimble, what do you think?" he asked.

Trimble stepped forward and leaned over the jewel, his ebony eyes reflected in the mirror of the gem. With one crisp fingernail he flipped it over and stared at the tiny writing on the back. "Definitely enchanted."

He turned the stone back over, reached in his pocket, and pulled out a silky black bag, closed with a drawstring, one cord of which was safety-pinned to his pocket. Wiggling open the bag, he drew out a pad of flash paper a few inches square. He ripped off two pieces, delicate as tissue, and wadded them into a loose ball. "Do you have a match?" he asked me.

"Oh God, no trips to the emergency room, please," I said.

"It's okay, I won't burn down the house."

"Yeah," said Larry, "we specialize in hedges."

The boys laughed, not sounding nearly as guilty as I wished. All except Justin, who continued to glare at me.

Nicholi crawled out from under the desk and grabbed a pocket on Justin's pants. Hanging on, he pushed himself onto tiptoe, peering at the stone. Justin swung Nicholi up into his arms.

Trimble extended his hands, colorful cotton sleeves dangling, slender fingers face down towards the jewel. All the boys leaned forward except Paul, who had found a place in the corner and stood with his back pressed to the wall, looking as if he didn't want to be there.

"What are you planning to do?" I asked.

"I'm going to see what you've found," said Trimble. "If you'll give me a match, that is."

I looked from boy to boy. Larry inclined so far forward his flat nose practically brushed Trimble's sleeves, his blunted hands up as if to ward off a blow. Case slouched on one hip and grinned, looking thrilled at the prospect of mayhem. Justin tossed his hair aside and watched the gem intently, hostile, both hands holding Nicholi tight. They were so in love with danger it made me shiver.

But what else could I do? Consult Dr. Harvey? Get a legal brief from Mr. Eastman? *Trust the boys, Mimi.* I hurried to the kitchen cabinet and came back with a matchbox.

Trimble took the match and curled his fingers around it. He held up the wads of flash paper and poised his thumbnail to strike. "I command you to identify," he murmured, and he lit the stick.

The match fizzed and tissue caught fire. Trimble tilted it slightly to let flames climb to his fingers, and then flung the burning wad into the air. With a whoosh the paper exploded, leaving a ball of flames hanging over the jewel's face.

Then the fire vanished: no smoke, no ash.

Hands spread into claws, Trimble tensed over the necklace as if expecting it to flee. The boys perched on their toes, not moving or breathing. I strained to see between them to the gem's face.

A desolate hush settled over my thoughts, a chilling fog in which I couldn't find myself. The floor hit my back as I slumped to the ground. Something bitter and harsh pressed forward, compelling me to speak. Whispers, my lips moving, the rough grate of Draconic searing my throat.

Open dark gates of death, let flesh escape, fill this hollow form with corruption's body, solid now as dirt—

I forced out a cry for help, but it was as if a hand closed on my neck. I opened my mouth, choking. Tears leaked and trickled around my nose. I fought to pull in air, scream, but he wouldn't let me. Coursing through me, he commanded the spell, words tumbling as fast as rapids, dragging me, a leaden weight, in the current.

"Get more matches!" Trimble's voice, high pitched and frantic, came from a distant room, blurry against the chant.

—breathing life from she who mouths—

Pancrizio emerged from another world, taking on outline, density, faint color, a ghost congealing into a man. His cape flowed over Justin's desk, that red that oozed butchery. Red on the scrawled algebra, red on the wooden desktop, red filling my eyes, the world fading behind a forest of boy's legs as I retreated far, far away.

Fire exploded in my vision and a scorched smell stung my nose. Powerful hands lifted the choke hold, lifted the leather strap and slammed the necklace face down on the desk. Trimble struggled with the stone, leaning his weight into it, steamy purple oozing between his fingers. Above his head, the sorcerer loomed, a weighty body suspended in the air, eyes cruel with contempt.

Justin's voice came into focus, panicked, furious. "Get away from her. Get away from my sister you son of a bitch or I'll tear your friggin' arms off."

"Justin, stay back!" Trimble thrashed over the desktop as if fighting an animal. "You can't damage him with your bare hands."

Case threw a match, fire exploded again, and the sorcerer vanished.

Paul knelt beside me, his grip holding my head. Shoulder to shoulder, Justin and Larry stood over me, guarding me with Mom's pickaxe, a wall between me and the space Pancrizio had vacated. Didoo jammed against my left side and Nicholi lay on the floor, squeezed against my right, pinning me between them.

"Are you okay, Mimi?" asked Nicholi.

I panted. "I don't know."

"Give her some space." Paul waved everyone back a few steps. "Can you breathe now?"

"Yes." I dabbed away tears, wiped my nose. "You could see him?"

"Heck yeah, any closer and he would have singed our nose hairs." Trimble cautiously released the stone, eyed the inert gold, and then turned up his scorched palms. "Paul?" he said, nodding at the dark, oval burns.

"Trimble!" I tried to get up, but Paul held me down.

"No worries," said Paul. Letting go of me, he dug a battered Altoids peppermint tin out of his pocket and pried it open with a chewed fingernail. Inside was brassy powder, flecked with salt-and-pepper grains.

"Need fire?" asked Case.

"No." Paul sprinkled a speck of powder over Trimble's hands. "There's enough magic bouncing around this room to unsnarl a Troll's beard."

Everybody laughed but me, who had no idea what was so funny. Paul bowed his head and muttered something, and as he passed his fingers over Trimble's skin, the burns rubbed away. I stared at the skin of Trimble's perfect brown palms, too astonished to speak.

"She okay?" Justin gestured toward me.

Paul nodded. "Trimble took the heat."

I flushed with shame, worse than useless. I was a liability, in fact. I should give them the Wyrmstone and get out of their way before I got us all killed.

Justin stepped forward and picked his pencil off his math book, looped the eraser through the leather strap, and lifted the gem off the desk. He dangled the sparkling facets in my face, the light too jagged, searing my eyes, and I squinted. Then he let the necklace fall around my neck, where its delicate mist enveloped my shirt front.

"Don't ever, ever take this off again. Understand?" Justin really did have that bossy voice down pat.

Steve had told me that wearing the stone was dangerous, so either he lied, or he didn't know. Or maybe Justin was wrong.

"Why?" I tried to sound brave, but I came off frightened and confused.

"Because for some bug-butt, cheese-monkey reason you can control it." Justin's amazed tone matched his awed expression.

"No! No, I can't!"

"Oh yes, you can," said Trimble. "We just frightened away

a Grand Sage, and I guarantee you it was not my warding that did it. You threw around magical weight like an 8,000 pound Godzilla. All I did was channel it."

I stared at him, speechless.

Larry cocked his head, twirling the pickaxe in his hands, and I wondered what Mom would think about him hefting her garden tool like a weapon.

"Mimi's a sorceress?" he asked.

Nicholi piped up. "Nope." All heads swiveled his way.

"Wizard?" asked Paul.

"Nope."

"A druid?" asked Trimble.

"Nope." Nicholi snuggled into Didoo's belly.

"What, then?" asked Case. "No one else can cast without a scroll." But Nicholi buried his face deeper and didn't answer.

"So, who's this Grand Sage, Mimi?" Justin gripped and ungripped his fists, pent up barbarian strength shoving against his self-control.

Paul scowled at Justin. "For creep's sake give her a minute."

Grateful to Paul, I closed my eyes, palms pressed into my wet lids, sure I'd shake apart if I had more stimulation than my hearing. I stole a moment just to breathe. "His name is Pancrizio," I said finally.

"No flip-a-friggin' way!" said Case. He shoved Trimble aside and slapped his bottom onto the desktop, grinning like a fool.

"Well, I'll be an orc," said Larry, planting himself on the floor. Justin collapsed into a cross-legged slump next to him, and motioned for Nicholi to crawl into his lap. Paul retreated back into the corner, and Trimble retired gracefully to the desk chair. Bewildered, I watched them settle in.

Case bobbed, his butt practically dancing on the wooden desk. "This couldn't be better if I'd written the history myself." The boys leaned toward him.

"Year 300: amethyst mined and cut by none other then—" Here he nods to Larry, "Gend—"

"Gendrad Stormhammer! Yo, baby!" Nothing but a heroic dwarf could make Larry's eyes mist with tears. "He knew how to die."

"Yep, and the mountain dragon who ate him had this thing for Yvess, so year 500, he gives her the stone in exchange for the title Emperor—"

"Carrach!" The boys yelled together.

"But was he really flesh?" added Paul.

Case puckered into a smirk and pumped his shifty eyebrows. "Flesh enough for the Empress, I guess. Who knows? Deathwish severed the final cord, still, they say that Carrach died a hundred times before Deathwish no-shit finished him off. But I digress."

His hand breezily wandered toward Mom's Night Veil, gathered it up, and fingered it softly. "About year 550: Yvess enchants the stone with epic powers of magical illusion and sets it to hide her city. The mountain dragon realm is placed so far off the map that a rainstorm couldn't find it. And here comes the best part: Snick—"

The boys gave a deep, collective groan and Larry rolled his eyes to the ceiling.

But Case was not deterred. "The almighty, glorious, un-surpassed phenomenon of Slyfoot Snick the Bright Raven—"

"Get on with it," said Trimble.

"—actually manages to *steal the stone* in the most reverent year 782—" Case pressed his palms together as if in prayer, and when he opened them, Mom's vial was gone.

"Case, Yvess friggin' slaughtered him where he slept. Rule one, Age of Dragons: stay alive in your sleep," said Justin. "And put the vial back on the desk."

"Okay, okay." The vial reappeared on Case's palm, and he set it on Justin's math book. "So he died. But he left behind two epic mysteries. One: How did he steal the stone? Any guesses, dragon fans?" Case waited in the rapt silence. "No? So I'll tell you, but this is a guild secret, so don't go blabbing it around if you value your *cojones*."

Case leaned his elbows on his knees and inclined so far into the circle of listening boys that I feared he might fall off the desk. His voice dropped to a theatrical whisper. "Snick lost his caravan deep in the Dolomites, wandering helpless, his undefended wagons piled with the treasure of Elvinwest—or so it appeared. Brilliant, eh? Saved him years of useless searching, because you can be abso-frickin' sure that Yvess found him. Snick sent his shadow away at a dead run, and while the Empress chased the shadow he sealed himself in a golden amphora." Case flashed his alluring, toothy-white smile. "The Trojan Slyfoot. Took more balls than a herd of Minotaurs. Admit it, you unwashed disbelievers, admit that you worship him."

Justin flipped him the bird, Paul laughed his shy guffaw,

Larry rolled his eyes so deep into his head that it looked painful, and Trimble gave a wisp of his sage frown. But I was willing to admire Snick. Imagine having the nerve to trick that regal, lethal empress? Never in a zillion years.

Case licked his lips. "Once the treasure was dragged into Yvess' city, Snickity snuck out—fine sneakin', dudes, and you know it. Here's the awesome part: he held a *mirror* to the amethyst. Made a reflection so real, Snick was tucked in bed in Covingdale before Yvess figured out that her jewel was gone. Moral of the story: even a lazy dragon will do your work for you if you're tricky enough."

"Case, the Night Veil," said Justin.

Case sighed and pulled the vial out of his pocket, placing it far on the other side of the desk where he couldn't easily reach it. "Satisfied?"

Justin nodded.

"So," continued Case, "epic mystery number two: where did Snick hide the gemstone?" Case stared around the circle, daring anyone to answer. "Lost three hundred years. Now that's a man who knows how to cache his stuff." He rubbed a hand over his budding moustache. "So now we get to Mama Mimi. Year 1194: the eldest son of Gino Sovrani, a sorcerer by the name of Pancrizio, is accused of a vile murder."

"What does that have to do with me?" I asked.

"Sovrani, your Mom's sorcerer bloodline," said Case. "So the murder is never proved, but Gino—"

"Wait!" I interrupted, "You knew Mom was a sorceress?"

They all turned to me with such incredulous stares that I flushed.

"We guarded her for years," said Larry.

"Healed her too," said Paul, contemplating his hands.

"She left me with this, every time she was too weak to protect it." Justin pointed to the vial of Night Veil, which had mysteriously crept into Case's fingers again. Justin kept his eyes on Case, who casually put the vial down.

"She never told me." Somehow this hurt more than any of Mom's other betrayals. All of those years, Mom trusted Justin but not me.

"Tell you or Dad? Reality check, Mimi. Dad was worse than clueless, and you were … what's the word, Nicholi?"

Nicholi tapped his temple with Didoo's paw. "Confusinated."

It was impossible to argue with that assessment. I blinked back tears. "So Mom told you about the amulet?"

"Hell no." Justin lifted Nicholi off his lap and stood up. "Mom was the only person in this house who kept secrets better than you, Mimi. She told us absolutely *nothing*."

Justin began to pace angrily: the room too small, the boys too big, so his pacing wove a figure eight around their drawn-in knees. "We watched her struggle, get weaker, Dad and Dr. Harvey throwing her into the loony bin like she was a banshee. She wanted to do it alone, Mimi. Sound familiar? That's why she died—died of her frickin' stubbornness. If she only would have told me, given me a war hammer and pointed me in the right direction—"

"Chill, Justin, it's over," said Paul, flattened against the wall, out of his way.

"It's not over!" said Justin. "Mimi just gave this Pancrizio dude form. He's out of the ethereal plane and into ours. He'll be busting his staff trying to grab the gem and ultimo-pown us."

"Yeah, he almost redecorated the room with our body parts," said Case, and for the first time in all the years I've known him, Case looked gloomy.

The boys collectively contemplated the floor, making me sick with dread.

Case sighed. "Dudes, serve up the fail pie, we were taken totally flatfooted."

Flatfooted: the ultimate slyfoot insult. Experienced adventures were ready for anything, anytime. Or they die. In the quiet of shamed silence Justin paced, feet slapping, big knuckles cracking. And it occurred to me; it was their mistake, not the threat of Pancrizio, that troubled them. Being outsmarted, not death, was the ultimate defeat, which didn't bode well for our future.

Trimble nervously scraped open, then scraped closed the match box. "Sit down, Justin, you're driving us nuts."

Justin plunked down beside Paul and dropped his head in his hands, his hair closing in a curtain over his fingers. "Go on, Case."

Case eyeballed the necklace in the center of my shirt, no doubt weighing its heft and worth with his gaze.

"So … as I was saying, then the stone shows up—tada! Out of nowhere." Case sucked in the rapt silence like oxygen. "Pancrizio takes—get this—a vial of Night Veil—" Case waved a hand with exaggerated drama and the vial appeared on his palm. Justin scowled and Case hastily set it on the desk, "—a splatter of dragon's blood, and the legendary sword

Deathwish," he raised an eyebrow at Larry, who nodded with approval, "and he sacrificed these three epic items to forge an amulet, which he called—"

"The Wyrmstone," I whispered.

Everyone swiveled to look at the jewel, the gold roots dull as if sulking, the gem steaming with purple menace. Even with its air of poisonous anger, it was still the most beautiful thing I'd ever seen. I could tell by the boys' quiet breathing that they agreed. Nicholi rested his apple-round cheek on Justin's T-shirt, eyes on the stone like he was mesmerized.

"Prettylicious," he whispered.

"The Wyrmstone," cooed Case. "Made to enslave dragons. They say it can raise reality out of illusion, and will hold Pancrizio's soul trapped forever in its roots. Or not so trapped, as it turns out. And now it's yours, eh, Mama Mimi?" Warmth oozed from his charming eyes. "Tell us how it came to hang around your noobie neck."

His suave condescension was irritating, but I kept my voice steady. "It was buried in the fig's roots."

Justin's head snapped up and he stared me in the eye. I flushed with guilt, remembering the day I dug it up.

"*Buried in the fig's roots.*' That's not a story!" Case flung up a hand with disgust. "We want drama, sweat, hopefully a little blood."

I laughed weakly. "There was blood. The roots hung on so tightly …."

Told in any other company, the tale of the fig's fight might have brought polite disbelief. But told to the boys, it brought satisfying nods and comforting *ahs* of understanding. Only

Justin listened passively, as if my deception the day I found the gem was to be endured, like the rest of the crap fate dealt him. I was beyond Carlo opening the box and on to my first nightmare about Pancrizio before Trimble interrupted.

"Wait, slow down, tell us exactly what Pancrizio said."

"Well, I can't really, because it wasn't in English."

Five heads cocked to the side, quizzical. Didoo stared at me with his bubbled glass eyes.

"He said," I closed my eyes, feeling the harsh words as they scraped off my tongue. "'*Proch mandatum niss calx sna* ….'"

"Stop!" screeched the boys. Justin looked at Trimble, Case looked at Larry, and Paul looked at Justin, and they all vigorously shook their heads in mystifying consensus.

"What?" I said.

I waited for an explanation, but all Paul said was, "Ooookay, it's all right Mimi, just chill-lax." He was the one who needed to chill; his whole body quivered. "Explain to us how you speak Draconic."

"In English, we don't want any unwelcome visitors." Larry jumped to his feet, surveyed the hall, and then elected to lean in the doorway with Mom's pickaxe over his shoulder.

Reaching deep for an explanation, I felt again that wisp of a path down into old memories. But the way was vague, my feet unsure; I couldn't follow.

"I understand everything the dragon and Pancrizio say. I even spoke with a swamp dragon, and last night I … well … spoke to Empress Yvess."

The boys didn't need to say, "You?" with incredulous

voices and dropped jaws; their doubt showed plainly in the crinkle of their noses and the curls of their upper lips.

Discomfort pushed my gaze down and I studied the gray pile of the rug.

"Okay, I agree. It's ridiculous."

"It's true, Didoo says so," said Nicholi. Now distrustful gawks turned to Didoo, snuggled against Nicholi's neck. The bear gazed back passively, holding his ground.

"If this is true," said Trimble, "then we have a fighting chance."

"If," said Larry, scrutinizing my face, no doubt looking for proof in my cream puff features that I was more than a girl, a friend's sister, and a good cook.

If he found confirmation I'd appreciate him sharing. I could use the support.

"Let's get back to the sorcerer," said Trimble. "Tell us the dreams."

I described them all, using way too thin a frosting of drama for Case, and I prudently translated the Draconic instead of speaking it. I neglected to mention the sword. Maybe the idea that the sword belonged to me seemed farfetched, and I didn't want to be ridiculed again. I mean, really—the first time I grabbed the blade I almost cut my hand off. Not the mark of an epic heroine.

"So, Empress Yvess," Justin gave a nod of respect, "told Mimi to separate the gold from the stone. Why?"

"She's a wyrm," said Larry, setting Mom's axe head on his shoe. "She just wants her jewel back, in that deadly dragon kind of way."

I guess you can't be the eldest of ten kids, or a Wielder level dwarf, without a healthy dollop of practical sense.

"Any idea how to break the Wyrmstone?" asked Trimble.

One by one, the boys shook their heads, no.

Trimble raised an eyebrow. "Mimi?"

I shook my head, no.

"Dang," said Trimble, and I suspect that he spoke for all of them.

Paul looked up, face drawn as if he, alone among the boys, was capable of fearing an early death. "So, where'd you get Vedette's vial?"

"Ms. Farr, the lady I work for."

"Dude, you are hopeless," said Case. "'*The lady I work for*'." He repeated my words with zombiesque stiffness. "Details, Mama Mimi: action, excitement, stimulating storylines. Like, what did she say when she gave you the vial?"

I made no effort to compete against his thrilling style. "She never speaks," I said flatly.

"Never?" Paul's expression morphed from anxious to thoughtful, and I wondered what he would make of Ms. Farr.

There was the pond, I explained, and her saucer eyes, staring as if the scene was so grim she couldn't look away. When I got to the part about Steve being her caretaker and selling her archeological artifacts everyone sat bolt upright.

"Whoa," said Justin. "What's this dude like?"

"A vulture."

Justin looked at Trimble, Case looked at Larry, and Paul looked at Justin.

"It's possible," said Case, but the other boys joggled their heads with doubt.

"What's possible?" I demanded rudely, tired of being out of the in-group.

Case evaded my question with a grin. "A vulture, good description. Maybe he's there to eat whoever dies."

Everyone seemed to think that was funny except me. Being left out of the loop might have dulled my sense of humor, but as far as I was concerned, *eating whoever dies* summed up Steve perfectly.

Justin turned out his pocket and palmed his dice. His roll was quick and sure, the answer definite: eighteen. "Open the vial. We've been guarding the sucker for years, it's time we knew what it is. Traps, Case?"

Case found the vial—again in his pocket—and pulled it out by the narrow neck. He held it inches away, studying each curve and groove, slowly turning it end over end. "It won't detonate."

There was nervous laughter. He sniffed the wax, then cautiously touched the tip of his tongue to where the black seal clotted the stopper. He recoiled in a hurry. "Whew, nasty," he said, "but not poisonous," and hopping off the desk, he passed the vial to Paul.

"What if it had been poison?" I asked Larry, who squatted next me.

"Case is immune."

"How?" I asked.

"Trial and error."

Errors tasting poison? Ah yes, Poison Control. I wondered

if Case's Dad—who worked night shift—slept, oblivious, through Case's mistakes.

Paul knelt and set the vial on the desk. He closed his eyes and began to rock, drifting forward then jerking back as though catching himself in sleep. His hands cupped the vial in a sphere of air. Everyone else sat in respectful silence.

After awhile Paul opened his eyes.

"I'd have to break the seal to be sure," he said.

Justin rolled again: fifteen. He nodded.

Trimble made a wad of flash paper and readied a match in case of disaster. I held my breath. The stopper squeaked as it turned, as if dragging the wax in a painful spiral. As the top drew out a scent escaped, oily, clinging, but soft as snake skin: Night Veil.

That aroma that once hung over our calendar, marking the days that Mom drifted away and Dad went after her, patient as a sheep dog. Marking the nights she laid cool fingers on my forehead and said, "Goodnight, *cara* Massima. *Sii forte.*" Be strong.

Massima the great one. Strong as my heart, that ached to fly apart and scatter this endless grieving over the earth.

In Justin's lap, Nicholi began to cry. "Shh. S'okay Little Dude," whispered Justin, kissing him on the cheek.

The boys sat in glum silence until Nicholi's howling stopped. Then Paul dabbed a smear of Night Veil on his wrist and watched the brown liquid turn silky gray, the color of cobwebs. The smell of ripe-to-rotten fruit filled the room, making it hard to think. Shaking his head against doziness, Paul forced the stopper back in place.

"Potion of Domination," he said.

"What's that?" I almost didn't want to know. I'd had a lifetime of wondering, fearing, worrying that she'd poisoned herself into insanity.

"Allows one mind to override another," said Paul. "It kept Pancrizio at bay."

I was flooded with relief. What a comfort that Mom fought back. Now that I knew who she stood against, I couldn't bear the thought of her bowing her head and submitting.

"What's it made of?" asked Trimble.

"Domination is tricky: vinegar, dry lovage, rue seeds, over-ripe fruit—that's easy enough. But then you have to unearth the right words." Paul placed the bottle back in the center of the desk and I wondered, which vinegar? He brought his wrist to his nostrils and inhaled, rubbing traces of oil onto the tip of his nose. "This is a particularly potent version. Vedette knew what she was doing."

"I wish she'd told us," said Justin. "We're clueless."

Case cleared his throat. "Not completely. We have a sorcerer calling dragons to war, channeled through a noob who—still processing this one—speaks Draconic. Said sorcerer is now, thanks to noob inexperience, in solid avatar form. But he hasn't yet, thanks to our bold wizard Trimble, crushed the bejesus out of us. And we have a gorked-out old lady who mysteriously snatched a Potion of Domination out of the air during an airplane explosion. An accident caused by King Adrikhedon, if the magnificent Empress Yvess—" Case gave a nod of respect, "—is not lying. But dragons never tell the whole truth. Oh, and a Wyrmstone that our noobie here," he turned to me, "knows how to use?"

I shook my head, a humiliated noobie 'no'.

"Do we have any weapons against dragons?" Justin asked.

No one answered. I inhaled, and then thought better of speaking.

"Out with it Mimi," said Justin. "Now's not the time for stoic-heroine-who-can-do-it-on-her-own."

"I … I have a magical sword," I said, embarrassed.

"Now we're talkin'," said Larry. "Let's see it."

"It, ah, doesn't actually exist in reality."

One look at Larry's face and I wished there was somewhere I could hide: in Justin's mess of a closet, or in one of his large shoes. Larry's big brother disgust was withering.

"If the dragons turn out to be in your imagination we'll be in great shape then, won't we? Crap. How'd we get such a novice in our party?"

"Larry, save your dwarfish temper for the enemy," said Trimble. "How do you know you have a sword, Mimi?"

"I've seen it in a dream. I forgot to mention it."

"She forgets to mention a magical sword," Larry muttered.

Trimble ignored him. "Can you draw us a picture?"

Nicholi slid off Justin's lap and went to the desk drawer. He grabbed paper and a crayon, which he pushed into my hands. Everyone huddled around as I drew.

First was the round disc of iron on the very end of the sword, the breadth of a big man's fist, adding weight and balance. Then the grip wound with braided hair, the strands various colors as though many heads lost scalps to it. Then the hilt with an iron hook.

"What's that for?" Nicholi pointed to the hook.

"For the forefinger. Holds the sword steady against a side blow." Larry's attention was riveted. "Keep going, Mimi."

The blade, carved with runes worn to shadows, the razor-sharp double cutting edge with the tip that stayed fat until the last second, then slanted to a lethal point. And the glow that emanated from the iron, burning away rust and nicks. I crayoned this in with yellow. I left out my blood stains.

When I put down my crayon, Trimble pushed the drawing toward Larry. "Well, weapons master?"

Larry scowled, flat forehead wrinkling. "I'd say a third century dragon slayer, judging from the cross guard and pommel. Italians favored that point taper. The runes enchant it to penetrate armor and scales. I'd say … " he looked at me with newfound respect, " … it's Deathwish." He broke into a broad, crooked-toothed smile.

Deathwish. Of course; the sword sacrificed to the gem. It made sense that the sword could be unsheathed from the jewel. I didn't know why it had been given to me, but I knew what I wanted to do with it. All I needed was Adrikhedon's slimy neck, and Mom and Dad could be avenged.

Then again, Yvess might be lying. There might be many reasons she could want Adrikhedon dead. Motive and means: was she setting me up for murder, or helping me to survive?

"Wielding Deathwish, we might put up a good fight before we die," said Larry with enthusiasm. Boys bumped fists with a hearty, "Yeah!", as if this were a positive development.

Trimble glanced at his watch. "Sharpen your blades and

wits, kiddies. We needed a plan yesterday, so think dragon army and Grand Sage, and bring me your best ideas."

"How fracked are we?" asked Paul.

"On a scale of zero to ultimo-fracked, I'd say we're skidding toward the final 'd'. But that's what makes it fun, right?" Trimble grinned, and the crazy idiots grinned back (except for Paul, of course, who closed his eyes and shuddered).

Trimble stood up. "It's time for the dreaded apology to Ms. Rossi. Who's coming with me?"

Everyone groaned as though they disliked this more than dragons.

As boys herded toward the door, I put a few slices of homemade banana bread on a plate and covered the caramel-frosted tops with saran wrap.

The boys were jovial, teasing, savoring being a group as they sauntered down the driveway in the icy drizzle. Nicholi held my hand, little fingers grabbing tight, taking two hops and a skip for every step of mine. As we approached Ms. Rossi's porch the boys gathered in a nervous knot. Larry rang the doorbell. The porch light came on, not adding much brightness to the dreary day. Ms. Rossi opened the door, zipped into a rose-patterned house dress an inch too long for her stooped frame. Her wisps of white hair were pinned into a bun.

"Yes?" She squinted through thick glasses, as though trying to make sense of the shadows that hung around her door.

The boys stepped back and nudged Trimble forward.

"Hi, Ms. Rossi." His voice squeaked with tension. "We came to say we're sorry about your hedge."

"Oh, my deep fried laurel." Anna stifled a smile and the

boys snickered nervously. Warm air wafted from her hall as she stepped aside to let us in. "I don't believe I know all of you."

"I'm Trimble." Trimble gave a majestic bow, and then made introductions all around.

"And this is Didoo," added Nicholi, pushing his bear into Ms. Rossi's hands.

She squeezed a furry paw. "Please, everyone, have a seat. Carlo!" Her voice cracked with the effort of calling. "We have company."

Carlo. With a tingle of last night's humiliation I imagined his ironic smile and his bank of eyebrows, hanging over those intense eyes. Maybe this time I wouldn't come across as a clueless fool, in need of rescue from her own stupidity.

As we crowded into the living room Carlo rose from the armchair. "Here, take my seat." He gestured for me to sit. Whatever his thoughts about my ineptitude with a chisel, my unattractive illness, my boyfriend disasters, and my inability to defeat a fig stump, he kept them to himself.

Determined to be gracious, I thanked him and sat down, then cringed as boys scattered over Anna Rossi's beautiful white couch, feet thankfully on the ground. They left the rocker for Anna. Nicholi sat at Justin's feet, walking Didoo in a little dance across the rug and humming to himself.

"Can I get anyone a root beer?" asked Carlo.

Six hands shot up in the air. No, seven; I forgot to count Didoo. I didn't raise my hand. I wanted a cup of Anna's tea, but it seemed demanding to say so. Carlo left for the kitchen, and Anna lowered herself into the rocker as the room went quiet.

Justin's friends are talented with tongue-tied silences. I suppose it's herd instinct; facing down the enemy as a group, tails whisking and horns lowered, all kicking when one member startles. In this particular case, they moved with unspoken unity to protect against awkward questions. No eye contact, no chitchat. Paul chewed his cuticles. Trimble crossed his legs, arms, and I suspect his fingers, no doubt preparing their defense. Case combed fingers over his shaved scalp as though having a bad hair day. Justin brooded, staring at haphazard swirls in the white shag rug. Larry sat slumped and edgy like a boy in a confessional, clicking his fingernails together. Nicholi was the only one oblivious to the weight of the hush. He flopped on his belly and waddled Didoo further from Justin's feet, towards the runners of Anna Rossi's rocker.

Ms. Rossi, dear soul, couldn't see their careful evasions of her smile. She sat quietly, a semi-blind old lady, resting at home in her rocking chair. Carlo returned with root beer, and with palpable relief the boys grabbed bottles. They sipped and burped softly until Carlo brought another tray. He handed his grandmother a china cup, and me a mug.

"I didn't know what you wanted, so I made tea. Hope that's okay." He had such a pleasant, quiet manner.

"It's perfect, thanks." Naturally he'd guessed. I couldn't seem to keep secrets from this man. Suppressing an irrational annoyance, I set the plate of banana bread in my lap and gripped the comfort of the mug in both hands. With nowhere else to sit, Carlo settled cross-legged on the floor by his grandmother's chair.

"So," he said, after a sip of root beer, "this is the

pyrotechnic crew. That was one awesome column of fire. How did you do it?"

Sheepish grins crept across the boys' faces.

"Gunpowder," said Case, and for a moment he looked as though he might launch into an enthusiastic instant replay of the explosion. But he must have thought better of it, because he took a fortifying slug of root beer instead.

Carlo shook his head. "The next time you decide to do something like that, let me know. I'd like to see it up close. And maybe I can help you engineer it so that no one gets killed."

Trimble uncrossed his legs and sat back, the rainbow of his robe shockingly bright against Anna's white couch. "I think we're done with gunpowder for the moment. We … ah … we're really sorry about the hedge. We were trying to … ah … well, things were taken out our hands."

Paul, Case, and Larry nodded.

"If I'm not mistaken," said Justin, "you look like the guy who saved Nicholi and Didoo. That was awesome, dude."

Carlo pulled Nicholi and Didoo from the fire! I inhaled with surprise, and tea caught in my throat and choked me. Sincere thanks and gratitude were swamped by sputtering and coughing.

"Dude! Where'd you come from anyway? You just like, dropped from the sky." Case's voice held a twinge of professional jealousy.

"I was on the roof setting rat traps."

"You *jumped* from the roof?" Case couldn't hide his robust admiration, as if he imagined imitating the stunt. It made me hope that Case knew how to call an ambulance as well as poison control.

"It seemed the quickest way down," said Carlo.

"*Awesome,*" breathed Case.

Carlo made another absolutely priceless shrug, as good as any in Rome. His fingers spread slightly, nimbly deflecting Case's praise. One eyebrow shot up in polite acknowledgement, while his gaze tilted humbly down. Collectable. It made my heart twist with sadness that Dad couldn't see it.

Meanwhile, Didoo had marched across the room via Nicholi's hands, and arrived at Carlo's knee. "Do you know the Chilkat robe?" asked Nicholi.

Carlo didn't blink at this non sequitur. "Nope."

"It's a gathering of spirit bears."

"Is Didoo a spirit?" asked Carlo.

"Yup." Nicholi put Didoo in Carlo's lap.

Carlo put his arms around the bear, and then turned to his grandmother. "Nonna?"

Nonna: Italian for grandmother. Dad claimed Italian was his worst language when, in fact, it was his best. Maybe one of the only lies Dad ever told, giving him a well-worn excuse to travel to Italy. He died flying home with an improved vocabulary, new shrugs, and my tanned and rested mother.

Why had they really made that last trip? Now that I knew the whole story, I doubted that Mom went along for the tan. Perhaps it had to do with Night Veil. I tried to remember if the vial had been full or empty when she left. Picturing it in her suitcase, it was impossible to say. I had never been allowed to touch it. Justin might know.

Anna sighed. "Well, this has been so pleasant I hate to ruin it, but I suppose we should get to the task at hand. The new hedge will cost twenty-five dollars a plant, if we get azaleas large enough that I'll live to see them bloom. Twelve plants ought to do it. That's a lot of money for you boys, I bet."

Three hundred dollars. Half a week's pay for me, and out of the question for Justin and his friends. The boys gave a glum, collective nod.

"Here's what I suggest, tomorrow Carlo will rip out the old hedge, then in spring he'll replant. If you're willing to help Carlo for two days, we'll call it even."

Justin looked at Trimble, Case looked at Larry, and Paul looked at Justin.

For once, I didn't mind being left out.

"That's fair," said Trimble.

"I'm in," said Case.

Paul nodded shyly, flushing to have all eyes on him.

Larry swallowed his gulp of root beer. "Okay, as long as my parents don't need me to baby-sit."

As a united body, the boys turned to Justin.

Justin didn't hesitate; he pulled out a twenty-sided die and gave it a shake. With a practiced thumb, he flicked it. Twenty eyes watched the red plastic lump rise toward the pink plaster of Ms. Rossi's ceiling, twisting and twirling, then drop, falling with the weight of fate. As it picked up speed, hurtling towards an answer, Trimble snatched it out of the air. Next to him on the couch, Justin heaved around, an offended barbarian with fury in his eyes.

Trimble didn't flinch. "What if fate didn't choose the

gunpowder? What if Pancrizio is tampering with the dice? Maybe you're being used, Justin." There was a four second standoff, during which the Master Wizard stared down the Barbarian Wolf King. The other boys tensed into red alert.

"I trust the dice. That's final," growled Justin.

His legs flexed underneath him, his big fingers spread and chest expanded. Sick with fear I gripped the armchair. I was a dinky barrier, but I'd throw myself between them if I had to.

Ms. Rossi, even blind as she was, must have sensed something terrible approaching. She rocked forward in her chair. "Justin?"

One final, steady squint, and Justin broke off his confrontation, turning toward the frail grandmother.

Anna coughed a creaky catch out of her throat. "I really hated that hedge. It didn't flower. The branches had been sheared so close that birds couldn't nest. It grew so tall that it cut me off from the exciting goings-on at neighbors' houses. Thank you for burning it down. If you don't want to help replace it, we'll just call it even."

She gave a guilty smile. "There, thank goodness that's out. It isn't fair to deceive you boys, you did me a favor."

Justin shifted uneasily on the couch, as though the friends on either side crowded him. Larry and Trimble slid over, giving Justin a few more inches.

"I decide things by throw of the dice," he said gruffly.

"Well, then, by all means," said Anna. She nodded to Trimble. With great reluctance, Trimble dropped the die in Justin's palm.

Justin rolled it around, then dropped it in the other palm.

Glancing at the number, he let out a long, slow breath, then broke into a smile.

"Maybe we did you a favor, but I'll help replace your hedge and—" his gray eyes sparkled with pure elfin mischief, "—and I guess we should apologize for only blasting a hole. Three more inches of gunpowder and we could have incinerated the whole butt-ugly thing."

Ms. Rossi shrieked with delight and collapsed into giggles. Her chair rocked raucously as she clapped a withered hand over her mouth.

"Oh dear, oh dear," she mumbled, "now I'm in trouble." Her clouded eyes searched in my direction. "I'm sorry, Mimi. I'm afraid I haven't kept my promise very well."

I could hardly hear her over boys guffawing and high-fiving.

"*Nonna*," interrupted Carlo, "*può darsi che per te le cose siano andate bene, ma Nicholi e Didoo hanno rischiato di rimmetterci la vi.*" The blistering Italian, peppered with I's and O's, reinforced with a muscular chop of Carlo's hand, sliced through the hilarity.

Justin froze, his face contorted. My parents' beloved language, voiced with authority, delivered one final counsel from the grave in flawless Italian. The party stuttered into silence.

Over the course of the tense argument Nicholi had crawled into Carlo's lap. Now, Anna laid a hand on his head.

"Forgive us, Nicholi," she croaked. "Carlo has reminded me that you were almost killed. I'm so used to ignoring death, I forget that some people have long lives ahead of them. We weren't laughing about your predicament."

A heavy blanket of guilt draped over the boys, hunching their backs, and they withdrew into tongue-tied safety. Carlo sat with Nicholi in his lap, supporting burned and battered Didoo with one hand as his gaze pursued downcast eyes, boy by boy.

Finally Trimble cleared a sticky sounding lump from his throat. "I let you down, Nicholi. There's no excuse."

"Yeah," mumbled Larry, "I knew better. Sorry, Bezerkidude."

Case tugged at the fine hair on his upper lip. "I screwed up, Little Dude. I'm glad you and the Didooster are okay."

Paul sat up abruptly. Taking one rapid, clipped breath after another he hyperventilated himself into a state where he could speak. With two strangers in the room it was possible that he might pass out before the first word. Fortunately his courage mustered before his oxygen level overwhelmed him.

"Nicholi, you and Didoo are so great I could never forgive myself if something happened to you. We shouldn't have put you in danger. Without Carlo's help I wouldn't have gotten to you in time." He took a few more deep breaths and looked so pale I wondered if he might faint after all. "And I should have stayed when the police came, to be sure you were all right." He extended a hand toward Nicholi. "Sorry, little buddy."

Meanwhile, Justin sat, weighty as a bronze statue, fist curled under his chin. I suppose he pondered remorse, its terrible size too much even for a barbarian to lift.

His friends, clearly feeling his misery, looked awkwardly at walls, shoelaces, and other fascinating things. Anna rocked quietly. Nicholi repeatedly pulled on Didoo's ear, whispering "oof" every time it snapped back. Carlo surveyed Justin's face. After a minute, Justin hauled his gaze off the floor and met Carlo's, then Justin's eyes dropped in submission.

"I'm sorry I didn't protect you and Didoo," he said. "I love you and … I'll try to be a better brother."

His back snuggled against Carlo's chest, Nicholi raised Didoo and pawed the air with his bear's arms. "Di*doo* Di*doo* Di*doo*," he whispered. Then he sprang out of Carlo's lap and threw himself at the couch, landing on Justin, Larry, and Trimble. "Tickle monster," he yelled, digging fingers into any ribs he could reach.

Boys squawked and fought to defend themselves. Paul and Case leaped onto the pile, grabbing legs and arms. They became one writhing, yelping bundle, thrashing on Anna's white couch.

"Knock it off, you're going to break Ms. Rossi's couch." I sounded just like Mom, but without the cute accent.

Justin swept Nicholi into his arms and stood, shedding boys like water.

"Ms. Rossi, do you need a new couch? We could destroy this one for you."

Again her laugh, as though her sense of humor was still in pigtails. "No, I like my couch. But I'll call you boys if I ever get sick of it."

Chuckling sheepishly, the boys collected themselves.

"Well," said Trimble, "we should go."

Carlo stood up. "See you tomorrow, and bring shovels. Ten AM."

Boys trundled into the hall, Anna creeping along behind to see them out.

As I rose to go, Carlo pointed to the plate of banana bread still clutched in my hand. "Is that for us?"

"Oh, yeah, this is for you and Anna." I held it out.

He wrapped his hand over the edge of plate, his fingers pressing mine, warm and strong. "If it's a tenth as good as your cinnamon rolls, Nonna's not getting any of it," he whispered.

For a second I thought he was serious and I blinked with surprise. Then I recognized the tease in his eyes and his look of quiet longing. He was flirting with me! My heart flip-flopped a few times, a fish gasping on Duke's dry dock.

"I … I … goodbye Carlo." Hastily extracting my fingers, I hustled down the hall, away from his gaze.

Outside, a hard rain drove down, pounding on our heads. Larry ran to catch the bus, Paul and Trimble hopped on bikes, and Case, hunched over and coatless in the eve of our garage, called his Dad on his cell phone.

"Do you want to come in, Case, while you wait?" I asked.

"No, I'm good." Slyfoot that he was, he leaned into the shadows and semi vanished, enduring the weather without complaint.

As Justin, Nicholi, and I arrived at our door I asked, "Justin, was Mom's Night Veil empty when she went to Italy?"

Justin nodded as we walked into the house. He waited until Nicholi had danced off, then said quietly, "It had been empty for weeks. Mom was worried, and the fig was dying."

"She went to Italy to make Night Veil."

"Yeah, I guess she must have. Though I don't know why she couldn't make it here."

Memories filled my nose, pungent with sweet decay, the scent of vinegar stepping forward like an old friend.

"Tuscan balsamic," I said. "Can't buy it here."

Lips pressed tight, Justin nodded.

"I was wondering, could you … you know … help me use the Wyrmstone?"

His eyes flew open. "Heck no. I wish I could. Controlling an artifact requires a deep bond with it, but your Wyrmstone is two things at war. The gold is a powerful dungeon. Pancrizio charmed his way out, but he'll return if we kill that body you conjured for him. The jewel is pissed as hell about being imprisoned and wants to be back in a dragon's claw."

Justin shrugged off his wet coat. "You're in way over your head, Mimi. Dude, you're in over Trimble's head, and he's a master."

I threw my coat over what I now considered to be Ms. Whitting's doorknob, and wandered into the chaotic living room. Shoving aside Age of Dragons texts, I collapsed on the couch. "Don't you have a book about the Wyrmstone somewhere?"

Justin sank into Dad's armchair. "Like what, *A Dummy's Guide to Enslaving Dragons*?" He snorted. "You're still wearing it?"

I touched the warm lump through my shirt front.

"Good, because Pancrizio is watching day and night, and the moment you take it off, he'll nab it."

The thought of Pancrizio stalking me was too creepy. "Won't he try for the gem while I'm wearing it?"

"Of course, but when we least expect it. And from now on, we expect it, right?"

I stared at him, too frightened to know what to say.

"He'll likely come while you sleep. We'll post Larry outside your door—"

"No! Absolutely not." I would not have boys hanging around the privacy of my room, risking their lives, then causing trouble by falling asleep in school the next day.

From deep in the armchair, Justin brooded out the window, studying the splintered, muddy fig roots in the garden, and I wondered if he still smarted over my deception. Then he took out a die and rolled it.

"Nineteen. The dice agree, so Larry guards you. First rule, Age of Dragons—stay alive in your sleep. Trimble's finding a shielding spell. Tomorrow we'll see if you can harness enough power from the stone to cast a barrier against Pancrizio."

My jaw dropped. "I have to use the Wyrmstone?"

"Well, duh!"

"What if I don't want to? Or can't? Or kill us all trying?"

I had once felt, after a feverish night of horrible dreams, that I might be capable of mastering dragons. But in the healthy light of day that was clearly a sick delusion.

Justin scowled, that blade that made mincemeat out of arguments.

"Around your neck lies our strongest weapon. Danged if I'm going to let it laze around while we fight a Grand Sage and his dragon army. Wield it, Mimi—that's obviously what you were made for." Then he stood up and stalked off.

I turned my gaze to the fig stump. *What I was made for.* There was a time when I would have laughed this off, but now destiny pushed into my stomach like a fist. Mom either sealed my fate, or did her best to keep me from it; I couldn't tell which. She'd bargained me away—twice—then buried out of reach the one object that might save us.

I fingered the warm stone and icy roots. *What I was made for.* Perhaps there were some things only one person could do. They could either give their gift to the world, or not. Still, there was no rational reason why I should wield the stone. True, I worshiped the jewel: an obsession that made other emotions feel thin. But loving beauty was hardly a mark of epic destiny. If Mom made me to wield the Wyrmstone, she kept among her secrets *how* she equipped me. I hungered for her to speak the truth, instead of leaving such confusing whiffs and flavors. Just for once, I pleaded silently, come to me Mom, and tell me what you know.

Meanwhile, rule number one: stay alive in your sleep. It seemed to me a better rule was *stay alive,* period. Dragons, avalanches, Pancrizio—one of the bunch was bound to slaughter me. And if I survived, I still had to break the Wyrmstone or face Yvess. Dad had been clueless, Mom was dust, and the adults who scrutinized me were worthless. *Trust the boys, Mimi.* But that wasn't enough; in the end, I'd have to trust myself. That was the beast that really made me cower.

Chapter 16

As the day progressed towards seeing Duke I became more and more anxious. I still didn't have a babysitter for Nicholi, and though it seemed outlandish that Duke might be a Doppelganger, I needed to get Nicholi out of the house just in case. Finally, in the late afternoon, I went to the kitchen and called Ms. Rossi.

Her sweet, creaky voice barely carried through the receiver. "Yes, dear, I'd be delighted. What time will you drop him off?"

I glanced at my watch, deciding that I had enough time before Duke arrived to bake her some sugar cookies.

"How about eight? Just for an hour, maybe less. Is that okay?"

"Of course. Bring a few books for us to read."

Justin spent the day studying Age of Dragons texts, sprawled on the floor belly down like a bull walrus. Around seven Larry arrived, toting an overnight bag on Mom's pick-axe handle, hitched over one shoulder in the manner of an adventurer's rucksack. I wasn't happy about it, but I let him in. So much for sending Justin to Case's house.

"This is a private conversation. I want you two out of the way when I speak to Duke, clear?"

The two of them were side by side and bellies to the rug, munching sugar cookies and reading. Larry glanced at Justin and Justin glanced at Larry, but they didn't argue.

After Nicholi's bath, I dressed him in pajamas and found *Millie and the Alien*. No way would he read *The Complete Book of Dragons* and scare the heck out of dear Anna Rossi.

"Ms. Rossi is going to sit with you and you can read to her. I'll pick you up in an hour." I crouched to look under the couch where Didoo had rolled during Nicholi's game of 'bear soccer'.

Nicholi stood behind me, one finger coiling thick, dark hair into ringlets.

"Why?"

"Why what, honey?"

"Why am I staying at Ms. Rossi's?"

I handed him his bear. "I need to have an adult conversation with Duke. It won't be long."

He shoved his nose into Didoo's face and rubbed back and forth vigorously, breaking off a few more dirty pink threads. Then he stared into the bubbly glass eyes. "Didoo likes Ms. Rossi," he said, and he went to put on his shoes.

I had a half an hour after I dropped Nicholi off, but I didn't dress for Duke. Instead I made myself a cup of hot tea and had a cookie, crumbling with butter. From the armchair, I watched rain flow over the tree stump that I didn't have the physical strength to remove. Tonight, in the dark with the patio lights off, I could barely see it: a black lump hunched over a gaping hole, tangled lie of roots exposed. The hole my parents left when they died, a cave where Mom buried her secrets. One by one I unearthed them, each mystery clawing for blood as it came to light. So many secrets still entombed. Things I should have asked Empress Yvess, like: what had Mom received in return for her promise?

The doorbell startled me, yanking my thoughts back to Duke. Dread rushed from my chest to my brain, erasing my articulate goodbye speech. I should have written him a letter. I didn't want another miserable humiliation.

With Nicholi's super slo-mo, I dragged myself to the door.

"Hey, Mimi." He looked drop dead stunning and held out red roses, smelling like the ferns and Baby's Breath. For a moment I wanted to believe he hadn't cheated. He stepped forward to press his lips over mine, but I turned to divert the kiss to my cheek.

"What's up?" He looked me up and down. "I thought we were going out."

"Come in." I turned my back and left him to maneuver the open door and his wet coat while I collected myself.

"What's the matter, babe?" He set the flowers on the coffee table and eased himself onto the couch. I could smell the seductive spice and ether of his aftershave.

For a full minute I couldn't speak. His hair, that elusive color between gold and rosewood. His face, carved with symmetry, skin smooth and lips sensuous. His chest and abs under the close fitting shirt. I savored his suave beauty as though I were packing my childhood into boxes, wrapping each treasured memory carefully, giving one last hug to immaturity before the lid closed forever. One straight, honey blonde tuft fell over his eye, and he shoved it aside, smooth as a cat, eyes sparkling. He was not a good man, but he sure knew how to pick a good restaurant.

"I was sick this week with Chlamydia." Determined to remain calm, I said this as flat as a crêpe pan.

"Chlamydia? Where'd you get that?" He was on full alert now, still sure enough of his ground to remain seated, but every muscle tensed if needed.

"From you. I've never had sex with anyone else."

"Me?" He looked genuinely bewildered. "Are you sure?" Amazing, really, his ability to lie. If I didn't trust Dr. Harvey so completely I might have doubted, even now.

"Do you have other lovers?"

His mouth dropped open. "Well, sometimes, I guess. Not often."

"Not often." My voice cracked like my heart. It took everything I had not to pursue this lead, demand to know who and when. But it didn't matter; why torture myself?

"Why didn't you tell me?"

"It … ah … never occurred to me that you didn't know. I mean—" he raked fingers through his hair, "—did I ever *say* you were my only one?"

No, in fact, he hadn't promised me anything. I had assumed. And why not? I was in love with him, and I thought he felt the same about me. But, in fact, aside from the certainty that he loved to date and sleep with me, I had no idea how he felt.

"Did you wear a condom the last time we were together?"

Finally he had the decency to look embarrassed. "Umm … well … I … probably."

"Probably?" I bubbled with fury. "I think the answer is 'no, Mimi, I didn't'."

"Look, if I knew I'd caught something I would've been more careful."

He leaned forward, fingers in a peak and pressed together with patience, as if he planned to reason with me. "We've had hardly any time together for months. I might be willing to make a commitment if I could see you."

"What do you mean?" I said between my teeth.

He bore down with the full weight of his charm. "Let me hire a nanny for those damned brothers of yours, so you can spend time with me. I don't like hanging out alone."

His smile reeked of pleasure and promise, and for a second I knew how he got whatever he wanted. But … *damned brothers?* That's what Nicholi and Justin were, then: a nuisance from hell. I was so irate I could hardly speak. I snatched up the flowers and tossed them in his face.

"Get out." I pointed to the door. "Don't ever call me again." I didn't need articulate speeches, I just needed him gone.

Anger twisted his mouth, a flash of stung ego and spite.

He stood up and my heart raced. His beautiful face distorted, yellow bleeding through the cracks, eyes shrinking to a pig's, a rat's, then melting completely. I gasped and backed up. Yellow slime shot to the ceiling and loomed like a tsunami. I coughed, wheezing in the ether of his perfume, thoughts screaming through cloudy confusion. He was going to kill me!

My hand fumbled for the Wyrmstone, finding, clutching the hot swirl of its face. I leaned into the strength of the stone, fighting overwhelming waves of sleep. Words flew unbidden, up that hidden path and into light of day, yelling, "*Yomorrtarr.*" *Deathwish.*

A sword appeared in my hand, runes glowing, edge a glinting razor. My head whirled, dizzy from his stupefying stench. Yellow folded down on me, teeth grinding over my head.

A pickaxe, spinning like a shuriken, flew past my ear and buried in yellow flesh with a thud. The slime wavered, blood running around the gash.

I thrust my blade upward, toward teeth, but it sliced air as the Doppelganger shrank with a snap. A lithe cougar body leaped over my head. I spun around to see Justin swing at the cat with a sledgehammer. With a grunt the cougar ducked, backed away, bleeding from the gaping gash in its side. Molding into Duke, he ran to the hall, pressed his leather coat into his wound, and threw open the front door. Seconds later I heard a squeal as the Lotus backed, zero to sixty in 4.9 seconds, out the driveway.

Justin and Larry stood panting side by side, Justin with the sledgehammer up and ready.

"Friggin' coward." Justin dropped the sledgehammer and nudged it under the couch with his boot. Weapons in the house no longer seemed like such a bad idea.

"They're all cowards." Larry strolled around me to retrieve Mom's pickaxe. He paused for a moment to gawk at the sword in my hand, and then under his gaze, it vanished.

"Awesome," he breathed.

I threw myself into the armchair, trembling all over, so upset I couldn't put a sentence together. I had to do something violent or I'd explode. Leaping up, I snatched the pick-axe out of Larry's hands, strode into the hall, pulled on Mom's steelshank boots, and yanked on her muddy garden jacket. With a few big strides I was in the garden, my blade poised over the dead fig stump.

"You bastard," I swore as I raised the axe. I swung with such force the blade sank three inches into dead wood. The fig shuddered but didn't crack. I wiggled the blade free and swung again, severing a large root off clean.

"You slimy butchering bastard." I lifted the blade. He'd murdered Duke. My sweet, playful genius was dead. My heart pained as if I'd slammed it instead of the tree.

Twenty minutes of chopping later I was drenched, filthy, and exhausted. I was still brokenhearted, but too tired to cry anymore. I staggered inside, combed grimy hair out of my eyes, covered my muddy clothes with a raincoat, and went to get Nicholi. Larry and Justin had discretely retired.

Thank God Carlo wasn't at Nonna's. If any man had tried to flirt with me just then I would have lopped off his head with Deathwish.

Nicholi slept on Anna's couch under a lacy crocheted afghan, cheeks flushed pink and his widow's peak a dark smear. His thick eyelashes fluttered with dreams.

"Was he good?" I whispered to Anna.

"Oh, yes. He's a sweetie."

I scooped my Bezerkidude into my arms and clutched a

paw of his spirit bear. I would protect my brothers, even if it killed me.

"What do I owe you?"

"Nothing, dear, my family takes good care of me. It was a pleasure." She patted me on the cheek.

"Thanks, Anna." I looked down on her bent head, feeling how much her friendship meant, hoping she could hear it in my voice.

"I'd be happy to sit again if you need it." She shuffled towards the door. "Oh, and thanks for the cookies. I had to fight Carlo for them, but I was cunning enough to get one or two after he left for work."

I shifted Nicholi onto a hip and buttoned my coat. I didn't mean to be rude, but I wasn't in the mood to converse about Carlo.

"He's in the family business. Hates it, poor boy, but he has to pay for college somehow."

I inched towards the door.

"For five generations we Rossis have stuck together, but he's determined to go on to other things."

So was I, and they didn't involve men.

"Goodnight, Anna."

Walking home, I paused at the hole in her hedge, burned like a fiery punch through waxy, stiff leaves. A void, slammed right through the heart of it. I ached to be home, curled in bed so I could cry again. I remembered my parents' twenty-fifth wedding anniversary. A friend, who had known Dad since high school, had asked, "Hugh, you ugly old bulldog, how'd you keep such an attractive woman to yourself, all these years?"

"It's easy," Dad said, "I love her for just exactly who she is." But he was mistaken; he never really knew who she was. He just loved her, regardless.

Chapter 17

That night Mom stepped out of the blackness of sleep and wavered, flimsy as a reflection.

"Mom!" My heart leapt, so desperate for her.

"Massima, *cara*, you must learn to cook with blood."

And then she disappeared, leaving me sobbing.

The rest of the night I had a horrible stomach ache. Maybe I slept a few minutes. Maybe I slept it all and only dreamed of tossing side to side, gut gnawing. In my dazed sorrow, I tried to remember recipes that called for blood. And though I pictured blood sizzling in the frying pan, steaming in the double boiler, roiling in the soup pot, it all turned a sickening yellow as it cooked, evaporating away. In the vapor floated everyone I'd lost: Mom, Dad, and now Duke, dissolving, beyond reach of my pleading. When dawn lit the windows I knew that grieving was a road that stretched to infinity, a road to be staggered one painful step at a time, every step cherished, because I didn't want to forget.

Six AM Sunday morning I threw off the covers and opened my bedroom door. Larry stood spread-legged in the hall, pickaxe across his chest, eyes wary. In my stubborn incompetence, I'd become a burden. Flushed with shame, I resolved to stop whining and do whatever the boys asked.

"I'm so sorry," I said, "can I make you breakfast?"

"Nah." He yawned and relaxed his vigilance. "I'll just go sleep for half an hour, if you're going to be awake, that is."

I found him a pillow and blanket for the couch, then went to the kitchen. Chili, I would make chili. The cool metal of the colander as I washed dried kidney beans. The warm wood of the spoon as I fried onions. Cumin, oregano, breathed in like comfort. The snap of the pressure cooker lid. Help me, Dad; please heal me before I am shoved back into life.

~

The boys arrived at ten and left soon after, looking like five of Snow White's overgrown dwarves, pickaxes and shovels over their shoulders. Nicholi trailed behind in Mom's garden coat, sleeves rolled up and hood covering three-quarters of his face. His own coat was lost for the second time this year.

Hours later I pulled on Mom's boots and trudged down the driveway to see the progress. The gloomy, dense barrier walling Anna off from the neighborhood was gone. In its place lay a swath of dirt, open to the light with rich, turned-up soil.

Trimble, Larry, and Paul tossed branches into Carlo's truck, testing how high limbs could stack before the pile collapsed. Carlo sliced trunks with Marty's, chain saw—the same chain saw that had taken down the fig after my parents died. I was surprised Marty would let it out of his sight. I guess I wasn't the only one to trust Carlo with precious tools. Justin fed larger branches into a chipper shredder while Nicholi jumped in puddles, preferably as close to another person as possible. Everyone's noses ran and fingers curled in their gloves from the cold.

"I'll have chili and corn bread in a half hour," I yelled over the roaring, squealing, machines. Carlo cut the chain saw engine and turned off the chipper shredder.

"What?" he asked.

"Chili and cornbread in thirty minutes." I smiled at him despite myself. "All invited." With the fedora pulled down over his eyes I couldn't tell if he'd accept this invitation. "Where's Case?" I asked.

"He went to get rope." Carlo lifted his hat and hair flew every which way in the wind. "When you have that load tied down, why don't you go on in and clean up," he said to the boys. "Justin and I'll be done here in ten minutes." He cinched his hat down and folded the brim against the rain. "And before you go, Trimble, take the curse off my grandma's house." To my surprise, his tone was deferential, as though he seriously expected that this could be done. I envied the ease with which he took the boys' world in stride.

With a yank on the cord and a flick of the choke the shredder started up, so loud it vibrated through my feet as I walked down our driveway.

Dad made cornbread with a hint of sage, and sweetened it with honey. As I took the airy, yellow loaf from the oven, the desert-dry scent of sage brought back the way his shirt smelled when I lay my head against it as a child. He would have loved to see me scooping the ladle into the chili pot, drawing a sharp knife through the bread's crust, sinking spoons in the sorghum and honey. When I graduated from high school, he'd kissed me on top of my head and said, "You have good, solid, common sense, Mimi. Use it well." I'm trying, Dad, I'm trying, but common sense doesn't seem to be what's needed.

Carlo showed up at the last minute, just as we were all seated around the table gripping one another's hands. He clamored into the room smelling like Ivory soap, and pulled up a chair between me and Paul. He glanced around the table at the clasped hands, then took mine in his roughened fingers. His gentle warmth felt wonderful, until I remembered the Doppelganger.

A shudder of loathing and disgust chilled me. How could I *not* know that a monster had replaced the man I loved? I'd sensed something strange, but I hadn't listened to myself. I needed a vacation too badly. Behind my closed eyes, Duke's playful smile cracked into the Doppelganger's sneer. He'd stolen Duke and slimed even my memories.

"May the circle be unbroken," I whispered, holding back tears. As soon as the hand squeeze traveled around the group I tugged free my fingers, leaving Carlo's hand alone on the table.

Carlo glanced at me and then tactfully looked away. He took a piece of cornbread, inhaled the aroma deeply, and set it on his plate. "So, did Trimble remove the curse?" he asked, nudging the pan toward Larry.

Case intercepted the pan and helped himself. "Yeah, dude, Trimble's awesome." He piled several pieces on Trimble's plate then passed the cornbread to Paul, bypassing Larry. Larry scowled at him.

"So, what was the problem?" asked Carlo.

Trimble buttered his cornbread, frowning as if he were reluctant to talk about it. "The curse attracted a Griefor to your grandma's porch." He spoke with his usual matter-of-fact dryness.

"How'd you get rid of it?" asked Carlo, snagging the basket of bread and passing it to Larry. Larry took four pieces, then gave a slice to Nicholi.

"Paul prepared a scroll so I could sanctify the area, and I happened to know a Griefor's true name, so …." Trimble's voice trailed off; for him, this was all in a day's work.

"Dudes! Can't anyone tell a story around here?" Case gestured toward Carlo with his spoon. "So here we are, under the cobwebby, moldy porch in the dark, trying to locate the Griefor. Trimble lights one flare of paper after another and matches are flying everywhere. It took a whole pad of flash paper just to get the Griefor's eyes to glow. Then suddenly this Raff-dead Squirrel comes flying through the air, claws out like the possessed thing that it is, and lands on Trimble's shoulder. Trimble hollers and grabs the thing with a gravewarden's glove and it bursts, puffing gross death dust all over us. It was friggin' fantastic."

Case took a huge gulp of milk and charged on. "Then the Griefor comes crawling towards us, 'cause he's too tall to stand down there. His flesh is blowing off his body like mist in Larry's flashlight and his eye sockets are shining green. Trimble starts chanting backwards this spell of creation and the Griefor dissolves one bone at a time until nothing is left but the evil runes that float over a Griefor's head. Trimble says the Griefor's true name and the runes start to fry. They were sizzling, dude, popping and splattering like eyeballs. You should have been there, Carlo, instead of putting the stupid shredder away."

"Gees, if I'd only known." Carlo considered Trimble, giving no clue as to what he thought of all this. "Any chance you could get rid of the rats?"

"Your rats are gone, cowboy," said Justin. "One whiff of Trimble's spells and they ran."

Carlo looked incredulous. "The rats are gone?"

Around the table, boys nodded.

"If that's true, I owe you guys a favor."

"Of course it's true," said Larry. "Trimble's a Master Wizard, he can handle a few rats."

The boys turned back to eating with gusto, fortified by their last battle and totally psyched for the next one. Did they really know what they were doing? I pictured a dragon war, and cringed. Dragons were violent just looking at you. I couldn't imagine them roaring through a city. Could bullets even penetrate their scales? Thousands would die before they were destroyed, assuming they could be destroyed, and the devastation would be gruesome. There was no way we could fight such a force. But the boys were cheerful! Arguing over second and third portions, elbowing and ribbing each other, joking like they had the best destiny ever bestowed. Justin was right: they desperately needed the Wyrmstone. But with or without it, they were dying to fight. I was on team crazy.

When everyone was stuffed with chili and Larry was picking at the last crumbs of cornbread, I turned to Justin. "Loan me a twenty-sided die."

Without comment, he reached into his pocket and handed me a blood red polygon with silver flecks.

"Okay, roll for dish duty." I turned to Trimble. "You first, ten and under clean up."

Trimble gave me a sideways glance, but he took the plastic piece and rolled it. "Thirteen." With a smile he pushed his chair back and settled his hands contentedly in his lap.

Case, next around the table, swept up the die. "What ever happened to girls doing the dishes?" he said under his breath.

I laughed. "We girls grew up. Roll, Case."

"Dude! An eleven, I powned it!" He tossed the die to Larry.

"I wish we did this at home. I get stuck with dishes every night." Larry rolled and practically leaped out of his chair with delight. "Natural twenty, Dwarves have skills!" He passed the die to Justin.

Justin took the die and rolled without a word. An eight. Apparently unmoved by his fate, he slid the die to Nicholi.

"I want a … four." Nicholi used Didoo's paws to sweep the die into his lap.

"No you don't, Little Dude, then you'd have to do dishes," said Case.

"I don't care." He rolled a fifteen. "Can I stay in the kitchen anyway, Mimi?"

"If you want to." I suspected he was mostly concerned with his Lego castle under the kitchen table. He handed the die to Paul.

"I … uh … I tend to drop plates and break them." Paul looked uncertainly at the plastic piece in his fingers.

"That's totally cheese-monkey," said Larry. "Just roll the dice."

Paul rolled an eighteen. With a sparkling smile, he slammed the die down in front of Carlo. "You're up, cowboy."

Carlo slid his eyes sideways. "Getting mighty bold there, partner," he said with a western twang. "You sure you wanna try to out roll me?"

Paul grinned. "Just draw, buster."

Carlo rolled a two and the whole table erupted in whoops and catcalls.

"Owned! You've been powned like a noob."

"Carlo, Carlo, he's our man! Wash those dishes, Carlo!"

Carlo pushed the die in my direction. "Help me out, Mimi. I'm getting stomped here."

"Sorry, I do enough dishes. I'm hoping for a twenty." I cupped the die and blew, wishing for a hot bath, or a good cookbook to read by the fire. Could I ever, in my *what I was made for*, get off my feet and relax?

I rolled a one. A one. Justin's dice have a nasty sense of humor.

Carlo, Justin, and I stacked bowls and collected silverware while fate's favorites, bragging and swaggering, filed out of the kitchen.

Nicholi crawled under the table and set Didoo in his Lego castle. "This is where spirit bears live," he explained, and then he left to find his box of loose Legos.

By the time I'd put the plates in the dishwasher, Carlo had established himself at the sink and scoured the iron skillet. Justin scrubbed around the gas burners of the stove, keeping his back pointedly towards me, and I wondered what he brooded about. Carlo? No, he obviously liked Carlo. He was probably as worried as I was about my upcoming attempt to use the Wyrmstone.

I grabbed a handful of used paper napkins and opened the sink cabinet under Carlo's feet. There in the garbage, torn into two-inch squares, was Justin's math homework. I tossed the napkins and picked up a fistful of paper scraps.

"Justin?" I spread the pieces on the counter.

Justin didn't answer. With rapt attention he wiped clean the grill on the burners. I pulled the trash can out from under the cupboard, digging for little pieces. Some of them had coffee grounds and grease stuck to them. Even if they could be taped back together, they'd be hard to read. No teacher would accept this as homework.

Justin finished wiping the counter and turned around. When he saw the pile of shredded pages, an elfin grin sneaked across his face. He pushed his bangs away just long enough to make eye contact, then he left the kitchen. A few moments later he came back carrying the broom. He proceeded to sweep gentle, lingering strokes, as though he thoroughly enjoyed rearranging flakes of garlic skin on the linoleum.

Carlo finished loading the dishwasher and turned, dish

sponge in hand. "Next?" he asked. His gaze traveled to the pile of scraps and his eyebrows shot up.

He tried to catch my eye but I shied away.

"Nothing left but this cornbread dish." I put the loaf pan beside the dish drainer.

"What's that?" he asked, pointing at the shreds.

"Justin's math homework." I busied myself taking honey and sorghum spoons from their respective jars, hoping he'd drop the subject.

"Why is it all torn up?"

"Oh," I screwed the lid on the honey jar, "it's complicated."

"No, it's not." Justin leaned on his broom and glared at me. "It's simple. I roll less than an eleven, I throw it away."

Carlo pinched a scrap in his thumb and forefinger. He turned it over and read what could be read on it. "How long did it take you to do this?" he asked.

"What, the math or the ripping?"

"The math."

"About an hour." Justin squatted and swept garlic flakes into the dustpan. Then, as though to make a point, dumped it in the trash can at my feet.

"Why did you rip up an hour's worth of work?" Carlo didn't sound upset, or even derisive, more confused and curious, as though he'd caught someone shredding a hundred dollars.

"Whatever fate decides is the right decision." This was so straight forward to Justin that he obviously didn't figure on a response. He picked up the broom and headed for the utility room.

Carlo called after him, "You think a roll of the dice can tell what's meant to be?"

Justin glanced over one shoulder. "Yeah, why not?"

"What if the decision killed someone?"

Justin turned and stared at Carlo. Carlo stared back. At first Carlo seemed to expect an answer: movement suspended, he waited for Justin to speak. But as the pain and loss in Justin's face registered, Carlo sucked in a sharp inhale.

"I see," Carlo said. And I believe he did. He saw what Justin saw: an airplane in a rolling ball of fire. I might believe that Adrikhedon killed them, but it was obvious that Justin didn't.

Carlo spun in his tracks and faced me, as though asking, "What can we do?" But he didn't say anything.

It was my father's chisel all over again: I was the wrong tool, without enough force, incorrectly applied. If this man could convince my brother that fate wasn't a good decision maker, I'd be forever grateful. But I was not going to stand there and feel like an incompetent fool because I'd failed. I crossed my arms over my chest, pressed my lips together, and gave Carlo my best "I-am-out-of-good-ideas" shrug.

"She wouldn't roll against me," said Justin.

"What do you mean?" asked Carlo.

"I told her I'd give her my homework if she rolled over a ten, but Mimi didn't like the price."

Carlo looked back and forth between us. "Price?"

"Drop it, Justin," I warned. I didn't like the direction he headed, but I couldn't think of a way to force him onto safer ground.

"Yeah. You know what I wanted? I was going to ask her to dump that A-hole of a boyfriend who gave her Chlamydia. For two days she was so sick she could hardly stand because of that slimeface and his Doppelganger dick. Then she dumped him anyways, so she could have had my homework for nothing."

"Justin!" If Justin had thought for a year, he couldn't have hit upon a better way to punish me. I blushed a livid, burning red, too infuriated to trust what I might say next.

Carlo, who stumbled into our family problems as naturally as a lost tourist might end up in the bad part of town, paused for a second. He must have spent that moment deciding which side of our feud he was on.

"I'll roll against you," he said to Justin.

Justin looked surprised. "For what?"

"Well, how about if I lose, I owe you free transportation to anywhere, anytime you call, until school is out."

"'Till June?" Justin sounded intrigued.

"Yeah, I mean, I can't leave my job or anything, but I'll keep my cell phone on and except when I'm at work, I'll drive you. But if you lose, you have to hand your homework in from now on."

Justin put down his broom and dug out the die, and Carlo extended his hand. "Including the math you ripped up today."

"No way, those were already decided." Justin dropped the little plastic ball onto Carlo's calloused palm.

"They're being re-decided right now, all or nothing."

"You're hard, dude." A smile of admiration, one fighter to another, spread over Justin's face.

"Yep, now let's see how lucky I am." Carlo took a deep breath and wiped his palms on his jeans. "Ready?"

Justin nodded, and Carlo dropped the die.

There couldn't possibly be anything good in Justin continuing to throw away homework. Fate had to see that; what screwball advisor would say otherwise? So I waited for fate to settle on a number. If the number was high I'd believe, trust that Justin was in good hands. I mean, we all took guidance from somewhere. But if the number was low—

And the number was … three.

"Aw, crap." Carlo threw down the dish sponge. He spoke for both of us.

With great sportsmanship, Justin picked up the broom, the sponge, and the die. "Keep your cell phone on," he said with a grin, handing Carlo the broom and sponge. Then he sauntered out of the room with barbarian macho. It was brave of Carlo to try to intervene, but fate clearly wasn't done jerking Justin around yet.

Carlo went to put the broom away. That left me alone in the kitchen, putting soap in the dishwasher and giving the counter a final swipe. So Justin wanted me to bargain Duke away. I would never have understood, nor gone along with the dice roll, had he told me the terms. Part of me still denied that Duke was dead, even though his murderer had nearly eaten me. I mean, *a Doppelganger?* Absurd. My reality was absurd. And if I had rolled against Justin, and the dice had decided to save Justin's homework instead of me? Justin didn't believe it could happen; dice made the right decisions. Justin's trust stood against us all. I had no such faith.

I wiped the counter for the fourth time, then turned to see Carlo watching me polish the same place over and over. I flushed and tossed the sponge in the sink.

"So, there's hope?" he asked.

I dried my hands on a dishtowel. "What do you mean?"

"This Duke, he's history?" The relaxed hang of his shoulders radiated patience.

"Duke's history, all right, but—"

I reached for an explanation, something that wouldn't sound trite. Nothing could express the knot of fury, grief, and confusion that was Duke's awful death.

"I don't want a boyfriend."

"How about a friend?"

"A friend?" I asked. "Like … someone to open impossible locks, pull Nicholi from a fire, bring homemade soup, and wrestle fate for Justin's homework?" His smile was so charming I had to laugh. "I guess you're already a friend."

"I'm trying." And he gave a classic Italian shrug, one Dad brought back from Rome early in his travels, that irresistible combination of "Who-knows?" and "We're-all-in-this-together."

I had an urge to reach for him, but resisted.

"Trimble is waiting for me," I said, hurrying out the kitchen door. As much as I dreaded using the Wyrmstone, the thought of hugging Carlo scared me more.

In the living room, boys clustered on the couch, heads together over *A Handbook of Weapons: the Brutal, Subtle, and Enchanted.* Justin stood when he saw me.

"We'll be in the garden shed. Mimi, you and Trimble take

the Wyrmstone and … well, just try not to die, okay?"

The others laughed, a hearty guffaw of macho bravery. I swear, this was their idea of funny. Justin dragged the sledgehammer out from under the couch, nodded to Trimble, and headed for the door with Larry, Case, and Paul.

"Take Nicholi with you," I called after them.

"He's safer than we are," said Justin, waving toward the kitchen. "Pancrizio's not going to attack a fortress of spirit bears."

Trust, don't trust. Belief, doubt. I didn't know where Nicholi was safest. None of us were safe. With a sigh of frustration I shoved aside folded laundry and made space in the middle of the floor so I could kneel across from Trimble. He faced me calmly, back straight, legs crossed, robe sweeping around him on the rug.

"Mind if I watch?" asked Carlo.

I glanced at Trimble with alarm.

"If you absolutely do not move or speak, no matter what happens. I mean it." He made eye contact with Carlo and held it. "Heroics could interfere in a dangerous way." Trimble's hair had grown long, and in the dim of the living room the beads on the ends of his cornrow braids glistened as they lay on the colorful fabric of his clothes. He looked like an Egyptian pharaoh.

Carlo nodded and took a seat in Dad's armchair. Maybe he'd provide a voice of sanity.

Trimble reached into the pocket of his robe and drew out a roll of parchment. "Wizards don't cast dragon spells, so forgive the awkward phrasing, I did the best I could." He unrolled the scroll. Flowing lines of Draconic filled the page. "They say this makes a rune to protect dragon property, usually used on a hoard. With luck, we can lock the house. If worst comes to worst, we'll attach it to you, at least protect the keeper of the stone."

"What does it do?"

"It's nicknamed 'Dragon's Doorbell'. Anything that tries to approach the protected area will be stopped at the rune and you will be alerted. You can choose to let them pass or turn them away."

"Does it work against social workers?"

He gave me a quizzical look. "Never occurred to me to ask. I don't suppose many dragons are plagued by social workers." Trimble swept up one of Nicholi's crayons, lying on the floor. Flipping over a page of Justin's graph paper, he started sketching. "Dragons evoke either their empress or their king to protect a hoard. I assume, since you will be evoking Yvess, the final rune will look something like this—"

The hexagon of Yvess, diamonds drawn inside. It looked familiar. No, I'd seen a pentagon, filled with interlocked triangles. Where? Scratched in dirt and overgrown by grass. At the base of Pancrizio's tower? I couldn't remember.

"What if it's a pentagon?" I asked.

"The five points of death?" Trimble shuddered. "Don't ever be foolish enough to step across a pentagon. That's the personal foil of Adrikhedon."

It must have been in *The Complete Book of Dragons,* because where else could I have seen Adrikhedon's rune? I didn't regularly visit dragons. I didn't need to, they seemed to find me.

Trimble handed me the scroll. "You can read Draconic?"

I silently scanned the spell, then nodded. Trimble narrowed his eyes in thought. Okay, so it was odd, but I refused to make a big deal of it. "Trimble, if I translated, could you cast this? It might be safer."

Trimble shifted uncomfortably and beads on the ends of his braids clacked. "I don't—I mean, I can't. Pancrizio is a sorcerer and I'm a wizard. Do you know the difference?"

I shook my head.

"He has magic in his blood, like a dragon, which allows him to handle dragon forged charms. I learn magic from books, and don't have the genetics to use the jewel. Pancrizio would overwhelm me in a moment, if Yvess didn't kill me first. You, however, have hidden talents."

"Very hidden."

Trimble laughed, and I envied his cheerfulness. "There's only one way to know if you can swim, Mimi. We have to throw you in water."

Water, or a dragon mire? I closed my eyes. I could feel Carlo breathing on the other side of the room, absorbed inhales, steady exhales, his gaze on my face. Nicholi whispered in the kitchen; if I wanted to, I could have heard the words. And the boys, honing blades and talking strategy in the garden shed, a tied knot of camaraderie. Far beyond us was the oblivious world, clanking along in the twenty-first century. Deep in the muck dragons stirred, heaving huge shoulders and stretching wings against the weight of slime. God, how swamp dragons smelled, rotted with greed. Around my neck the gem glowed hot, the purple bottomless and silky. At the jewel's edges, gold marred the stone, corroding the surface with a caustic clutch, leaving rough cracks. I opened my eyes. The gem's surface misted, steamy dampness drifting down the buttons of my shirt to the floor, seeking escape.

"Ready?" Trimble asked.

I shifted to get comfortable, squeezed my hands together in my lap, and closed my eyes. My heart pounded, each thump a flash of frightened light on the dark of my lids. Mom flitted like a ghost through my inner darkness. Whatever she'd told me, I thought with shame, I'd heard only by accident, too busy with reality to listen. The scent of Night Veil hung like an old calendar, pages turning, Mom's actions fluttering by too fast to understand. But her aroma clung, tenacious as her grip on my life.

"We need Night Veil," I said.

"Where is it?"

"The dresser. I'll get it."

When I came back, Trimble had balled-up wads of flash paper and arranged them with a box of matches around the hem of his robe. His black drawstring bag lay open and resting in his lap. I handed him the vial.

"If I start to go under, douse me with it." I sat down.

"You sure?"

"It's what Mom did." I swallowed. "I think."

I was terrified, absolutely tingling on the edge of the abyss. The sorcerer would lead me like a dumb puppy. If only teen boy invincibility was infectious. I took a peek at Carlo, who studied me with fascination, then I shut him out of my mind and raised the scroll.

"Draconiŭ y Draŭtox, sna rŭ chroot ...." I whispered.

Dragon Empress, I greet you ....

Yvess' silver blue eyes appeared through the page, considering me with reptilian cool, causing a riot of panic in my brain. My words faltered, and I sat paralyzed with fear. I must speak, not waste her time, annoy her. Struggling to bring the spell into focus, I stuttered on. *R—raise about this p—p—precious treasure ....*

The disk of gold, roots tickling, sank, buttery, into my skin. Then I felt his icy presence. Hair on my neck lifted and quivered with warning. "Come girl, you meddle where you can do nothing but die. Tell the children who prod you to play somewhere else." His Draconic was syrupy, like honey flowing over splintered wood.

" *... Arahm tss eirstatu laaft ...* "

Let those who seek to pass .... I drove forward over his voice, refusing to flinch.

Dots of delicate lavender appeared, suspended in the air between Trimble and me. My focus sharpened, willing them into the shape of a gauzy hexagon. If I could just add inner triangles—

With a snap, my head bent back, his hand pulling the weight of it down, my throat to the sky. Above me, his face snarled, the force of his breath ruffling the collar of my shirt. He roared a torrent of Latin, the words soaring and diving like crazed hawks, ripping at my spell with vicious beaks. He reached for my neck, his hand solid as ice. With clawed fingers he grabbed the amulet and heaved at the leather.

And I sank, deep into thrashing darkness, desperately

chasing each word of my spell, screaming as I caught them, hurling them against his onslaught ... *whisper ... your ... exalted ... name ... that ... I ... may ... be ... warned ...* I couldn't see the rune, but I could feel the prickle of its presence, swelling, becoming heavier.

"Carlo! Sit down for God's sake!" Trimble's voice was panicky.

A splash of peppery heat hit my neck, smelling of oily, cloying sweetness, and I knew, rather than felt, the sting of Night Veil. There was a small explosion and the scent of burnt paper. I could hear Trimble chanting something but he was far away, and I couldn't move .... *and ... rise ... with ....* My neck would break; any second, the unbearable pain as bones gave. The gold loop refused to yield against the taught leather. My mother's soldering held .... *your ... vengeance ....* Any moment my head would flop free, the vertebrae crushed as the leather cord yanked through my bones. Die for the spell or save my life. For Justin and Nicholi, I had to do better than die.

"*Morrtarr, dledz Pancrizio.*" I gasped the curse that willed the sorcerer's death, and felt a tremendous surge of power. I lifted my talons and raked across his face, then swung the back of my claws in a stunning blow to his head. He cried out, a sound like a furious crow, and he let go of the amulet.

I opened my eyes. Light hurt, making me squint. Trimble knelt before me holding Night Veil in one hand and his nose in the other. Carlo hovered behind him, pale with worry. Blood leaked between Trimble's fingers.

"Are you okay?" I whispered.

Trimble grinned. "Me? Are *you* okay?"

I throbbed, aching all over as though I had been beaten, my mind thick with exhaustion. I wanted to stare for an hour, quiet as Ms. Farr.

"I think so. I attacked and he let go."

My fingertips grazed the brush burn on my neck and I cringed at the sting, then I remembered talons and jerked my hand to my face. I must have dreamed claws. What a relief to see fingers.

"I failed, didn't I?"

Trimble stood and found Kleenex on the desk, and Carlo took the opportunity to crouch beside me, pressing my hand with sturdy warmth.

"Yeah, you failed," said Trimble. "But, gees you're strong. When he reached for the gem I thought we were dead, and then you backhanded him like a tennis ball." Trimble began to giggle, then to laugh, blood still trickling from his nose.

"An epic moment, I'm sure." I wasn't a bit impressed by my feeble fight. "What happened to your nose?"

"I was kneeling too close."

"Are you okay?"

"I'll recover." He found another Kleenex and threw the soaked one in the garbage. He couldn't seem to stop grinning.

"Why are you smiling?"

"Because this is going to be one hella-cool fight!"

I scowled. "Age of Dragons players are twisted."

Trimble laughed and Carlo shrugged an eloquent "Okay-by-me." I sighed and stood up, the sole keeper of the group's common sense.

Trimble handed me the cinnabar vial. "Keep this in your pocket, you might need it in a hurry."

I tucked the gem under my shirt and the vial in my jeans. "Next time, my strength won't surprise Pancrizio."

Trimble stood over me, still mopping his nose. "And it won't surprise you, either. Meanwhile, I think someone had better continue to guard you at night. No, not you, Carlo."

Chapter 18

Vedette lied, the vixen. That is not a human child she conceived and hid behind delicate features. I hover over the pretty head: dark rivers of hair, eyebrows thin and straight as slashes, mouth sweet as red grapes. The scent of Night Veil still clings to her, disturbing her dreams so that she turns and tosses. I long to crack the life out of her with my staff, but she would not die with the first blow, not with that blood in her veins. As we fought, the silly boy guarding the hall would be upon me, axe swinging, and I'd bloody my robe and barely escape with this body intact.

Whom did Vedette trick into fathering such a monster? Adrikhedon had the will for such a deception, but Vedette would never have had him, despite how hatred joined them. The others of his kind slept this last six hundred years. Besides, hers was no common dragon sire; this child carries the blood of royalty.

I drift to the likeness that hangs on the wall: Vedette, and that toad of a man she married. Was the poor toad cuckolded by an ice wyrm? It seems impossible that a mountain dragon would entangle himself in such human affairs, even to possess a woman of such beauty. Unless, of course, she showed the stone. No, that would have been far, far too risky. The stone laid bare in Yvess' realm would bring the empress herself, screaming down from the sky. I would have known, too, had the stone travelled; I was trapped within its setting. Yet the child is at least half dragon, no doubt can deny it. I have been made a fool by a little sorceress who could not cast beyond a middling spell. It is infuriating to be bested by such mediocrity.

Van Gees' painting of my tower leans against the wall near my feet. He made such a desolate ruin of art, Van Gees. Even the fields of sunflowers are dreary. This toppling tower was his elated depiction, I assume, of my demise. Ha! The dead have a way of returning when one least expects them. Vedette, for example, whose small hands grip at my throat with the scent of Night Veil. Where did the child get that vial? One that was buried, Adrikhedon swore, under the sea. The dragon betrayed me—nothing new in that. But did he give it to the child as a present? For five thousand years he has lived without generosity: it seems odd that a fancy for gifts would suddenly strike him. Was it a dragon's courtship offering? One is left with the absurd impression that Sovrano females are irresistible to dragons. Or the even more absurd idea that a half-dragon whelp stole such a prize from Adrikhedon's hoard. This bedroom is full of mysteries.

But the girl wakes and the dwarf who guards her senses danger: I must go. She will use the stone again, and I shall be ready. Far easier to kill her than to control her.

Chapter 19

At school on Monday Nicholi gave up Didoo without a struggle, kissing us both goodbye at Ms. Greer's door. I was as delighted as Ms. Greer appeared to be. I hoped she had lots of gold stars for her chart.

In a gesture of diplomacy, I set about to cook Mexican for Steve. I chose a shoulder roast with a good sized bone, fresh cilantro, plump scallions, Serrano chili peppers, and dried pinto beans. Steve was out when I arrived, and Ms. Farr dozed in her chair. Relieved not to fight about it, I wrapped Didoo in the Chilkat robe and set him on the kitchen table.

As I sliced meat into cubes, I thought about the bills. Last night I'd paid the mortgage, light, and gas, but the phone would have to wait until my paycheck came. Water and garbage bills would be arriving soon. Which would we be better off without: water, garbage service, or the phone? I rolled meat in a mixture of pepper, garlic powder, and cumin, and then set it to sauté. Then I prepared broth, throwing cilantro stems, pork bone, onion, and oregano into a quart of water. If I didn't feed Justin's friends I might be able to afford all of my utilities. I imagined telling Case, Larry, Paul, and Trimble that they couldn't stay for dinner anymore. I imagined selling Steve my gemstone; no chance, now that I knew what it was. Then I set about peeling onions, tears slipping from my burning eyes.

Snapping the lid on the pressure cooker, I flicked on the heat. When the broth was done, I'd be back to cook beans. Meanwhile, it was time for Ms. Farr's tea. I put Didoo-in-robe under my arm and went to her room.

"Hey, Ms. Farr." Easing into the chair beside her, I laid a hand on her hair and stroked the thin gray wisps. "How are you?"

She opened her eyes and that big, round gaze lovingly traveled my face. I held out a cup of tea but she ignored it, pointing a shaky finger toward the pond.

The pond was steel gray, placid and cold as a polished blade. At the roots of the cedars, overhanging branches reflected in the watery universe. The waterline had crept to just yards from her window, swallowing tufts of brown grass in the strip of unmown lawn. I could have sworn that the house tilted forward to meet the pond, as though they were lovers.

Lately, I didn't have much trust in lovers.

"Does the water always come up this high?" I set a saucer in her lap and closed her fingers around the cup. She didn't answer.

"Ms. Farr, is this dangerous?"

Purple black clouds drifted overhead, making the pond's reflection dark. She sipped her tea, pensive. In the background I could hear the shrill, far off shriek of the pressure cooker. The air was tinged with the scent of cumin. Underneath us, the house gave a deep groan and settled into the earth. Goose bumps rose on my skin, cold from a damp that seeped through the floor. For once, I wanted Steve to come home. I peeled the coverlet from her bed and wrapped it around her knees, then went to the living room.

Lights were off and the room was empty. I sat backwards on Steve's smelly couch, waiting for him, my arm around the thick bulk of Didoo and blanket. In the soft light I could make out shadows of Ms. Farr's artifacts. The knobs on the fertility goddess' head were rubbed smooth by darkness. The black eye sockets of the bronze mask seemed deeper in the dimness. The Aztec knife—the Aztec knife—was missing!

I rose off the couch, hurrying to the shelf. The African spear was gone, one of the Grecian pots, and the miniature portrait of a Medieval lady. Thank God he hadn't sold the Chilkat robe.

Frantic, I spun in a circle, whirling with fury and mistrust. A dealer who sells to museums should be a man in a well-cut suit and an avant-garde tie who speaks with good grammar. He should smell of aftershave instead of swamp mold, and have cufflinks on his sleeves instead of grease stains. I paced the shabby living room rug. But then, I'd never met a museum supplier before. Maybe they all looked hideous and threatened people. If I sold Steve my gem he might go away to Mexico and leave Ms. Farr alone. It was almost worth it. He might be a better match for the son-of-a-bitch sorcerer as well.

I paced through Ms. Farr's room to the kitchen, where I plunked Didoo down on the counter and grabbed the solid comfort of a cutting board. As the pressure cooker steamed, I chopped chilies and cussed Steve. He obviously wasn't stupid, as far as IQ, but I couldn't understand how someone with so few ethics and such a dearth of purpose came to be in custody of Ms. Farr's affairs. He was Mr. Eastman's nephew, which explained all. Mr. Eastman, who was too busy with important things to pay attention to Ms. Farr's interests. I had to negotiate a truce with Steve, somehow.

I yanked the pressure cooker off the stove and quick-released steam with the back of a spoon. Here I was, taking the money from her artifacts and spending it: thirty dollars for lunch today. And Steve would eat most of it. It infuriated me. In a frenzy, I washed beans, strained broth, and refilled the pressure cooker. Calm down, Mimi. There was nothing I could do about Steve. It was not going to help if I totally lost it with him.

Twenty minutes later the beans were ready to refry, fragrant with the broth they'd boiled in, and my hands weren't shaking anymore. I sautéed celery, then added pork, cilantro, cumin, and a large handful of hot peppers. In a half hour the pork would be simmered tender to the point of melting in the mouth. I had time to make Steve sopaipillas. You know what, Dad? Diplomacy wasn't easy. It was a strain to set the table for someone I despised.

Steve's timing, as always, was perfect. He wandered in as I lifted the last frying golden disc out of hot oil and sprinkled on sugar. He scowled at Didoo, but I didn't care what he thought about the ratty bear dressed in the precious robe he'd fought so hard to protect. If he wanted cleanliness, he could vacuum his hairy couch, or cut his disgusting fingernails.

"What's that?" he asked, waving toward the platter.

"Sopaipillas."

"You're amazing." Something akin to admiration, with just a hint of sleaze, crossed his bony face. He reached to pinch a Sopaipillas, but I batted his hand with my wooden spoon and he jerked it back.

"The pond is rising," I said.

The tip of his tongue slipped out and wet his upper lip. "Have you ever thought about going to Mexico?"

"No. I'm too busy for vacations." I dumped oil out of the frying pan, wiped the iron clean with a paper towel, and set the pan back on the stove. While my back was turned, Steve grabbed and devoured a Sopaipillas. I grit my teeth and ignored him, tossing a tortilla into the hot pan. "What about the pond?"

He gave a backward glance at Didoo, sucking sugar off his fingers. "Winter, rain, wet ... you know, nature."

I searched his face, all shadows and sunken cheeks, no humanity. "You're not worried?"

"Worried? Why? When's lunch?"

"Because water is yards from the house!"

He didn't answer. He just licked his long fingers and watched me flip tortillas.

It was impossible to keep the irritation out of my voice. "You sold the Aztec knife."

"Is that what's eating you?" His gaze wandered to my throat and his green eye closed, studying the leather cord of the Wyrmstone with just his squinted blue eye. "Have you thought about my offer?"

I lifted my spatula, blade toward his skeletal chest. "Forget it, Steve. Go get Ms. Farr, it's time to eat." The snarl on his face curdled my blood, but he backed away and left.

Ms. Farr ate three quarters of a burrito and two sopaipillas. Steve sprinkled ten shakes of Tabasco sauce over his mountain of pork and beans—the spices already so hot they made my mouth glow—and ate everything else. Every last fiery bean.

Leaving that afternoon, I passed the shelf of dwindling objects, Didoo tucked under my arm, and worried that I hadn't hidden the Chilkat robe well enough. It lay on the bottom of Ms. Farr's chest, pressed to the cedar floor by books, papers, and a few spare clothes. I gave it a fifty-fifty chance of being there tomorrow. It was the best I could do; it wasn't mine to take home. I dreaded what would happen to Nicholi's cooperation if it vanished.

I forgot the parent-teacher conference with Ms. Greer until Nicholi didn't show at the roundabout, and Justin, alone and anxious, ran to my approaching car.

"Where's Nicholi?" he huffed, face drawn.

"Oh! Ms. Greer's room, we have a conference. Could you do homework in the library for half an hour?"

Looking relieved, Justin slung his heavy knapsack over one shoulder and lumbered into the elementary school.

Ms. Greer had restyled her straight, blonde hair such that it hung in a chic diagonal over one eye. Her navy suit coat swooped out and then in, showing off her narrow waist, and a substantial span of her slender legs were exposed by her short, navy blue skirt. She had a fluffy pink scarf at her neck.

"Sit down, Mimi. How are you? I'm so pleased we could meet." She rearranged her papers nervously. "First of all, do you have any questions for me, any particular concerns about Nicholi?"

"No, he's always been a good student."

Nicholi, who had greeted me long enough to get a hug and his bear, occupied himself with a spelling game on the classroom computer.

"Yes, he's doing very well academically. He tested this week at a fifth grade reading level, and his math is two grades ahead. He also seems to have calmed considerably." She gave an approving smile, and I tried to keep my expression neutral as I thought about the hidden Chilkat robe. "I wondered, would you consider moving him up a year?"

"Skip a grade?" Great timing: as if the child wasn't under enough pressure.

"Yes, now, before the school year is too far advanced."

"Why?"

"First grade isn't much of a challenge for him. Emotionally it's been a tough year, but given how well he responds to behavior modification I think we could provide the structure he'd need." The whiteness of her beautiful smile seemed to lend credence to this outlandish idea.

"But he'd be in with seven- and eight-year-olds. He's too young."

This had to be the dumbest idea Ms. Greer had ever had. It made star charts look genius.

"It would be an adjustment, certainly, but look at his work." She held out a book report on *The Complete Book of*

Dragons, bound with a homemade book cover and containing several essays, including ones on the temperature of fire and the anatomy of human vs. dragon eyes. I suppose this was unusual in first grade, but it was pure Nicholi. Ms. Greer appeared to be mistaking my brother's looming fears for academic sophistication.

I pointed to the fire essay. "These facts are from Wikipedia."

"Are you saying he copied without understanding?"

"No, he wrote it, and he understands, it's just … "

It's just that he is a little boy who copes by collecting facts, like other boys might collect stamps or worms, and that made him seem wise beyond his years. Not to mention that he lived with siblings who thought that dragons were about to attack the modern world. "He's still quite immature in many ways."

"Oh, I know that. We *did* go through the bear episode together, didn't we?" She gave me a conspirator's nod, as if Didoo were about immaturity, and not about love, loss, and protection in the face of terror. "But he might relate better to older children. Certainly he'd be less bored in class."

This was a terrible idea, but it was hard to articulate rational reasons. "But we're fighting the Sorcerer Pancrizio right now," I might say, or, "Can we wait until the dragon war is over?"

I settled for, "No. Keep him right where he is."

"Why? I'm offering quite an opportunity."

"I—I can't say why. I just don't think he'd be happy."

"Well, I think it would be best for him. We still have some weeks before Christmas. We could move him right after the holidays."

She looked superb in her determination. Contempt for my poor judgment made her cheeks flush pink, to match her scarf.

Then she brought out ample evidence of Nicholi's intellect. He had mastered addition and subtraction. His fat, wobbly numbers tumbled across the page wildly, but added up correctly. His spelling tests had equally poor handwriting, but the scores, written in red at the top, were 100%. He'd even cut neatly on the line when making his paper Thanksgiving turkey. I gathered this was important.

I half listened when she took out his standardized reading scores, my heart desperate for Mom. Ms. Greer pointed to bar graphs and compared percentiles while I, dazed and churning inside, remembered the picture Nicholi drew to place under Mom's memorial stone. Stick figures of Mom and Nicholi side by side, round faces smiling, blunt stick arms fused together. They stood in a white bubble, a dazzling circle of rainbow, brilliant in crayon colors, all the way around them. And every inch of paper outside of the rainbow was colored black. If Mom were alive, perhaps the world would not be closing in on Nicholi, and academics would seem more important.

"Here's your copy of his report card. Any questions?" She checked her watch briefly, letting me know that, with other parents waiting, questions were allowed but not encouraged.

I rose to go. "No, thanks. Come on, Nicholi."

Nicholi, bear at his feet, sat joined with the screen in *Spelling Adventureland*.

"Turn it off, honey, we have to go."

Nicholi gave no sign of moving, too motionless even for super slo-mo. Ms. Greer walked over and clicked off the monitor. "Goodbye Nicholi. See you tomorrow."

Boy and bear ambled with dragging feet out of Ms. Greer's classroom. "Why does *i* have to come before *e*?" he asked, as we rounded the corner by the library.

"I have no idea."

"Why doesn't Ms. Greer like me in her class?"

I figured he'd listen in on the conference. Perhaps he was right. Perhaps our family's chaotic, imaginative, grief-torn world overwhelmed Ms. Greer, even though she didn't know the half of it. "I think she wants you to be challenged in school."

"I don't like second graders. Smudge called me a baby and pushed me off the swings. I don't wanna be in class with a Smudge."

"Smudge?"

"That's what Didoo calls him. Anyway, Didoo likes Ms. Greer."

"Really?" What a surprise. I wondered what Didoo saw in her. Well, I guess that settled it. I put an arm around Nicholi's moping, slumped shoulders. "If you don't want to go, you don't have to. I'll just say no, okay?"

"Good." He took a few skipping steps to the library, flung the door open, and sang out at top volume, "Justin! Time to go!" If I could face down Ms. Whitting, I could face down Ms. Greer. Right then, however, I had to face down the annoyed librarian.

Pulling onto our street a half an hour later, I saw the

procession of neatly lined-up garbage cans and my heart sank. My life simply did not include remembering to put out the garbage on Monday. It was as though the jam-packed can, almost too heavy to drag and certainly too full to put more garbage in, was someone else's problem. Unfortunately, garbage collection wasn't one of those things that ran smoothly without me.

I crept down the street, swerving around kids playing in the brisk November afternoon. I edged to our driveway and looked enviously at the cans by the laurel-less clear-cut. If I didn't pay the bill it wouldn't matter: they'd never get the chance to pick up our garbage anyway. Then I recognized our can, vacant, knocked on its side, next to Ms. Rossi's.

My first thought was Duke, who came back to say he was sorry and took the garbage out. No, Duke was dead. I wanted him alive, even if I never kissed him again, even if he never had intended to propose to me, even though he and I were doomed from the start. My eyes teared up and I suppressed a sob.

"What's wrong?" asked Justin. But he had little sympathy to waste on Duke, I was sure.

I swiped off tears and parked the car. "Did you take the garbage out?"

"Have I ever taken the garbage out?" Justin unlatched Nicholi's car seat and grabbed his backpack. "Carlo did it, I saw him from my bedroom window."

"Carlo?"

"Yeah, he's been doing it for weeks." Justin jumped out of the car, Nicholi trailing behind, then slammed the door.

I should be accustomed to Carlo, appearing in holes in my competence, darning those holes without effort, and then vanishing unthanked. I should feel grateful. But I couldn't bear being a hopeless charity case. And he couldn't just step into the void Duke left.

That had been the issue all along, I realized as I unlocked the front door; from the moment I saw Carlo I felt an idiotic desire to attract him. My unfaithful heart was embarrassing. My love was ridiculous. Duke wasn't right for me, but I found plenty of excuses to fall in love with him. I was *not* going to do that again with Carlo.

I let my brothers in, and then stomped down the driveway. Snorting like one of Justin's Minotaurs, I dragged the cans rumbling and bouncing down the gravel driveway and heaved them into the garden shed. Next week I would remember my own dang garbage. If I was still alive.

After dinner, I spread Dad's cookbooks on the living room floor and began planning Thanksgiving.

We'd never had Thanksgiving without Dad. I wanted to make him proud. And what remained of our family badly needed Jovel comfort.

The turkey, of course, was not to be tampered with. I would make it as Dad always had: fresh rosemary and lemon halves stuffed in the cavity, roasted under a butter-soaked cheese cloth, breast down to keep it moist. If I was lucky with dice, Justin might even help me flip it over halfway through so the breast would brown.

In Dad's kitchen, Thanksgiving side dishes followed two unbreakable rules: the food could never have been served before at a Jovel Thanksgiving, and the recipe had to be intriguingly odd. Ideas were stolen from the most famous Northwest chefs—baby green salad with blood oranges and shaved parmesan, crispy corn meal onion rings with sour cream dip—i.e. nothing the Pilgrims would recognize. We had giblet gravy made with Dad's chicken stock, of course, because how else would we drown moist white slices of turkey? But everything else was a feast of discovery.

Case, whose mother died years ago and whose father worked at night, had been a fixture at Thanksgiving for seven years. Larry snuck away from the chaos of ten siblings and arrived just as we sat down to eat. Paul's mother embarrassed Paul mercilessly by calling every year to make sure he was welcome, protesting that we wouldn't want such a bother as Paul on a family day. "We can't possibly eat all of this without Paul!" Dad would say. And Trimble, whose parents preferred that he spend the day with his own family, usually arrived halfway through the meal, guilty but excited. Dad kept a plate warm in the oven for him.

This year, planning the vast, most outlandish spread of the year was in my hands. Hopefully war with Pancrizio's dragons would wait. Nervously, I swept Nicholi's dirty socks off a patch of living room rug, flopped onto my belly, and searched for untasted delights. Some I rejected as too weird (frog legs in fava bean purée), others were too expensive (Dungeness crab with pomegranate), and others seemed unlikely to be eaten, even by the adventurous Age of Dragons crew (wild mushrooms and chicken livers with spiced pecans). But roasted yams with caramelized mango looked promising.

I chose eight things that would make a curious banquet and drew up a shopping list. I was searching for unusual desserts when Justin loped in, shoved aside books, and plunked onto the couch.

"I want the party to camp here. We need to relieve Larry at night, and we need a war conference. And you've got to try again with the Wyrmstone." His manner—elfin eyes burning through his sheet of bangs, barbarian size dominating the sofa—made me feel pushed around.

"You just had a party, remember? It ended with you in the police station." I opened a book of homemade ice creams and slowly flipped pages.

"Not a party, *the* party, the A.O.D group. We have a serious problem with dragons and a sorcerer, remember?"

Citrus meringue with Bing cherry ice cream. There were frozen Bings at QFC grocery. I'd put Dad's ice cream base in the refrigerator tonight.

"Are you listening, Mimi?"

"Yeah, I'm listening. What do you think about rhubarb bread pudding with strawberry sorbet?"

"What in the heck is the matter with you?"

I put aside one chef and reached for another. "Don't you need Thanksgiving? Don't you want *something* to be normal?"

He gawked at me as if I were written in Draconic. When he'd recovered his power of speech he said, "Yeah, I want Thanksgiving. You know how much I love Dad's feasts. But what are you doing about the Wyrmstone?"

Despite my effort to control myself, I laughed.

"Doing? I'm dreaming about blood and yellow slime. I'm wearing a piece of jewelry and thinking I'm going to die." My tone sounded crazy, even to myself. Palms down on a cookbook, I tried to collect my sanity. "I'm begging a dragon empress to save me. I'm splashing around in Night Veil as if I knew what I was doing." I was on my feet now, yelling. "I'm turning into Mom, that's what I'm doing. And if I don't cook, I'll lose it completely. So get out of my face and let me plan Thanksgiving, because cooking is the only thing that gives me any peace of mind."

Justin held his breath, stunned. When I didn't say anything more, he let out a long, slow exhale. Turning away, he swept *A Handbook of Weapons: the Brutal, Subtle, and Enchanted* off the floor. Trembling violently, I watched him page through the book.

"We'll roll for it, let fate decide." His voice was gentle, as if he cajoled little Nicholi.

I looked down at a cookbook, dropped at my feet, fallen open to a recipe for white chocolate soufflé. Soufflés collapse if anything bumps the oven, which was likely on a crowded Thanksgiving day.

"I need to cook." I sat down. "And not with five boys camped in my living room." Just for a little while, things would be normal again. Plain, dull, reality. Ugly as it was with Child Protective Services and squabbles with judges and teachers, reality tasted sweet right now.

Justin flipped through his book, studying enchanted bracers, helms, and hammers. Finally he said, "I'll do Thanksgiving dishes and hand in my homework. I'll release Carlo from his bargain, take out the garbage, and clean my room."

Holy Moly, he was offering everything he had. "You mean a straight across deal?"

Justin stared at Gemini's Lance, a steel pole with a nasty hooked blade. *This legendary weapon*, said the caption, *nicknamed 'The Gemini Solution', makes the user appear as twins. The opponent is drawn into attacking the false fighter while the real fighter lies in ambush. Like all legendary weapons it is extraordinarily difficult to destroy.*

Justin said, "No, I mean roll, winner takes all." I guess it's hard to negotiate a compromise when you have invincible, indestructible options.

Justin wins: homework remains in the hands of fate, Carlo runs up a heck of a gas bill taxiing Justin around, and I do the Thanksgiving dishes. Plus, I would cook a feast while surrounded by an encampment of teen boys with pickaxes, sledgehammers, spell books, and poisons. Perhaps while being strangled by a sorcerer or eaten by a dragon.

I win: Carlo is free, Justin hands in his homework, his room is clean, the garbage goes out, and the Thanksgiving dishes are not my problem. And for a little while, just long enough to feel like my feet are back under me, I can pretend that this hot, light weapon that I'm terrified to even look at right now, is just a necklace. I could see why people became gamblers: the lure of paradise inches from your grasp. A fifty percent chance looks big through the lens of winner-takes-all. But then, fate and I hadn't been getting along very well lately.

"No."

"Mimi, we have to act, *now*."

"Pancrizio is not bothering us." Perhaps if I believed hard enough, it would be true.

"Don't be an idiot." His way of snarling 'idiot' made it into a swear word.

"The last time I acted I almost died. Don't push me, Justin, I'm standing at the edge." I stacked cookbooks. "You have a doctor's appointment tomorrow."

Justin crossed his arms over his thick chest and glowered with barbarian displeasure. "Why? I'm not sick."

"We're about to lose our health insurance. You need a checkup and your teen shots." And Marcella's condom lecture, not to mention that I plan to corner Dr. Harvey and push him again to tell me what he knows about Mom.

"*Shots?*" He dug in his jeans pocket for dice. "You've got that friggin' Wyrmstone around your neck and you're worried about *shots?*" He shook the die in his cupped hands.

"Justin, you need to see Dr. Harvey."

He spilled the die from his hand and it rolled across the couch, tumbled onto the rug, and whacked into a miniature plastic troll. A four.

"Crap!" He stood and raked hair out of his eyes. "You are so friggin' stubborn. You have to do everything your own stupid way, but you're clueless. You know Mom failed because she fought alone. She should have trusted us. Now you're acting just like her. Why did fate have to leave me with *you?*"

Then he stomped to his room and slammed the door.

Perhaps, before he ate me, a dragon would answer that question for both of us.

Numb and exhausted, I re-filed cookbooks on Dad's kitchen shelf, deliberately distracting myself from the silence in Justin's room. I had slammed a lot of doors when I was Justin's age, but this was the first time a door had ever been slammed at me. "If you didn't hate me now and then, I wouldn't be doing my job," Dad used to say with philosophical calm. I think translating at the United Nations gave him a worldwide perspective. Exactly where, in the spectrum of humanity's crises, would Dad place our problems?

Nicholi wandered in, Didoo tucked down his shirt front, a filthy pink bear nose peeking out of Nicholi's collar. He slipped a hand in mine. "Didoo and I love you," he said.

I kissed Nicholi's forehead. "Tell Didoo 'thanks'."

"Let's read *Brave Ant* tonight," he said.

Thank God, no dragons. Brave Ant, who has, in his abnormally prolonged insect childhood, met and prevailed over every disaster known to ant-kind. We all take solace from the heroes who are blessed by fate.

Chapter 20

Tuesday morning there was a note on Ms. Farr's front door. From the narcissistic lack of a signature, I figured it was from Steve.

"I won't be here today. Leave me a phone number. I need to call you about Thanksgiving."

As I entered, my gaze went automatically to Ms. Farr's shelves, straining to see if anything had been sold. The Aztec knife must have paid well: nothing else had been pressed into sale. Greatly relieved, I dragged groceries to Ms. Farr's room and set them on the bed. The Chilkat robe, thank God, was still in her cedar chest. I snatched it up and hugged it. Too bad I didn't have a 'Gemini Solution' to twin the robe, let Steve cart off and sell the duplicate while Didoo kept the original.

I placed a robed Didoo in Ms. Farr's lap and kissed her cheek. "How are you?"

She reached for my hand, lacing thin fingers through mine. Her eyes didn't leave the pond, so I squatted to her eye level. The pond spread like a sheet of warped glass, rippling with light rain drops, a vast pool from the far bank all the way to Ms. Farr's foundation. Muddy water slapped against concrete block as though demanding to be let in.

I looked at her, alarmed.

"Does Steve know? Has he told Mr. Eastman?"

She continued to study the water, motionless, as a cat in a window might watch a prowling pit bull. That must be where Steve went off to, why he left the note. I felt the floor; the rug was dry. It was hard to say how far under the foundation water seeped. I would call and leave a message for Eve Tavick so she could inform Mr. Eastman.

I gave Ms. Farr's hand a squeeze. "It's you and me, today. I'm making sea bass in Thai red sauce, and a green papaya salad." I let go of her hand and her fingers went to her cheek where I had kissed her. "Let's eat in here so we can keep an eye on the pond." I hauled groceries to the kitchen, and then looked on my cell phone for Eve Tavick's number. No one answered, so I left a message to call me right away.

Red sauce made in the summer is divine enough to serve to the empress. In winter, tomatoes are not as sweet and tend to be mealy, but stewed in spices they still make an outstanding dish. I peeled tomatoes, red debris clinging to my fingers. It reminded me of cooking with blood. Whose blood, Mom? Blood drawn from sacrifice, as with the Aztec knife? I shuddered and washed scraps of peel off my hands. So like Mom; even when she haunts me, she's bizarre. I set the tomatoes to simmer in chilies, cilantro, and white pepper, and when the ingredients began to blend I turned off the gas and put on a lid.

I washed rice, wondering what Mr. Eastman would do about Ms. Farr's sinking house. I couldn't bear to think of her in a nursing home, staring at the walls. Maybe the water rose every year, no big deal. Maybe the pond would retreat again, having risen for its annual lover's kiss.

I poured hot water in the rice cooker. Once again, I wished Steve was here: great irony! I actually wanted his phone number in case of emergency. Hilarious that I considered him so reliable. I clicked on the rice cooker.

As I sliced green beans, papaya, and cabbage, I realized that Steve's note said he wanted to talk about Thanksgiving. Maybe he wasn't aware of the flood. I tried Eve Tavick on my cell phone again, leaving a second message. But that was silly; Steve couldn't live here and not be aware that the pond encroached on the back door. He wasn't so sluggish that he'd let his livelihood sink, even if he didn't love Ms. Farr.

I poured lime juice in a salad dressing jar, then added Thai peppers, sugar, fish sauce, and garlic. Dad always said that Thai food was perfect because it contained stimulation for every taste sense: sour, hot, sweet, salty, and bitter. But Dad went beyond taste. He cooked with instinctive flashes of genius, straight from his soul. Dad pretended he hated fantasy and imagination. "Spells, swords, and grandiose delusions just kill the peace," he'd joked. "I will not tolerate such heroics in my Barcalounger." Then he'd swept Justin's Age of Dragons miniatures off his armchair. But he didn't fool me; his cooking was magical. I shook the dressing and poured it over green papaya salad.

Dinner prepped, I brought Ms. Farr her tea. She huddled in her chair, shoulders hunched and eyes wide, a portrait of worry, hugging Didoo to her chest with the fringe of the

Chilkat robe tickling the floor. I found my Mom's sweater folded in her wooden chest and draped it around her, then handed her a tea cup. Hopefully Steve would come back before I had to pick up my brothers. I didn't feel comfortable leaving her here alone.

As the tea and sweater warmed her, she began to relax, and she watched with interest as I set lunch, aromatic with lime and fish sauce, on the coffee table. I handed her a fork and she scooted forward. Leaning over the table, she began to eat. With chuckles and chortles she ate everything, every last grain of rice, and took a second serving of salad from the bowl. Then she gave the smile we cooks cook for.

"I'm so glad you liked it. Thai is your favorite, huh?"

She leaned back with a satisfied sigh. Well, Steve wouldn't be eating Mexican for awhile. If he was going to sell her precious artifacts for groceries, he was going to eat what she liked.

Back in the kitchen I washed up, watching salamanders scuttle nervously around the feeder, fretting among the half-eaten slugs. I'd delay as long as possible, but if Steve didn't return soon I'd be forced to leave Ms. Farr alone.

By the time I finished the dishes dusk grayed the trees around the pond, but there was still no sign of him. I checked the water line. With all the rain, the water had risen another inch. I shook her shoulder gently. "Ms. Farr?"

She woke, sweet in her sleepiness.

"I'm going to pick my brothers up from school. I left my home number and cell number by the kitchen phone. Call me if you need me, okay?"

She didn't answer, but it was the best I could do.

"Do you put yourself to bed?"

Again, her bright, warm gaze, but no answer.

"Call me. Please call me, if anything happens." I gave her a hug and walked reluctantly out the door.

~

Justin looked sour as he stood waiting, buffeted occasionally by bumps from Nicholi, who hopped around him on one foot.

"Do I really have to get shots?" he asked, as he climbed into the car. I wondered if my barbarian, who swung a sledgehammer with such ease, was afraid of needles.

"I don't know, it's just a physical."

He studied passing scenery as Nicholi said an effusive hello to Didoo.

When kisses and snuggles were over, Nicholi announced, "Ms. Greer made me visitolate second grade."

So much for having a say in Nicholi's schooling. Nicholi's face, buried in Didoo's singed fur, was hard to read in the rearview mirror, so I couldn't tell if he was as angry about this as I was.

"The teacher's Ms. Blue, and she said everyone had to be niceish to me, even Smudge."

"How did it go?"

"They had a beetle in an aquarium. Ms. Blue called it a Ground Beetle." Nicholi and Didoo rubbed noses.

"Oh?"

"So, did you know that there are over five million kinds of beetles? In Egypt they have a beetle god named Kehpri."

"Ms. Greer let you on the internet?"

Nicholi held Didoo up to the window. "Yup, she said grownup second graders get to go to the library and look things up on Wikipedia."

The sneaky little fashion snark. "So, what do you think about second grade?"

Nicholi and Didoo considered each other. "Smudge is uber-awful, I have Wikipedia at home, and there's Ground Beetles in Mom's garden."

I laughed aloud. That's what Ms. Greer got for messing with a smart kid. Her determination was daunting, though: tough as a legendary weapon. For Nicholi's sake, I couldn't let her push us around.

As we entered Dr. Harvey's office, Becky called out a bright, "Hello, Jovels!" Nicholi established himself beside Becky at the desk, little fingers on the spare keyboard. Justin flopped into a chair and patiently examined the rug.

"This expires Monday," said Becky, scanning my insurance card.

"I know."

I had to ask Mr. Eastman for health insurance. Being an adult seemed to entail endless unwanted confrontations. I should have taken Assertiveness Training instead of An Introduction to the Wider Uses of Unusual Vegetables.

Marcella was fast in calling Justin back, putting a mothering hand on his thick forearm and sweeping him out of the waiting room. Now was the moment to plot a path around

Dr. Harvey's ethics. All my life he'd been a towering figure, respected and beloved, so no tactic seemed right: tricking, bullying, or deceiving. And I didn't dare be honest. I sat in anxious silence, head in my hands.

I was still deliberating when I heard uproarious male laughter. Justin and Dr. Harvey burst out the door to the back office, both laughing so hard they could hardly walk. "Well, here he is, then, healthy as a horse, and twice as smart." Dr. Harvey biffed Justin on the shoulder. "Take care, young man. I don't suppose I'll see much of you 'til next year. Don't get any taller or you'll look down on my bald spot."

"Goodbye." Justin reached to shake the old, familiar hand. "Thanks a lot."

"My pleasure." He turned to go.

It was now or never; I'd just have to trust to instinct. I stood up. "Could I see you for a minute, Dr. Harvey?"

"Of course."

He didn't even glance at his watch. "How can I help you?" he asked, once we were in the sanctuary of his exam room.

"Is everything … ah … okay … with Justin and Elina?"

His smile flattened to a closed line. "I assure you there's nothing to worry about. Give it a year or two, and we'll talk again."

He sat on the edge of the exam table, hands folded patiently, while I struggled to finesse my next question. He had such a gentle face, born to save lives.

"The Wyrmstone is dangerous, isn't it?" I blurted out.

He frowned. "Are you hearing voices? Seeing things?"

"No." My lie was immediate and instinctive: a hand jerked

out of the fire. "But Mom buried it because she was afraid of it, didn't she?"

He smoothed creases from his white coat. "Your mother loved you very much. Everything she did, she did out of love for you and your brothers. Her actions were strange, but her motives were absolutely clear."

Bargained me away out of love? Kept secrets, mistrusted, hid what would protect us, and kept us ignorant about the threat. Love did that? I stared at him, looking for a chink in his ethics, a ploy, a crack I could peek through to see what he knew. He might know why I was chosen for the stone. He might know how Mom planned to destroy it. He might have even had forewarning of her accident. I had nothing to appeal to but his compassion.

"Please," I begged. "I know the stone had something to do with their death. I'm frightened."

His eyes teared up and his jaw tightened. "I can't," he said. "Please don't ask again."

If only I could cling to his white coat, throw myself on his mercy, dissolve into tears and tell all. But I didn't dare. Distraught, I spun around and headed for the door.

"Wait, Massima, I know you're losing your insurance. If your family needs me, there won't be a bill."

I couldn't tell him: the next time we needed medical care, it would be too late. I kept on walking, and he didn't stop me.

Chapter 21

The day before Thanksgiving dawned windy and wild. Branches hit the roof as I tried to find my bathrobe in Mom's and Dad's closet. If we lost power I was sunk; the sauces and dishes I had planned to cook ahead would be doomed, and Thanksgiving would be reduced to whatever I could cook on Thanksgiving morning. Not to mention the food that would spoil in a warm fridge. I only had half a day as it was; I'd leave Ms. Farr's early because Justin and Nicholi came home at noon for the holidays. And Nicholi would likely play under my feet and hang on my legs all afternoon. I could only move so fast, dragging an alligator.

I woke the boys and made breakfast, listening to the radio. Due to flooding, schools were closed in outlying Snohomish County. School busses would be an hour late in north Seattle, Bellevue, Kirkland, and Kenmore. The police requested that drivers treat all nonfunctioning stoplights as four way stops. The radio DJ cheerfully reminded us to have flashlights and extra water at hand.

What an absolutely lousy stroke of luck; a major storm the day before my Thanksgiving solo. Dad would have made the feast happen. Nothing ever stood in the way of Thanksgiving for Dad.

A few minutes after seven the phone rang and I recognized Steve's low croak. "Don't come over for a few days. My uncle's taking the old lady to some relative's house. He'll bring her back Monday."

"Which relative?" I asked.

He snorted. "I don't know. Who cares?"

I cared, a lot. I was glad Ms. Farr had family willing to take her in. Hopefully they were kind and loved her. "What about the water at the foundation?"

"It rises and falls, no big deal."

I didn't believe him. Rationally, there was no reason why this couldn't be true, but then, Steve's and my relationship had little to do with 'rational.' Well, at least she had relatives if her house went under.

"So—" He breathed into the phone and I instinctively shifted the receiver away from my ear. "I'm going to Mexico."

I was tempted to say, "Who cares?" but I restrained myself.

"Do you want to go with me?"

I yanked the phone down and gawped at the holes in the earpiece. He had to be abso-frigging nuts. Whatever gave him the impression that I would go anywhere with him? Putting the receiver back to my ear, I mustered a fortifying ounce of tact.

"I have other obligations." Said with only a sprinkle of disgust.

To my overwhelming relief he hung up, finishing the conversation.

Justin stomped into the kitchen, uncombed, untucked, and only partially buttoned. He flung himself into a chair at the kitchen table.

"How come we don't have the day off, too? How does Snohomish rate?" he grumbled.

Pulling myself together, I set four slices of cinnamon toast and a large glass of orange juice in front of him. The burden of going to school for three hours that morning didn't dampen his appetite. He crunched down the first slice in three bites.

"Did you think any more about having the A.O.D party move in for the holidays?" he mumbled, mouth half full. "I'm still willing to roll—dishes, homework, garbage, release Carlo, and a clean room." He arched his usually glowering eyebrows, highlighting the irresistible nature of this deal.

I was getting all kinds of offers this morning. Why didn't fate send me bids to pay my bills, or to kill my sorcerer, or fulfill Mom's promise to Yvess? Justin tried to catch my eye, but I escaped into dicing tomatoes on the cutting board.

Justin must have sensed he was making no headway, because he changed tactics. "The whole of Seattle will burn, Mimi. Don't you have any sense of responsibility?"

I turned my back and broke six eggs into a bowl, beating them to a froth with a fork, wishing he and his question would just go away. Did we have a wisp of a chance against what threatened us? Grating cheese, I explored the far reaches of my wits for a response. Still searching, I plopped a dollop of sour cream into the eggs. It floated precariously on the bubbly yellow surface, and then sunk. I folded in cheese and tomatoes, shook in a dash of dried basil, then poured the batter into a skillet.

"Roll for it. Let the dice have a say," said Justin.

I might withstand the onslaught of meddling teachers and vindictive CPS workers. I might muddle through our financial problems and dodge Steve's horrid sliminess. We might even survive the decisions of Justin's dice. But I had no talent for wielding great power through dragon stones. I didn't want to confront Pancrizio again. I'd do it when I was forced to, and no sooner.

"If I lose, it will be my last dice roll, ever," said Justin.

My jaw dropped. In fact, I almost dropped the skillet as I spun around. "Really?"

Justin hesitated, but only for a fraction of a second. "Yeah, the dice would be gone for good. I'd take my direction from you. You're the boss, applesauce."

"Why are you doing this?"

"You tell me. You're the one who wakes up screaming."

The edge of the omelet crisped and pulled away from the pan. I stared at its succulent perfection. "Sometimes I'm so terrified it overwhelms me," I said. "Other times the whole mess is hazy and far away, impossible. I mean—dragons attacking Seattle? It depends on whether I think like Mom, or Dad."

Justin glugged down his juice. "You're not Mom or Dad. They died and left us in a friggin' maze. We have to walk our own path." Wise advice. Maybe the kid really was half elf. He pulled out a red plastic die and slapped it on the table.

"Roll, Mimi."

If only I trusted myself as much as Justin trusted his dice.

With a jolt from my wrist, a perfect omelet rose out of the pan, folded in midair, and settled neatly back into the butter. It was crazy, but it might be worth it if I could get rid of the dice. And maybe my luck was changing.

"Okay, I'll roll after breakfast. Go get Nicholi out of the shower. He's been in there for twenty minutes and we're going to be late for school."

I slipped the omelet onto a large plate and cut it into three uneven pieces. A few bites for Nicholi, a few bites for me, and the barbarian's share for Justin. Lose or win, he needed fortification to bring us through.

Nicholi, pink from his long shower, jabbered through the meal, excited about his upcoming Thanksgiving vacation. Justin and I ate in silence, contemplating, or perhaps trying to sway, the decisions of fate. When the plates were rinsed, the iron skillet tempered, and the table wiped, Justin took a handful of dice out of his pocket. We stood across from each other at the kitchen table, leaning over the shiny surface still damp and smeared from my sponge.

"What're you doing?" asked Nicholi, reaching for Justin's leg.

"Stay back, Little Dude." Justin picked him up and set him on a kitchen chair, then dragged the chair aside.

I lifted one of the dice and rattled it in my cupped hands. Every rational cell in my brain protested, begging me to reconsider. Too late for the rational. With a leap of faith, I let the die fall.

The die rolled, clattering across the table with little hops and bounces as if it were alive. Capriciously, it turned a circle on its twelve little points, dancing lightly in front of Justin's tummy, then it settled with a shiver on the wooden table top.

A ten.

"*Yes!*" Justin thrust his fist into the air, his face relieved, determined. "You can do this, Mimi. I know you can. I'll tell the group to bring sleeping bags."

Crap! Now the five of them would camp in my living room, bugging me to death about the Wyrmstone while I tried to cook.

"Don't I get a luck point?"

Justin laughed. "No way." He swept up the die. "Luck is for players. You are fate's beast."

What a lousy, insulting excuse. I glared at him, fed up. But Justin trudged away, big shoulders swinging.

"Elina can't spend the night," I yelled after him.

Justin turned around. "Elina is a cohort."

"I don't care what she is, she can't spend the night."

"She doesn't exist, Mimi. She's an imaginary companion to a game character."

Imaginary? How dimwitted; of course the girl didn't exist. Justin's friends hung around like flies on barbeque. If she existed, I would have seen her ages ago. No wonder Justin and Dr. Harvey just about split their sides laughing.

In a fervor of nerves I threw sandwiches into lunch boxes, and gathered up coats, hats, and gloves. "Let's go," I said impatiently to Nicholi who sat, short legs kicking, in the too-tall chair.

"Didoo says you want to kill a lot of dragons and save

Seattle," he said, his chin resting on the bear's battered head. I stared at the disheveled stuffed toy. For once, Didoo was dead wrong.

~

Between the wind, driving rain, and blackened traffic lights we were late, even though school had been delayed an hour. I shopped for Thanksgiving ingredients, then back at home I stacked cookbooks, piled with the relevant recipes face up and the bindings spooned. I accomplished only half of what I'd hoped by the time I had to pick up the boys. As I drove to the elementary school, wind threatened to push my car off the road and streetlights swayed riotously on their cables. Justin and Nicholi had taken refuge under the school's awning. They both looked anxious to go home.

"What's a potlatch?" asked Nicholi, as Justin buckled him into the car seat.

"I have no idea. Why?" I pulled out into the thick, slow traffic, congealed around the school.

"That's what they make Chilkat robes for."

"Oh?" I braked to avoid colliding with the car ahead and skidded on the slick pavement, nicking the curb of the round-about. In the center of the traffic circle the flagpole trembled and shivered in the wind, barely holding onto the frantically flapping flag. Traffic crawled forward, gusts of rain falling so hard I could hardly see.

A few minutes later Nicholi said, "Maybe spirit bears come from British Columbia."

I flicked my eyes to the rearview mirror. Nicholi hugged Didoo, his cheek dented by the bear's round ear. "You looked up Chilkat robe on Wikipedia."

"Uh-huh. Ms. Blue gave me a goldish star in reading group and I got to go to the library."

"You were in Ms. Blue's room again?" In my estimation, Ms. Greer just slipped beyond 'snarky', sliding on her little high heels toward 'hellcat.'

"Just for reading group. Smudge kicked the back of my chair three times, then he knockovered me in line." Nicholi affected a brave face, but his blue eyes looked unhappy.

I stopped at a dark street corner. A drift of thrashing cedar branches had pulled down a wire, leaving tangles and darkness where the street light should have been.

Confronting Ms. Greer moved up on my things-to-do list, becoming something I actually *wanted* to do. Nicholi was not transferring into second grade at six years old, and that was final. I eased around the corner and down the block. Our house was blessedly intact. Branches had been ripped off and tossed in piles on the roof, and the gutters were so clogged with needles that they overflowed. The stubborn roots of the dead fig lay submerged in a stream of swirling mud that snaked through the courtyard garden and washed a gully down the driveway. But the house stood. I hoped Ms. Farr's house had survived as well.

Justin was no sooner inside than he began to arrange furniture for the war summit, taking folding tables and chairs out of storage, hauling books to the table, and choosing miniatures from his box to arrange on the grid-like map.

"Can I order pizza?" he asked, as I hefted the frozen turkey from the fridge.

"I spent my last dime on Thanksgiving. I won't have any money until Friday. You can order pizza if your friends pitch in to pay for it."

"Okay." He left for the phone to dock his friends, or more likely his friends' parents, for the needed thirty bucks.

Nicholi crawled under the kitchen table and began adding thickness, Lego by Lego, to his already dense castle walls. He was so much less clingy since the Chilkat robe. With Steve in Mexico the robe should be safe for the weekend, if it wasn't submerged in water. But what about next week?

Boys began to arrive as I prepped lettuce, car doors slamming and parents calling 'goodbye' at the door. Case sauntered in and looked disappointed that only cold, green things were being prepared. He leaned his elbows on the kitchen island, watching me swing water out of the leaves.

"No cookies?" he asked, his mournful look a comical contrast to the tough guy shaved head.

"Not today." I put aside lettuce and picked up a knife to chip at the ice in the turkey's cavity, trying to dislodge the frozen bag of giblets. "Today it's pizza, and only if you can pay for it. Tomorrow, you feast."

"Just one batch?" He twinkled his eyes, as though I were a giggly teen girl, likely to be influenced by his allure.

"Maybe, if you'll tell me something."

"What?" His expression slid from sweet to guarded in an instant.

"How did Snick double the stone?"

"Hmm." Case studied the way I stabbed at the frozen, bloody ice. "No one knows for sure. Most stand-alone Gemini spells don't last long when humans cast them, so I suppose he must have had a Gemini mirror." He hesitated, then added, "You should have Larry sharpen your knives."

Dad used to keep the knives honed, and I'm sure Case knew that. We made eye contact, and for a moment I think Case felt genuine empathy for another human's sorrow, unfettered by calculating the angles.

"Where do I get a Gemini mirror?"

"You don't get one, you make one. Trimble knows the spell, though I doubt he's ever used it. He prefers True Naming to Illusion."

I studied my frozen turkey, the skin slick and white under my pink, cold hands. "How long would a mirror illusion last?"

"Human casted, one hundred hours. Dragon casted, one hundred years."

One hundred hours: roughly four days. That might be a way to protect the Chilkat robe. But I'd have to bring the original home, which was essentially stealing. I thrust a hand in the turkey cavity, gripped a corner of the soggy giblet bag, and tugged, but the giblets were still stuck to the inner ribs.

Case sidled closer and poured on the sunshine. "I'd say that bit of intelligence was worth *two* batches of cookies."

I looked into the brilliant warmth of his hazel eyes. "Scram, Case, I have work to do. Or better yet—" I held out the bloody knife, "—dig the giblets out for me."

"No thanks." He vanished into the living room.

Case must have spread the word that Mama Mimi was grumpy, because Larry, Trimble, and Paul barely poked their heads into the kitchen to say hello. For several hours the boys were remarkably quiet. Relieved to be left alone, I stayed out of their way.

By two o'clock the giblets were thawed, diced, fried in onions and garlic, and simmering in gravy, and I felt significantly calmer. I made ginger snap dough for Case's cookies and the spicy smell filled the kitchen. Maybe by the time the feast was prepared I'd be able to bear my Wyrmstone responsibilities. I was selecting herbs from the spice rack when the doorbell rang.

"Justin, would you get that?" I hoped it was Carlo, I reluctantly admitted to myself, as I shook basil into the gray. It was probably the Pizza guy.

Justin didn't answer, but I heard the front door open and the rumble of an argument.

"Just get out," I heard Justin snarl. He sounded as if his barbarian half was getting the better of him. He wouldn't speak to Carlo like that; it had to be Duke. How nice if it could be Duke, I thought sadly, but Duke was gone, and visiting us wasn't a Doppelganger's idea of a good time. I turned off the gas under the giblets, pulled cookies from the oven, and went to investigate.

Steve stood in the hall. A black plastic slicker hung from his skeletal shoulders, soaked and dripping around his ankles. He looked tall in the low hallway.

Justin occupied the entry into the living room, a granite rock of resolve, sledgehammer held across his chest. He stood backed by Larry with the pickaxe, Case with his fists in his pockets, and Trimble wielding Mom's sharpened bamboo pole. Together they blockaded the entrance. Paul cowered by the Age of Dragons table, pale as his character sheet.

"I'm doing your sister a favor, so go find her, mutt." Steve's tone had an edgy rasp that made me cringe, as though he was losing what little patience he had. My first thought was that something had happened to Ms. Farr, and I rushed forward.

"It's okay, Justin." I tried to sound reassuring, reassure myself, as I worked to squeeze my way past the boys. But they weren't moving. "Is it Ms. Farr?" I asked, standing on tiptoe and peering over Justin's thick shoulder.

Justin jerked a thumb toward Steve. "I don't want this—this—*polymorph*—in my house."

Polymorph? I'd never seen Justin so snarly and aggressive. I had no idea what he was so upset about.

Steve smirked with contempt.

I stared helplessly at Justin. He outweighed me by a hundred pounds and was rooted to the ground, eyes locked on Steve's. A human wall, not to be reasoned with. I scrambled desperately through my parenting repertoire for some way to make Justin listen. I couldn't afford to have Justin in Officer Dray's jail again, this time for assault with a deadly sledgehammer. I didn't want to have to explain this to Mr. Eastman. Worst of all, Steve didn't even look nervous, clearly confident he'd prevail if it came to a fight. I didn't like the creep, but I didn't want him hurt, either. I shoved my way around Trimble and stood between Steve and my brother.

"I thought you'd gone to Mexico. Is Ms. Farr okay?" I asked.

Steve grinned, all yellow teeth and malice. His hair glinted with damp oil, hanging like dirty ropes. In the dim light of the hall, deep scallops of shadow sculpted his bony face, making him look spectral.

He flicked a hand toward Justin. "Tell the puppy to sit," he said, a rattle of venom in his voice. I turned and caught Trimble's eye, beseeching him to help me.

Trimble glanced nervously from me to Justin, and then laid a finger on Justin's arm. "Hey dude, I can't cast and Larry can't swing in such close quarters. Let's back this up a few feet," he said softly.

Eyes never leaving Steve's face, Justin drew back a step into the living room. He still obstructed the way, but the pressure eased in the tight entryway. Nicholi slipped around the boys and stood with Didoo in his grip and his back against Justin's knees. Justin put a hand on his head and shoved Nicholi around behind, where he peeked through Justin's legs.

Steve turned to me and slid his gaze slowly up and down. The first time he did that, weeks ago in Ms. Farr's kitchen, I'd felt undressed. This time he seemed to appraise my worthiness. He must have decided that I merited favor, because he reached in his coat pocket and pulled out a scroll of parchment.

"I wrote this out for you." He handed the scroll to me.

"Don't take any gifts from him," growled Justin.

"It's just a piece of paper, Justin." I unrolled the page. Handwritten lines of Latin flowed across the page, reproduced from the original engraving like a master forgery.

Natus, semines quae terram efficiunt,
Sanguis qui ullum marem transit.
Tribuete natus huic mulieri,
Omnis eorum maior quam posterum,
Quoad uterus centum reges foras ederit.

Underneath was an English translation:

Sons, the seeds that make the land,
The blood that crosses any water.
Grant this woman sons,
Each larger than the next,
Until her womb has pushed forth a hundred kings.

I whispered the translation to myself, the words reverberating with power. Icy fingers crawled up my back and crept through my hair, tugging at the roots until they tingled. The inscription was sickening. I cleared my throat to push down revulsion. "What does it mean?"

"If your mother hadn't locked me in a ridiculous cage, I'd be more inclined to tell you."

My mother? Inside I staggered; Mom embroiled with Steve?

Steve leaned against the door, relaxed enough to slouch, enjoying my inner turmoil. His eyes slid to my chest, blue eye and green eye united in their greed.

"Show me the stone."

I took a moment to recover, then blurted out, "You knew my mother?"

Steve began to laugh, a sound like steam leaking from a rusty throat. "No one knew your mother. She eluded every one of us. Show me the stone and I'll tell you what I do know."

The boys grumbled, pressed forward, shortening the gap between them and Steve. But finally, here was someone willing to divulge secrets, so I pulled the necklace out from under my shirt.

Steve reached forward very slowly. At first I thought he was trying not to startle Justin, then I realized it was the gold that he distrusted. He pushed aside the collar of my blouse and pinched the leather between long, filthy fingernails. Cautious as a man with explosives, he lifted the leather until the jewel dangled, and without touching the setting, twisted the cord and let the stone flip over. He studied the writing on the back. Except for ink and metal, his copy and the engraving were exactly identical.

"We were as close to allies as Vedette would allow. When she buried the stone it could no longer give her children, so I taught her to cast these words without Pancrizio's aide." He twisted the cord and the inscription of the fertility charm glinted. Then he sneered at Justin. "You, wolf cub, were born from my instructions." Justin stiffened with resentment. "Only you, little reptile, with your love of bears," his blue eye stayed on the amethyst while his green eye wandered to Nicholi, "only you are a mystery. You fight wild, like a Druid, so I suspect that you carry your father's seed. An accident, no doubt born of years of pleasant effort." Steve laughed again, and the harsh sound made Nicholi hide behind Justin's thick leg. "He could have been great, your father, had he not denied what he was. He could have been useful."

Nicholi whimpered, and Justin put a hand in his curls, his other hand squeezing the hammer.

"Who are you?" My voice shook.

Steve closed moist white fingers around the leather, avoiding the gem.

"Better you should ask that question of yourself. Who are you, Mimi?"

He took a step closer, so that his dank heat seeped into my clothes. Hot breath blew down my collar, foul and sticky. "I offer you a place by my side *Massimaŭ y Draŭtox*, daughter of Prince Vasborya and granddaughter of Yvess. You have refused me once, but by courting ritual you must refuse five times. Will you remain a tiny human, or would you be a dragon queen?"

"Adrikhedon!" gasped the boys, and even Justin stepped back.

I stared into his mesmerizing blue eye and light poured in, illuminating all the way to the forgotten. There had been a crack of eggshell over my head and sudden searing sunshine, my inner lids snapping shut against it. The snarl of challenge from my nest mate and I bit blind, taking off a scaly foot with my strike. The yowling hunger with which I devoured him, gobbled the next siblings who hatched, even ate their shells. The massive blue-scaled paw that swatted me into the walled-off nursery, and soon after a woman, Vedette, I realize now, who lifted me like a lap dog and held me to her heart.

Dr. Harvey lied; he did not deliver me. I was born of my mother, but born a dragon: muscled, cunning, with magic in my blood. It must have taken great skill for Vedette to charm me into something delicate, gullible, practical, and human.

"What say you, *Massimaü*?" whispered Adrikhedon. "Together—you, me and the stone—nothing could stand against us."

In my depths stirred dragon hunger: the desolate mire of loneliness, bitter pointless greed, a sucking emptiness that nothing could ever fill. This raging need echoed in Adrikhedon's whisper, blended and mixed with mine. It bound us together in a thick web; two monstrous flies, joined and hanging side by side for thousands of years, our ravenous craving keeping us alive.

Nothing could stand against such craving: not teachers, judges, social workers, not Pancrizio or even an army. My gem glistened, and I imagined Yvess coming for her liberated jewel. With Adrikhedon at my flank I could defend it, send her yowling back to her Dolomites. My jewel, soothing my need every time I gazed at it, forever in my claws.

Nicholi stepped out from behind Justin's knee. "You don't need him, Mimi." I looked down at the mop of black curls, large blue eyes, and forehead, split like a heart by his widow's peak. He was so frail, this human child, and would live such a short, short life. Defending humanity was like defending a field of flowers; they died in a very brief season, so why bother? But so beautiful, those cornflower eyes, with love as pure as a diamond.

I reached for Nicholi's warm hand.

"I refuse you, Adrikhedon," I said.

A grimace of satisfaction twisted Steve's face, as if he guessed I would be stubborn. "That's only two out of five."

His fingernail slid down the leather, peeling a strip off the cord.

"Pancrizio has made you sterile, and he will make you beg, as your mother did, for every child. Such a waste, *Massimaŏ*, when I would give you offspring for free."

He raised the jewel, his green eye reflecting purple from the facets, and his blue eye gazing directly into mine.

"*Jilsara cassar, jilsara rhoffver ....*"

He whispered the rolling Draconic, enveloping me in dark softness. *Never refuse, never resist ....* His eyes pinned me, green as Emerald, blue as lazurite, caught in their sparkling power as his long fingernail scraped along the cord, slicing through layers of hide, thinning the leather to a faint thread. Then he jerked downward, straining against the last fiber that held the amulet to my neck.

My claws shot up to stop him.

"Break enchantment!" Trimble lunged forward, fire balls exploding around a blur of rainbow cloth, bamboo pole thrusting past my ear.

But Steve was too fast. He gave a final yank, and when the leather refused to snap he whirled and disappeared out the door, into the storm. Boys poured past me: Larry bellowing, pickax raised; Justin howling with fury; Case, the swiftest runner of the three, was beyond the others within paces and disappeared silent as an owl. Wind tossed rain and leaves into the hall. Out in the blustery gloom, trees creaked and branches snapped.

I stood stunned, wits slow as thick batter, will numbed into silence. Paul hovered over me, his grip keeping me from collapsing to the floor. Fumbling with fear, he pulled a black plastic film canister from his pocket.

"Drink," he said, snapping off the round lid.

"I just need to sit down." My voice sounded far away.

"No, drink." He held out the canister. "It's mithridate."

It was citrus and salty and definitely not water. Whatever mithridate was, it washed through me like a flood, driving paralysis before it.

With a stomach full of Paul's potion, more rational thoughts intruded. Adrikhedon nearly stole my stone! And Justin, Case, Trimble, and Larry were out in the storm. What were they going to do if they caught the dragon? I didn't want to think about it. Even in human form he would be formidable. And where was Nicholi? He must have dashed off after them.

I had to pull myself together. Tamara Whitting was right: I needed skills to deal with life. I had allowed Adrikhedon to enchant me, and then let the boys endanger their lives as I stood stupefied.

Mustering Ms. Whitting's parental expertise and my dragon heft, I pulled free of Paul's grasp and extended my pointer finger toward the door.

"Go. Bring the party in out of the storm before someone gets killed." My tone was harsh and commanding; poor Paul stood immobilized by my reptilian glare. "Go on. We have a war to plan." He turned and fled into the furious rain, slamming the door behind him.

One hand protecting my thin thread of leather, I stumbled to the kitchen and grabbed the wooden spoon that rested in cold giblet gravy. Holding the round handle reminded me;

simple events, like stirring a sauce, were valuable balm for life's wounds. My father taught me that. Not my dragon father, who spawned and then forgot me, but my human father—a druid who denied his abilities, Steve claimed. A man who loved me no matter what.

I started a gas flame under the gravy and listened gratefully to the soft sputter as it reheated. The remains of Adrikhedon's spell, slogging through my veins, faded as I stirred.

A few minutes later I heard the boys return, grumbling and trading pursuit stories in angry voices. When they arrived at the kitchen door they fell quiet.

Cooking spoon in hand, I faced them.

They stood in a two lines, filling the doorframe—Larry in front twisting his axe handle. Paul beside him, staring at the floor. Trimble was squeezed against Paul, his expression arranged into careful neutrality. Case stood behind, squinting through the rain on his lashes, leaning a shoulder into the frame. Justin was planted next to him, feet spread and chest out, ready to take on all comers. They were wet and disheveled from the storm.

Nicholi slipped between their legs and crawled on sopping knees under the kitchen table.

"So, now we know why I speak Draconic." I pushed my hair back, self-conscious of the gross deception of my human face, wondering how Vedette had accomplished it. Wondering how I hadn't known.

No one moved or spoke, quiet except for the slap and scrape of branches hitting the roof. I remembered how I'd felt in the presence of Yvess—cowed and terrified. The boys had a lot more fortitude in the company of dragons, or at least half dragons, than I did.

"Do you still trust me?"

It was too much to ask them to rush forward with a hug, but a smile, even eye contact, would have been so reassuring. Justin looked at Trimble, Case looked at Larry, and Paul looked at Justin. But no one answered.

"Dragons lie." With pleading eyes I searched their faces. "They eat their children. They covet riches with a hunger you humans cannot imagine. It says right in your books that I will never be a true ally. Should I have gone with Adrikhedon, or am I human enough for you?"

Case fiddled with the hair on his upper lip, Larry rubbed his thumb over the axe blade, and Trimble laced his fingers into a loose weave. Even Justin, big hands palm to palm, rolled a die around in circles and refused to look at me. Outside, the wind howled.

Only Paul had the courage to drag his eyes off the floor and meet my gaze. Bless his heart; he had the makings of a hero cowering inside him. "We'll trust you just exactly as much as you trust us," he said.

The dragon in me wanted to laugh; such a fair, wise, deeply flawed offer. Dragons didn't care for fair, and we grew too old for wise. Only humans could barter trust for trust.

But then, I was half human, wasn't I? Human enough to fear being alone.

"I'll trust you," I said.

Larry finally looked at me, cautious, cool, but at least eye to eye. "You'll take our advice?"

I nodded. I desperately needed advice.

Case shifted uneasily. "Follow our methods?"

I nodded. The boys were foolhardy, but so far they were still alive.

"Respect the dice?" asked Justin.

I wasn't crazy about this, but I nodded.

"And you'll kill other dragons?" asked Trimble.

I hesitated. That's right, I'd have to kill my kind, wouldn't I? I needed to be sure which side of this war I was on. I knew where my dragon interests lay; I'd lose beside the boys, and win allied with Adrikhedon. But I had no illusions about how far I could trust *bechmukk*; dragons didn't love, they made treaties, and then they ripped them to shreds. Only humans are willing to die rather than lose the other. And I had had a human heart for all but a few days of my life.

"If you'll believe, then I'll believe, that I won't betray you."

There was a tense silence as each boy considered my response. This was a deal that wouldn't be easy for either side to honor. And obviously I hadn't answered Trimble's question. They made a prickly barricade, standing there with hostile expressions. An unbearable wall that I had no idea how to approach, and my heart sank.

"Mimi, I'm hungry." Nicholi huddled under the kitchen table, surrounded by his Lego castle, looking wilted and abandoned. Oh my God, I'd never fed the child lunch. I put down my cooking spoon and grabbed a loaf of bread.

"Get the books and bring them here," said Justin, and he turned away.

The others paused, and then quietly filed out.

I laid out two slices of bread and slapped peanut butter on one, listening to them whisper in the living room, trying not to panic. Even my dragon hearing couldn't catch the words, drowned out by the buffeting gusts of storm, but I heard the tone: I was on probation.

Maybe trustworthy. They were in no hurry to decide.

I took a plastic honey bear from the cupboard and squeezed slow drizzles onto the bread, then put the sandwich on the table. Nicholi scooped it up and carried it into his castle where he hugged Didoo and ate. Boys returned, toting books and a map.

Determined to be one of them, I set parsley on a cutting board and carried it to the table where they gathered. Trimble and Justin inched aside to let me in. The landmarks on the hand-drawn map Trimble unrolled were oddly familiar: a ragged, winding road through the woods; a house jutting out at all angles; a rough-edged, massive pond. Ms. Farr's house and land. Amazed, confused, I pointed to the drawing. "What's this?"

"Ground zero, dragon lands." Justin sat down heavily, avoiding my gaze. "I'm afraid your description of a vulture with a hoard of ancient artifacts was a dead giveaway."

"Ms. Farr is a dragon? No way!" I said.

"She's human." Paul planted his chair backwards in the corner, leaning on it as though the rungs made a rampart. His glance skittered over my face. "She's likely a Guardian who stands at the border and guides magical items across. Or keeps them out. An ideal location for a swamp dragon garrison."

Of course: Adrikhedon, unlike Yvess and I, had to eat magical items for his power. Steve wasn't selling her things, he was consuming them.

I pictured the Aztec knife, the giant bone, the miniature portrait, resting side by side in the dark cavern of his dragon belly, magic leeching into his gut. Such a painful way for her beautiful treasures to end.

"She helps Adrikhedon?" I asked.

"No." Larry settled into a seat across the table, eyes on me like I might make a sudden move.

I ignored his scrutiny and lined up parsley sprigs on the cutting board, chopping confidently, deciding not to take it personally that he still had his pickaxe gripped and battle ready.

"She's been his prisoner for a long time, and from your description she's keeping Adrikhedon's army from fully awakening." He glanced at Case, who stood with the curve of his backbone resting against the wall by the door, hands in his pockets, studying my every move. "You sure they're in the pond?" Larry asked.

"Positive." Case didn't take his eyes off me. "I scoped it yesterday. We've found them."

I stared at Case, stunned. They asked for my full cooperation, but there was obviously a lot they hadn't told me. Case stared back, gauging my reaction.

"Young dragons, or twenty wouldn't fit," said Larry.

Justin stood and began pacing, round and round in little circles in front of the table, the small space hampering his long stride. Trimble took a seat on my other side to get out of

Justin's way. "We don't know the depth of that water." Justin collapsed back into his chair. "Adrikhedon is ancient, well over five thousand years. Probably closer to six thousand. We could be up against twenty gargantuans."

Everyone nodded, and thrilled smiles crept onto their otherwise serious faces. Either grandiose delusion or confident skill stood between us and disaster; I couldn't tell which. But I'd sworn to do it their way, so I squashed my nervous doubts.

"How do we kill dragons?" asked Trimble.

I cringed. There was a weighty silence.

Larry, who had been flipping through *The Complete Book of Dragons*, slammed the cover closed with a thump. "The usual method is to drop something heavy on them. A massive stalactite, or an ice mountain," he said.

"That house is just a shell," said Case. "You could bring the whole friggin' thing down on their heads and they'd just sneer at you. I don't suppose we can conjure an ice mountain?"

The boys pivoted toward Trimble. Trimble gave a barely perceptible shake of his head, and everyone slouched in their chairs. Except for Case, who still inclined against the wall watching me like I was a wild animal.

In the glum pause, my knife crunched through parsley, releasing a green, wet, reassuring smell.

With a wily smile, Case scraped fingernails over his shaved head. "What about Whiff of the Enemy?" Discouraged frowns curled into broad grins as they nodded their approval.

Whiff? One fought dragons with *whiffs*? Whiffs of what? I bit my lower lip to keep from laughing. Trust them, Mimi. If nothing else, the dragon in me was going to be entertained before I was slaughtered.

Case's stare was starting to unnerve me. I stood up and carried the parsley to the stove, where I brushed it into the gravy pan.

"Great thinking." Trimble opened *The Epistemic Arcane* with enthusiasm and rifled through its well-worn pages. He settled on a page deep in the back of the book, marking it with a scrap torn off a corner of the map.

"Big pond," said Justin. "Absolutely no way to get to the middle of it. One splash of an oar, one ripple of a breast-stroke, and they're on us."

The boys pondered this insight in silence, while I puzzled over why we might need to get to the middle of the pond.

"Paper boats could do it," said Nicholi. The five bigger boys leaned under the table and looked at him. Didoo in his lap, he continued to add Legos to the spirit bear castle, the walls now three inches thick under his fingers. He snapped a yellow square on top of a red square.

Trimble's cautious exhale whistled in the thoughtful quiet. "Yes. It's possible, very risky. Mimi would have to cast the illusion, or it would never fool old dragons."

Larry snorted. "Make a half dragon the pivot of our defense? What are we, idiots?"

Paul straightened in his corner and glared at Larry. "She's not going to betray us."

Larry glowered back. "Maybe not, but we need a stronger defense than some noobie half wyrm—"

"She acts more human than you do, Larry," said Paul.

Trimble raised his voice. "We cannot fight this war without the Wyrmstone—"

"Enough!" Justin's fist hit the table, and map, books, and pencils bounced with the impact.

In the weighty silence, everyone glared off into neutral distance except Case, who still stared at me.

"One visit from a dragon and we're squabbling like kiddies." Justin pushed hair out of his eyes, appraising his friend's faces. "Are we that easy to manipulate? Get a grip, dudes."

I grabbed my wooden spoon, anxiously burying the parsley in gravy. I was suspect because of my nature. Not what I did, but who I *was*, was unacceptable. Promises by my human half were not going to change that. Dragons waged war without trust, but humans couldn't. Perhaps my best shot at helping them was to leave them alone. I set aside the spoon and spun around.

"Trimble, take the stone." I lifted the fragile leather off my neck and held the jewel out. "Use it to get us through."

Trimble's eyes went wide, and his brown complexion paled to gray. Slowly he shook his head, 'no.'

Justin dropped his die on the table and it clanged against the wood, making everyone cringe. A seventeen. "Case, sense motive?" he said.

Case's gaze slid off of me, over the map, over each of his friend's faces, and finally onto his feet, encased in muddy sneakers. "She wants two things: her brothers alive, and the jewel around her neck. Dragons are hard to read but, that's the gist of it. Oh and," he grinned at his shoelaces, "she'd like a date with Carlo."

My cheeks burned with embarrassment, my motives and hidden desires splayed open and dissected, guts out. Had Case's charming eyes always seen through me so easily?

Paul put a hand over his mouth and snickered. "Is that human enough for you, Larry?"

Larry set his axe down and tilted onto the back legs of his chair. "Yeah, that's about as cutesy as it gets: a dragon king in competition with the boy next door. Here's our big chance to see real romance."

His belly laugh hooted overtop of everyone else's. As humiliated as I was, I felt grateful. Better that they laugh at my expense than be wary of me, dislike me, and abandon me. I breathed in relief.

"So, how much Whiff would we need, Paul?" asked Larry when he'd recovered his breath.

"Twenty dragons? We'd need—" Paul's eyes rolled up, "—about thirty Styrofoam cups worth." He leaned around his chair so he could see under the table. "Nicholi, you'll make the boats?"

Nicholi nodded.

"Case will string them together," said Trimble. "I'll float them and Mimi will make them dazzle. Agreed?"

"I'll need kite string and strong glue," said Case, soaring right past the *Mimi will* part, not leaving me time to agree or disagree, or even to find out what *make them dazzle* meant. But for the moment, at least, I was accepted, and I hung onto that with my whole half-human heart.

"Kite string and glue are in Mom's garden shed," said Justin.

"Styrofoam cups?" asked Larry.

"Mom's garden shed," said Justin.

Case eased over to Paul's corner. "Will you help me make the Whiff?"

Paul stiffened. "I don't do poison, it's against my creed."

"Is it your creed to fight twenty instead of one? Come on Paul, bend your morals just a little. They won't break." Case had an exceptionally refined tone for wheedling.

"You're not poisoning people, Paul," added Justin. "No one's going to dock you your cleric robes for killing dragons." Justin wiped his bangs aside and his gaze sought mine, locking on, oozing elfin mischief. "Unless you go after my sister, in which case, you'll be too dead to worry about your vows."

My eyes filled with tears, and for a second I thought Justin's might have, too.

Paul scowled. "Oh, all right."

I brought ginger snaps to the table and set them down, letting the boys grab them up still warm off the sheet. Within seconds there were only two left. Well, they trusted me enough to eat my cookies.

One cookie in each hand and chewing thoughtfully, Trimble said, "So assuming this works, that leaves one dragon standing that we'll have to fight."

"You still have that claw?" Case asked, brushing crumbs off his black sweatshirt.

Justin shook his head, swallowed, and reached for the second-to-last cookie. "It attacked me. I dismantled it."

"Do we have wire to make another one?" asked Case.

"Yeah, Mom's garden shed," mumbled Paul, Trimble, and Larry in unison, mouths full. Then everyone laughed.

"I wish Mom were here," said Justin.

No one tried to answer. Instead they dusted cookies off their hands, wiped any remaining film of butter onto their jeans, and stood up. Chair legs squeaking and boots thumping, everyone cleared out, leaving Trimble alone at the table.

"Come on, Little Dude," called Case. "We need you."

Nicholi climbed out of the castle and hurried after them.

Trimble reached in his pocket and drew out his flash paper pouch. He undid the safety pin that attached pull cord to pocket lining, then shook out the contents. "Here," he held out the empty sack, "I know it's silly, but it makes me nervous to see that amulet hanging from a thread. Put this around your neck and keep the Wyrmstone inside."

I took a seat beside him and accepted the bag. It was feather light, cool, and smelled of Cinnamon, the silk as soft as down.

"It's made of Phoenix hide, impermeable to blindsense, so other dragons can't see the stone unless you expose it. The cord is nothing near as strong as the leather your mother enchanted—that is a work of mastery. But it's a good back up."

"Thank you." Grateful for the help and friendship, I put the cord around my neck and slid the Wyrmstone into the sack.

Trimble eyed the last cookie, then tented his fingers and closed his eyes. "There are some things you need to know."

"Yeah, like how to *make things dazzle*," I said.

"No, that's not what we need to talk about. I was referring more to … " he repositioned himself uncomfortably in his chair, his gaze on his lacing and unlacing fingers, " … dragons mating."

No way! A dragon sex lecture; this was too much. Now I knew exactly how Justin felt when I showed him the condom package. I stood up and walked to the stove. "I have no intention of accepting Adrikhedon, this is not an issue."

"Just hear me out," he said, and he took a deep breath. "It's traditional for him to offer you a gift. If you accept it, you must accept him."

"So, I won't take any gifts from him." I put a lid over the gravy and pulled Bing cherries from the refrigerator. As Trimble pondered my response, I went back for the ice cream base.

"It's not that easy. The gift will be carefully chosen, such that you won't be able to refuse. If you take the gift, you must either accept him, or give him back something of even greater value, otherwise …." he watched me chop cherries in half, " … otherwise he will fight you to the death."

Holy moly. I plunked down the knife and stared at Trimble's worried face. I was half dragon, Adrikhedon was full dragon; I had the Wyrmstone, he had five thousand years of killing experience. This was not a fight I wanted to pick.

Trimble tugged nervously at the ends of his braids. "Likely he has already set in motion how he will trap you. You must accept no gifts, no matter what the cost of refusing, Mimi."

"I understand." I stirred cherries into the base and watched red swirls stain the white. It was ridiculous, really, to worry about one more way to die. There were so many ways I could be finished off, long before it came to a fight with

Adrikhedon. What an odd feeling, to be so hardened to a fear of death. There were good things about being part dragon.

"What about *making things dazzle?*" I asked.

Trimble eyed the last cookie again, then looked away. "As far as I'm concerned, that's a backup plan."

"What do you mean?" I poured cherry ice cream base into the electric churn, snapped the toggle, and it whirred softly.

"Think about it Mimi: if we kill every last swamp dragon, Yvess' clan will be unopposed. It won't be long before your relatives wander out of the mountains, discover they have no enemies left, and begin to—forgive me," he nodded with respect, "—terrorize the world. Dislike of swamp dragons, Adrikhedon in particular, keeps them holed up."

"Oh!" I carried the stirring spoon to the faucet and rinsed it. Gazing out the sink window, I watched the top third of a huge cedar tree bend, then whip straight again in the raging wind. That was quite a storm, still seething outside.

"So Plan A: you send them back across the border."

"The one Ms. Farr guards?"

"Yeah. The dragons live, they won't be able to bother us, and the mountain dragons stay put. Maybe Ms. Farr can help you."

"She doesn't speak, Trimble."

"But you do." He pulled out a blank scroll and opened *The Epistemic Arcane* at his little paper bookmark. "I'll write a banishing spell. You'll have to translate it so they understand, but with the command of the stone behind you I'm pretty sure the words will send them home."

He held out the plate with the last cookie. When I didn't come forward to take it, he waved it back and forth. "Killing dragons is hard, Mimi, even if we have to kill only one. And I think you'll be surprised by your sympathy. Your human half may not be able to betray her dragon blood. Don't force fate to tempt you."

He set the plate on the table and took the cookie himself. "There is only one thing you need to accomplish: get them back across the border. If you can't, then control the final survivor until we've killed it." He looked up and met my gaze, and in his eyes I saw hope, faith, and trust. "Oh, and, hang on to the Wyrmstone." He took a big bite of cookie.

I wasn't fooled: that was three things, not one, and I didn't know how to do any of them. "May I make Thanksgiving dinner now?"

Trimble laughed. "We'd all be very disappointed if you didn't."

An hour later my cell phone rang, vibrating on the kitchen counter as I took drying bread crumbs from the oven. I set down the hot tray and ran to snap the phone open. "Hello?"

"*Ahhh ... ahhh ... eiiiahhhh ... uuhhhh ....*" The odd squeaks and groans made my insides quiver. It was either a nasty prank call or a very poor connection.

"Who is this?"

Creepy crackles, moans, and guttural vowels leaked through the receiver. I was a second away from slamming closed the top when Nicholi said, "It's your workolady. I think she needs help." He stood in the kitchen door, Didoo shoved up under his shirt.

"Ms. Farr?" My heart leapt. "Ms. Farr, is this you? Are you okay?"

The squeaking and groaning became desperate, pleading. I realized with horror that Nicholi was right. I was sure of it.

"What's the matter?" What a stupid question; she couldn't answer. I needed to think straight. I clutched the phone with both hands. "I'll be right there. Hang on, okay? I'll be right there." I slammed closed the phone.

"Nicholi, put on your shoes. Hurry."

I dashed into the living room, yelling. "Justin! Justin! Something's happened to Ms. Farr. We have to go."

At the narrow rectangular table, five pairs of startled eyes looked up, and their hands stopped tying a long chain of paper boats.

Case recovered first. "What's up?"

"My friend Ms. Farr. Something terrible has happened. She needs help."

Justin stood abruptly, knees hitting the table and it rocked, almost flipping over. "It knew it. Come on, let's go." His expression was both grim and thrilled as he headed for the door.

"What's up?" Larry reached for his pickax.

"The dragons are rising, dudes. Get in the car. Come on!" Justin wedged his feet into untied sneakers and shoved them around, trying to force his shoes on and grab for his sledgehammer at the same time.

"We can't all fit in the car," said Trimble, hurrying to the hall and taking up coat and bamboo staff.

Justin whipped out his cell phone. With a few rapid presses he dialed.

"Carlo? Yo, it's Justin. Are you at Nonna's? Come over right away, dude. We gotta go." He closed the phone. The front hall filled with boys, furiously putting on coats, hats, and boots, clutching weapons.

I gathered up my purse, shaking so badly I couldn't feel my car keys in the hall drawer. I took a deep breath and searched again, my hands finally closing on pointy key edges. Flashlights. We might need flashlights. I grabbed the only two I could find in the kitchen utility drawer and hoped they had batteries. On my way past the kitchen table I saw the scroll Trimble had written for me and I stuffed it in my jeans pocket. I checked the other pocket for Mom's cinnabar vial.

Nicholi stood barefoot in the kitchen door. "Where are we going?"

"To fight dragons." Justin swept him off his feet.

"I'm scared," said Nicholi.

"Never show fear to a dragon. It just gives them more power." With a few lopes Justin was at the table, Nicholi on his hip. He squatted and pulled Nicholi's shoes out of the castle with his free hand. "You're going with Mimi," he said, handing Nicholi his shoes, then he turned to me. "Larry and I will follow in Carlo's truck. Paul, Trimble, Case, you go in the Subaru."

Outside the rain fell in torrents, whipped into stinging sprays by the howling wind. Justin and Larry dashed down the driveway, their shoes kicking up splashes of water.

Case stood on the porch with a large plastic sack, stuffing in boats and string. He shoved the sack in the back of the station wagon and scooted into the back seat. Paul leapt into the front seat and set a cider jug of murky fluid on his lap, stacks of Styrofoam cups at his feet. Trimble helped Nicholi with the car seat buckle.

Carlo's truck waited at the end of the driveway, the yellow headlight beams lighting up cones of pouring rain. It was reassuring to watch him pull in behind me and follow. I broke the speed limit down our otherwise deserted street. At the first stop light I dialed Ms. Farr's number on my cell phone. No answer. I handed the phone to Paul in the seat next to me.

"Keep dialing," I said. "If you reach her, tell her we're coming."

Paul looked nervous, short red hair rising straight up in front and quivering like his hands as he took the phone. He rolled his eyes anxiously towards Trimble and Case and then redialed. "Busy tone."

I gunned it when the light turned green, fishtailing through the inch of water on the road, racing for the freeway. I should never have left her there, alone with Steve. He was a lying, thieving, stinking dragon and I knew it from the moment I saw him. Someday I would learn to listen to myself.

Chapter 22

I switched lanes going 70 miles per hour, veering onto the highway exit to Ms. Farr's, the car's rear end swinging wildly in the wet. Applying the brakes, I skidded towards Ms. Farr's road. As we approached the security gates the boys fell silent. The security guard wasn't there, so I punched in the code and gripped the steering wheel, impatient for the gates to open. I glanced in the rear view mirror to see Carlo right on my bumper. I could see his profile in the street light as he turned to speak to Justin. No doubt Justin was explaining to Carlo how to fight dragons with whiffs and paper boats. Talking about half dragons, too. I cringed, wondering how Carlo would feel about my genetics. No time to worry now. His truck slipped past the gate behind the Subaru.

In the clash of the storm the forest felt alive. It thrashed and fought an invisible foe, trees creaking violently. I prayed nothing big would fall on our hoods, or heads. The car shuddered as it left the pavement and bumped onto the gravel. It bottomed out as I hit potholes at too fast a speed. I slammed on the brakes a short way down the deserted driveway. It was dusk and the light was gray, fading fast. There was no hint of life. A hundred feet down the road the house hunkered low on the forest floor, as if resisting the wind. Or giving in to gravity. I jumped out of the car, flashlight in hand, and was about to propel myself through the furious rain to Ms. Farr's door when Larry grabbed my shoulder.

"Case first, always," he said, "unless you want to die in a trap."

He said this right in my ear, so the wind wouldn't blow it away. He rested the head of Mom's pickax on his boot, and with a firm grasp on my forearm, held me to the spot.

Justin, Carlo, and Trimble hurried from the truck behind us.

"Stay in the car, Nicholi. Don't get out, no matter what," said Justin.

Nicholi! Stupid—I should have left him at Nonna's! To emphasize his point, Justin motioned for Nicholi to lock the door and stood watching until Nicholi forced down the old fashioned catches. A car would be useless against dragons, or Pancrizio. Protect him, Didoo, please, please, please.

Case slunk into the surrounding woods as rain pelted and wind roared. He crept behind a tree trunk and didn't come out the other side. I searched the woods—wind whipping debris in swirls, branches breaking and scattering—but he'd melted into the furious chaos.

Side by side in an arc facing the house, we blocked the driveway in the icy rain: Trimble with staff half raised, Larry with Mom's pickax on his boot, Justin bareheaded with wet hair plastered to his face and the head of his sledgehammer in his big grip. My hand shook, clutching the silky bag that hid the Wyrmstone. Paul sat behind the wall of our bodies, hunched at our feet like a turtle, his arms pulled deep into his coat sleeves. Carlo stood next to me, pressing against my shoulder so that his bulk cut the wind. I shivered and Carlo's warm fingers found mine. Without turning his gaze from the house at the end of the driveway, he gave my fingers a squeeze. I laced my fingers through his and hung on. Nicholi and bear observed out the car's back window, Didoo's chin on the backseat and Nicholi's chin on Didoo's head, motionless.

It was probably no longer than five minutes, but the wait seemed endless. Our group inched together tighter and tighter as rain soaked our coats and dusk gave less and less light.

After awhile I heard a muffled boom, followed by a series of pops, but no one jumped with alarm except me and Carlo. Perhaps the boys were expecting this, or maybe they were frozen in place, but they didn't look worried. I fought the urge to dash to Ms. Farr's side.

None of us saw Case approach. He rose suddenly off the frozen mud of the driveway, startling Trimble, and causing a growl of surprise from Larry. He was filthy. He nodded once, then went to Dad's Subaru and opened the hatch. From the trunk he pulled a round cork disc Mom had used to protect her floor from houseplants, the plastic garbage sack poked and tented with paper boats, and a coil of rope. He slung the rope around his chest like a sash, then retrieved Paul's gallon jug of hazy, brown liquid. He handed the jug and Styrofoam cups to Paul, the cork disc to Trimble, and picked up the sack. A Skeletal Hand of Power dangled from his belt by a wire loop.

"They're awake," said Case, "and waiting. Four traps, three out of four dismantled. Couldn't find the forth, so be careful. The entry is clear now, Mama Mimi. With the stone you should be able to pass Adrikhedon's rune."

He met my eye, and I knew in that moment that he still wanted to love his Mama Mimi as he always had. I hoped I could live up to his trust.

Trimble turned to me. "Take the Wyrmstone out," he whispered.

With shaking fingers, I lifted the jewel out of the sack so that it lay, steamy and brilliant, on my coat zipper.

"Okay," said Larry, slapping a flashlight into my hand. "Go." He put a few fingers in the middle of my back and nudged me down the driveway.

"Alone?"

"We're right behind you. You just won't see us," said Case.

"But wait … what do I do?" I turned to Trimble, frantic, panicked.

Trimble's gaze was steady. "When you see the birds, think treasure. Reach into your dragon soul and think of all you need to fill that void. Give it to the birds."

"Birds? I don't understand!"

Trimble smiled. "You will. Trust yourself, *Massimaǔ*."

Trust. I imagined creeping through the storm and opening the door that led into Steve's smelly hole. Every step of the way was irreversible, like tumbling off a cliff, striking the rocks, and shattering.

Soaked, freezing, terrified, I stared down the driveway, suddenly not a bit anxious to dash down it, even for Ms. Farr.

"Remember, never show fear to a dragon. Especially, don't be afraid of yourself," said Justin, and he kissed the top of my head. That was the first brotherly kiss Justin ever gave me. Perhaps he thought it was his last chance.

Carlo stepped forward. "I'll go too."

"No way." They said it together, moving as a unit to block Carlo's path.

"She goes alone. It's what the dragons expect," said Trimble, and everyone murmured in assent. "Anyone with her would just alarm them. Believe me, you don't want to alarm twenty dragons."

Carlo gave an exasperated grunt. "Be careful," he said, and he kissed me on the cheek. If I hadn't been so terrified, it might have felt good.

Ms. Farr, I reminded myself. Gentle, lost, adorable Ms. Farr. My brothers. I loved my brothers. Seattle, innocent and unprepared. I had, like it or not, a responsibility. I took a few steps down the driveway, wondering what I'd find beyond the door. Then I turned around for one look back, but the boys and Carlo were gone. Only Didoo's and Nicholi's blue eyes watched me, the glass eyes resigned and the human ones wide and anxious.

Nicholi shouldn't be here. I absolutely should have left him with Anna Rossi. But it was too late to change that now.

And then, of all the strange things, I remembered Ms. Greer. Sucking in cool confidence, radiating authority. And Ms. Whitting, bless her sandal-wearing soul, with her severe, sour face and witchy swagger. I turned, walking down the branch-strewn gravel. Never show fear to a dragon, ladies, not even to *Massimaü y Draütox*. You give me parenting advice, and I'll teach you things you never imagined.

Closer to the house, wafts of rank pond water gusted into my face, blown by the wind. The house shuddered and cracked. Adrikhedon's pentagon had lifted from the earth and hung before the door. That's where I had seen it! Was that only two weeks ago? *I give you two weeks*, Steve had said. And it appeared that he was right; that was just about how long I would live. His pentagon shone, wide as my reach, lit with a malevolent, golden gleam, filled with triangles to make a multifaceted eye. The gate to slaughter.

"Hello, Adrikhedon," I whispered, "I hope you're in Mexico."

I took a breath that filled me all the way to the depths of my belly. Refusing to be terrified, I pushed into the symbol, into the tingling burn of magic. Molten gold assaulted my smell, my taste: bitter, as though I were eating metal. Under the roar of the storm I heard the faint clicks and creaks of twenty dragons tensing. With a shudder, I forced through to the other side.

"Ms. Farr?" My yell was swiped away by a blast of wind. I put my key in the lock, trembling with adrenaline. Bracing myself for dragons, I opened the door. "Ms. Farr?" I bellowed, letting the chutzpa of Greer and Whitting propel me into the room.

Empty. No answer except for the storm.

I stopped in my tracks, stunned by the devastation. Her house was gutted. The beautiful floor-to-ceiling circular window overlooking the pond was blown out. The whole back wall and most of the roof were gone, as though something huge had burst through, leaving a ragged hole. The house sloped at a precarious angle into the deep, rank pond, which now seemed to extend forever into the forest. Waves lapped at the platforms above the sunken living room, which was now submerged. Ripples grabbed at wood, hinges, and doors. Water had dragged Steve's couch deep into the mud and reeds, almost engulfing it.

"Oh my God," I whispered.

I shone my flashlight into the dark shadow of the flood, fearful for Ms. Farr. No bodies floated in gruesome death. Nothing showed under the impenetrable murk of the wind-thrashed waves. My light passed over the shelves: empty. Every single artifact, gone. Steve had eaten everything, and I wondered about the Chilkat robe. In the white flashlight beam the barren, looted walls were ghostly.

My light flickered back to the pond, and it was then that I knew them.

I knew them first by a burden. The weight of their souls, seeping like venom, soaking into my heart, mixing with my dragon blood and recognizing its own. Then I saw their eyes, slits, suspended over the agitated waves, a lake full of crescent moons. But the slits peered from scaly skulls, and the skulls floated with alligator patience, bodies submerged in the murk. *Green for little alligators and red for big ones*, Nicholi had said. But these eyes were, without exception, a menacing golden yellow.

The instinct to freeze, run, cower, weep, and beg for my life flooded me. Fear swept aside any hint of rational thought, pounded to bits any swell of bravery. My heart felt lighter than a leaf, throwing itself against the wall of my chest. Some stubborn audacity held me to my spot in Ms. Farr's entryway.

Audacity, or the sheer weight of my dragon soul.

With a sucking hiss, a dark mountain of a body rose from the murk. Taller than the devastated ceiling, muscles rippling, he pulled his scaled legs and claws from the muck. He wove his long neck with its skull of a head into the room until the lethal tips of his horns were a foot over my head. His chin and jaw glistening as he dripped swamp water.

"Belez, Massimaŭ y Draŭtox. Aaa niss sith cree rü, Calx Orosiss?"

Greetings, Massima. What do you want of us, Stone Master?

His breath seared, caustic in my nose, smelling of steaming gore.

Adrikhedon, unbound from Mom's spell. I knew the mesmerizing depth of his eyes. My gaze couldn't move from his malevolent glare, the beam of my flashlight trembling over his face. I could feel his loathing for the gold around my neck. I could feel the glow of the captured jewel, dragging him into submission. I could feel his hideous, magnificent strength. And deep in my heart, he was mysteriously, unspeakably beautiful.

I hesitated, suffering a dragon's miserable, unquenchable greed. What courage, cunning, and sheer will it took to withstand a dragon's centuries. What were humans going to do to this creature? Trimble was right; I didn't want to kill him.

Breathing in a tiny inhale, I crawled the fingers of my free hand across my chest and grabbed the Wyrmstone. My other hand fumbled in a pocket and pulled out Trimble's scroll. But I didn't need it; I knew the words to send a dragon home.

"*Adrikhedon, proch mandatum niss calx sna rů gethrix—*" Then I started the banishing spell, my voice a cracked whisper.

And then my breath stopped, cut off. I tried to inhale, but I instead a boom of a voice poured from of my throat, commanding, rushing forth Draconic as though I were a hollow pipe to blow through.

"*Up, lazy scum. Take whatever you want, rip apart whoever dares to obstruct you. Flatten, burn, and eat. The city cowers before you.*"

Pancrizio stood so close that I could smell dusty grass from the tower. His hand gripped mine, holding my fingers to the Wyrmstone as he dragged us backward, into the frame of the open front door, where he held me braced against the wood.

"*Be gone,*" we screamed.

I tried to silently conjure my sword, willing it desperately into my hand. It was beyond reach—I saw only my feet on Ms. Farr's mud soggy rug. Craning to look behind me, I searched for the boys: only darkness behind us, even the rune, gone.

"As you wish, *Massimaŏ,*" Adrikhedon smiled, teeth corroded to sharp points and slick with acid, his grin an ecstasy of destruction. Rain hammered the roof overhead, deep and violent.

He backed out of the cave of Ms. Farr's living room, into the vast pond of watching golden eyes. Heaving open his massive wings, he crouched to launch. Other scaly bodies hauled, dripping and creaking, up from the mud. *Liss!* I tried desperately to shriek at them, *liss!* No, no, no! But Pancrizio's fingers crushed mine, silencing me as effectively as a grip, tightening on my throat.

Then a light, soft and blue, floated by. A disc, glowing with fairy radiance. Behind it trailed tethered birds, white and frail, strung in a line. Beautiful doves, flapping against impossible odds. I felt the sorcerer tense, studying the filament of silver and the leashed, winged creatures. Illusion, or a dangerous animation?

How dangerous? I knew his confusion and surprise.

When you see the birds, think treasure.

I had seen treasure, unbelievable mounds of it, gleaming and breathtaking as the Dolomites where it was hidden. My father's treasure, Prince Vasborya sitting blue and terrible on the heap of it. And how I had ached for every gem and coin, my little dragon heart heavy with greed. *Cartsüm har drem, Grustiler. Raise this dream, grandmother.* Vasborya's treasure. Help me now, if for nothing else, then to save the stone. My lips mouthed the plea as my heart filled with longing.

The birds teetered, their backs burdened with gold, jewels, crowns, and pearls, dripping with coins that splashed into the devastation of the flood and sunk in the ooze.

Twenty dragons smelled treasure and turned, considering the long rope of birds. It wove among them like a thread, tangling in little loops around their spiked tails and horns. Dripping jewels, dazzling and sparkly, onto their armored hides. Bird wings fluttered soft as death, and dense vapor flowed from their feathers. Vapor that turned dark, settling on dragon scales.

I felt Pancrizio's will leave my throat for one brief moment, probing at the enchantment. Yanking free, I lunged forward, out of his reach, fumbling to feel if the leather strap had broken. Intact.

"*I command you to stay, dragons,*" I screamed in Draconic, and Deathwish was in my hand, solid as muscle. Forty yellow eyes burning with loathing, turned to study me.

The silken thread broke in a hundred places and the birds vanished. Paper boats tumbled bow over stern, spilling the contents of Styrofoam cups, spraying eyes and coating the scales of confused beasts. Snarling with alarm, they reared, rising over the ruined house in a great flock, fighting into the storm, violent as the wind that bent the trees beyond the torn roof. I wanted to run out the door, down the driveway, and back to the car where I could cower with Nicholi. Oh God, Nicholi!

The dragons hovered, wings rushing and snapping, searching for the enemy. I could see myself in their gaze, frail as a twig, sword raised in the shattered room. The sorcerer had retreated into shadows by the doorway. God how they hated the fist that drove and ruled them. Their blindsense probed the hunk of gold that hung around my neck, no heavier than a bird's egg. A tiny tangle of roots to keep them from chewing me to bits.

Then Whiff of the Enemy sunk its poisonous teeth into their hearts. With earsplitting shrieks they attacked, tearing into each other's flanks, and clawing each other's wings. Pain seared through me as they tumbled, jaws biting, necks whipping. Some fell into the pond, squawking with fury, teeth snapping at crusted underbellies. Dark blood mixed with the wind blown rain. Their helpless screams mimicked the storm.

"*Liss, liss, liss,*" bellowed Pancrizio, raising his hands to the tangled war of bodies. He leapt into the water in the sunken living room and struggled around the half-submerged furniture, staff high and sparking with power. And I wanted to run with him, stop the slaughter, protect my beautiful kind. Already some were dying, sinking below the oily waves with final, horrible cries.

Pancrizio turned his fury on me, advancing through mud as though the sword in my hand were a toy.

"Idiot child. I told your mother it had to be a boy. But she tricked me. She promised me yielding and compliance. 'Your voice will be her guide, *Nonno Sovrani.*'"

Nonno. Grandfather in Italian. He clamored up the stairs and stood within a foot of me. I could have thrust my sword into his gut. He could have knocked my head off with his staff. *Nonno.* Kill a Sovrani ancestor?

"It took me twenty years to eat my way out of her trap, only to find that she'd left me a deceitful half-dragon bitch. Give me the stone child, or I will fry it from your neck."

"*Liss,*" I hissed at him.

I pulled back my sword, ready to strike, disembowel the man who threatened me. But I doubted myself. *Nonno.* What human kills an ancestor? A dragon would do it. No dragon would hesitate. The reptilian child of Prince Vasborya would bear her teeth and bite.

"Get down," hollered a voice behind me, and a powerful hand slapped me to the ground. A ball of fire blazed over my shoulder, hitting Pancrizio square in the chest, knocking him backwards. Larry leapfrogged over me, swinging his pickax and howling. Carlo sprang off the catwalk above the sunken living room, grabbing Pancrizio and pinning his arms.

"I will find you a horrible death," Pancrizio gasped, backing away from Larry, struggling in Carlo's grip. He glared at me, then vanished.

Everyone stood still, panting, waiting for Pancrizio to reappear. Trimble aimed the burning tip of his staff into the shadows; Larry snarled at the agitated water; Carlo balanced on the balls of his feet, searching up into the broken rafters. When the sorcerer didn't materialize, Carlo helped me off the floor.

"Okay?" he asked, brushing off my coat.

"Yes," I said, because it was easier not to explain that my dragons were dying. Inside I was a seething mass of furious, miserable, jelly.

Larry stared at my sword, dangling from my trembling grasp. "You really know how to choose your weapons."

They choose me, I wanted to say. Instead I said, "I'm still alive."

Trimble, Carlo, and Larry grinned.

"Fun, isn't it?" asked Larry, and Trimble laughed.

"No." All of this useless death wasn't my idea of entertainment. "Stand back," I commanded, waving them around behind me. "Be ready if Pancrizio returns."

I watched them cautiously obey. Then I lifted the stone.

The amethyst glinted with inner light, the jewel almost too hot to touch, the golden roots clinging ferociously. This time I didn't whisper, I boomed up toward the stormy sky, where dragons tangled and plummeted in thrashing pairs. Swooping up, they dove at each other again and again, teeth, claws, and tails thrashing, now lost behind the clouds, now flashing wet scales in the rain.

"*By the power of the stone I command you,*" I thundered, filling my Draconic with their longing for a cold, solitary swamp, deep with mud, paved in its depths with consoling treasure. Chanting the spell to call them home.

One by one they tumbled from the sky, splashing up huge wakes of filthy water that rushed up our knees and sopped our already drenched clothing. Some flapped, dying. Some listed, mortally injured. Some, however, tunneled deep into the pond toward the gates. They would survive.

Gradually the turmoil of their bodies disappeared beneath the waves, and all that remained were the floating dead, slapped by wind, hammered by rain. Adrikhedon and his kin were gone. I was the only living dragon left in the modern world.

I dropped my hands, letting the icy gold warm my frozen fingers. Carlo stood beside me, watching me cautiously. He didn't reach for my hand.

"Where are Justin and Case?" I asked.

"Around back, looking for Ms. Farr." Trimble stared at me in awe. When I raised a questioning eyebrow, he turned away and stuck the still smoking end of his bamboo staff into the water. The staff steamed and bubbled.

"Where next?" asked Larry.

I pointed a quivering finger across the fetid water. "Over there. The door, hidden flush with the wall."

Larry glanced at the door, then up through the torn roof at the racing storm clouds. After a moment, his eyes met mine. "*Graven portenz*," he said, *good hunting.* He mangled the Draconic, but the camaraderie of the ancient battle cry came through. Then he turned and waded into the sunken living room, into the blackness of waist deep slime. He didn't hesitate.

I hesitated, and I had the flashlight. The water was freezing cold and reeked of decay. It was too murky to see below the surface, even with the torch beam. We would never find a small, practically weightless human body, trapped underwater.

Ms. Farr: I dreaded the brush of her dead hand, shuddered at the thought of tripping over her lifeless leg.

Stumbling over lumps of submerged furniture, I started across the room, groping ahead in the rancid water with my free hand. Dragon scales, sharp as glass, floated on the surface. Dragon blood, thick as warm tar, clung to our clothes with the mud. Carlo and I slipped and slid cautiously forward, but Larry plowed on, heedless of what he might step on.

Trimble sloshed toward the perimeter, headed for the empty shelves and the only unsubmerged remains of the room. He pulled himself up onto the catwalk, robes dripping, and began to make his way along the ledge. Halfway around the room he stopped, standing above us with his hands thrust into the shelves' recesses. Gloom gathered around him as he muttered, eyes closed.

"What's he doing?" I called to Larry.

"I'm not sure. Wizard business." He didn't pause in his wading, his powerful legs making a 'V' in the slime.

When we reached the other side of the room, I searched with my boot for the stairs, struggling to get a foothold. My legs were numb and I was nauseated from the scum that clung to my sopping clothes. I just wanted to find Ms. Farr and get out of there. Back to little Nicholi, waiting in the car, with only a flimsy Subaru and a stuffed bear between him and all of this horror. What would Ms. Whitting say?

Stay put, Nicholi, I prayed.

I scrambled up the steps, pushing to get through the bedroom door. Something held it fast. I shoved one shoulder against it. "Ms. Farr!" I yelled.

Larry and Carlo climbed up beside me. Nudging me aside, they threw themselves against the wood. The door gave a mighty crack and buckled in the center.

"A tree," said Carlo. "There's a tree in the way. Stand back."

He slammed his boot against the door and the top half shattered. Hoisting me by the waist, he raised me up to the opening. I wrestled with branches, dragging myself through the hole, and then dropping into the room.

A cedar tree had fallen into the atrium by the kitchen, ripping through the bedroom wall. The top branches tangled in the bedroom and pressed closed the kitchen door. Ms. Farr's bed had been washed against the bathroom and lay crushed under thick black boughs. Her chest of photos and clothes was submerged, sunk in the mud, the photo of her love, ruined. And the Chilkat robe?

Later, I thought, Ms. Farr first.

I shone my light toward her seat watching over the swamp, but the window was gone, and her chair had floated to the middle of the pond. It bobbed there in my flashlight beam, a vanquished throne amid dark humps of dead dragons. I turned away, guilty and aching, sure that she was dead.

Carlo and Larry had beaten in the rest of the door, scrambling over the barrier of limbs into the room.

"Where else?" Carlo asked, as I flicked my light around.

"The kitchen, by the phone."

I waded across the room and we climbed through the tree branches, pushing at what remained of the kitchen door.

"Let me," said Carlo, raising his boot. With one powerful blow, the door came down.

Through dark branches, I could barely see the sink end of the kitchen, where inches of water lapped at the lower cupboards. The fallen cedar filled the atrium, crushing the salamander feeders and bursting through the picture windows, making a hole that let in a biting wind. Branches, smelling of torn evergreen, thrust into the room. All was lit by an eerie, flickering, orange glow.

My blindsense tingled as something moved in the atrium. I tensed, raising my flashlight. Case and Justin appeared in the beam beside us and brushed quietly past, through the branches, to plant themselves by the sink. Feet spread and shoulders together, they stood side by side with wire claw and sledgehammer raised.

I hurried forward to join them, but then instinct raised a chill on my neck. I froze in my tracks. Spinning about, I looked to see what they stared at.

And there she was.

My heart rose into my throat, choking my shout of relief, jolting me with a pounding fear.

At the far end of the kitchen, she crouched on the table, gripping her knees to her chest and shivering violently. The telephone cord was slung around her neck and the phone dangled by its torn line, a weight resting against her shins. Her round eyes, shocked wide open, stared into some terrible void. Her face, framed by a filthy, sopping, terrycloth bathrobe, was as pale as death.

"Ms. Farr!" I gasped, and she raised pleading eyes to me.

On either side of the table stood salamanders. Not wet, slithering little things that burrow with cold feet under dead logs. No, reality had completely deserted us. These were two Age of Dragons Basilisks—heads brushing the ceiling, bodies of muscular men, tails of a serpent, skin on fire. The ceiling above smoked from their heat. Their flaming, snaky tails were hot enough to boil the water that sloshed against them. Rain, blowing in through the shattered wall, caused their fiery skin to sizzle.

They stared back at us, ugly reptilian faces twisted in malicious snarls, clawed hands raising metal spears as long as their bodies.

I think, had not the will of the sword surged through me,

my frail human self would have run for her life. Instead, Deathwish sprang into my hand, and the sword attacked.

The Basilisk's spear was significantly longer than my blade, but with the first swipe, Deathwish shortened his weapon by two feet. Larry was right behind me, sinking his pickax into the muscled arm that rose over my head to strike, and shoving me out of the way so he could swing again at the serpentine body. I rolled aside, away from the thrashing axe and burning, switching tail. Rushing with adrenaline, I crouched for cover.

Overhead, Case's claw winged through the air and stuck solidly to the Basilisk's face. Larry surged forward with a hailstorm of blows as the creature screamed and dropped his severed spear to struggle with the gripping claw. Lashing his tail against Larry's blows, he backed into the atrium. Cedar branches smoked and steamed as the Basilisk pressed into them. A fire alarm, set off by all the smoke, erupted into high, painful squeals, blasting through the chaos.

Then, with a fantastic leap, Carlo soared over my head into the second beast, his boot landing square on the Basilisk's hand and knocking free the spear. The weapon clattered against the cupboards and fell to the floor. Justin leapt for it, grabbing the shaft in his free hand, and then swinging his sledgehammer before him as he sprang to Carlo's side. Carlo kicked at the beast again and again as it snarled and clawed, driving it back against the wall beyond the table. His boot was on fire and the air stank of burning rubber and the bitter reek of Basilisk. Cornered and furious, the beast lunged, and its fiery hands seized Carlo by the waist. Tail whipping wildly, it squeezed, crackling flames searing through the fabric of Carlo's coat. Smoke billowed up in black clouds. Carlo twisted and struggled, grimacing in pain.

But Justin lunged forward with the spear and stabbed the thrashing tail, pinning its tip to the floor, then pounding it hard with his sledgehammer. The Basilisk heaved Carlo with a shriek, sending him soaring into Justin, who sprawled sideward, the sledgehammer flying from his hand. The hammer's iron head sailed past the Basilisk's ear, punching a hole in the wall, as Carlo crashed to the floor with a horrible thud and rolled under the table.

Carlo! He lay on his side, burning coat smoldering in the flood, the waves sloshing over his cheek. He didn't move, didn't cry out from the smoking burns. Panic gripped me. I couldn't tell if he was unconscious or dead. Could he even breathe, half-submerged in the water? The Basilisk glowered over him, hands out to take on the next attacker.

Justin dragged himself to his feet, grabbed up the kitchen chair, and smashed off a leg. Bellowing and cursing, he struck at the creature still pinned by the spear. The Basilisk thrashed, twisting to get a grip on him, as Justin bludgeoned its howling face again and again with the chair leg.

I had to do something; I was just cowering there, terrified, of no use at all. Leaping around Justin, I swung Deathwish, a heavy, awkward slice that hacked off the Basilisk's tail and sent the burning snake of it wiggling away. The beast staggered toward me, screeching.

"Stand back," screamed Trimble, and Justin shoved me to the floor, diving on top of me. Trimble bellowed a word I couldn't understand, pulled from some range deeper than even my dragon voice, and a ball of ice hurtled past our heads. The blast thumped into the Basilisk's scaly abdomen, whitened into frost, then vaporized. Trimble bellowed again and another ball of ice exploded in a cloud of steam beyond Larry, whose pickax still harried the other Basilisk. The room filled with a dense, cold fog, and it was impossible to see. Through the fog, two red glows pulsed where the Basilisks burned.

Scrambling out from under Justin, I lurched across the room. My hand swept blindly across the table, fumbling for Ms. Farr's skinny legs. I found her, icy and stiff, and put an arm around her waist. Carlo lay underneath. I needed to shield Ms. Farr and get Carlo's face out of the rancid water. My blindsense tingled, and I knew hot claws were rising over my back. Deathwish twisted to strike.

"Down," screamed Trimble.

Gripping Ms. Farr, I dove, pulling us to the floor as a freezing hail of stones seared over my head, grazing my scalp. Beyond Justin's furious bellows, beyond the grunts and the whacks of Larry's swinging axe, two red glows hissed and went out. With a crunch of pickax against plastic, the fire alarm stopped.

The room was still. I could smell fresh rain, blowing in around the toppled tree. I could taste the tang of thawing, scorched wood. I could hear the storm, howling over the roof. But I couldn't see an inch into the compact fog.

Rising to a squat, I set Deathwish down and wrapped an arm around Ms. Farr, tight over her quaking shoulders. With the other hand I reached for Carlo and lifted his head into my lap. He lay limp and heavy, half-concealed by mist.

Tears sprang to my eyes. He had to be okay. This was a world of invincibility. A world where teens best the most powerful and the heroic dead are resurrected. Just ask Case, he told legends about it. Carlo could not die.

But Mom and Dad? Died in an airplane crash, or Adrikhedon murdered them; I couldn't remember anymore. I wasn't breathing and the pressure in my chest was rising into a scream. I swallowed and tried to remember how to inhale. My fingers stroked the bristle on Carlo's cold cheek, wanting to warm the skin.

"All clear." Larry's voice was hoarse.

Careful as a tiptoe, silver light crept into the room. The fog receded. Justin stood over us, guarding Carlo, Ms. Farr, and I with his sledgehammer. Larry had his axe across his chest, facing the fallen tree where the last glow of Basilisk had vanished. Case lounged by Larry, looking about with wary eyes, wiping blood off his singed wire claw and onto his pant leg. Trimble stood in the doorway with his staff raised, light glowing from the staff's blackened tip.

"We need you, Paul," said Trimble, and everyone turned to look at Carlo.

Chapter 23

From behind Trimble's rainbow robe, Paul peeked into the room. Dead Basilisks, crushed wall, fallen tree, flooded floor, thawing ice—his gaze stopped on none of these. He studied his battered comrades one by one as they rushed forward to crouch around us. Then he contemplated Ms. Farr. Having made these rounds, he pushed by Trimble and strode straight to Carlo.

"Give me room," Paul said, and they all stepped back. He kneeled. I moved to shift Carlo's head off my lap and onto Paul's. "No, don't move. He's happier where he is," said Paul, and I flushed. He ran fingers over Carlo's face and down the sides of his neck, then over his ribs, arms and legs. He grasped Carlo's wrist, then put a cheek near Carlo's lips.

"Unconscious, breathing, nothing broken," he said.

I exhaled, choking on tears of relief. Overhead, the boys patted each other on the back and softly bumped fists.

Paul grinned. "I have smelling salts, but he might prefer a kiss?" He raised his red eyebrows.

"Don't go there," I said, but I cupped Carlo's chin and held him closer, ignoring the snickers over my head. "He's okay, then?"

"I'm not done yet." Paul peered under the jacket where two huge, scorching handprints had melted holes in the fabric. "Oh, dudes," he said, turning pale.

"What is it?" I craned to see.

Paul lifted the coat. In the glow of Trimble's staff light, two gigantic black palm prints lay wrist to wrist on Carlo's belly, ten singed claws wrapping around the thick muscles of his waist. Carlo stirred and opened his eyes, gazing with stunned confusion into my face.

"Can you feel this, Carlo?" asked Paul, brushing a finger across the burn.

"No." Carlo smiled at me, staring into my eyes.

"Crap, third degree burn. We have to get you home, cowboy. I don't have enough of a power source to heal this here," said Paul.

"Can you draw on the storm?" asked Trimble.

Paul shook his head. "That's Pancrizio's toy. He doesn't like to share."

"I'm just fine," said Carlo, in a dreamy tone.

"Home," commanded Paul.

Justin and Larry reached forward, each taking an arm to lift Carlo.

"Wait." Carlo shrugged them off and sat up. He rubbed his face and looked around, then shoved up his coat. With his thumb and first finger, he pinched the black scar. It tented and lifted, peeling away like a second skin.

"Yo!" gasped the boys, and they all leaned forward.

"Under Armor," he said. "Justin called me just as I came home from work."

Trimble lowered his staff and the full brilliance of his light fell on the thick, tan cloth that covered Carlo's trunk.

Case flashed a smile, radiant with admiration. "Assassin wear. Dude, what the heck do you *do* for a living?"

Carlo said something, but I missed it, because as he spoke another voice screamed: high, terrified, and one hundred percent Nicholi. "*Mimi!*"

Larry was out the door first, scrambling over the fallen tree with Mom's pickaxe raised. Justin loped behind, still holding the broken chair leg in his left fist and his retrieved sledgehammer in his right. Case and Trimble followed.

Carlo pulled himself to his feet and limped after them.

I lurched up, lifting Ms. Farr to a stand, my heart wrenching in two.

"Go, Mimi. Ms. Farr's going to be fine. I'll help her." Paul stood and put his arm around her. She shivered and stared, silent as death.

Hoping the shy, crew cut healer knew what he was doing, I ran.

The living room was a dark cavern under the gaping roof, wind swirling rain into our faces. We stopped at what had been Ms. Farr's bedroom door, me caught half in the branches of the fallen cedar, and the boys' dark outlines up against the shelves on the wall. No one dared move. No one could catch enough breath to speak.

Pancrizio hovered below the shattered rafters, dominating the room, lifted by some magic that caused him to glow. A little black bear dangled in one hand, gripped by the paw and swinging with each gust from the storm. Nicholi drooped from the other hand, seized at the nape of the neck like a puppy. He hung limp, as though all effort at a fight had been shaken from him. Behind them, the relentless storm surged through the torn hole in the roof.

Adrikhedon crouched, a huge slick mass in the deep water of the pond, neck thrust into the living room, steam drifting from his sunken nostrils as he sniffed Nicholi's sneakers. Every one of his inhales sucked the wind out of me. His defeated kin bobbed and sank, battered corpses filling the murky pond.

Impossible that he was still here. Impossible that he had disobeyed the stone. All of Ms. Farr's objects, taken in one huge gulp, must have given him unspeakable power. How well he lied and pretended.

"Do I have your attention, child?" Pancrizio roared into the wind. "We trade, a little boy for an amulet, and the dragon gets the bear. Or perhaps you'd like to use the Wyrmstone, see which of us controls it? Because, given a choice, the dragon would prefer to eat the boy."

I wanted to cry out, "I'll give you the stone," but I couldn't speak. Terror filled my mouth and packed the words against my tongue.

Case appeared beside me, silent as a cat. "Distract him," he whispered in my ear. "Buy us two minutes."

Mind blubbering with fear, I pulled myself free of the cedar branches and plunged waist deep into icy water. I waded into the flood, cold gripping more and more of me as I pushed through the slimy muck.

"Didoo doesn't swim," called Nicholi.

What a brave little boy. His voice didn't waver. His complete trust in me rang through his terror, denied his peril. Or perhaps he remembered that you never show fear to a dragon. I was crying now, swearing to myself, to Judge Burrows, to Ms. Whitting, to anyone who would listen, that if I got him out of this alive I'd never put him in danger again.

"Mimi, you need to listen now," called Nicholi. "Didoo wantinates to tell you something."

"Tell me, Didoo." I tried to match Nicholi's courage, but my voice cracked at Didoo's name.

"Come closer, so you can use your listening ears," said Nicholi.

Pancrizio said nothing, watching me wade in, chest deep in scum, dragging Deathwish, my sword arm impeded by thrashing waves. Hoping, maybe, that I would reach for the stone smoldering on my coat. Studying me as I put myself within reach of Adrikhedon's jaws. Pleased, no doubt, with how my every stagger forward weakened my position.

A few yards beyond me, Adrikhedon's monstrous flank glistened and stank. He bent his long neck and considered me, a look colder than the water that numbed my skin. Was it inside of courting etiquette to eat the intended? Trapped as Steve, I had imagined him having some trace of human emotion, but it was clear that this dragon had never had a single tender feeling. Lust, yes. Love, never. His crescent eyes flicked up, glancing briefly over Pancrizio's head, and I followed his gaze.

Two human shadows, one on either side of the hole in the roof, rose from a crouch and fought the wind to stay upright.

Two small phantoms, outlined in Pancrizio's glow. With a lift of hope I calculated the striking distance to Pancrizio's head, but he hung between and below them, out of reach. And Adrikhedon had clearly seen them.

"I can't come any closer," I said, wondering whose side the dragon would take. To keep the sorcerer's eyes on me, I waded in another foot, until my shoulders were wet and the edge of the floor would soon give way to the depths of the pond. Oil and scum sloshed up my neck, bitter and rotten, and I fought the urge to vomit.

Nicholi made no effort to fight, hanging limp as his bear. Beyond Pancrizio's head, one rooftop silhouette threw the end of a rope. It uncoiled across the gap in the roof, slithering in the wind, striking through the air with the precision of a snakebite. Across the gap, the other rooftop shadow caught the knotted end, and the rope tightened, a feeble bridge over a long drop. I held my breath as Adrikhedon's golden eyes watched them. But he said nothing.

"Hold on," yelled Nicholi, "Didoo changofied his mind. He wants to say something different." He peered up at the adult who held him; my little frenzied bezerker sizing up the sorcerer's malicious stare. This was no Ms. Greer. This would require no ordinary tantrum. No, Nicholi, he's too strong for you, don't do this!

"What will it be, girl? I'm out of patience." Pancrizio shook Nicholi, and held him over the dragon's steaming head.

Someone ran along the slack rope, surefooted as a cat, light as a mithril blade. The silhouette paused again and again to balance as the storm whipped the rope side to side. It was incredible; no one could keep their footing. But he kept moving forward, teetering on the swinging rope between his sprints.

"He says—" Nicholi sucked in a deep breath. He was going to bezerk. Hurl himself into a thrashing ball of fingernails, heels, and hammering fists. Drop himself right into the opening jaws of the dragon.

"No, Nicholi!" I screamed.

"Turn the dragon into a man!" yelled Nicholi.

Then he began to kick, arching his back so that his feet rammed into ribs, scratching at the tough hands that held him, yowling with the force of his frenzied fury.

Pancrizio gasped with shock and reeled from the blows. Nicholi's coat ripped, and he dangled by the torn yoke. Pancrizio dropped Didoo and seized Nicholi in both hands, battling to hang on. I held my breath as Didoo floated, suspended in the air for an instant, glowing in the pale gleam of Pancrizio's light. Then he fell.

Above Nicholi's raging tantrum, the shadowy man slid off the rope. Barely catching the rope in the crook of one knee, the rescuer swayed dangerously. Then he dropped again, one foot looping the rope, and the rope swung free, an end released. Sweeping forward, he veered toward the tumbling Didoo in a precarious arc. His foot, twisted in the loose rope, seemed too tenuous for all that weight and motion. How could he not fall? But he snatched a furry paw, oscillating back to grab Nicholi by the shredded coat. Momentum yanked Nicholi free, flinging bear, boy, and rescuer into a wild arc. The foothold gave.

Together Nicholi, bear, and rescuer dropped like a dead bird, torn coat flapping. My stomach dropped with them, clutching as they smacked water before the dragon's chest. The dragon lunged for where they had fallen, shoving aside debris to dive underwater, every tingle of his blindsense reaching for their warm, soft bodies.

Turn the dragon into a man.

Neck deep in mud, scales, and the blood of dragons I pressed my thumb against the Wyrmstone. Tell me how I do this. I opened my heart, my soul, to all I knew. Trusting myself to speak the words. You made me for this, Mom. You trusted me to save us.

Draconic poured from my throat like a gush of acid. "*Ehlar da char cartsüm ....*"

Body that life brings forth ....

I could feel the sorcerer's mind pressing into mine, bending the words toward a velvety slither of Latin, shoving aside the singed Draconic, twisting another spell out of my power. I wasn't going to succeed: my spell was drifting. The dragon, snapping and rooting in the muck before me, sloshed up slimy waves that filled my mouth.

I sputtered, dug in my submerged pocket, and took out the cinnabar vial. Holding it above me, I flicked off the top. Waves knocked me side to side as I aimed. With a wild fling I splashed toward my face. Missed. Splashed again, wondering if I had wasted the last few drops in the bottle. Night Veil slapped into my pores, the pungent smell stiffening my will.

"*Ka trajikalor niss vitthrik ....*"

Precious substance of human ....

One by one the words pounded, thinned, then ripped through Pancrizio's Latin. In a rush, I spat out the final phrase, rasped into the wind. Before me, Adrikhedon wailed in fury and turned on me. His long neck slid upward, aching over my head, his face all teeth, horns, and spikes. He opened his jaws, and I gasped into the corroded depth of his throat. Then he vanished, leaving a bobbing human body.

I struggled against the backwash, quaking with adrenaline and cold. My eyes strained to see Nicholi's little head. A furry, wet paw. The face of his rescuer.

Case? It must be Case. Who else would try such a stunt? I saw no one.

Underwater? Hiding among the dead dragons? Frantic to see over the waves, I jammed Mom's empty vial into my pocket and plowed forward, dragging my sword.

A force of light smacked my head, knocking me dizzy. Pancrizio hovered over me, hand raised. Another explosion fired from his palm. I sank beneath the slime, no time to take a deep breath as light whacked the water and shook the waves. Blast after blast lit the scummy murk before me, sharp claps stabbing in my ears. At least with the fleeting light I could see. I gripped Deathwish and swam deeper, searching for curls, a widow's peak, or a bear's tattered ears. Where were they? The water was absolutely black and thick. Scales sliced, stinging my face. My head ached from the sorcerer's blow and my eyes burned as I peered through slits. I needed my four inner eyelids to shield me from the murk, and my ability to breathe underwater. A breath of air. Pancrizio floated above, exploding his rage down on me. I had to find them.

I had to have a breath. There was no sign: no shoe, no shred of cloth. Just one breath, so I could search again.

Squeezing my sword, I squirmed to the surface. As the ball of light hurtled down on me, I threw the blade over my head. My body jolted with pain, but Deathwish deflected the blow. Was this a horrible enough death for me, or would the sorcerer have preferred something else? I gasped a lungful of foul air and dove again.

I could sense fathoms below me—that sinking terror of depths that causes every cell to shrink away. The floor of the house had given way and the pond was dreadfully deep. Not a pond, a submerged cavern, burrowed into the earth. Far below me: the border crossing. I tuned my senses to warmth, skin, and beating hearts, reaching blind, feeling with every dragon cell for human hearts. Nothing.

Something floated before me, hard, slick, and scaled. A dead dragon. They must be on the other side, hiding against its bulk. I stuck my sword in my belt and pressed a hand against the cold flesh. Hand over hand, I pulled myself along the submerged belly. Jagged edges of scaly armor sliced my fingers. My sword made me clumsy. Light exploded again and again, and the massive carcass rocked as it absorbed the blows.

I reached a drifting broken wing, a folded tent of bones and leather. Diving deep, I kicked, pushing under the spiked elbow, then popping up above the surface. A roof of snapped bones and twisted skin arched overhead, translucent with trickles of veins when backlit by the sorcerer's fire.

No Nicholi. No Case. No bear.

I treaded water, peering through rips in the pelt. Every-where, dead dragons obscured my view, dark as hilly graves. Nicholi and his rescuer couldn't be gone. My heart labored with unbearable weight, deep and desperate. I trembled in the water, tears mixing with the rain, more bitter than the foul water in my mouth. When Mom and Dad died, I thought nothing would ever be worse. But this loss I could not sur-vive.

Something moved from the crevice under the dragon's shoulder.

I surged toward it. "Nicholi?" My nose smelled hostility and Deathwish was in my hand, rising up in defense.

"I didn't eat him. In fact, I would have preferred the bear."

Steve. Even in the dark, covered with muck and dog pad-dling, head barely above water, I knew him. I felt his blue eye appraising Deathwish, his green eye warily watching the stone around my neck, hanging by the cord's thread. Sensed his calculations on the sword's angle and the thread's strength, as he inched away from the dead dragon's side, coming closer.

"Where is he?" I asked, angry, hopeful, devastated.

But Steve only snorted. "Enjoying your toy?" He nodded at the amulet.

One handed, I tucked it back into its bag. "I thought the stone would send you back across."

He grinned, yellow teeth exposed by the distant flash of another attack of light. "And leave our courtship incomplete? You think too much and know too little. Did you find my gift?"

I panted with exhaustion, fighting to stay upright, freezing cold. Squinting at the choppy surface beyond our hiding place, I hoped for another blast to illuminate the water and show me a little curly head. "Basilisks?"

Steve laughed, scraping and cynical. "No. They were for Ms. Farr, to remind her not to steal cinnabar vials from dragons. I left you something more pleasant. Ask your wizard, Trimble. Perhaps he planned to keep it for himself."

"I won't accept it."

"We'll see." He looked around, a frosty, calculating inspection. The sorcerer's blasts were closer now. One seared our hide roof, fizzling in the water a few feet away, exposing the storm that raged overhead. "Well, I suppose it's time to end this. Shall we go to Mexico?"

The thought turned my stomach over. "No." I raised Deathwish. "I'm going to kill you for murdering my parents."

Steve laughed. "So you believe her. Why? Because she's your grandmother? I didn't kill your parents, she did. Vedette was too weak for Pancrizio, incapable of breaking the gold. Yvess decided that you were more likely to succeed."

I poked with my sword point, and he retreated. "But you had the Cinnabar vial."

"Ah! Clever. That just proves I was there, not that I killed them."

He grinned, backed up against the dragon carcass. I should whack through his filthy throat, slice that disgusting leer clean off. I could feel Deathwish, surging with the will for it. But he was right; Yvess had more motive for killing my parents than he did, and how lucky for her if I slew Adrikhedon in revenge. I lowered the sword.

"Turn me back into a dragon. I could do it, but it would waste too many artifacts. Human bodies are worse than useless."

"What are you going to do?"

"Whatever you ask, pretty *Massimaŭ*."

My hand slid to the Wyrmstone. There was only one thing I could trust him for. "*Mert Atarviss*," I whispered. *Kill the sorcerer.*

"With pleasure." And Steve sunk underwater, gliding away as I mouthed the spell.

Adrikhedon burgeoned from the pond with an explosion, startling Pancrizio, who floated in the turbulent wind just above us. Waves slammed me against the carcass in his wake, and I clung on to keep from sinking.

With a flap of his wings, Adrikhedon struck upward, snapping at the floating sorcerer. His lunge drove Pancrizio higher, out of reach of his fierce jaws.

Pancrizio fired and hit the dragon square on the forehead. "Do not challenge me, Adrikhedon," he snarled.

The dragon shrieked and lifted heavily from the water, taking flight.

Pancrizio attacked, exploding bursts of power on wings, neck, and flank. But Adrikhedon circled back, flapping in the rain and wind, acid spraying from his mouth with every scream. They rose high above me, lashing at each other in the sky, swirling in streams of acid and cracks of fire.

Defeat him, Adrikhedon. For eight hundred years you

have dreamed of tasting his blood. Now comes a dragon's revenge.

I ducked underwater, out from under cover of the wing, searching with my dragon sight for a little foot, a tiny hand, lit by the wrath of their fight. Nothing but dark and wild, branches floating, corpses sinking, waves in a frenzied dance. I was exhausted, defeated, so far beyond cold that I was numb to my shivering. But there was no giving up.

Get help?

I looked back to the cave of the living room. The boys stood in the light of Trimble's staff, up on the platform and out of the flood, attention riveted on the pond. Carlo's thick silhouette, pacing the walkway; Larry squatting, short and coarse as a rock; Trimble thin, with wet robes twisted around him; Case slumped against the wall and half hidden in shadows.

Nicholi trusted me, the boys trusted me, and I'd failed. I would lose Justin, too, to a broken heart.

Wait—Case?

Then I saw a lump, hunched on the platform at Case's feet, tricky to see in the shadows. Too big to be Ms. Farr. Two heads—Paul and Ms. Farr? No, there was Ms. Farr. Paul had her wrapped in his coat and stood over her in the shelter of the front doorway. Justin holding Nicholi? It had to be. My heart bounded, and then faltered. Was Nicholi alive?

I thrashed in the water, my crawl impeded by the sword. With an impatient wave I willed the weapon away, feeling the hilt vanish in my grip.

When I hauled myself out of the slime, Larry stepped off the platform.

"Who is it?" he demanded, axe up, peering into the dark.

"*Massimaŭ*." I spoke without thinking, as if only my strongest self could face them, bear up under such failure.

"Thank God." Carlo stepped off the platform and threw an arm around my shoulder. "When we saw the dragon fly, we were sure we'd lost you."

"Not yet." I pulled away from the warmth of his hug and kneeled on the catwalk by Nicholi. His little head was covered by Justin's coat. Justin's skin was ashen under his strings of dark hair, and his pained eyes lifted to mine. I tugged aside the coat. Nicholi's eyes were closed. His widow's peak lay flattened by filthy water. His lips looked blue in Trimble's light.

"Sweetheart," I whispered.

He opened his eyes. "Didoo is dying," he said, and out from under the coat he pulled the grimiest bear any boy had ever loved. "I couldn't keep his head above water." My tears fell on Nicholi's face, and he swiped them away with a balled-up fist, lips trembling. "Help him Mimi. Get him the Chilkat robe." And in that moment, I knew Adrikhedon's gift.

Chapter 24

"Let's go." Paul hurried across the room, sloshing through mud. "I can't do much here, and several people need serious care."

Justin stood up, cuddling Nicholi like a doll.

"Wait." I turned to Trimble. "There's a gift for me?"

"Is that what it is?" Trimble pointed to a shelf. "It's so shrouded in Conceal I couldn't get a good look. Case?"

Case drifted out of the shadows and over to the shelf. On the warped and musty wood, visible only when Trimble's blue light fell directly on it, was a patch of—well—nothing. A rectangular box where space stopped and a delicate void began.

"Awesome, dude, the forth trap. Knew it was here somewhere, but I couldn't sniff it out." Case slipped a hand into his pocket and took out a slender pick. "What's my luck, Justin?" he asked.

Still snuggling the wrapped up Nicholi, Justin worked a die out of his pocket and rolled it on his palm. "Fourteen. Hurry, we've gotta go."

Case grunted. He poked once, cautiously, as though the cavity were a beehive. Then he stuck in both hands, working blind. There were clicks and snaps, and he grimaced. "Who conjured this lock? It's beast." He drew his fingers out, scratched and bleeding. He put a hand in his pocket and took out a wad that looked like chewed gum. "Hold your ears." He plunged both hands back in, then rapidly snatched them out again.

There was a pop pop pop, like gunfire, and everyone took a step back. A package appeared, wrapped in my mother's soft, green sweater and tied neatly with cord, as if it had been delivered by UPS. Case looked at the handwriting on the envelope, pinned to the front. "Yours," he said, and he sauntered a few steps and handed it to me.

Massimaŭ y Draŭtox, the writing said. I ripped at the bands of string that lashed the parcel together. It was so effectively bound that I could only expose a corner of the cloth underneath. Gold and black, coarse textured and hand woven: thank you, Adrikhedon.

Trimble left the knot of onlookers and hurried to my side. "Mimi, you know the rules."

"Anyone have a knife?" I pulled aside more sweater, exposing the fringe.

Trimble put a steadying hand on my sleeve, restraining me. "Think about what you're doing. You have the option to put it back."

I pushed his hand aside. "No, I don't."

"You'd trade your life for Didoo's?" he asked, face ashen.

I didn't answer.

Everyone gathered around; Carlo behind Case, Larry with his axe slung over his shoulder, and Paul supporting Ms. Farr.

Nicholi struggled in Justin's arms, and Justin set him down.

"The robe!" Nicholi staggered forward, offering up his limp, disheveled bear. "Hurry Mimi, hurry."

"Give me a knife," I said. *Worth more money than you'll ever make, from now until you die*, Steve had said. I had nothing to equal this robe: nothing but my Wyrmstone. I should be frightened, but my fear was worn out. I was a beast of fate. Life was a bag of groceries, and all we could do was hope to make something palatable from its contents.

Case rummaged in a pocket and came out with a switchblade, stained with dry blood. A responsible adult, one who had taken parenting classes, would have asked whose blood. I just gripped the razor sharp knife and sliced through the rope. Then I closed my eyes, embraced my fate, and spread my arms, unfurling the swath of cloth. The long white fringe tumbled free and the white spirit bear of the Tsimshian people grimaced in his black frame.

"Whoa!" gasped the boys.

Nicholi snatched at the robe, struggling to fold its heavy thickness over his bear. "Help me, Mimi." I lifted the robe and wrapped it around the sliced cloth of Didoo's body, torn as if by dragon talon, half the stuffing gone and the tummy now gaunt. Mud from Didoo's fur stained the magnificent cloth.

"Who gave you this?" Justin reached for the envelope and saw that it had no return address. He shook the envelope, and a folded letter fluttered out. It drifted between us, and slid into my hands. The boys crowded around to read over my shoulder. It was dated today.

"Massimaŭ,

I knew you would choose wisely. What do you own that means as much to me, as Didoo's life means to you? Or perhaps we shall go to Mexico, after all. Then again, it is more pleasant to fight things that taste sweet when the fight is over. I look forward to your next choice."

Trimble draped Mom's sweater over my shoulders and gripped me with both hands, squeezing tight.

"Did Ms. Farr give the blanket to Didoo?" asked Nicholi, rocking Didoo in the bulky swaddling and peering at the poor, silent woman who drooped against Paul.

Justin grimaced with revulsion. "The dragon sent it, Nicholi, not Ms. Farr."

"Why would a dragon give away his treasure?" Nicholi twisted the blanket and face to face, the bears studied each other.

Justin cautiously fingered the fringe on the blanket. "What have you done, Mimi?"

"Nothing you wouldn't have done. Let's go." I jumped off the platform and slogged through water, headed for the door.

Above us, the storm abruptly stopped. Winds that had torn forests to shreds, fell silent. The rain quit slapping the roof. For a moment, there was blessed quiet.

Then, into the silence, came the wavering, shrill howl of a fire truck.

"Firemen, and where there's firemen, there's police," said Case, slinging his coil of rope over his shoulder. "Let's get out of here." He sprang off the platform and glided through the flooded living room without seeming to disturb the water.

Boys snatched up belongings and hurried after. Paul and Larry carried Ms. Farr. Nicholi straddled Justin's shoulders, Didoo, robe, and the sledgehammer all cradled in Justin's arms.

"Thanks for saving Nicholi, Case," I said as he, Carlo, and Trimble caught up with me.

"Oh, you have Carlo to thank for that. I just threw the rope."

"Carlo, you walked that rope?" I was more than surprised; I was stunned.

We were at the door. Trimble gave one glance back at the destroyed house before dousing his staff light.

"Yeah." Case elbowed Carlo in the ribs. "This dude's a ninja," and he chuckled with awe.

Carlo shrugged, eyebrows up, gentle lines of his lips smiling. "That's-what-friends-are-for," and "Anything-for-you," said the gesture. A shrug that went into *my* collection.

The dragon rune was gone and the driveway pitch dark. The storm had blown over and trees creaked and sighed with relief. A piece of moon came out from behind dark clouds. It was a blessing not to be rained on. From down the end of the driveway, flashing lights and sirens cut through the black.

"See ya," said Case, and he stepped off the porch and vanished into the forest. The boys accepted their slyfoot's desertion without so much as watching him go.

Cars and trucks bumped and rocked down the driveway, rolling over downed branches, through ruts and deep puddles. A police car pulled to a stop and a uniformed man got out, his body striped red and blue by the swirling lights. He flashed his overhead spotlight around the scene, and then focused the beam on us.

"Police! Hold it right there. Hands up."

I squinted into the blaring light, one hand over my eyes. Now they arrive, when all the trouble is over. Well at least they could help us get home. Just don't let them insist on Ms. Whitting's emergency room.

Justin put down the robe and sledgehammer and slung Nicholi off his shoulders. Paul and Larry set Ms. Farr on her feet and put up their hands. Trimble raised his staff. Carlo showed empty, spread fingers.

The policeman, backlit by the red, blue, and white, stepped into Ms. Farr's devastated front yard.

"You're under arrest. Put down everything you're carrying."

"We haven't done anything," I said.

Trimble dropped his staff, and it clattered and rolled to a stop at the policeman's feet. Larry dropped the pickax, and Paul and Justin showed empty hands. Nicholi inched forward and dug his bear out of the robe, then backed up against Justin's legs.

"I think there's been a misunderstanding, officer—" I started.

"You too, son." The man gestured for Nicholi's bear.

"This is Didoo," said Nicholi, stuffing the poor, torn-up bear down the front of his shirt. "He belonginates with me."

"Put him down."

Nicholi stood stock still, hair filthy, clothes plastered in mud, face white in the vibrant light. "No," he said, with that edge of warning that made me brace myself. No Nicholi, please.

The policeman took a step forward. Other police came out of obscurity, tall shadows streaked by the light, closing in. Groups of firemen hovered in the background. Nicholi shrank back and hung onto Justin's legs.

"Just put him down, son." The officer inched closer, gun drawn now, holding out a hand for the bear that Nicholi frantically stuffed deeper in his shirt.

Then Nicholi made his move. With a shriek, he dashed off the steps, leaped over the robe, pickaxe, sledgehammer, and staff, latched onto the officer's leg, and bit.

The man yowled and staggered backwards, a little alligator glued to his shin. More police sprang from a car. From all sides men closed in, reaching to subdue my frenzied brother.

I pushed forward, desperate to get to Nicholi. "Stop, wait, he's just a kid!"

They had him surrounded.

Police rushed forward, seizing Larry, Justin, and Trimble by the arms. Paul slumped to the ground and curled into a little ball.

I circled the ring of struggling men around Nicholi, distraught and frantic.

"Noooooooooooo," Nicholi shrieked through his mouthful of leg, thrashing in the midst of them, driving them back as they danced around his kicking legs.

A gun went off, the *pow* echoing in wet air. The reverberation ricocheted off the trees and slammed against my heart, knocking the wind out of me.

Nicholi let out a blood curdling scream. The commotion stopped, frozen mid fight. The red and blue flashing lights abruptly dimmed and mist hung over the pure white scene. Everyone stared in amazement as Nicholi screamed and screamed and screamed, loud enough to shame the storm.

I staggered forward and fell to my knees, tears streaming down my face, reaching for my fallen baby brother. The bitten policeman, petrified with dismay, stood clutching his gun, mesmerized by the blood.

Justin heaved aside the man who held him. He launched off Ms. Farr's doorstep and headed for his brother, clothes disheveled, hair in his scratched face, closing in with furious, heavy strides. He looked powerful enough to snap the poor, distraught policeman in two.

"Stay back!" Three police trained guns on Justin.

Justin stopped in his tracks. With a smooth plunge into his pocket, he pulled out his die. He flipped the little red plastic piece into the air and it tumbled across the dirt. With a bounce and a skip it rolled and turned over.

A one.

Justin stared at the number, transfixed by fate's decision. Fate had commanded that he stand by, powerless, while Nicholi bled. Fate, the rough teacher who dragged us all through life's lessons, gave Justin one final and terrible instruction.

Justin took a step backward, his face contorted with helplessness. Then, something inside him snapped. Like a slave splitting his shackles, Justin raised his arms. He bellowed, all the sadness and suffering at the hands of fate pouring out. He howled a misery that silenced even Nicholi. He staggered forward and kicked aside the die. It sailed, hopping across puddles and bouncing over rocks, and landed with a whack against my leg. I seized it in one hand. Collapsing at the policeman's feet, Justin gathered his little brother into his lap. Everyone drew back as he put his hands on Nicholi's belly, into the terrible, hot, red dampness.

"Nicholi, Nicholi." He forced Nicholi to uncurl, squeezing Didoo's sagging tummy through the shirt.

"Are you all right?" Tears streamed down Justin's face.

"Noooooooooo. He shot Didoo," wailed Nicholi. "He shot Didoo."

Justin's face twisted with anguish. "Don't die," he whispered, rocking back and forth. "Don't die."

My fingers tightened over Justin's die, clutching it hard enough to hurt. I could not accept the scarlet stain, wet on Nicholi's side. I wanted to squeeze so hard that the die was crushed. I wanted to squeeze so hard that fate obeyed me. I crawled toward my brothers.

Paul slipped between the stunned police and laid hands on Nicholi, searching under the bloody shirt. "Shh, now," he murmured to Nicholi. "Bring me the robe," he said over his shoulder. Hands red with blood, Paul too began to rock back and forth, whispering in Nicholi's ear.

"Miss, step aside with your hands up." A policeman stood over me.

"The Chilkat robe, hurry," Paul insisted, looking back to see if anyone responded.

But Carlo, Trimble, and Larry all had handcuffs on.

"That's my brother," I said numbly. "He needs that Chilkat robe." I stood up, pointing. Nicholi's eyes closed and his breathing quieted.

"The paramedics are on the way. Hands up, miss, you're under arrest." The policeman waved his flashlight as though to direct me back to the guarded knot of boys.

"For what?" I walked backwards toward the robe, staying out of his reach.

"For murder." He slid a flashlight beam over the broken ground to the base of a fallen cedar. There in the roots, mangled and horribly broken, lay the sorcerer's body. Next to him slouched Steve, sneering at the policeman's gun in his ribs.

"I'm not leaving my family." I fell to my knees, and grabbed the robe. Dragging its weight, I staggered across the yard and wrapped Justin, Paul, Nicholi, and Didoo in its blessed peace. Then I hung on to them with all of my strength.

Chapter 25

Life had rolled the die, packed its suitcases, and accepted fate's decision to walk out on me. Every time I opened my eyes, the bare jail cell looked bleaker. The plastic chair, crushed by some past prisoner and tossed in a corner. The cot, bolted to the wall with huge rivets, as if we criminals were too much for legs to bear. One blanket, too thin for warmth. And dark, it was so dark in there, as if the fluorescent light overhead had given up hope. Every time I closed my eyes, Nicholi's chalky face appeared, immobile and tear streaked in the vast blackness behind my lids. Everyone I cared about rolled in the void in my head, waiting to see how fate would toss us. No one came with any news.

The boys were all in jail: juvy, I hoped. Or at least together so they could defend each other. I couldn't bear to think about it. Except Case. God only knows where Case was. No one revealed that he was with us, and if the police searched, they never found him. A slyfoot didn't worry about right or wrong, I reminded myself. They protected themselves and their own—in that order. But I couldn't imagine how he could help us, even if he was willing to risk himself.

Ms. Farr was homeless, abused, and robbed of everything she owned. My dear, precious, helpless friend, whom I had last seen wrapped in Mom's sweater, being hustled into a squad car. Surely they had not put her in jail. Mr. Eastman would stick her in the first nursing home with an open bed. In a hurry, as always, to get the job done.

And Carlo. A good man wanders into the bad part of town too often, and sooner or later it catches up with him. Those invisible strings that repeatedly snagged him into my problems, now tightened around his neck. Romantic interest in me was the kiss of death. And I couldn't tell either Duke or Carlo that I was sorry.

The body Pancrizio had forced me to conjure lay in the morgue, demanding an explanation. His soul had fled back into the gold, per Trimble's whispers in the squad car. Trimble was surely right, and just as surely, would not be believed if he said so. I had no idea what to do about any of it, too scared and overwhelmed to hardly think.

My arraignment loomed, but even if they offered bail and release conditions I didn't have the money to post bond. The public defender hadn't known what to make of my story when we met early this morning. In the end he had recommended that I, "stick to the facts." I wondered which facts those were, and how they would compare to the facts the boys were selecting.

And my Wyrmstone, the one that was supposed to give me such power, burned like a hunk of hot lead, searing a hole in a plastic bag in Officer Dray's locked drawer. I could feel it like a sore on my blindsense. Evidence, he'd said. The only thing it proved was my knack for catastrophe. At least he'd locked it up. Perhaps it wouldn't get it's clutches into anyone else before I'd served my time.

I lay on my cot looking at the ceiling. White, I suppose, but in the shadowy room it could have been any color. I kept my eyes open until they burned. I didn't want to close them and see Nicholi. I couldn't bear the guilt and pain. I'd give anything to be in Ms. Whitting's emergency room, taking a tongue lashing for my incompetence. Instead, Nicholi was alone there. I shuddered to think what would happen if they took Didoo away. Maybe Nicholi was too injured to fight back. No, I couldn't think that way. He was okay. He had to be. Even if I was never allowed to see him again, please, just let him live.

There was a bang on metal, echoing off the walls, and the door to my cell slid open.

"Arraignment," said the guard.

I sat up and cringed, bruised all over from yesterday's fights. I swung my legs off the bed and hauled myself to my feet. Time to patch together some of those elusive facts, try to tell a story that someone would believe.

It was the smallest room that could possibly squeeze in five people. The stenographer hid in a corner behind the bulk of Judge Burrows. A table, piled with papers, took the rest of the room. My attorney pressed shoulder to shoulder with the prosecutor, facing the Judge, backs against the wall and whispering together so low that even my dragon hearing couldn't catch their words.

Judge Burrows fiddled with his papers impatiently then

coughed: a harsh, tired sound. "Do we have a decision, gentlemen?"

"Yes." The prosecutor, a lean, athletic looking man, shoved a ream of documents across the linoleum table. "We have a full confession to the murder from Steve Eastman. Ms. Jovel had no motive and, given the amount of damage to the corpse, likely lacked sufficient strength. Reviewing the evidence, I have no probable cause to hold the defendant."

My heart leapt, joy trying to bound over my wall of doubts. Steve confessed! He took the fall for us. Why? Whatever devious plans Adrikhedon hatched, I was eternally grateful.

Judge Burrows raised a weary eyebrow. "You're dropping the charges?" He sounded disappointed.

"Yes. Steve Eastman claims he killed the front man who was blackmailing him for a cut of the stolen artifacts. Our lie detector seems to think this is the truth."

King Adrikhedon's mind, probed by the wires and chips of a lie detector; there is so little honesty in Adrikhedon, it's a wonder the machine didn't implode.

"The destruction of property charges?" asked the judge.

"Being investigated. So far, there is only evidence of the worst storm in fifty years," said the prosecutor. If he didn't mention dragon corpses, then I wasn't going to either.

"And the resisting arrest charges?"

By this point, Judge Burrows was starting to glower, and I kept my head down submissively, for the first time in my life hoping to look the sweet and innocent creampuff.

"The police haven't filed any charges yet," said my attorney, a wizened old Hispanic with a gentle, persuasive voice.

"Officer Dray is asking for a final statement from Ms. Jovel." I cringed inside, hoping I could keep my facts straight under a Dray-style grilling. "Unless there are further charges against her, you have no grounds to hold my client in jail."

"Well then," Judge Burrows tossed his reading glasses onto the table with disgust, "case dismissed."

I stood up. In the dark recesses of that horrible jail cell I'd rolled a ten, and life had just given me a luck point. I was unable to contain the storm of my emotions: tears of joy and squeezing guilt and the sudden irresistible urge to sprint to the emergency room.

"Can I go now?" I asked.

Judge Burrows put his glasses back on and studied me, looking, I suppose for traces of my guilt. But his 'sense motive' was not nearly as good as Case's.

"You are a difficult little miss, aren't you? Relax, Ms. Jovel. The jail staff will process your release in due time."

Due time turned out to be three hours. It was past noon when my cell door finally opened, startling me out of my obsessive pacing.

"Let's go," said the guard. She led into the visiting room. I sat in the musty little booth with a dirty plastic ashtray and picked up the phone, peering through the wired security glass to see who had come for me.

Marcella?

How odd to see her here, out of the context of the office, sliver drifts of her hair tangled in the nap of her fleece coat, and that open, lovely face. She clutched her receiver. "Are you okay, Mimi?"

"Well, I—" Her gaze, so motherly in its concern, over-whelmed me. I put down the phone and burst into tears. I couldn't lie and tell her that I felt fine, and I didn't have the strength to tell the truth.

"Never mind," the receiver warbled from table top. "We'll talk about it later." Marcella took a Kleenex from her pocket and, realizing that she couldn't hand it to me through the glass, used it to dab at her own eyes.

I collected myself and lifted the phone. "Nicholi?" I asked, and I held my breath.

"Your little brother wasn't hurt. The bullet went through Didoo's belly and hit the policeman in his own leg. The ER doc who took care of the policeman thought he'd be okay."

"Thank God. Oh, thank God." I filled with hot, rushing relief. Grateful tears poured down my cheeks. Shaking so hard I could hardly swipe, I used the cuff of my orange jail suit to wipe my nose. "And Didoo?"

Marcella hesitated, taking solace from her sopping Kleenex, and my heart clutched. "Dr. Harvey tried, but—" fresh tears came into her eyes, "the bear just fell apart in his hands."

No. I closed my eyes. Not Didoo. Nicholi wouldn't be able to endure life without him. The pain was too much, and I put my head in my hands, sobbing. Soft round ears, frayed pink nose, his whole being a love and comfort. Oh, my poor little brother. When I could finally speak again I asked, "Where is Nicholi now?"

Marcella reached over and laid a restraining hand on the glass, as if to contain my reaction. "He's been released to Dr. Harvey."

"Released to Dr. Harvey?" My pulse sped up, and I felt lightheaded.

"Yes, they called Ms. Whitting. As you can imagine, she was none too pleased."

My pulse leapt wildly. "Am I going to lose custody of my brothers?"

"She's trying. There is an emergency hearing this afternoon."

"Today? But I wasn't notified!"

Judge Burrows had said nothing, and it would have been so easy for him to mention the hearing at my arraignment. What had I ever done, besides being small and female, to make him mistrust me so much? Maybe he knows I'm a dragon. If I hadn't been so upset the thought would have made me laugh.

Marcella dragged down the corners of her lips, making a heart-shaped frown. "Three o'clock. I bet Ms. Whitting planned to send you notice at two fifty-five."

God, how Whitting must hate me. Thanksgiving Day, and here was the Jovel family, back to haunt her on a major holiday. A court hearing instead of turkey. She was no doubt stuffed, from sandal to Patchouli-dabbed earlobe, with pent-up revenge.

I looked around at the guards standing against the wall, the buzz-locked doors, and the cracked, barred security glass. "I need to get out of here," I said with desperation. "I need to get to that hearing."

"You have a few hours yet. I brought you some clothes." She held up a paper grocery sack. "My God look at you.

Didn't they let you have a shower?"

"A brief one, no shampoo."

"Phew." She wrinkled her nose.

"Is my friend Carlo out?"

"Anna paid bail early this morning. I called him. He's waiting to drive you to the hearing." What a relief to know he's free, that he'll be there.

"And the boys?" It was too much to hope they'd rolled high numbers, too.

Marcella hunched a little shrug. "Still waiting for final word from the police department on charges."

I leaned toward the glass. "Do you know anything about Ms. Farr?"

"The ER treated her for shock and released her. Carlo and Anna took her home with them, and she'll follow up with Dr. Harvey next week."

So we might make it through with no one else dead. Mom, Dad, Duke, Didoo: the list was already too long. I had to get my brothers back, then put an end to this Pancrizio jerk. And, my human self decided, I'd do it with no more lost loved ones.

"Where's Dr. Harvey?" I asked.

Marcella scowled. "In the waiting area, contemplating his sins." She wrapped her sweater around herself and clenched her arms across the overlapping flaps. "He's coming in next to apologize, and to explain." She did not use 'we', she used 'he'.

"Apologize? Explain what?"

She shook her head, a defiant flip worthy of a teed off beauty queen. "I'll let him tell you that." She leaned over and blew me a kiss. "Call me when you get home. Let me know how I can help."

"Thank you, Marcella." I ached to throw my arms around her, smell her baby powder and rubbing alcohol, and hold her tight.

Dr. Harvey hesitated at the booth, as though not daring to trespass. I nodded and gestured to the chair.

"I hoped you'd say that," he mouthed. He removed his coat and lifted his cap, then sat down and surveyed my face with a professional eye. "You've changed into a formidable young woman," he said into the phone after his brief exam. "I'd say rescuing old ladies is good for you." He set his cap on the booth table.

If he only knew the half of it. "It wasn't good as far as Ms. Whitting was concerned."

Dr. Harvey wrinkled his forehead with disgust. "I think her zeal for a good night's sleep clouds her professional judgment." Then he sat back, his spine as straight as the line of his lips, and I wondered what he had to say that caused such a pensive look.

I shifted the phone to my shoulder so I could push filthy hair out of my eyes. "Thank you—" I swallowed hard, "—for trying to save Didoo. And for taking responsibility for Nicholi. Foster care would have been—"

"Yes." Dr. Harvey cringed, as though I'd rapped him on the head. "Unthinkable. Actually, I sent Nicholi home with Anna Rossi."

"Thank you." Nicholi in his own home, asleep. Nothing in the whole world could be sweeter than that. And then I imagined him without Didoo and my heart twisted.

Through the wired glass I contemplated the old man, so stiff with British reserve. He'd stood by my family through every illness we'd faced for twenty years. But I never thought it was in his job description to accept legal responsibility for Nicholi in the midst of a crisis, or to make house calls to jail. I sat tongue-tied, wishing I had Case's 'sense motive.'

Without raising his gaze off his cap, Dr. Harvey said, "Marcella has finally agreed to marry me. After thirty years."

"Oh? Congratulations. But … ?" Now I was really baffled. I glanced at the clock on the wall behind him, wishing he would get to the point.

The smile dissolved off Dr. Harvey's face. "Well, yes, that's what I'm here about, isn't it?" He gripped his hands, running his fingers over veins and wrinkles. "Doctoring is not … well, it's not all it's made out to be. There is a part of the job that takes more of a toll than the deaths and the late hours. You see—"

He looked up, a vulnerability in his old face that no amount of resolve could hide. "—Of all the weights that I've borne with a stethoscope about my neck, the task of keeping my patients' secrets has been the heaviest. I keep a secret whether I approve or not, whether it helps or injures, whether it festers or rots."

Sadness wrung his voice dry, and he cleared his throat in an effort to go on. "Marcella is unable to tolerate this unbreakable rule. She vowed years ago that she'd never marry a man who let rigid regulations force him down the wrong path. I'm human, she reminds me, with as much responsibility for my soul as any other human. 'Propose to me when you are in a position to be ethical,' she said, 'I'm not interested in the just-doing-my-job type.' So, she has loved me for this eternity, but refused me—" His cheeks flushed a little. "Then she found out that my silence endangered your lives."

The tremor in his hand made his fingers dance across the plaid wool of his cap, and he steadied himself by gripping the bill.

"When Justin came to the office the other day, he told Marcella that the Wyrmstone now possesses you, Mimi."

I nodded cautiously, tense tingles prickling my chest, not sure how far could I trust this rational man of science with our irrational troubles.

"Justin told Marcella that she could believe him or not, but if either of us knew anything about the Wyrmstone we should speak up. Of course, she knew nothing. I, in my ethical wisdom, didn't talk about Vedette's mental health problems. Not even to Marcella."

His gaze held such regret that I panicked. What was he about to say? How ironic if, after roasting in the crucible of magic, I was diagnosed with an inherited mental disease and transferred to the psych ward.

"When Ms. Whitting called to tell me that Nicholi was in the ER, Marcella pried from me all that I knew, insisting that your lives depended on it. She was furious when she heard that I had refused to tell you. It was she who sent me to collect Nicholi. She told me it was finished between us if I didn't tell you the absolute truth. So, I don't know if this will help or damage, but here it is."

He took a deep breath, pulling air in slowly all the way to the bottom of his lungs, taking his final breath as the keeper of confidences. His exhale was an exhausted sigh.

"Vedette was ecstatic when she brought you to me. There was a—" He raised his bowed head and his eyes travelled over my face as if he might not go on, then he hung his head again. "There was a hole in Vedette. Perhaps from her sterility, which drove her to despair for the first six years of her marriage. But your baby giggles and cries filled that hole and sealed it. With you in her arms, she was absolutely radiant. I had never seen a woman more breathtaking, more charismatic. Vedette at her best." His eyes flitted up to mine with a sad smile.

Despite my anguish, I was compelled to smile back. Vedette at her best, and she had loved me. Who couldn't help but love her back?

"When I saw her two months later for your next set of shots, her whole demeanor had changed. There was a nervous desperation about her, as though she worked every second to keep the façade glossy. She adored you, I could see that. It was not the dreaded issue of bonding that nursery staff fuss over. It was something else, and she wouldn't tell me what troubled her." He held the phone in one hand and laced the fingers of his other hand through his hair, gripping. "It was not until you were six months old that she confessed to nightmares, to paranoid fantasies that the Wyrmstone stalked you. She was absolutely convinced that the soul of a sorcerer, trapped in a piece of gold and controlling a powerful dragon stone, put you in terrible danger."

He stopped. He gulped, and gulped again, and I realized he was swallowing an overwhelming grief.

"For the next seventeen years, I treated Vedette for a psychotic depression." His face contorted as though he tore every word from his throat. "We tried every medication available, and some that were off label. Vedette never for a moment believed that she was hallucinating. She believed every terrible vision that came to her was real. But she hoped, nonetheless, that medication could make her fears retreat." His head shook back and forth, back and forth, as if it were all too horrible to bear.

"There were times when she was worse. Once, when the fig tree in her garden was split by a storm, I thought I might have to hospitalize her for weeks."

"The fig tree?" I whispered. Dr. Harvey studied my face and I realized that my whisper squeaked and cracked.

"Yes. She claimed that that tree was all that stood between Seattle and gruesome destruction. She had conceived you, she told me, with a—" he cringed, but went on "—a dragon prince from the Dolomite mountains. She said that you were born to do terrible things, but that you must never know this truth because if she could only destroy the Wyrmstone, none of this would matter. You can see, can't you, why I didn't believe her?"

I nodded. Who would believe her? And when I gave my statement to the police detective, who would believe me?

Dr. Harvey stared at the wall, shook his head. He looked ashamed beyond anything his stoic demeanor could hide. "I forgot, you see, the most basic, fundamental principal of

medicine: if the illness does not respond to treatment, reconsider the diagnosis."

Tears leaked from his blue eyes, trickling into the crevices
of his wrinkles, washing the flush from his cheeks and leaving
them sallow.

"Two days before your parents' final trip to Italy your father came in alone, distressed and agitated. He told me that
Vedette was worse than she'd ever been. She had divined the
secret to destroying the Wyrmstone. They were going to Italy
to make the last piece they needed to take it apart."

My heart began to pound, the rushing in my ears almost
drowning out his voice in the receiver.

"Hugh brought with him a tiny red stone vial, apparently
made to hold a powerful potion. But it was empty, and at least
a drop of the potion was needed. He claimed that with this
potion, a certain sword, and dragon's blood, the stone could
be unmade. Your father hoped that with the necklace dismantled, Vedette could be healed."

The edges of my vision grayed and buzzed, as though I
might faint. Cooking with blood. And I had thrown out my
pants. Last night, when they stripped off my stiff and muddy
clothes and prepared to bag them, I had said, "Just throw
them away." "Can't do that, Miss," the guard had responded.
But when she got one whiff of them she'd recoiled, then nodded. "Maybe it would be best," she'd said.

Over my frantic thoughts, the doctor spoke softly, gently, a
tone polished by years of experience with breaking bad news.

"Your father never believed, over all of those years, that
the necklace held any power except in Vedette's imagination.

Magic, he explained, was a childish delusion. A facile explanation for fears that Vedette couldn't face. She was not crazy, he explained, just grasping at straws to make sense of life's accidents."

Yes, of course it was that way. My father and his unbendable truth. I remembered their wedding photo on the bedroom wall. Mom in cream lace, too grave for one so beautiful, not yet the lighthearted companion to Nicholi's playful world. And Dad in his black Tux, smiling as though his joy was barely contained. My God how he had loved her. How it must have torn him apart not to believe her. In every other way they had been a perfect match. But facing the Wyrmstone, they had lost each other.

And I had thrown away my pants. My pants with the cinnabar vial in the pocket. Someone was going to empty a garbage can, and my only chance to destroy the stone would be lost. I rested my head on the table of the booth, pulling the phone cord to its limit.

"He wanted to know—he asked my medical opinion: if he helped her to break the necklace, would it save Vedette, or push her over the edge? Because Vedette claimed a dragon was trying to kill them. Your father was convinced that Vedette would die of this fantasy if the necklace was not destroyed."

Vedette, whose adoration of my father knew no bounds. My father, who wanted to heal and fix the world. They had stayed together, one believing, one not believing. They had died together, still in love.

My temples, squeezed hard between my hands, started to

ache. I had thrown away the cinnabar vial. The glass and walls were closing in. I had to have that vial back.

The doctor who had tended me all of my life reached for me through the phone. His voice was tinny and thin, but it touched with the skill of a healer.

"What do you need?" he asked.

"I need my pants. The ones I told them to throw away last night." I looked up into his wretched shame.

"Why?"

"The cinnabar vial was in the pocket."

Dr. Harvey blinked. "Vedette was right all along, wasn't she?" he asked.

I nodded.

"I'll make sure they find those pants." He grabbed up his cap. "I'm terribly sorry," he said.

"I understand. There was a time when I wouldn't have believed her either. You didn't deliver me, did you?"

"No, and you are not your father's child. Your mother forbid me to tell you. But you did punch me in the face the first time you met me—a smack I richly deserved." Dr. Harvey set his cap on his head. One hand found his coat. "Take an old doctor's advice: avoid secrets. It appears that this is as important to a long life as eating one's vegetables." He gave a faint smile as he put on his coat.

I laughed, despite everything. After all, what do humans know about a long life?

Chapter 26

On the small TV, hanging from the ceiling in the waiting area outside of Officer Dray's office, Case looked heroic and battle worn. His shaved head was streaked with mud. His shirt was ripped in shreds across his chest. The dirty skin around his eyes crinkled, as though looking ahead to a daring adventure.

"So after she calls we go tearing over there, and arrive just as the whole back wall of the place blasts sky high, glass flying everywhere, roof shingles pelting down on our heads."

Such breathtaking showmanship, such a shrewd and irresistible pretender. His lies made me want to stand up and cheer. Case's voice dropped an octave to heighten the drama, and the TV reporter moved in closer to catch every word in the microphone.

"You think that destruction was the storm?" Case snorted. "No friggin' way! He wasted that wall with a bomb. Can you show some footage of Ms. Farr's house?"

Everyone who walked through the hall on police business paused to watch TV. They stayed to give Case their full attention, gathering like the voting public in front of a reality show. The TV flickered and scenes of Ms. Farr's flooded living room came onto the screen.

"The storm's howling like a dead thing, and the house is sinking into Hell's slime under our feet. We're searching for poor Ms. Farr, tearing through flood and fire, while the killer keeps his head down in the shadows."

Case wiped his hand over his shaved scalp then glanced sideways at the camera, his smile confiding. "Ms. Farr had all this cool archeological stuff from all over the world. The creep took everything, then wanted to burn her alive to shut her up. The guy's a psycho killer. Order of the Dragon. They'll never keep him in jail."

Case leaned into the screen, eyebrows raised with pleading, even managing to look innocent. "And the police are trying to blame us. Gees, if it wasn't for us, the poor lady would be dead."

Photos flashed over the screen: Ms. Farr cringing in the bright light, squeezing Mom's sweater to her chest as she was escorted out of the squad car; a puny, filthy Paul in handcuffs, too timid to look at the camera; Trimble's wise and noble smile; Larry standing by Mom's garden shed with the pickax on his shoulder and an open-mouthed guffaw of joy; Justin in a rare moment with his hair out of his elfin eyes; and a photo of me in my kitchen, holding up a wooden spoon like a Slice-O-Dice-O model. In Case's photos—when had he taken these?—we appeared far too benevolent for murder.

A thoughtful silence settled over the watching police staff. Small notes of eye contact passed back and forth. More converts to Club Case. I retreated against the wall and buried my face in *Modern Mother* magazine, hiding my gratitude and amusement, and my relief to see Case alive.

The TV announcer, considerably cleaner but much less charismatic than Case, appeared on the screen. "And there you have it, word from one of the heroic teens who saved an elderly lady from fire and drowning and foiled the escape of a murderer last night. The boy was interviewed from his place of hiding. At last report, the police were still holding the other teens involved in the rescue pending charges for murder, theft, and the destruction of property. Charges our witness swears they are innocent of. Information about the identity of the man found dead at the scene should be called to Bellevue Police Department ...." A picture of Pancrizio's dead body filled the screen and I closed my eyes against the gruesomely battered face.

I put my mind back to willing Officer Dray's door to open. I had studied the precinct hallway for twenty minutes already and I knew every soggy coffee cup, dog-eared magazine, and metal folding chair. I was determined to surprise Ms. Whitting and be at that custody hearing. I glanced again at the wall clock, wishing my dragon heritage conferred the power to open sealed doors. One hour before the hearing.

" ... A massive grassroots internet protest is underway. Wireless lines are overloaded all over Seattle, calling for the teens' release. Comments to the police about their treatment of the heroes can be filed at www.freetheheros.com. And now we go to Sandy Trice for an update on ...."

I watched the second hand take another minute. When they gave me my property box, the ruined clothes had not been inside. Confiscated as evidence, the jail claimed; talk to Officer Dray. The cinnabar vial could have easily disappeared into someone's hand before the transfer. Or it could have fallen out during my struggles and be lying in the bottomless depths of the pond.

"Ms. Jovel," said a voice.

Finally. I stood up, wincing from stiffness. It would take twenty minutes to drive to the hearing. I might still make it. I followed so close on the secretary's heels that I almost stepped on them.

Officer Dray sat with his chair pushed back, hands on his round belly and polished shoes resting in the center of his desk blotter. He was nowhere near as formidable as a dragon. This gave me courage as I met his smug gaze.

"Miss Jovel. I suppose you've come to make your statement?"

"Yes, sir," I said, arranging Case's facts in my brain.

"No lawyer?"

"I'm in a hurry, so if it's okay with you, let's get this over with."

There was only one extra chair: the little low one directly across from his desk that Justin once occupied, only feet away from Officer Dray. Close enough that he could see every worry line on my face.

He put his feet down with a thump, reached across his desk, and snapped on a recorder. "I understand that you work for Ms. Farr?"

I kept my voice flat. "Yes. I'm her cook."

"Could you tell me what happened last night?"

Thank God dragons are such marvelous liars, and slyfeet are so clever.

"Well, uh, Ms. Farr called at around three-thirty …."

The whole story took about ten minutes. It would have taken longer, but I left out details of swamp dragons rising for war, spells that brought bodies into being for sorcerers to inhabit, how to kill Basilisks, the complications of wielding a Wyrmstone, and the intricacies of dice and fate. Taking my cue from Case, I limited myself to facts that reality could stomach.

When I was done Officer Dray snapped off the tape recorder and leaned back. He was quiet for awhile, just looking at me, and I could sense him trying to read my mind. I was suddenly aware that I was smelly, scratched, uncombed, and hungry. I ran my fingers once through my hair to untangle it, and then gave up.

"Well," he said finally, "That makes a whole lot more sense than what your brother and his friends told me."

I gawked with surprise. "Justin spoke to you?"

"Yeah."

"I'm so glad."

Justin was rolling good numbers today. But no, his dice were in custody, and one die was in my jeans.

Officer Dray chewed his plump lower lip, as if tasting for the right thing to do. Then he said, "He and his friends told me about a sorcerer planning a war against Seattle, and a dragon king hiding in a pond with his army." He paused to consult his notes, wetting a thumb to flip the pages. "I was given a detailed description of an ancient hoard, stolen from a priestess."

He flicked his eyes back and forth between me and his pages, as though he didn't want to miss my reaction. I gave him a docile smile.

"But the sorcerer was killed by the dragon king." He flipped ahead a few pages on his yellow note pad. "Meanwhile the priestess was saved by a barbarian king in a rage, a … mmm—" more glances through the notes, "—a Wielder level dwarf. Do you know anything about these levels?"

I widened my eyes and shook my head, 'no'.

"Hmm." He stroked his pink, shaved chin. "Wielder is high level, I gather. With a pickax, no less." Again he studied me for a reaction, and I did my best to assemble a confused but cooperative shrug. "How about NPC—do you know what that means? No? An NPC assassin who slack-rope walked through a windstorm? No? Oh yes, then there's the slyfoot whom we can't seem to locate despite the fact that every TV reporter in the county has interviewed him."

He cleared his throat and paused, as though expecting that now, surely, I might comment. When I didn't, he went on, reading rapidly, clearly ready to be done with this nonsense.

"And thank heavens the wizard was there to cast Spew Ice, or you all would have died fighting flaming Basilisks. And, of course, the magical bear—oh, excuse me, spirit bear—who protected the innocent child from being eaten by the dragon. But the spirit bear was shot by our officer and bled to death." I winced but quickly put a hand up to cover my face, as though wiping away my hair.

"Miss Jovel—" Officer Dray leaned forward and pressed the tips of his fingers into his forehead, watching me from under the protective arch of his hands. "I understood your brother better *before* he was willing to speak to me. Back then, I thought he was just a stubborn spoiled brat. Now, I see that he's … well … crazy."

Insanity defense. It was a good one. It might be our only hope. "Are you going to prosecute the boys for resisting arrest?"

Officer Dray exhaled, and I could smell the chili he'd had for lunch. Chili with too much rancid oil and not enough Cumin. The smell, and his large torso, hemmed me into my chair.

"That depends on you. You have a potential wrongful injury claim for little … Nicholi? Is that his name?"

"Yes." No lawyer would take up a case for Didoo, I was sure.

"Is the child all right?"

"Yes. At least, they tell me he is."

"Good. And we have resisting arrest charges. Perhaps we can come to an understanding?"

I nodded. It was a deal I could to live with.

"Excellent. Paul has kindly explained to me that some people have—" he consulted his notes, "—Wyrm Fog in the presence of dragons, and lose their ability to rationally assess threat. As interesting as that is, I suspect that we could not use it in our officers' defense."

Dray leaned back in his chair, his weight making the swivel mechanism creak as he allowed me more room to maneuver. "Heroic boys on YouTube are more popular than overreacting officers. Case is almost as loved as he is difficult to catch. I think there would be a riot if I put Seattle's favorite slyfoot in jail, or kept your brothers beyond tomorrow."

I could tell from his professional frown that he was not pleased about this. But I was, oh I was!

"And Steve?" I asked, with a pang of guilt.

"He's ours. Though Justin has warned us that holding a dragon against his will is almost impossible. You, he claims, are one of the few who can do it."

I raised my lying eyebrows with disbelief.

He reached into his desk drawer and took out a clear plastic baggie. The air in the bag had expanded, puffed up with heat, and a penny-sized spot of plastic had melted to the gold inscription on the back of the amulet.

"With this," he said, "you could keep Steve locked up forever. True?"

He slid the facedown necklace across the table to me, watching my eyes, and I was so glad that he was not Case.

I laid my hand over the Wyrmstone to feel its reassuring heat. With my gaze on Officer Dray's fleshy, round, pancake of a face I prepared myself for his most piercing scrutiny.

"It's … ah … just a necklace," I said.

With fumbling fingers I drew it from the baggie. A small scrap of plastic had melted to the gold. I picked at the scrap nervously, but it stuck, hard. I gave up and put the frayed cord around my neck, dropping the amulet into the Phoenix-hide bag.

"Of course it's just a necklace," he said.

As dragons wisely say, sometimes the truth doesn't exist. And now I knew how that was possible.

"And this?" he pulled my cinnabar vial from his desk. "What's this?"

I almost leapt up and snatched it. Instead, I met his curiosity with convincing eye contact. "A perfume vial. It has sentimental value. My mother used to wear that perfume." This lying became easier and easier.

"Ah, then I can see why Dr. Harvey called and insisted that it be returned to you. It's not Ms. Farr's then, or Steve Eastman's?"

"No. It was my mother's." I gave him a mournful smile, willing him to look away with shame at his rough treatment of an orphan. And he did. "Do we have any idea where Ms. Farr's artifacts went?" I asked.

Officer Dray raised a neat eyebrow. "The ancient hoard?" An ironic curl lifted one corner of his mouth. "The boy Trimble claims it's been swallowed into the belly of the dragon king. Consuming magical items greatly increases a dragon's powers, I gather."

"Well … ah … I see." Hence, Adrikhedon resisted the Wyrmstone, and he hoped to become even more powerful by swallowing Didoo, I could have added, but I didn't.

Officer Dray sighed, clearly smart enough to suspect that the truth had evaded him, but wise enough to know when he was beaten. "Where can we reach you if we have further questions?"

I wrote my cell number on a scrap of paper and held it out to him. "So you will release Justin and his friends?"

Officer Dray leaned forward and looked me hard in the face. "Yes, once we are sure we are done with them. But you should seriously consider a psychiatric evaluation for Justin. The young man is sick."

Psychiatric evaluation: we had made progress since his need for grief counseling. I laughed with relief, which brought a look of mild confusion to Officer Dray's face. He leaned back and eyed me as though he wondered about my mental health as well.

I rose to go, one hand cradling my cinnabar vial, one hand clutching my Wyrmstone. One of Justin's dice, returned with my purse and car keys, dug through my pocket and pressed a bruise into my leg. Fate had let me wiggle out from under a few of my real-world troubles. I owed fate, and a swarm of unknown Internet supporters, *lots* of cookies.

~

Carlo waited by the police station front door. He opened his arms, hugging me to his canvas coat. "You know that Nicholi is okay?" he said in my ear.

I rested my head against the sturdy feel of him, wishing I could just go to sleep there. "Yes, thanks. Apparently it was the guard who was bleeding." I could hear Carlo's heart, steadily thumping, and smell ivory soap and oregano.

"In the squad car, Paul told me about the bullet wounds." There were dark rings under Carlo's eyes, making his face look worn. "The bullet went into Didoo's left side and came out the rip in Didoo's belly."

I blinked. "I don't understand. The bullet turned? Inside a fluffy stuffed animal, it changed directions?"

"It's kind of hard to argue with bullet holes," said Carlo.

I stared into his face, walloped dumb with amazement. "What do you think happened?"

"I think," Carlo took a deep breath. "I think Didoo loved Nicholi as much as Nicholi loved Didoo." He reached to wipe away the tear, sneaking down my cheek.

We hurried across the parking lot, his arm around my waist. The afternoon sky looked bruised with purple clouds. A faint wind twisted the curls under the brim of his fedora. We arrived at his truck and I stood aside as he unlocked the door. He turned to face me, close enough to raise my pulse. He reached and laced strong hands into my hair. His blunt fingers pressed gently into my scalp in slow hypnotic circles. He stroked my hair, pushing the knotted snarl of it against my skin. Then he kissed me, one light brush across my lips, waking every cell to lean into him, tangle, and melt.

In my head I heard the Doppelganger laughing, a seductive wheeze, mocking my surge of love. Romantic interest in me was the kiss of death. And Carlo? He had saved my family over and over. I owed him more than a life of danger, bad luck, and tragedy. Guilty and confused, I jerked away.

"We should hurry," I said. "I don't want to be late for the custody hearing." He opened the truck door for me and tucked in the tail of my coat before he closed it.

Evidence of the burnt out storm lay everywhere as we drove through Bellevue. Cars had been abandoned in ditches, trees choked the roads, and power lines looped and tangled. Much of the city had lost its electricity. We drove on in silence as I thought about his kiss.

"Carlo," I asked, "how did you walk the rope like that?"

He glanced over from his driving. "Hmm?"

"Over the sorcerer's head. In the storm."

"Oh, that." As if it were nothing.

"So?" I insisted.

"It's what I do for a living." He didn't say anything more, watching the road with absorption.

A clutch of worry drove me on. I could be such a dupe. Feeling foolish, I forced myself to ask, "Are you an assassin? Is your family Mafia?"

"Assassin? *Mafia*?" Carlo burst out laughing. "If I didn't like you so much, I'd be offended. No, I don't kill for a living, and I'm not Mafia."

"So, what do you do?"

Carlo sighed. "I'm one of *The Rossi Brothers*: five generations of high wire, trapeze, and slack rope acrobats."

Tightrope and trapeze. Of course: the strength, the inner balance, the ease with the unknown and risky, the team work.

"I'm speechless. That's truly amazing."

"You think so?" Carlo glanced my way, studying my face. I couldn't read his guarded expression under his dark brows. "I'm going to graduate school to study business. I don't plan to swing from the rafters and soar through rings of fire all my life." He turned on the blinker and waited at the stoplight to pull into the court house parking lot.

"But to be part of such a tradition—"

"In my family, tradition is deadly." He drove the truck into a parking space and turned off the engine. "I perform three times a week, thirty feet up in the air. No net—that's the family trademark. In five generations we've lost five family members. My father, Nonna's oldest, was one of them. At any minute my attention might not be perfect, my brother could miscalculate, my uncle's strength might fail. I want to live to be a husband and a father, Mimi." He leaned forward, such that I could feel his whisper on my face. "Don't you think that's a good idea?"

Yes, it was a wonderful idea. I wished that he would kiss me again, but he didn't. He stepped out of the truck and came around to open my door. "I'll wait in the lobby." He glanced at his watch. "Time for Ms. Whitting."

In the empty conference room, Tamara Whitting hunched over a computer monitor tapping at her notes, alone at the end of a long table. The streaks of gray in her hair looked dull in the fluorescent light. Where was everyone? She glanced up as I came in, narrowed her eyes into little slits, and wrinkled her nose. "*Miss* Jovel," she spat out.

"Hello, Ms. Whitting. Surprised to see me?" I found a chair near her end of the table but scooted the seat back to allow for distance.

"You and your brothers managed to get yourselves into trouble again."

I winced, but maintained eye contact. "I'm afraid I don't have very good luck."

Ms. Whitting tapped a few commands on her keyboard, and then closed the lid of her computer with a snap. "Is an enraged attack on the police, complete with a destroyed house, a dead body, and a gunshot wound, considered *bad luck*?"

I caught my breath and forced my teeth down on the tip of my tongue. I couldn't afford to say anything stupid, not with Nicholi's fate in the balance and Justin still in jail.

"There were lots of extenuating circumstances—" I started.

But she scoffed, interrupting my defense with a roll of her eyes and an impatient shuffle of her sandaled feet. "Well, you missed the hearing. So much the better that you weren't there." She sniffed. "You smell like a homeless runaway. Your case was better served in your absence."

I stood up, feeling my fury swell. "What do you mean I missed the hearing?"

"Sit *down*, Miss Jovel." She waited, steaming with self-control, sending deep, coffee-smelling breaths into the air between us.

I sat down.

"The hearing was moved forward an hour so we could all go home for Thanksgiving dinner." She smiled, and it radiated vengeance.

I did not smile back. "You never notified me. Isn't there some law that I get to be there?"

"Well, what's done is done." She could not have sounded more satisfied.

I wanted to grip her head in my dragon claws. "And what was the outcome? Do I have custody or no?"

Her hands reclined on the smooth case of the computer as though resting on their laurels, or procrastinating.

"Did it ever occur to you that, regardless of the circumstances, children should not be dragged into that kind of danger?"

I bristled with frustration. "Steve Eastman almost killed

Ms. Farr. She's a very sweet old woman who can't even speak to defend herself. He stole everything she owns. He's a confessed murderer."

"That, my dear, is why we hire law enforcement professionals."

"I was afraid she was going to die—"

"You and your brothers are not the police," she interrupted. She stood up, revealing polyester pants of a shocking light blue. "I want you to ponder, Miss Jovel, that you might have exceptionally poor judgment." She picked her briefcase up off the floor, not looking at me, attention instead on opening the case.

I sat, punched into silence, gagged by the appalling picture of Justin and Nicholi in foster care. I took a breath, floundering for words to fight with.

She unplugged her computer power cord and began to roll it up. Her machine was clearly more interesting to her than I was. I watched the black cord slither off the floor and into her hands. My failures snaked in a long, wandering line before me; mistakes so profound that I had almost killed the people I loved. I could feel Justin's dice, hard and round in my jeans pocket. Every roll seemed cursed. Everyone faces good fortune and bad fortune. I was nothing special. Was it my awful judgment, my terrible destiny, or my even worse luck, that made all of my roads lead to disaster?

"You'll get a letter in the mail within a week," she said, still absorbed in her packing. "I'll let the judge tell you the verdict."

It was her tone that did it. That snide splash in the face, taunting me with the prospect of seven miserable days, waiting in agony. The swagger of a bully who thinks she has the bigger fist. My hand went instinctively to the Wyrmstone, hidden under my shirt. My fingers passed over the scrap of plastic, rough on the back of the polished setting. I could feel the sorcerer, hiding from me, much more dangerous than this social worker in Birkenstocks.

Obscurla slavik. Enough already. If she wants a fight, I'll fight.

I raised my head, the ice of my gaze forcing her hostile glare off the work of packing, dragged her attention to my face. My dragon temper bored into her flabby skin. "Tell me now, not by letter. Tell me if you've taken my brothers away from me. Tell me to my face if you truly believe they'd be better off raised by strangers."

She cringed—for who can face down a furious dragon? Her enviable self-possession caved and she looked away, unable to meet my stare, terrified of my reptile ferocity.

"What was the result, Ms. Whitting? Did I lose them or no?" I hissed.

She didn't answer, still as a rabbit under my growing anger, her gaze on her scuffed and dented sandals. The Wyrmstone felt hot in my hand. I wanted to draw Deathwish and lop off her head.

She made no effort to move, frozen by my dragon wrath, as I stood up and walked around the desk. I opened her briefcase, then her computer. Hitting the power button, I booted her computer up. Her files were a sloppy mess, all over the dashboard, labeled with surnames. There were at least a hundred names, a hundred families she grappled with. I found Jovel.

Our file ran to five pages, quote after quote. She had interviewed everyone she could think of: neighbors, teachers, even Carlo.

I read aloud the first quote, and she flinched at the harsh rasp of my voice.

"'Always has Nicholi's best interest at heart. Very bonded to the child. I highly recommend that they not be separated.' Ms. Greer."

Ms. Greer said that? The snarky educator who looked at me with such disdain? Perhaps that had not been dislike on her face. Perhaps she was overwhelmed by our grief, without the strength to face our loss. I was ashamed at how poorly I'd understood her when she had obviously looked very carefully at me. I cleared my throat and kept reading.

"'A very bright young woman who clearly adores Justin. Doing an excellent job managing the teen despite her youth.' Mr. Peppercain."

"'Reliable, efficient, competent, what more is there?' Mr. Eastman."

"'Generous, kind, works her tail off for those kids. I bet you won't find anyone willing to say a bad thing about her.' Carlo."

I caught my breath and stopped reading. Tears blurred the words. Statements from Anna Rossi, Marcella, Becky, Mr. Masters, even Officer Dray. It went on and on. She had done an exhaustive search, and Carlo was right: no one was willing to say a bad thing about me. And I had felt so inept.

At the bottom of the page, Ms. Whitting had summarized her thoughts. I read them silently while Ms. Whitting wilted in the stuffy, coffee tinged air.

"Justin's grief must be overwhelming," she'd written, "matched only by his loyalty to his siblings." And, "Nicholi's IQ is through the roof. A hard child for any parent to raise." Ms. Whitting wrote that. Regardless of how she felt about me, she cared about my brothers.

I snapped closed the computer. "I won, didn't I?" My voice was a whisper. My dragon gone, I released her to speak.

Finally she dragged her gaze off the dirty tile. "I didn't have a single witness against you." Her voice trembled. "Nicholi was shot at by an overwrought policeman who was declared unfit to carry a gun. Steve's confession is ironclad. Justin and his friends are heroes as far as Seattle is concerned. Charges will be dropped. I didn't take your brothers, Miss Jovel. Judge Burrows wouldn't let me."

It took a minute for her words to sink in. She stared at me, her face sagging, drained of all emotion. For a moment I could see how profoundly tired she was, how much the long hours taxed her. One hundred families struggling as I struggled, lifting the boulders that life dropped in our paths. And one woman, trying to keep all of those children safe. I felt a pang of sympathy for her. Then I wondered how she might fare protecting children against Pancrizio, or Adrikhedon.

"Thank you for trying so hard to help my brothers," I said. And I meant it.

She rose from her chair. Without another glance at me, she grabbed her briefcase and walked out. The door slammed, wafting a sad gust of Patchouli Oil into my face.

Outside a soft rain fell, so light it did not even feel wet.

Carlo drove me home, pulling his truck into our driveway. The house was silent. Sometime during last night's disaster the wind had taken down our electrical power. I opened the door and climbed out. Carlo leaned over the vacated seat and smiled through the open truck door.

"Can I help with anything?" he asked.

"No. I just need some rest. See you tomorrow? Come to dinner, and bring Nonna and Ms. Farr. We'll celebrate the boys' release."

"Yeah." He sat up and looked through the windshield, face obscure in the unlit carport. "Ms. Farr's staying in the spare bedroom, so I'll go to my mom's. I suppose my family will put up with me long enough to let me stay the night."

"You don't get along?"

"No. They think graduate school is a waste of my talents." He fiddled with the brim of his Fedora, his calluses smoothed by the late afternoon light. Then he put his hat back on. "I'll be at Nonna's early to clean up from the storm." He leaned, reaching for my fingers, kissing them on the tips. "Take care, *Massimaŭ* Sovrani Jovel."

"See you tomorrow, Giancarlo Alberto Ettore Rinaldo Rossi."

He smiled and turned away without any more kisses, backing out of the driveway.

Ms. Farr sat in Dad's armchair by the fire, watchful eyes on Nicholi. My sweet Lizbeth, looking warm and pink in another of Mom's thick sweaters. She glanced up at me when I walked in and smiled with serene pleasure. It was such a relief to see her looking well that I hugged her and hugged her.

Nicholi lay curled on the living room floor, surrounded by his spirit bear castle, covered by the Chilkat robe. I'd never seen him without also feeling the presence of Didoo, and I expected him to be diminished somehow. But soft gaslight from the fire wavered over his sleeping face, and he looked older, stronger. I knelt and buried my face in the cranny between his shoulder and neck, cuddling him to my warm tears, smelling his newly-washed little boy scent.

"Thank you, Didoo," I whispered. "Thank you, fate."

Lizbeth stood and came over, laying her hand on my shoulder. I took her bony fingers in mine. "I'll walk you back to Nonna's," I said, and she kissed me on top of my head.

The refrigerator was full of warm, festering food. On the stove dried, shriveled giblets lay in the spoiled gravy, the parsley on the surface wrinkled and brown. The turkey sat on the counter, smelling a little sour. The power was out, and within hours the heat in the house would be gone. I had no money for groceries. I had no job. It was Thanksgiving night and there had been no feast. The boys slept in jail. And soon, with a cinnabar vial, Deathwish, and Adrikhedon's blood, I had to destroy the Wyrmstone.

Still, this was the most grateful Thanksgiving I could imagine: tomorrow Justin and the boys would be free. Nicholi was alive, resting in innocent exhaustion. My brothers were still mine.

I lifted Nicholi and the Chilkat robe out of the fortress of Legos and carried them to the couch. Lying down, I folded

Nicholi against my belly and spread the Chilkat robe over us. The thick fringe, pungent with animal oil, rested against my cheek. The white face of the spirit bear snarled over us like a guardian.

Chapter 27

The phone woke me from a deep, dreamless sleep. I stumbled off the couch and into the kitchen.

"Miss Jovel?" said Mr. Eastman's clipped voice. He was rushing around on Thanksgiving night, even at—I glanced at the clock—was it really ten PM?

"Mr. Eastman, thank God you called. Ms. Farr's house sank in the storm yesterday. Your nephew took Ms. Farr's—"

"My nephew?" He sounded inpatient, as if he wasted his time correcting me.

"Steve Eastman, your nephew."

"We're not related. Where is Lizbeth?"

Of course they weren't related—Adrikhedon, such a brazen liar. I smiled despite myself. "She's staying with my neighbor, Anna Rossi. She's safe and—"

"I've found a nursing home for her. I'll send someone to pick her up."

"But, where will you take her? She's—"

"They will be there first thing in the morning." He hung up.

That was it. Fate might jerk me around, murder my parents, attack my brothers, eat my boyfriend, endanger my friends, and spoil my Thanksgiving dinner, but Mr. Eastman was going to *listen to me.* Even if it took five whole minutes.

Furious, I redialed his office. The phone rang six times before he picked up. "Yes?"

I mustered Ms. Greer's poise, my dragon ferocity, and Ms. Whitting's indignation. With this cast behind me, I took a deep breath, so that I could blast it all out before he hung up on me. "Mr. Eastman, this is Mimi Jovel. Don't you *dare* interrupt me. I have something to say to you."

There was a clipped gasp, as though he had been hit in the solar plexus.

"Ms. Farr is a sweet, kind, helpless lady, and you left her in the care of an amoral bastard. He stole everything she owned and abandoned her to die. You are so *busy* that you almost killed her. You owe that woman. You will *not* put her in a nursing home. I won't stand for it." Adrenaline surged through me, causing my hands to shake and my voice to crack. I quaked on my feet, unsure where to go next with this suicidal conversation.

On the other end of the phone there was a shocked silence, and I expected any second to hear a click and a dial tone. Instead he said, "Steve stole her belongings?"

Where had he been for the last twenty-four hours, in a fantasy world? Didn't he own a TV?

"Yes, instead of selling her artifacts as he was supposed to, he walked off with them."

Slowly, as though his motor had cut out and he couldn't quite get it running again, he stammered, "What—w— whatever gave you the impression that—that Steve was supposed to sell her artifacts?"

"To pay the bills. That's what he said. That was his job."

"No. That was not at all—" He coughed, and then collected himself. "What did he sell?"

"The Aztec knife, the carved thigh bone, an African spear, a Greek pot. I don't know. All of it. Then he murdered the front man he sold through."

"Oh, Jesus." His voice was a thread. I hoped he wasn't having a heart attack.

"Then yesterday, he told me she was going to relatives, and he left her alone while the house burned and sank. If she hadn't called me she would have died. Don't you watch TV?"

In the traffic jam of Mr. Eastman's life, a car exploded into flames and snarled the roads for miles around. Mr. Eastman was left muttering, "Oh, Jesus. Oh, Jesus."

I couldn't tell if it was a prayer, a curse, or a beg for forgiveness. Perhaps he imagined his face on the front page news, or pictured his name in a lawsuit. Or maybe he actually cared about Ms. Farr.

"Mr. Eastman, I'm very fond of Lizbeth. We're friends. Even if you won't pay me, I'll find somewhere nice for her to live. I'll watch over her. You may *not* stick her in a nursing home."

When he spoke again he sounded relieved, as if I were the fire department and several tow trucks. "Okay, Miss Jovel. We'll work it this way: I'll continue to pay your salary, and you'll find a place for Lizbeth and take care of whatever she needs. Call Eve Tavick if you need anything."

"No, I want your cell number. Eve Tavick was not in the office yesterday when Lizbeth almost died, and I couldn't reach you. And I need one more thing. If this is going to be my job—" I sucked in enough air to last until the end of my next sentence, because if I paused too long, I'd lose my nerve. "If this is going to be my job, I'll need health insurance for my brothers and me."

"Health insur—" He stalled. The phone crackled slightly as he thought. Finally he said, "You drive a hard bargain, Miss Jovel."

"I have two brothers to support."

He laughed: not a sound that I ever expected to hear. It was a rapid fire hey-hey-hey, rough and grating with grudging admiration.

"Fine. I'll find you some insurance. Anything else?"

"That's all. Thanks. Have a good Thanksgiving, Mr. Eastman."

"Thanksgiving? Oh, I guess it is, isn't it?" And he hung up.

I put down the receiver. A bubble of hope lifted from my chest, floated across the room, and bounced on the devastated kitchen counters. Tomorrow, I would face the dead turkey. I would use one of my last three matches to boil water and wash dishes. Maybe some of the food in the refrigerator could be salvaged in a cooler. First thing in the morning I would attack the kitchen. Then, the Wyrmstone.

The next morning, as soon as everything was scrubbed, I took out my Mexican cookbooks.

Mexican corn pudding, done well, has the texture of velvet, with little ribs of sweet corn, clinging to the shape they held on the cob. The flavor is dotted with an occasional burst of cheddar cheese. The world's best recipe uses something not Mexican at all: quark.

Pork cooked in beer and Tequila makes a wonderful, tangy Enchilada. I would smother the plump rolls of tortilla in deathly hot, red chili sauce, and garnish with fresh cilantro. The mail with my paycheck came at ten. I could fold the laundry while I waited to go shopping.

Nicholi woke at noon. He wandered out in rumpled pajamas and sat right in the middle of what was now a clean kitchen, clutching the Chilkat robe, his complexion too pale for my liking. He watched me with bleary eyes as I veered around him.

"What are you making?" he asked.

I found the eggs and reached for a mixing bowl. "Breakfast. And Drunken Pork Enchiladas with Mexican corn pudding for Adrikhedon."

Nicholi spread the Chilkat robe on the floor near my feet and lay on it, curling the fringe over his legs. I didn't like how gray he looked, but it didn't seem bad enough to call Dr. Harvey.

"You're going to askingvisit a dragon?" he said.

I broke a few eggs into the bowl and whisked them forcefully. "I have to. You'll stay with Nonna and Ms. Farr, okay?"

Nicholi was quiet for a minute, and then he said, "Yes."

I added salt and pepper, and then poured eggs into the pan.

Nicholi watched me scramble his eggs dry, as he liked them, and then slide them onto a plate. He sat down at the table and picked at the eggs. He swallowed a bite and said, "Didoo says take dessert, too."

I froze in place. Slowly I turned around, searching his expression for some hint of an explanation. Maybe his grief was too much, and the bear simply could not be gone. "Does he?" I said cautiously. "Where is Didoo?"

Nicholi's little fingers combed through the fringe that brushed his leg. "I'm too oldish for stuffed bears. It's time for me to wear a spirit robe."

"He's in the robe?" I whispered.

Nicholi nodded. "With all the other bears. It's less lonesad for him in there," he smiled a mischievous grin, "and Ms. Greer doesn't have any rules about Chilkat robes."

I started laughing. Grateful clutches of giggles and guffaws hurt my sore ribs, but felt so good. Nicholi sat with a wisp of a smile, holding his fork, watching me pant and wipe my eyes.

"Three dozen macaroons?" I asked when I could speak.

"Yeah, that's good." Nicholi finished his eggs then got up. Dragging the heavy blanket behind him, he came and put his arms around my legs. He hung on as if we were still riding a storm. "Be careful, Mimi," he whispered.

They had transferred Steve to King County jail in downtown Seattle. It looked like any other skyscraper except for the bars on the windows. The warden shuffled paperwork and made phone calls for fifteen minutes. Fifteen minutes of my stomach tied in anxious knots before they agreed to let me see him. Then they led me into a glassed-in room, guards at the doors with their hands on their guns. As if guns would make us any safer.

Steve sauntered in and sat down, not bothering to look up and see who visited until he'd made himself comfortable. Then he lifted his eyes, slow as a snake. A sly grin crept across his face when he recognized me through the wired glass. He picked up his phone.

"Mimi Jovel." He nodded.

"I brought you something to eat." I pushed forward the Tupperware of enchiladas and the tinfoil wrapped pudding dish. They rested against the glass that separated us.

"Did you put a metal file in it?"

"No, sorry. I volunteered for X-ray inspection, metal detection, taste testing ... but they won't allow me to give it to you."

Steve laughed, a guttural, lost sound. "That's okay. You didn't come all of this way to feed me. What do you want?"

I leaned forward so the guards couldn't hear. "Blood," I whispered into the phone.

He threw back his head and all I could see was his boney Adam's apple swallowing, anger rolling down his throat with his spit.

"You didn't kill enough of us?"

"To release you."

His head snapped forward, his eyes narrowed to slits. "What? You think I can't walk out of here any time I want?"

"No, I mean—" I fumbled under my shirt and pulled out the Wyrmstone. "Ms. Farr's artifacts will eventually dissolve, and then where will you be?"

I turned the stone over, away from the inscribed back with the plastic still stuck to it, showing instead the breathtaking amethyst. Then I took the gift box of macaroons off my lap and opened it, offering it toward the glass barrier that divided us. "I'll destroy the amulet, but I can't do it without pure blood." I took a plastic bottle from my purse, drank the last few drops of water, and set it beside the Macaroons. "Just a few drops." My eyes shifted to the bottle.

He stared at me. His face was thinner since I last saw him, his eye sockets sunk deep into the shadows of his skull. He looked at me with a hunger that was too powerful for even a dragon to hide. A shutter of fear coursed up my spine. This was the man who wanted to take me to Mexico. This was the beast that left Lizbeth to die by flood and Basilisks.

"It would be very nice to have offspring with you, Mimi Jovel. Are you sure you refuse me?" He murmured, and a flash of tenderness crossed his face.

This scared me even more than his stare, but I didn't shrink away. "I refuse you," I breathed.

"But you took the gift, and now we've reached four out of five refusals."

His blue eye centered on my forehead, and I shuddered, wondering how good his 'sense motive' was. Excellent, I was sure.

"I'll leave the bottle and food on my doorstep." It surprised me that my voice was steady. "After I remove the gold, the amethyst is yours. A fair exchange for the robe."

"Mine? Aren't you clever."

He leaned forward, bringing his acne-scarred face to within an inch of the glass separating us. "Let me give you some advice. Don't take anyone down with you." He curled his upper lip into a jagged smile. "When things go badly, dragons die alone."

"I will. I promise I won't summon you." Or Justin, Carlo, Didoo, or any of my friends. They were safe now. I would not endanger anyone but myself, ever again. "Thank you for all you did for the boys."

He laughed, and for a moment I could feel his hot, acidic breath on my face as though it had passed through the glass. He lounged back against his chair. "You think I confessed to save that prickly little snack of kids? No, *Massimaŭ*, that's not who I did it for."

No frozen tundra, no searing desert could be more inhospitable than his four chambered heart. A heart built like a human's, but so wicked that even his own children would never love him. So, was it a clever lie, or did I see devotion when Adrikhedon looked back into my eyes?

With shaking hands I set the box of macaroons next to the other dishes, and stood up. "Thank you." My voice was a choked whisper.

He rose, looking down on me like a vulture. "I'll come for the stone."

"It's yours, I promise."

For a moment Steve considered me, his thoughts hidden behind the ugly mask of his face. "Dragon bonds are brittle." He stopped, wiping a slow hand across his mouth. "Revenge is better than love. You can suck it out from between your teeth." Then he turned and walked back towards his cell.

I watched him go. His spine was a line of desolate mountains poking through his thin shirt, his shoulder blades, two folded wings.

Chapter 28

The power came back on. Carlo arrived and cleaned the gutters, took the branches off the roof, and carted the mess away in his truck. Nicholi spent the afternoon on the couch wrapped in the Chilkat Robe. Gradually the gray left his cheeks, and he slept deeply.

Carlo drove Justin home from jail in the late afternoon. After holding Nicholi for awhile, Justin came to find me in the kitchen where I made dinner. He gave me an affectionate hug, and then said, "There's food on the doorstep."

"Hmm?" I had hoped to avoid this conversation.

"Cookies and pudding and enchiladas," he said.

"Leave it alone. Someone's coming for it."

"Someone?" His elfin eyes considered me, trying to add the food plus my expression into a plausible story. "Do you need help?" he asked.

"No." I reached up and pushed hair out of his face, so I could see his eyes. For a brief second he looked fully grown, and I knew who he would become. With tremendous relief I realized; he would do well as an adult. Even without me.

"I know what I'm doing," I said.

"Whatever you say, *Massimaü*."

He didn't ask to roll his dice, a pair of which still poked in my pocket. In fact, he never rolled his dice outside of the game again. He went and took a shower, then split his time between reading to Nicholi, playing Xbox, and talking on the phone.

I found Justin's copy of *The Epistemic Arcane* on the bookshelf in his room and carried it into Mom's closet. *Imagine having the nerve to trick that regal, lethal empress? Never in a zillion years*, I had once thought. But, like slyfoot Snick, I saw a way to risk all and win. At least for a short while.

There were several Gemini spells, mostly having to do with battle, none pertaining to a mirror, but I could adapt them. I found Mom's folded mirror, one that had two hand-sized sheets of glass with a hinge in the middle. I closed the closet door and stood the mirror on the floor, open like a screen. *Human casted, one hundred hours,* Case had said. *Dragon casted, one hundred years.*

Pulling out the Wyrmstone, I cast the spell, weaving into it all the illusive power of the stone. The mirror looked no different, but my dragon self could feel the pull of magic on the glass. To test my work I doubled Justin's red plastic dice, and set both copies on Mom's desk, next to her perfume bottles. I couldn't tell them apart; identical little twenty-sided balls, and the weights were twin ounces. Perfect. I wrapped the mirror in a plastic drugstore bag and stuffed it in Mom's drawer.

To keep from feeling depressed about my upcoming fight, I pretended that it was Thanksgiving. I had no turkey, but I took melted chicken broth from the defrosted freezer and added vegetables, noodles, tomatoes, and beans, making *ad hoc* minestrone. I baked a few dozen biscuits, and used melted ice cream and vanilla pudding mix to make Cherry Bavarian Cream. It was not an exotic feast, fit for the most important of Jovel holidays, but it was all I could salvage from the wreckage. Maybe next year I would live up to the Jovel tradition. Assuming I was still alive.

At around five the doorbell rang. "I'll get it." Justin dashed out of his room.

I arranged silverware for six places at the kitchen table, telling myself that this tiny gathering was a perfectly good Thanksgiving, so stop moping about it. There would be other chances to prove my loyalty to Dad. If Dad were here, he would marvel at this disaster; it would become legend. It took gale force winds, floods, twenty dragons, several near misses with death, police action, and a power outage to bring the Jovel feast to its knees. If Mom were alive, she'd tell the story over and over. And she would include the magic. She'd roll her R's and accent her I's, hopelessly garbling the English as the story came to its dramatic conclusion. In my imagination my family sat down to this small, simple meal. We would laugh, all five of us around the table again. The Thanksgiving of the Dragon.

I folded napkins under the forks, poured milk, and called, "Nicholi, Justin, come to dinner."

The house was oddly quiet. No Xbox zipping and exploding, no tapping at the computer keyboard. I walked into the living room. A cold breeze blew in from the hall. Justin must have left the door ajar when he answered it. I stepped into the hall.

There, crowded together with sheepish grins on their faces, were the people that I loved. Nicholi pressed the robe to his face to keep from giggling. Carlo held a turkey. Justin carried a Spanish flan. Paul had a fennel and cucumber salad. Trimble had carrot ravioli, and Case and Larry huddled together, supporting a huge cake decorated with hazelnuts. Anna Rossi leaned on Lizbeth Farr, who carried a basket of blueberry muffins.

"Surprise!" The yell almost knocked me over with joy.

"We made a potluck," said Paul. "I hope that's okay."

I was speechless, grateful beyond words. As grateful as my father once hoped I might be.

Nicholi bounced into the kitchen and added forks, knives, and spoons to make enough place settings. Carlo put the turkey in the center of the table and carved. Larry found serving spoons and put them in the various dishes. Case guarded the cake from stray fingers. All except his own, that is. Paul danced around slapping high fives and generally getting in the way. Nonna helped Lizbeth find enough chairs.

We gathered around the table, taking hands in a circle. Our hand squeeze traveled from person to person. Then Justin's voice resounded over our heads.

"May the circle be unbroken," he said, sounding like a man.

Chapter 29

That night, Steve escaped.

I woke, knowing his dragon blood with my blindsense. Through my parent's bedroom wall I felt his pleasure as he devoured the pudding, enchiladas, and macaroons. I felt his fleeting pain as he slit his forearm with a talon and let blood drip into the plastic water bottle. I felt the tug of his last yearning look at my shuttered window. Then he spread his wings and heaved himself over Mom's garden, stirring the fallen leaves into whirls of fright.

When I was sure he was gone, I tiptoed to the porch and picked up the bottle. He had filled it to the cap. If my efforts failed, it would not be for a lack of dragon's blood. Now to find a moment when all were safely out of my way, and I could face the sorcerer, alone. I hid the bottle in Mom's dresser, next to the Gemini mirror.

The following day, boys burst into the kitchen as Carlo, Nonna, Lizbeth, and I prepared lunch. They were raucous with excitement.

"Gone!" yelled Larry, waving his short arms. "They say he blasted a massive hole in the ceiling."

"Oh my!" Nonna sat bolt upright in her chair at the kitchen table.

Carlo looked up from filling water glasses. His eyes met mine and held them, offering support. I smiled but turned away. Please don't make me lie to you, Carlo.

"I knew they couldn't hold him." Justin swooped Nicholi onto his shoulders and strutted around. "It was just a matter of time."

"Dragons, dragons, dragons," chanted Nicholi from his high perch.

"Dude," said Case, "dragons are *awesome*." He snapped his fingers and danced across the kitchen floor. Noting that my hands were full, he swiped a strip of stir-fried chicken off my platter.

"Where's Trimble?" I asked.

"His parents won't let him come over anymore. They think we're a bad influence," said Larry.

I stopped still, stunned and sad. "I'm sorry."

In fact, it was amazing that any of the boys' families let them near me.

"Yeah, it sucks, dude." Case hung over the table, poking the bowl of papaya salad with a finger then selecting a peanut, which he popped into his mouth.

"He'll be back," said Justin, swinging Nicholi off his shoulders, "just as soon as they calm down."

"I hope so. Please put the silverware on the table, Justin." I tried to keep my voice steady.

Carlo took the heavy platter from my hand. "You knew he was out, didn't you?" His tone was quiet, right in my ear.

"What's going on, *Massimaŭ?*"

"It's okay, Carlo," I said.

Carlo put the food down and took his place at the table. "That may be the case, but this afternoon the boys and I are taking the axes and shovels to Larry's to be sharpened. We may need a few decent blades."

"Yeah," said Justin, sitting down and helping himself to four servings of rice, "never trust a dragon." He said this without thinking, I'm sure, so I didn't take it personally.

"I think you had better leave Steve Eastman to the police," I said.

"No friggin' way." They chanted this in unison: Justin, Larry, Case, and Paul, as though one mind possessed them. The problem with Age of Dragons players is that they live for adventure. Brushes with death and imprisonment had only a brief impact on their enthusiasm. Even Paul's.

Well, it didn't matter. I would handle Adrikhedon before they got to him. I'd send Nicholi to Nonna's, and with a good roll and some luck points, have the amulet apart before they returned. I reached my hands to form the circle. May the circle be unbroken, I prayed, begging not to be the next missing link.

~

In the silent house I opened the cupboard and examined every pot. Steamer: too small. Wok: too flat. Soup pot: too thin on the bottom. Fry pan: no tight fitting lid. When my hand fell on the pressure cooker, my fingers closed tight, steadied against the familiar feel. I placed the pressure cooker on the kitchen island. This was what my father would have used, had he lived.

Pressure Cooked to Perfection does not have a section on cooking enchanted necklaces. The hardest beans, Cannellini, take thirty-seven minutes to soften. A large, dense beet takes twenty-eight. Of course, they are not being boiled in something as corrosive as dragon's blood. I'd give the amulet forty minutes, and hope that I had enough time left to wrench the stone from the gold before the boys came home.

Leaning against the kitchen island, I took the Wyrmstone out of its silky pouch. Light stirred in the six facets, like a promise, far off in the haze. The beauty pulled and ached, collapsing all human thoughts and raising the desire of dragons. The urge to consume, to hoard, to corrupt my belly with crusts of priceless splendor. Irresistibly sweet and worth any price, this depraved and sensuous clutching. Never soothed, always roused: an abyss of bittersweet misery.

Then I understood. Adrikhedon craved Yvess' stone: that alone explained his allegiance to me. He knew, even better than I did, that my dragon fiber loathed giving it up. When the stone was free of taint and embraced bare in my fingers, my blithe human promises would be worthless. Deep under a slimy, fouled pond, he plotted to have me, and then kill me for the stone.

I had no time to be afraid. The era of worrying about whether or not I had the strength was over. I would do this now, quickly, to protect those whom I loved. I no longer had the luxury of doubt.

I hurried to the laundry room and found my father's tool box. Setting it on the kitchen island, I opened the lid. His tools were all there, neatly spooned as Carlo had left them, the damaged chisel on top. How long, long ago it seemed that I had chipped that blade. I chose a screwdriver and set it aside, then lifted the lid off the pressure cooker. The rubber seal jostled into place with a touch of my fingertips. With the screwdriver, I tightened the pressure valve in place. The steam release floated, well balanced. I secured the screw in the handle so the grip wouldn't twist during my alchemy. I slid the cooker onto the stove.

Pulling out cutting boards, working by instinct, guided by the same gauzy faith Dad trusted: there was no recipe, and never would be one. How does any chef know what it takes to create a magnum opus? The ingredients mix and meld to create flavors we know in our bones.

The blood and Gemini mirror still lay in Mom's drawer, and the cinnabar vial stood on her vanity. It was a moment's work to carry them into the kitchen. With one last sniff of the Night Veil, clinging to the vial's interior, I wrapped it in cheesecloth and set it on a cutting board. I'd have to pray there was a drop of potion in the bottom, because I had no way to make more. Raising the hammer, I smashed the vial to a damp powder. It squeaked under each blow, and I did my best not to cringe at the sound. The burnt-orange dust hissed as I shook it off the delicate cloth and into the cooker.

I replaced the used cutting board with a clean one. Then, pressing my trembling thumb against the Wyrmstone, I closed my eyes. The sorcerer stirred in the gold, waking to my plan, scrambling to craft a defense. I ignored him. Bring me my sword, I commanded.

Razor sharp blade and iron pommel clattered and bounced on the cutting board, stretching the width of the island. One last, sad look at the tip that could pierce any enemy: dragon, sorcerer, Basilisk. I dismantled all my weapons, one by one, and would meet my enemies with only my cunning. *Legendary swords cannot be broken except by extraordinary means*; I'd read this over Justin's shoulder. I suppose that meant that if I raised my hammer and struck the faded runes, trying to snap the blade in two, the blow would bounce. Smacking again and again would not so much as dent the metal. Fortunately, Mom had given me the extraordinary. I closed my eyes and focused all my heart on the stone, steaming in its gold setting. Help me Yvess.

So wily and wyrm this empress, snaking her way through alliances and betrayals. I could feel her probing, calculating, deciding. How much longer would her patience with me last? She knew, now, that the stone would soon be broken. She would prepare for her journey across the border, be here by nightfall. She would not be easy to fool. But Snick had done it, and so would I.

"*Nagrij cadeth dleedz, za robst Yomorrtarr jolke.*" Her voice in my ear, that abrasive rasp. *Reclaim a hero's portion, and leave the sword to ash.*

A hero's portion. The might of faith, the brutality of victory, the path of a legend: that is what a hero took.

My hands hovered over Deathwish. Tingling. Burning. Sucking. Drawing forth the conquest that refuses to know surrender. Gathering certain victory like a fistful of storm. My dragon screamed with menace, and under my shaking hands the blade vibrated. Cracked. Crumbled. It took all my strength to lift the board, pour the ash into the pot.

Gray mixed with orange. The dirt of what had once ruled.

The plastic bottle crackled as I squeezed it and screwed off the top. Red blood, rich to the depth of ancient wine, clotted with centuries of ferment. The gamy smells of wickedness and cave water. How much to use? All of it. Shaking the bottle to get the very last drop.

I turned on the eye, gas fire licking the sides of the pot. My wooden spoon smoked as I stirred, getting hotter until I yanked it out, wiping the rounded cup of it against the lip of the pan. Flecks of gold rose in the soup. From the cinnabar, the sword, or the dragon blood? I didn't know. It was time to throw in the Wyrmstone.

Now comes the sorcerer, his staff of darkness raised, no body to give him form, but in my mind his power rages. His blows fall in my skull and pound with pain, striving to knock me senseless. I raise the gale of my dragon breath against him. Blow that blood red cape back around him until it binds like fiery chains. He twists and contorts in the smoke of his burning. But still his assault of jolts, faster than I can evade, stronger than even I can withstand. In a fury, he claws his cloak to shreds. I have no sword to raise against him. No Night Veil to warp his will. No shield but my ability to endure, moment by moment, all that is flung at me. I rip at the amulet around my neck, trying to throw it into the pot. The leather holds, the strength of the frayed thread to be the death of me. The sorcerer floats closer, battering at the tearing fabric of my consciousness. I'm reeling in mist. The light around me dims.

It takes a piece of soul, Yvess whispers. *To break the spell, you must sacrifice.*

Dragon or human, into the pot? I grab blindly, unable to separate them, tearing off a little corner of both, gasping from the shock of it. It falls, crying like a newborn, into the pot. Missing forever like a lost puzzle piece, my picture never again complete.

Then I yank with all my strength at the necklace. The leather holds, but the soldered loop that catches the cord, Mom's clumsy drop of molten lead, gives way. The Wyrmstone jerks free and tumbles, gold over flashing stone, plastic scrap and broken loop, into the pot. Lifting arms heavy as victory, I slam down the lid. With an agonizing twist, the lid catches and snaps into place.

~

I woke on the floor. My heart lurched; how long had I been here? I listened for sounds of the boys. Overhead, the pressure cooker's jabbering steam blew from the valve.

No voices. Maybe there was still time.

The room weaved when I sat up. I collapsed back to the floor and closed my eyes to keep from vomiting. When I opened them again I could see a sinister fog of vaporized dragon's blood, drifting over the ceiling, foul as gaseous rubber.

My head pounded: clouded, poisoned. I couldn't lie here, I had to act. With a groan I rolled over and crawled to the back door, stretched for the doorknob and could not reach it, so I kicked the door open. Let in the cold air, the clean rain. The washed chill cleared the ache and left only a concussed haze. I willed myself to my feet and, hanging onto the counter, I coached my shaky legs to the stove.

The pressure cooker spit murky steam, screeching. I turned off the fire. With three layers of my father's hot pads, I gripped the handle. Heaving the heavy pot, I tested its weight, jiggling the contents. The Wyrmstone scraped across the bottom.

What now?

Perhaps I'd come this far and didn't know enough. Perhaps the one relevant cooking tip wasn't in my smoggy brain. I took a breath to calm my panic. I knew how to cook, I reminded myself. It was the one thing in this insanity that I could be confident of.

Blanching, peeling, spicing, and roux. Icing, leavenings, and roasting times. Basting and caramel sauce. Taffy—yes! The hard-crack stage of candy. Jostle the pan to make the blood crystallize. Crystallize around, and then crack the gold.

I tilted the pot. It took a few seconds for the necklace to scuff from one side to the other. The blood was sufficiently thick. Grabbing the handle with both hands, I shook vigorously. Shook until I was exhausted and my forearms ached and burned. Until nothing in the pot moved. I was about to carry it to the sink when I heard a voice say, "Not done yet.

Let the crystals work at the gold for a minute, it'll make separation easier."

I put the pot down and glanced around, heart racing, breathing cautiously.

There was no one but me in the kitchen. I had gotten used to hearing voices, others' voices: dragon, empress, sorcerer. But this was my voice, that warble of lilting ups and shallow downs that never sounded the same outside as it did in my head; *that* didn't usually ambush me.

I waited for the voice to speak again. When it didn't, I lifted the pot.

"Rapid release the heat, then hurry to the workbench before the gold cools. Use Dad's pliers. It'll ruin them, but at this point I don't think Dad cares."

The voice vibrated in my fingertips, quivering. It was coming from the pressure cooker! I almost dropped it, I put it down so fast. I yanked my hands away and stood panting, frightened.

"Hurry up. They'll be back any minute. You spent thirty-five minutes out cold on the floor."

That was me in there, that piece of soul I gave to the spell, melded into the steel alloy. My hands flew up and crossed my heart. This was horrible. I'd live forever in there, helpless and dependent. Maybe Trimble, if I was ever allowed to see him again, could pull me free. The absurdity of living in a cooking utensil.

"Come on, *Massimaŭ*, move."

I picked up the pot and heaved it into the sink. With a spoon on the valve and cold water gushing over the lid, I released the last of the pressure. Then I cranked open the lid.

Foul gas poured out, reeking of rot. Inside, the dragon's blood formed crystals, obsidian claws crawling up the sides of the pan, scratching at the golden roots, expanding in the cracks between gem and setting, cracking and popping.

Talons, grasping for the jewel. The scrap of plastic lay loose, untouched.

I grabbed Dad's pliers and pried at the amulet. Crystal claws hissed and steamed. The pliers' tips bent, softening. I ripped and twisted until I had tugged the amulet free. So light, so deceptively insubstantial.

Snatching up the Gemini mirror, I dashed out the back door and lay the amulet on Dad's plywood table. The wood smoked, darkening. Back in the kitchen, I turned on the tap and filled the pressure cooker with water, then tipped it over so the dark sludge oozed, frothing and gurgling, down the drain. I rinsed the pot clean. On the way back to the workbench I collected Dad's toolbox.

Outside in the light drizzle, I slipped a nail through a gap between roots and pinned the gold setting to Dad's workbench. With hammer and chisel I pried and chipped. Pounding. Panting. Grunting. Golden roots snapped and scattered. The stone wiggled in its setting. Splinters of gold fell at my feet, sparkling in the mud as I dented the chisel again and again, completely ruining the blade with my hacking. With a final *ping* the stone sprung free and lay glistening and steaming, fresh and hot. My heart leapt, buoyed by a joy that expanded all the way to the sky.

Overhead I heard dragon wings, whomping past the roof. I had but seconds. Standing up the Gemini mirror on the workbench, I set the sparkling amethyst between the two faces of glass. Three magnificent jewels glowed with lavender mist, one in each side of the mirror, one in the center. I closed my eyes and began the spell: *Real is but an illusion, dream is but its twin* … Draconic sighed from me, easy as breathing. I finished and opened my eyes.

Three stones, which was the real one? It was impossible to say. I lay a hand over two of them, and as the dragon landed I scooped them into my palm and dropped them in the Phoenix-hide sack around my neck. With a swipe I brushed away the mirror and it fell, shattering at my feet.

Adrikhedon's hideous mass filled the driveway. He snapped closed his wings, blowing hair back from my face with his foul stench. He wobbled forward, holding out a gnarled claw, talons dark with filth, grasping toward the naked jewel on the workbench. A hiss steamed from between his moist teeth.

Free from the gold, worlds of riches sparkled in the jewel's depths. As if all that Yvess had amassed in her glittering hoard—splendors made by human hands, in earth's fires, by dragon magic and dwarves' skill—lay within its six perfect facets. Irresistibly beautiful. I snatched up the stone and closed my fingers over it, wondering if it was the real amethyst.

A slow, menace of a smile crawled across Adrikhedon's face. He took one stealthy step towards me, heaving his huge haunches. "I thought so," he snarled. His golden eyes fixed on me, pinning me to the spot.

I held in my hand the will to fight. To sprout wing and rise, screeching into the sky, to slash and bite to the death this beast that threatened my riches. I had the will for it, the naked instinct to protect my hoard. But he would shred me easily.

In a hundred years, when the Gemini illusion wore thin, I would be ready for him. Then, it would be a toss of the dice which one of us would kill the other.

I opened my hand and offered the stone, the amethyst purple as a fresh bruise on my palm.

Wary, reckoning for angles and wily tricks, Adrikhedon inched his talons closer. "I can't say which I like better in you, *Massimaü*, the human or the dragon." He seized my hand, trapping my fingers and the stone in the crush of his massive claws, squeezing hard enough to draw blood, and I gasped.

"Come to Mexico," he rasped.

Tears of pain sprung to my eyes. "No." I stood ready, teeth bared and wings poised to sprout. Adrikhedon hung in the balance, teetering between lust and greed.

Then Carlo's truck pulled into the driveway. Five furious young men poured out, brandishing shovels, hatchets, and a sharpened pickax.

Adrikhedon let go, clawed Yvess' amethyst from my grasp, and opened his wings. "Goodbye *Massimaü*. You're too costly a treasure."

And he launched heavily into the sky.

I collapsed in the dirt, knees on fragments of splintered mirror and gold, tears streaming down my face. I had survived my first deception.

Tonight I would set the second stone on the dead fig

stump, and she would come. Cowering in my bed, praying that she didn't see through my ruse, I would hear her creak across the yard. I would hear her hiss of satisfaction as she found the stone, the snap of her wings opening, and the violent gusts against the roof as she flew away. And for a hundred years I wouldn't know if the true stone lay with her, with Adrikhedon, or with me. My dragon self thought this very funny, and I began to laugh.

Boys clattered around me.

"Holy crap, you broke it!"

"The Wyrmstone! How did you take it apart?"

"Dude, you're *awesome*."

I picked slivers of gold out of the glass and muck, gathering them onto my palm like a prize, for what dragon can resist gold? I still had one more task. With my fingers, I pressed gold shards into my skin, and my blindsense probed for the sorcerer. Where was he? Empty metal. No threat, no dark presence. Where had he gone? My mind replayed the Wyrmstone's destruction.

And then I knew, I knew, and it was the greatest joke of all. I started laughing so hard I was crying.

"Why are you crying, Mimi?"

Maybe because it was over. Maybe because we'd survived my parent's death, and made good of all they'd left us. Maybe because of the love that now lifted me to my feet and gathered me in its arms, while the sorcerer, trapped in a little piece of plastic, had washed down the drain.

Epilogue

It was four months before Trimble was allowed to visit. He showed up unexpectedly on my nineteenth birthday. I hardly recognized him. His corn rows and beads were gone, his hair was trimmed close in a military buzz cut. His robe had been replaced by a pair of pressed khaki slacks and a neatly tailored shirt with a suit coat. He wore leather shoes instead of sneakers. He looked like an Ivy League freshman, not a wizard. I let him in and followed him to the study where the boys and Carlo played *The Battle for the Universe.*

"Dude," said Case, putting down his controller. "Good disguise."

"Yeah, well, it fools my parents." Trimble grinned and Larry gave him a high five.

"Ranked match, same team?" asked Justin, holding out a controller. "We have time for one more game before we leave for Nonna's."

Trimble shook his head. "Thanks, but I want to see Mimi's famous pressure cooker."

He tailed me into the kitchen, hands stuffed awkwardly into the pockets of his pressed pants.

"Sorry about your clothes," I said.

Trimble's tone was stoic. "Robes don't make the wizard." In Trimble's case, that was certainly true.

My magical pot reigned permanently from the middle eye of the stove, becoming grumpy if I put it in a dark cupboard. I woke it with a polite tap.

"This is Trimble," I said.

It shifted slightly on the burner. "You've come to try and dismantle me, wizard?"

Trimble startled, and then a smile ripped across his face and burst the seams of his tailored life. "Sweet!" he said.

By then, I was used to my intelligent pressure cooker. The broth it produced made soup that cozied the heart into tranquil peace. Beets emerged, red as rubies and sweet as peaches. Its beans made a cassoulet rich enough to start a love affair. But I had never gotten used to my voice coming from the metal, an echo of me that had escaped time and transcended my youth. An older, more sardonic Mimi who could never be intimidated by a Ms. Greer or Ms. Whitting. A Mimi who wouldn't dawdle before attacking a nasty sorcerer.

"You want me to take this apart, really?" Trimble's face contorted with conflict: his eyebrows up with awe, his temples pulsing with fear, his mouth closed tight on his qualms.

I had considered this over and over in the last four months, but I'd been unable to make up my mind. It was disconcerting, what I had created: a monstrosity that might beg someday to be left in peace, like one of Ms. Farr's artifacts. A creation that might be revered or enslaved, used for charity or wielded for wickedness, or swallowed by a dragon and drained painfully of its life.

I wrapped my grip around the sides of the pot, feeling the iron and carbon in the steel. It pulsed with thought: logical, clever, inventive, and fearless. We Sovrani were a headstrong lot; who knows what the pot would become over eight hundred years? Whatever it was, with that mind in it, it would make a fate of its own choosing. Then it occurred to me—there was more freedom, really, in being this pot, than there was in most short human lives. More potential for evil, but more potential for good, too.

Taking my hand off the metal, I said, "No, leave it be. If it veers out of control, my great great Sovrani grandchildren will know what to do with it."

Trimble coughed out an inarticulate word of relief. "In that case, I'll go help Carlo plant Nonna's azaleas," he said.

The boys had chosen a riot of colors: red, orange, yellow, white ... arguing at the nursery over who got to give Nonna the pink one. They sweated and huffed, digging most of the morning. When they came in for lunch, grimy and weary, I had only made tuna fish sandwiches. I was preoccupied. Once again, I was determined to contend with the fig stump.

It was true that the fig had protected us; its roots restrained evil, its leaves spread a shield, its sap flowed with a charm without which I would never have lived long enough to seize my destiny. But all graves must close, someday. And this was a magnificent spring afternoon.

There had been a lot of argument among the boys about what kind of tree to replace it with, and in the end it was decided that there must have been a reason for a fig. A fig it would be, then, once again. But you can't plant figs until the worst of the frost is over. So we waited for the first day of March, my birthday. There are twelve varieties of fig they claim will bear fruit in Seattle, of them, the 'Brown Turkey' fig is the hardiest. "The most reliable fig tree in our region," promised the Rainstorm Nursery catalog. "A sweet golden flesh, two large crops a year."

I was no innocent when it came to figs; I knew I would never taste a single ripe bite. Every September, ants would crawl across the patio, seeking the shrunken green fruit that I hadn't swept away. Every April I would hand sift worm compost and crumble alfalfa pellets to mulch around the roots. Pining for roasting heat and prolonged equatorial sunshine, the fig would do its damnedest to die. But I ordered it, and I was going to plant it.

The tree had arrived two days before. It leaned inside the garden shed, hardly fatter than a twig, bare branches wrapped in twine and delicate roots in a canvas bag. It didn't look up to Mom's root-hog-or-die garden. But then, who knew how a mere twig could grow?

As the boys did the lunch dishes, I went to the garden shed and found the pickax. Then I stood before the stump, trying to muster some courage. Months of rain, snow, and ice had slid mud back into the excavation hole. The wood had hardened, condensed, practically petrified over time. The roots were slimy and impossible to grip. I could only hope the little whip of a tree that replaced it would someday become so strong.

I lifted the pickax and slammed it into the stump. The handle vibrated, sending familiar shocks of pain up my arms. Grief for my parents had softened to a gentle sorrow. I had no anger, now, to help me. I raised the pickax and swung again. Since their death I had done many impossible things. So, I would take out this stump.

"Stop! What are you doing?"

I was surprised to see Carlo behind me holding a shovel; I had thought he was inside with the boys, washing dishes. It was a warm day and he wasn't wearing his fedora. Curls blew about his head like dark laurels. He had his sleeves rolled up, showing the muscles that kept him suspended high above the show floor with his brothers and uncles. But not much longer. Next year he would start school for his degree. Perhaps someday we would open our restaurant.

I wiped a few loose strands of hair out of my face, smearing wet mud across my nose.

"You can't take it out with that," I said, pointing to the shovel. "I've tried."

He grinned, and then laughed out loud. "Are you lecturing me on tools?"

"Why not? I have it on good authority that advice on tools makes one irresistibly attractive."

He stood, shovel gripped in both hands, considering me. A stripe of yellow sunshine cut across his feet, lighting the patio around him with playful colors.

"You're flirting with me," he said, finally.

I looked down at Mom's grimy garden gloves, molded once to fit her fingers, now changing to fit mine.

"Our first and only kiss was four months ago," I said.

"When I kissed you, you didn't react as I had hoped."

I met his gaze. "I was having a bad week."

Carlo shrugged, another for my personal collection. "How-was-I-to-know?" said the rising shoulders, and "So-what-are-we-waiting-for?" asked the affectionate eyes.

He walked forward, close enough that his face blurred a little, letting the heat and man-scent of him waft over me.

"So, you're ready now?" he asked.

It was only a slight reach to his warm, smooth lips. A passionate kiss, and I was so keen for it. We fit together like those hammers and pliers long ago, in Dad's tool box. The kiss was sultry, intense and … well … short.

Because the boys started whooping and yelling.

"Yo, Carlo, good choice."

"Get a room, dude."

"Boom-chicka-wow-wow!"

They stood by the door, flapping their shirts and punching the air with their fists. One of those moments when I wondered if I would miss them when they grew up and moved away.

Carlo didn't even wince. He turned around and eyed them calmly. "Hey, make yourselves useful. Case, get the new fig tree out of the shed. Paul and Trimble, I need two bags of steer manure. Larry and Justin, get your badass fighter arms over here and dig some dirt." He turned back to me, surging with enthusiasm. "Let's do this thing," he said.

He stuck his shovel in the dirt pile and heaved a spade full onto the roots.

"What are you doing?" I asked.

"Filling in the hole."

"Why?"

"Because you don't pull up a living tree."

"It's dead!"

"No," he pointed to the back of the stump, "it's not."

Sure enough, out from between two roots, shooting up from the thickness of the trunk, a little sprout of youthful green investigated the light.

About the Author

Dr. Lisa Murphy has been a practicing physician for over twenty-five years. She is the author of two published novels: The Turkish Mirror and The Wyrmstone, both works of Magical Realism. She is currently working on a four volume series of historical fiction that extends from 1832 to 1864, encompassing the Civil War. She says of her work: "I am particularly fond of language: ancient, modern, ethnic, upper class, gutter slang, the language of thieves or the idioms of doctors, the words a mother might choose, or a wizard. I collect vocabularies and marvel at speech patterns. We have delightful ways of expressing ourselves, we humans."

The Turkish Mirror

Umut's brown, callused toes touched lightly from rock to rock, graceful with excitement. Foamy hands from the Mediterranean grabbed his ankles, shocking blue green, frothing too white against his skin. That far out the jetty waves thundered from deep below, their curls surging higher, up his calves, hindered by boulders as he scrambled around to where the path was flat. Overhead gulls drifted, screeching harsh calls as inarticulate as the boy's. I never understood Umut's garbled Turkish, but I knew what he was saying: they were coming. From my place on the cliff I could see them. Around the thick jaw of rocky teeth that protected Incir's bay came small wooden boats, painted blue and trimmed with red and white, diamonds of green and yellow on their cabins. Behind the boats, the sun descended into the sea, pouring blood red on the agitated waves. The fishermen were coming; spared by the sea one more day. *Maşallah.*

Children on the beach—digging holes with branches, tossing bulbs of seaweed like balls—glanced up. They saw Umut's stick-thin arms waving and his tattered flapping trousers and they dropped their wood and seaweed. In a dash to be first they ran for the village, taking the goat path up the cliff, going home. Like so many crows, they took up the call: their fathers were coming.

Xiao Lian sat high on a rock at the root of the jetty that pushed into the bay. Xiao had been writing. A letter home. I knew because Mizou told me. His curled hand dipped brush into ink, forming character after character of elegant Chinese calligraphy, an inkstone balanced on the uneven rock by his knee. He took his eyes off the wind-ruffled page and peered down at Umut, leaping below him on the slippery boulders.

"Umut!" He waved, and the child looked up. Just *un petit instant.* Umut took his mind off his feet *un petit instant*—and he was gone. Slipped into the sea without a sound. Swallowed. *Mon Dieu!*

Xiao stood and dove: a fluid, singular gesture from sitting to swimming. He plunged without hesitation into brilliant Mediterranean blue, unconcerned for rocks that shattered the waves, or undertow, or the menace of that dreadful mirror.

His hands were the last that I ever saw of him. They thrust out of foam, gripping the boy's waist. With a heave they threw the child onto black, wet rock: battered, frightened, bleeding. We never found any trace of Xiao Lian, though Incir's boats searched coast and open sea, and the fishermen threw their nets where currents might carry him. I paced the jetty where he disappeared a hundred times in the next few days, wishing I had the courage to throw myself in after him.

But I didn't. Because of you, my girl. Xiao's death marked the beginning of your life, sweet daughter, and the end of my childhood.

~

"And now you know what became of your father, *ma petite*," says my Maman. Maman is parked in her sumptuous armchair by the window, the gray light of Paris buffing color off her blonde hair. She closes thin lips and sucks in a stiff inhale, exquisite in her hoity-toity suffering. I stand over her, a towering six feet, too much of a biffa to ever come across so frail. Her porcelain skin, same white as mine, looks cold. I am so disappointed. Of all the things I dreamed my real mum might be, I never imagined such a ghostly aristocrat.

I'm not in a warm-hearted mood, having just stolen, lied, and done a runner from London with the police on my arse and this effing mirror in my rucksack. No mood to be sweet to this snooty nonstarter of a mum, even if it is the first time I've ever laid eyes on her. I yank out the mirror by its handle. It's swathed in a snippet of silk the color of dead goldfish. Much as I fear that mirror, I love that red orange silk—royal orange in the sunlight, an eerie stain of red in the dark.

"Right then," I say, "Dad died. But that doesn't explain *this* bit of trouble, does it?" I chuck the mirror in her lap. She jerks away her hands, avoiding what just landed in the folds of her wool dress. The silk slides apart. Painted waves wash up the mirror's handle and reach for the monster sculpted in mosaic tile on the back. "I want a full account, Maman. You owe me."

She raises her eyes: fearless. Wealth is always fearless—Emma, George, the whole upper crust. Maman is as confident as her antique *fauteuil,* from which she can glance out the window, clock the spring buds on the trees of posh Square Barye. No matter how seriously I give it a go, I can't rattle them. But I haven't finished trying yet.

Her eyes lock onto mine and I dare her to hate me. Sixteen years after she abandoned me, let her tell me to my face that she doesn't want me. Let her demand to know how I found her, and threaten to punish the lot who snitched. But she smiles with well-bred restraint and contends with the silk, righting the mirror's handle under the cloth. She tops off her demitasse with coffee, then lounges back in the armchair's crewel upholstery. I see that I've inherited my stubbornness from her—that steel that drives Emma into a dark room to suffer migraines.

"*Eh bien*, I can tell you only half the story, as much of it took place in China." She raises her cup, sips, and swallows. "China's revolutions shaped your father, Xiao Lian Chin, scarred and raised him to the hero he was. Patriotism, sacrifice, torture … these were not things that made sense to me at the time. *Mon Dieu*, I was an artist, obsessed with beauty, a mere girl of twenty! I was lost, spoiled, furious … well, perhaps a bit like you, *non?*"

Non, I think, you don't know a bloody thing about me. But I keep my gob shut. She sips again delicately, as if each taste in her mouth were a meal to be savored start to finish. So absoeffinglutely French, my Maman.

"And you will judge what I did, *n'est pas*? That is why you have come." She laughs. I can't tell if she's having a laugh at me, or if I make her sad. Either way, it's not a cheerful wheeze. Her gaze travels from the fine scar above my left eye, across my cheek to my ear where the cartilage thickens, having re-healed poorly after one of my fights. She studies my hacked off hair, dyed blue.

"Sit down, *chérie*. You look uncomfortable, standing there in those heavy field boots. This is a long story, so you may as well enjoy some coffee as I tell it."

Then, as though the mirror were harmless, Maman scoops up the handle and lets silk fall away. She gazes at the inlaid tile on the mirror's back, not a bit intimidated by the horrid three-headed beast who glares back at her, dog jaws slobbering. She sets the mirror in her lap. "I know how hard a child can be on a parent," she says. "When I was young, I laid full blame on my father, your grandfather, the formidable Boris Trotoskov. Because of Boris I fled to the tiny Turkish fishing village of Incir, where I met Xiao."

She leans back and closes her eyes. For a minute I worry she will have a kip, leave me wondering what she's on about. Finally someone who knows my Chinese half—a hero of some sort, no less—and she's ready for an afternoon snooze. But then she continues in a voice soft as a misty spray of golden paint.